SORE LOSER

Mike McAlary

SORE LOSER

A Mickey Donovan Mystery

William Morrow and Company, Inc.
NEW YORK

Library of Congress Cataloging-in-Publication Data

McAlary, Mike.
  Sore loser : a Mickey Donovan mystery / Mike McAlary.
    p.   cm.
  ISBN 0-688-15610-X
  I. Title.
  PS3563.C2647S67   1998
  813'.54—dc21   98-36716
                                                         CIP

Printed in the United States of America

FIRST EDITION

1   2   3   4   5   6   7   8   9   10

BOOK DESIGN BY CATHRYN S. AISON

www.williammorrow.com

For Ryan

SORE LOSER

Opening Day, William Tweed Field, the Bronx

Children grow up screaming in this neighborhood.

By Bronx standards, the crumbling stretch of Jerome Avenue wasn't a particularly vicious or murderous place, but kids playing in the park had to screech and howl to be heard over the passing subway trains. Melanie Morgan stood on the infield grass with her back to the field as the elevated train began to grind in the distance. The metallic roar grew as the umpire, facing the chain-link backstop and wearing an oversize navy blue sweatshirt and cut-off blue jeans, took a superstitious hop over home plate and dug into her pouch for the game ball.

"Here's a fat pearl," she said.

Morgan turned to face the pitcher's mound and whipped a single beaded blonde braid against her rubberized black mask. Her ceremony was deliberate. She raised the unblemished white leather softball to her left ear, cocked her biceps, and pumped once before snapping the ball out to a freshman pitcher.

The ump's left-handed hurl was startlingly hard and painful. The pitcher bit her lower lip and muttered a quick judgment. "Blue bitch," she said, knowing her insult was impossible to hear over the train.

3

The varsity pitcher was a grassy, suburban kid playing for an asphalt, urban school, the only college of any sort that had offered her an athletic scholarship. She was witty, hip, and scheming, your typical Tweed kid. Her school was just coming off NCAA probation after a point-shaving scandal involving the men's basketball team. Following a month in the dirty field house, she could curse with the foulest Bronx rappers. She spit on the mound as Puff Daddy blared over the grass field. Take me out to the ball game, indeed.

Some coltish outfielders, dressed in the school's new dollar-bill-green pin-striped uniforms, preened like models working a runway and finished their limbering tosses as a southbound IRT number four began passing over the field. On average, five trains crushed past them in a single inning.

"Yo, this isn't a booty call," the umpire yelled over the steel clamor. "Play ball, girls." She thrust her left fist in the air and the foam chest protector rose against her sweaty bosom. Even on this blustery late spring afternoon, the ump felt the mask wet against her face. She was fifteen pounds past her own playing weight but as serious as a Randy Johnson knockdown pitch.

From somewhere above the field came a deliberate crack—like a broomstick being snapped clean in half. The team's spindly short-stop, who had grown up dreading the same noise in a park next to the Soundview Houses, stiffened with terrified recognition.

Gunshot.

As the train rumbled off, the umpire stepped onto the plate and crumpled, falling on her back. Some players, believing the ump was fooling around, giggled as Morgan gasped and flopped like a speared bluefish.

"Don't play John McSherry on me, girl," the catcher said, smiling. On opening day in the bigs several years ago, a portly umpire had toppled over in mid-bellow and died of a heart attack.

"I can't feel my tits," Melanie Morgan said, almost calmly. She clutched a white plastic pitch counter in her right hand and pawed at a tiny circular tear on the left side of her blue chest protector.

As more players and coaches gathered around the pale umpire, Morgan's blood puddled on home plate. Everyone understood the umpire's sudden, gray silence.

Morgan tried to say more, but only a pink mist escaped her lips and she died with her mask on. By then, as the train rolled to a stop in the Jerome Avenue station, the shooter was again seated in the middle of the train's last car, the pistol warm against his belly. As the terror spread over the field, the players, coaches, and fans began to shriek. It was impossible to hear them over the next passing train.

ONE

Home Plate, William Tweed Field, the Bronx

The red-clay base paths were blocked off with the powder-blue sawhorses stenciled with the words "New York Police Department." A lieutenant from the crime scene unit, Brenden Bailey, stood over the body, writing furiously in a worn red notebook. He wore a black Burberrys suit, a white carnation in his jacket lapel, and severely polished black shoes. He had topped his practiced, funeral-parlor look with a neat black homburg. Occasionally, he would stop writing and sniff the white flower.

"This one's over five feet, too," Bailey said, whistling. He was adding figures on a palm-size page. The detective working over the body rolled his eyes as a civilian wearing a tweed jacket over a kelly-green sweatshirt walked up to them.

"I'm John Francis Xavier Cummings Junior," the man said, offering his hand. "I am the athletic director at William Tweed College and a personal friend of the mayor."

"Are you now?"

The academic offered a soft hand to the serious man who studied it over his bifocals, as if it were a bug, and continued writing. The insult was practiced.

The school's athletic director, a sweaty man with a nervous eye on the television cameras, took a step forward and studied the body. Bailey nonchalantly wiped the dust from his black loafers against the back of his black slacks, and asked, without looking up from his pad, "Was Miss Size Twelve here a friend of the mayor, too?"

"No."

"Then kindly step back toward the dugout, sir. The undertaker will contact you about visiting hours."

"What does the woman's size have to do with it?" he asked.

"Nothing," said the cop. Lieutenant Bailey looked up from his worn red book and waved his pen hand at the intruder, shooing him away like one of the black flies beginning to investigate the corpse.

"Can you put a blanket over her or something?" The nervous administrator sniffed, jabbing a thumb over his shoulder in the direction of the reporters. "It looks bad for our school."

The cop returned to his book and snapped his tape measure closed. The inscription on the tape could be read easily: "Compliments of South Brooklyn Casket Company."

"By my measure, this one is seventy-two inches long," Lieutenant Bailey replied. "The last five have all been better than sixty-five inches. Jeez, I'm on a roll."

"Sir?" the athletic director said. "I don't understand."

The cop smiled and placed his notebook back inside his jacket. "This makes an even four miles for me," he explained.

"What?"

"Yeah," Bailey continued. "I keep track of them. Sometimes it's pretty easy. But sometimes, say when the killer saws his victim's leg bones in half or stuffs the torso in an oil drum, it's hard to be accurate."

"I don't think I need to know this," the athletic director said, stepping backward.

"Oh, sure you do," Bailey said warmly. "Kids are the worst, especially the ones under two feet. And we had this Colombian hit man in Jackson Heights a couple of years ago. He used to melt his victims with sulfuric acid in his bathtub and then fold them into Pampers boxes. Maybe he killed fifteen people. I lost twenty yards with him."

"This is sick."

A uniformed cop with eagles on his shoulders appeared behind the lieutenant. He had been standing about fifteen feet away, next to a patrolman, listening.

"Good evening, Loo. I see the odometer is still running."

"Salutations, Inspector Donovan. I was just explaining my homework here to this inquisitive college fellow."

"Easy on the customers, Brendan," Donovan whispered.

"Well, Mickey, you know how I endure this wretched work. I've been laying my homicide victims end-to-end for twenty years, now. Thirty-six feet a day was my personal best—unless you count Happy Land. I had four hundred that night, but smoke inhalation doesn't count. As I was just explaining to the gentleman, our lady here is six feet tall. She gets me to exactly ten thousand, five hundred and forty feet of dead decade. That's two miles of bodies in the nineties alone."

"I'm going to be sick," the athletic director said.

"Don't corrupt my crime scene with your footprints," Lieutenant Brendan Bailey said. "And please extend my regards to the mayor."

"You'll be demanding frequent dier miles next, Loo," Mickey Donovan said as he watched the athletic director stagger off. By the inspector's own estimation, he had worked only a few hundred yards of murder cases with the crime scene supervisor.

"Now there's an idea, Inspector."

A couple of cops, who had been watching and listening, snickered. Brendan Bailey and his mileage chart was part of department folklore. Everyone respected his nuttiness so they quickly completed their canvass.

"Whattayagot, Brendan?" Deputy Inspector Donovan asked. As the head of the special investigations unit, an elite, highly secretive force in the NYPD, Donovan's job was to investigate jarring public cases and bring them to a quick close. He oversaw a staff of twenty detectives throughout the city.

"Somebody shot her from the train, I guess," Lieutenant Bailey said. He pulled a bottle of Ice Brut aftershave from his hip pocket. "Want some?"

"No thanks," Mickey Donovan said.

"I still got this taste in my mouth from this floater we pulled from the Gowanus this morning," Bailey said. "He was a ten-gallon ooze stuffed in a five-gallon can." Brendan Bailey brought the bottle to his lips, sipped a bit, gargled, then spit a green stream at home plate through his perfect teeth.

"I remember the first time I saw you do that with anisette at the Palm Sunday massacre in East New York," Mickey said.

"I prefer Stoli," Bailey explained, "but if I was still averaging seven bodies a day like I did when we hit twenty-five hundred in ninety-one, I'd be in the clinic with Boris Yeltsin. Incidentally, what brings you out in the blue bag, Mickey?"

Deputy Inspector Donovan, who normally worked plainclothes in his role as a city-wide detective, touched his seldom-worn blue tunic.

"I was at an honor legion meeting in the Purple Plaza when I got beeped. I had to go upstairs and the commissioner gave me his best hangdog 'Go up there and protect me' look. So here we are."

"First blush?"

"Yeah."

"We got stupid, but lucky target practice by one of our feral Bronx youth on his way home from school," Bailey said. "Probably riding between the subway cars and pegging shots. My math is rough but it looks like we got a single bullet, fired from thirty feet above the field, that traveled a hundred and fifty yards from a moving train through a five-foot-wide knothole of greasy thickets, broken fences, and barren trees."

"An amazing constellation of chance, Brendan."

"Yeah, and the umpire wound up on the wrong end of a one-million-to-one shot. By the way, Mickey, I'd play her numbers. Four, four, nine, and three. I got 'em from a Lotto ticket she had in her back pocket. I always play the numbers I find on them. And anybody that dies this unlucky, you got to take a chance with them."

"Well, Brendan Bailey," Mickey said, sighing. "Only a few miles to go before you rest."

"If she'd been hipper, she'd still be alive. She dies a fashion victim. In South Jamaica and East New York, kids wear Kevlar shirts or bulletproof hats. This is after that basketball referee in Baisley Pond Park got whacked for his overtime call in a crack dealer's game."

The deceased was unmarried, the detectives quickly discovered within the first hour, and at age thirty-three, Donovan guessed, probably unloved, too. She'd been a natural-blonde weight lifter with a loathsome mouth, the kids were saying, thunderous thighs, and a black barbed-wire tattoo wrapped around her left bicep, just above the entry wound. The exit wound in her muscled back could have been filled with a regulation softball.

"Any idea on the caliber?"

One of the detectives working with the morgue attendants had been leaning over the body with his own ruler as his supervisors talked. He heard his cue, and coughed. He stood up, offered a practiced, bored look, and snapped off his bright yellow disposable gloves before speaking.

"She was hit with a single Teflon-coated exploding bullet. I found a flattened dime-size slug about ten feet up the first-base line."

"Was it rolling fair or foul?" Mickey asked, smiling.

"The bullet pierced her foam chest protector," the young detective continued, "and I believe, passed through her ninth and tenth rib. I imagine the ME will discover that the bullet tore through her liver, spleen, and lungs. It will look like someone set off a bomb inside her chest cavity, Inspector."

"We'll see," Mickey Donovan said, clapping his hands. "Have your squad fax me all your DD5's to the parish office. Brendan, see you around campus."

And then the cop was gone, as quickly as he had appeared.

Even in a city where mindless, random violence was common, the chance murder of Melanie Morgan stood out. This one was better than when a kid riding another elevated train behind Yankee Stadium pegged a wild shot at the Bronx criminal courthouse and managed to shoot a judge in the ass as he lifted his robe in a bathroom. Detectives from the crime scene unit, the only New York City cops who traveled around in station wagons that could double as hearses, rushed to Tweed Field with their lasers, notepads, and tapes to survey the tragedy. Together with Bronx homicide detectives, in an hour less time than it takes the Yankees to play a ten-run, nine-inning game, they measured and weighed critical distances and interviewed witnesses. Then, the investigators bagged the body and zipped up the mystery.

TWO

Waiting Room, Dr. Bernard Klobes's Office, East Seventy-eighth Street, Manhattan

The clock was torture. The agony it produced could not be avoided, or endured. It hung above the receptionist's desk in the doctor's office. Each passing moment was announced with a dreadful, metallic click. She imagined it sounded like a revolver being cocked. It was the last sound you heard before you died.

She did not want to be reminded of time. The baby was inside her, she knew, but still only a vague presence. Perhaps she deserved the torture.

It was odd, but when she'd been a kid, sitting in the backseat of a green Volkswagen Beetle on some deserted country road, struggling with a teenager's desire and those impossibly rolled Trojan condoms, she'd thought getting pregnant was easy. Once she'd gotten married, it became impossible. They had worked for six months to get pregnant. In the beginning, when she'd announced that she was ovulating, he had come running. No one was going to call *him* barren. They'd been married two years before. Sex was great the first year, until they realized it wasn't producing anything.

"Just get off the pill, woman."

"I'm not on the pill."

Once lovemaking became a chore, it lacked passion and affection. The idea of sex as work was brutal and dehumanizing. He once said he had been reduced to shoveling dirt into a hole. Their love withered as his poisonous rage grew. He became limp to her desire.

She'd imagined that this room would be different. It was mauve-colored and kind. There wasn't a single magazine about families or kids on the glass table in the abortionist's office. Women waited to see the doctor while reading *Vogue, Vanity Fair, Allure,* and *Cosmopolitan.* She used to see the same magazines scattered around locker rooms in every great tennis stadium in the world. Perhaps, afterward, a woman could lose herself in fashion.

Her husband was a beautiful man to look at. He had a permanent tan, a seriously muscled chest, a stomach as flat as home plate, and a gymnast's high, steel derriere. Their fiery unions were great physical exercise, better than step acrobics. But in thought and conversation, the groom was as dense as one of his ash baseball bats. He worked in a manicured, green, fabled, and perhaps even sacred place where men never heard a clock.

Shane Dale Heath played right field for the New York Yankees. Behind his back, the other players called him "The Schemer," chiefly because Shane had no conception of baseball strategy or method. This was jock humor, sort of like calling the slowest guy on the team "Bullet" or the skinniest fellow "Tubby."

Unfortunately, Shane was only an average major-league player, a journeyman outfielder. One writer pointed out that although the words "Dale" and "Heath" were listed next to the word "field" in a thesaurus, this guy was a big-league talent in name only. Still, what Shane Heath didn't have in talent, he made up for in conceit. The rockhead was convinced he was on his way to becoming the next stone marker in Yankee Monument Park.

They'd met when he was still playing in the minor leagues, and human decency was possible. She'd been playing an exhibition match in Columbus, Ohio, at Ohio State University. Shane was playing for the Yankee triple-A farm after three years in Nashville (double A) and three years in Albany (A). Some guys who do five years hard on the bus become readers. Others just pick up the books left behind. Shane had been carrying a popular novel, *A Confederacy of Dunces*, when she first saw him. That made him an intellectual in her sporting world. The book, a delightful absurdity, was scary, too. Ginny knew that the writer, John Kennedy Toole, never wrote another novel. He'd committed suicide, at age thirty-two, before the book had been published. She'd watched Heath thumbing through it in the dugout between innings. She was delighted that a jock even knew about the book. It was her favorite work of fiction, too.

At dinner that night, they'd joked about naming their first child Ignatius Reilly after the book's main character, a hilarious genius. Shane was a corker, too, she felt. But as they began to date more and more, the ballplayer read less and less. He measured out his life over coffee while reading the box scores. He had no patience for anything deeper than *USA Today*. He was a six-paragraph man, tops, and joked in the clubhouse that he got through college without reading anything longer than a miniature baseball bat. But Shane read every box score of every printed game in every league and spoke in his sleep of going four for four with six runs scored and eight ribbies. Shane played that dream box-score combination—four-six-four-eight—as his daily lottery numbers.

She had a clock pounding in her head and the guy was likable enough. In the beginning, Shane was decent and caring. He made her loneliness disappear. By the time she realized she had been tricked by the vacuous ballplayer simply play-acting the role of misunderstood genius, they were married.

"Why did you carry around that book?" she once asked at the end of an argument.

"One of our pitchers who played in the Ivy League said it got him laid," Shane admitted. "Chicks are crazy for jocks who can think."

"That's grotesque."

"Maybe," he said, snickering. "But I shagged you."

He cursed at her the same day, and they were never really right as a couple again.

Once Shane was called up to the bigs, or "The Show," as the minor leaguers called it, he was ruined as a husband. In the Yankee clubhouse, Shane unpacked his gear, putting it in an open wooden stall next to the petrified Plexiglass-enclosed locker of the great, dead, Yankee's catcher, Thurman Munson. Steadily, like most legitimate ballplayers, Shane became callous to life beyond the ballpark. By mid-season, the baseball writers all agreed that Shane was a world-class prick.

He quickly tired of his own strikeouts. The fertility business was a maddening and humiliating secret. It was like a major-league curve-ball for him, a confounding mystery.

"Why do I want kids anyway?" Shane had sneered one night, curling his lips in disgust. "Kids are so fucking common. Shit, *fans* have kids."

He suffered through the indignity of the fertility tests, too. On the sultry summer morning the night after hitting his first major-league home run in the Bronx, but well before anyone really could recognize him as a Yankees' star, Shane Heath rode the subway to the doctor's office on the Upper West Side. He had a bottled sperm specimen in his front pocket. The doctor had told him to keep the sample warm. When a transit cop spotted him, nervously shifting the plastic red-capped vial from one pocket to the other, he walked over and asked Shane for some identification. The cop suspected the vial contained a popular new liquid herbal drug, one nicknamed Passion.

"Don't you know who I am?" the rookie whispered to the cop. "Shane Heath. I play for the Yankees. My photo's on the back page of today's *Daily News.*"

"Oh, really?" the cop said. "And I thought you were Michael Irvin and played for the Dallas Cowboys. Please step off the train, sir."

Embarrassed, the rookie outfielder was frisked. The cop, who'd grown up in Co-Op City and had once struck out Bobby Bonillia in a Little League game, hated baseball. He refused to recognize the new Yankees' right fielder, and laughed when he heard the explanation behind Shane's sample of bottled ecstasy.

"You mean you jerked off in a jar?"

"Can I just go, Officer?"

"Was it during the game?" the cop persisted. "Did your team-mates cheer you on?" In the cop's mind, carrying jars of semen on the subway qualified as a quality of life crime. He let Shane go but called the *New York Post Standard* as soon as he got off duty. Page

Six carried a gossip item on Shane Heath and his near arrest the next day under the headline: "Shame on Shane: Bronx Bomber Fires Blanks."

Later, when he'd finally reached the safety of the fertility specialist's office, Shane's wife had called. Come home directly, she'd insisted, I have good news for you. Shane threw his semen in the garbage, where it landed, ironically enough, on his own image.

Shane's homer on the night before had won the game and earned Shane his first back-page splash in the *Daily News* and *Post Standard*. His image had started to seep through the New York subway system, which is how fame begins in the city.

"Yo, rookie," one guy yelled from across the subway car, holding up the *News*. "Is you him?" Shane looked around and got scared. He was embarrassed by his ordinariness. Real ball players didn't live in Manhattan or ride the subway.

As he exited the subway, Shane made a decision. He had just come back from a road trip to the Midwest. He had spent one night with a teenager at the Phister Hotel in Milwaukee and another in Cleveland, where he'd picked up a Fiona Apple look-alike at a bar in The Flats. By the time he'd landed in Detroit, at the Pontetrain Hotel—they were racing Indy cars outside his room—Shane was a fully engorged sports hero.

Shane Heath strode into their apartment and announced his verdict on their marriage: "I want out."

He was a big leaguer, he continued, a New York Yankee. He did not belong to her exclusively anymore. He belonged to America. Then he turned and was gone.

She stood, quivering, for a good, long while. The plastic stick was still on the kitchen table. He never saw the results of the early pregnancy test. She stared with disgust at the blue mark that had so excited her. She was alone and pregnant.

Perhaps she'd gotten lucky. That is what she would tell herself later. Baseball players were unworthy of the attention. This guy could grow up to be a walking hard-on or a wife beater like so many big-ticket players. What then? Suppose she'd had two kids with him by the time he came home and announced he belonged to America? She wasn't going to wait around. She had money. She had a career. Even later, when she'd called him to tell him she was pregnant, he hadn't responded.

"You can't have my baby," he'd said. "I forbid it. The stress from this will mess up my batting average."

She had hung up on the insufferable prick.

So she sat in the kind, mauve-colored room listening to the clock. There was a part of her that watched the clinic door for him, hoping he would come rushing over the threshold to save the baby they had worked so long and hard to make. He never came. And by the time they called her name, she was fine. The sound of the vacuum and the machine surprised her. It covered the sound of the clock.

On the way out, another young patient recognized her. The woman stood and announced, "Oh, my god, *it's you*. I saw you beat Billabong at Wimbledon. I am your biggest fan. Imagine meeting you here. Are you getting one, too? Where is Shane? Oh, right, the Yankees are on the road this week. Shane is in Baltimore. Of course, how witless of me."

Americans, particularly New Yorkers, were amazing in this way. They had no sense of etiquette, place, or even their own lives when they came face-to-face with a sports celebrity.

"Could I have your autograph?" the woman pleaded. She pushed a pen, and a piece of paper at her—an appointment card for the abortion clinic.

She shuddered against the absurd morning, but pushed through her exasperation. With a cold, controlled hand, she completed her signature.

Her name was Ginny Glade.

Center Court, Mt. Cranmore Tennis Center, North Conway, New Hampshire

She could manage defeat.

Ginny Glade masked disappointment with chilly elegance. As

soon as she was good enough to play winning tennis, she had learned the importance of losing well. Her own dad, unlike those shrieking embarrassments who scurried over sidelines now, had taught her to mask her emotions. She maneuvered after even the most numbing loss with canny, almost frosty agility. The abortion nine months before hadn't improved her disposition. Instead of chasing somebody else's kid on center court, she should be nursing her own kid in the shade of a stadium box. In public, there was nothing she could do to rage against the pain. Public tirades and outbursts were banal, even slovenly. To sob in public, she'd decided long ago, was to be defeated again. Ginny never surrendered to tears.

Her real name was Virginia, but she'd gracefully softened that, too. Ginny endured losses and survived life on the Tour by keeping her emotions at room temperature. She could use her icy blue eyes to freeze an opponent in place or silence an inquisitive journalist. As a teenager she'd been pretty wild and hot-blooded. But one day, about twenty years ago, she had just started to freeze over like a Maine pond in early November. Winter became her permanent season. Shortly after she became a pro, the *Post Standard* in New York had nicknamed Ginny Glade "the Morgue Girl."

In recent years, unfortunately, the fading professional tennis player had had plenty of practice in handling public disappointment. She sailed through the most howling defeat with the sturdy, engaging confidence of a Parisian model on a catwalk during the spring show in New York's Bryant Park. The tennis writers liked to call the cold star "winning impaired." Ms. Virginia Glade, they wrote, has too much dignity and not enough backhand. Surrounded by teenaged players and their braying idiocy, the elegant player's composure had become legendary. The greater Ginny's defeat, the greater her poise.

Over the last few years, Ginny's age equaled her world tennis ranking. She was thirty-five this summer and that was a tough number in each category.

Ginny was a year from being over as a female professional tennis player, and she knew it. She had been losing on most fronts lately. Her marriage was over. Everyone who read the gossip pages knew her story, and most appreciated Ginny's simmering anger.

The frosty lady's dilemma this early August afternoon in the Volvo Classic—her first tournament final in two years—was even too much for a cold, ancient fish like Ginny to shrug off. As she prepared to serve for the match in the third set, someone in the box seats behind her opponent held a mirror up to the sun, creating an insufferably blinding light. Ginny mishit her first serve. Staring into the box, Ginny bounced the ball three times, and recognized the father of her opponent, a notorious cheater who liked to call himself "The Jackster." Ginny assumed he was trying to distract her with one of his absurdly large diamond rings, and thought she saw someone sitting behind him who looked vaguely familiar. She focused instead on her serve. She hit a flat second serve that the kid returned deep to her forehand. After an exchange of ten ground strokes, Ginny rushed the net and the kid tried to lob over her head. Grinny, waiting at mid-court, absolutely crushed an overhead winner. She watched the yellow Penn ball hit the back line, leaving a tiny red mark on the white plastic tape. Ginny, even in victory, bowed her head with the proper humility.

But no one made any call for ten seconds.

"Game, set, and match, Ginny Glade," squawked Bud Calloway, the barefoot television announcer told his audience, prematurely. "Look at that ball mark. Please replace your divots on the way out."

The deliberate silence continued.

"Hold it. Where's the call?"

And still no word from the chair, one way or the other.

The crowd favored her blonde, teenaged opponent, Rory Bliss, age fifteen. Miss Bliss danced, wiggled, strummed her racket like an air guitar, and blew kisses to the ball boys. She had so many beaded braids on her hair that she looked and sounded like Methuselah trying to outrun a basket of rattlesnakes. Every fingernail, and each of her toenails, was painted a different color. She flaunted those toenails, hanging ten over the television lens during a break in the second set as she changed her Nike Zoom Air sneakers. She wore Greatful Dead headbands and had a JERRY LIVES bumper sticker pasted across her Wilson/Marvel Comics racquet cover.

"I'm only playing tennis to make enough money to snow-board across America," she'd said. "If I stick with this much longer, my agent says I'll be a Playstation video game. The computer geeks expect me to be hotter than Lara Croft in *Tomb Raider II*. Wait until you get a load of my graphics. Damn, I'm gonna be one righteous babe."

After a decade of cheering boring Europeans, Miss Bliss was "the next one," and the crowd loved her. She reeked of chance. By contrast, Ginny was an anachronism. She was just starting to listen to CD's in her car. And she still wore white Fred Perry outfits. No one under forty cheered ice. Cool just wasn't cool anymore. Rage was the buzz in sports. Ever since McEnroe had exploded on center court at Wimbledon, passion was hot in tennis. Self-control bored American fans.

"Uh-oh," Ginny whispered to a ball boy.

The crowd was howling, showing a willing blindness to the evidence. There was no call from the linesman and the spectators filled the uncertainty with noise. Some kids began to shriek, "Go, girl."

Ginny could see the mark on the tape. It was as clear as a bloody palm print. She looked up to the man in the chair and pointed her racquet to the evidence. With a win, Ginny might be seeded at the U.S. Open the next month.

The mute linesman put her hands over her eyes. Now the chair had to make the call.

"Out," the umpire bellowed.

The umpire, Blinky Hammond, one of the last men still sanctioned by the United States Professional Tennis Association to umpire women's matches, would not even look at Ginny. Right then, Ginny realized that he couldn't see the ball. Blinky Hammond needed glasses but was too vain to wear them. Even when he squinted, he could barely see the lines. The players called him "Senior Squint." But Blinky Hammond was too conceited to be embarrassed. "Hey, even a blind ump is right half the time," he liked to say.

The crowd detonated with wild noise. The blonde kid, who was wearing oversize denim shorts, began to pulsate. She pulled off her oversize white T-shirt, revealing a very mature Demi Moore chest that spilled out over a multicolored Speedo bikini top. The crowd roared. Hundreds of fans, men and women, pulled off their own shirts as The Spice Girls blared over the sound system. They started to body-surf a fan through the grandstand. It was impossible to tell where the women's tennis tour ended and MTV began. The grandstand section had become a mosh pit.

"Yo, baby," yelled a fuzzy-faced ball boy at the newest champion on the women's tour. "Lap-dance over here." The little creep actually waved a twenty-dollar bill over his head.

Ginny wanted to vomit. It was over. Really over. Not just the match, but decency in American sports. Ginny was on fire, burning down in front of five thousand people, with another million watching on cable TV. She patted her white Fred Perry skirt and jogged to the net. She waited two minutes for the kid to show up and shake her hand. All anyone saw was the cool, easy smile. Ginny even raised her racquet in appreciation to the maddening umpire as she walked off.

By the time Ginny was dressed in her endorsements, the photographers were focused on a brand-new red turbo charged 960 Volvo GO sedan. Today's champion drove it home. They parked it over the ball mark on the plastic end-line tape. But Miss Bliss wasn't old enough to drive a John Deere tractor in New Hampshire. The night before, Rory had been turned away from an R-rated movie at the Waterville Valley Mall. In junior high school, the kid was working as a tennis pro to the sound tracks of Alanis Morisette and Green Day. She slid into the black-leather seat and immediately punched a CD in the deck. A song by TLC blasted across the man-made amphitheater.

The teenager, who loved to chase waterfalls, squealed. It was her favorite tape: *CrazySexyCool*. "Oh Gawd," Rory Bliss screamed as she cranked the music even louder. "Now I just *have* to get a license."

The Jackster jumped down from his box. A monument to excess, the Jackster was standing on the court in bright-red Nike shirt, shorts, and sneakers. He was working on his third Nike contract and his fourth wife this decade. If Ted Kennedy had been a tennis dad, he would have been Jack Bliss. A swollen man with slick, glistening black hair, Jack wore two gold bracelets on each wrist. In his day, the Jackster must have been the catch of his trailer park. Seeing him, Ginny wondered why tennis parents felt compelled to come to their daughters' matches dressed to play. Thankfully, hockey dads and jockey moms left their pads, hockey sticks, riding crops, and helmets at home.

"As soon as my Rory is old enough, she'll get a license," the

Jackster yelled after grabbing the ump's microphone. And then he faced the network cameras in his Nike best and boomed, "Next stop. Indy Five Hundred." He laughed and wondered how much Valvoline motor oil would pay him to wear their stuff in his hair.

"Who said cheaters never prosper?" Ginny snapped. "As soon as Rory learns your old dead-ball trick, she'll be in the top ten."

"Oh, Ginny, bitterness does not become you."

After revealing her bikini top on national television, Miss Bliss was now singing a tune made famous by a female rap singer who always appeared on stage wearing a condom over her left eye. Ginny strode off the court and was led by an assistant tournament director into the clammy interview tent. She dug a plastic bottle of Gatorade out of the icy chest and took a seat at the folding table. The only reporter in the front row, Arlon Kettles, worked for the *Manchester Union Guardian*. Ordinarily, the crew-cut reporter covered politics. "Commander Buzz Lightyear," as they called Kettles in William Loeb's old newsroom, had made a name for himself during the state's presidential primary the last time around. He'd caught a Democratic hopeful from the Midwest dancing with a transvestite in a homosexual nightclub. The story in the state's second city was headlined, "Welcome to the Queen City, Senator." In advance of the Volvo Classic final, Kettles had authored five columns on the perils of lesbianism in women's professional sports.

"Hey, Ginny," he said, scratching his crew cut. "Answer me this. How can you, a freakin' pro, miss an easy overhead like that? Don't women on this tour do anything straight?" He roared over the silence.

"At Hampton Hills—where they gave me a free membership when I came with Pat Buchanan last year—even I could put that shot away," Kettles continued.

Ginny swallowed her Gatorade and smiled. Kettles was legendary, too, as competitive. Ten years ago, he'd lived with his father but worked for a competing newspaper, the *Concord Monitor*. When the story broke about a teacher hiring one of her students to kill her husband, Kettles had slashed his father's tires and beat him to the story.

"Thank you very much, *Commander*," she said. "By the way, how's your dad?"

The other reporters began to laugh and wheeze. On the way out, Ginny passed the blonde wonder and "Father Nike." Rory was never sure what her father was up to, and who whetted his sexual appetite. So the kid had developed the habit of addressing every woman she met over age twenty five as "Moms."

"Nice win, kid," Ginny said. "Good luck with the driver's test."

Rory was plugged into a CD player listening to Boyz II Men. "Sorry you missed the overhead, Moms," Rory Bliss replied. "Life is bitchin'."

"I am so sorry, sweetheart," the Jackster said, pulling Ginny aside. "Personally, I thought an attractive lady like yourself would put that ball away. Tough way to lose. But Rory and her new mother are going to take the new car to Boston. I could drive you to Logan Airport myself."

"The ball was in," Ginny whispered. "You saw the mark."

Like some nocturnal lounge lizard, the Jackster flicked his tongue at her and actually grabbed her ass. Ginny waited until the last reporter left the tent, then slapped the Jackster hard across the face. No one saw her rage.

"Damn," the Jackster said. "I was only kidding."

"Touch me again and I'll snap your spine," Ginny said, smiling. "Although I would be surprised to find you had one."

She waved him off, and left. The reptile was probably screwing his own kid. Ginny stepped past him and bumped into Blinky Hammond. A large man, with a prickly melon head, the umpire was sweat ing profusely in the August humidity. At this rate, he would melt by New York and the U.S. Open. Not that Ginny would mind.

"The ball was out," Hammond stammered. He pushed a pudgy hand past Ginny and plunged it into the sweating, plastic ice chest. He came out with two green Heineken bottles. Ginny was colder, and greener.

"You never even came down to inspect the ball mark, Blink," she said. "The linesman missed it and you let the crowd make the call. You are a cowardly little man."

"I saaaawww the ball out," he stammered.

"It is physically impossible for you to see anything below your nipples," Ginny said. "You cost me fifty thousand dollars and a return to the top twenty."

———

As she walked from the interview tent down the hill to the parking lot, Ginny could see her teenaged courtesy driver, a stringy-haired surfer dude who called himself Stimsky. He was dressed in a white T-shirt, white spandex shorts, and red Dr. Martens boots. Ginny decided that from this distance he looked like a used tampon. Stimsky opened the back door to the taupe-colored Volvo station wagon. Ginny closed it and opened the driver's door.

She wanted to stop by her room at the Black Stage Inn and drive directly to Boston in time to catch the last shuttle to New York City. She could be out of this tourist hovel and in her own bed on the Upper East Side by midnight.

"I'll have you at Logan Airport by eight o'clock, man," the surfer dude said. Ginny spotted a rolled joint tucked behind his right ear.

"Thank you, but I'll take it from here," Ginny said. "Please instruct the courtesy driver to meet me at the New York shuttle in five hours."

She roared off, leaving the teenager at the bottom of the Mt. Cranmore skimobile. Ancient red-and-green metal chariots chugged up the mountain. In that moment, Ginny saw herself as an old machine. By five o'clock she was checked out of the hotel and hurtling south toward Boston on Route 3. As Ginny cleared Laconia, she began to cry. Losing at tennis was a lonely, miserable life. Once, she had been a grand accomplishment. She had grown up three hours south of Mt. Washington Valley in New Boston, New Hampshire, where she'd skied in the winter and played tennis in the summer. But there was never enough sun to grow world-class tennis players in New Hampshire, or enough snow to grow Olympic skiers.

The ball was in.

She said it again, out loud in the car. Ginny kept coming back to that. She checked the rearview mirror to make sure she was alone. No one was watching.

"COME DOWN HERE, you lazy turd, AND LOOK AT THE MARK." Her fury surprised her, but she was comfortable with rage. Professional sports, she had come to realize, were just controlled anger.

As she drove on, Ginny looked at her legs. She fit the car perfectly. She was five feet eight and one hundred and thirty pounds. Some of the younger girls had what she called Erma Bombeck thighs, but her legs were perfect. She checked her face in the mirror, again. She had an unlined brow. Although an infatuated Park Avenue plastic surgeon had offered to clear a couple of lines by her mouth for free, Ginny's eyes were free of crow's-feet. She still had a teenager's neck and hands. She had a nice behind. In New York, where construction workers gathered over lunch pails to rate pedestrians, Ginny still heard crude appreciation when she walked down the street. Although she liked being looked at, she hated being ogled.

The New York City fashion designers loved her. There was one guy, Isaac Mizrahi, who said he wanted to adopt her. She got a note from him saying she had inspired him to bring back the jumpsuit in the fall. But his stuff was too expensive. If she was going to afford it, she needed to remain in the top ten. She pulled her black Donna Karen jacket tighter and turned the Volvo air-conditioning up a notch. They laughed at her in the clubhouse because she had frozen people out of the room. Soon Ginny Glade was cold, dark, and happy again.

She got off the highway at the exit for 101 West, Bedford, and pulled into the Sheraton Wanderer. There were only a couple of large hotels near the highway, so every Democratic front-runner in the state's presidential primary after Eugene McCarthy had used the Sheraton Wanderer as campaign headquarters. Ginny walked into the hotel restaurant, alone, and immediately felt a dark, brooding reality.

No one cared.

Three hours south of the state's only professional sporting event and no one recognized her. Ginny ate quietly. The waiter wanted to know if she had heard the Red Sox score, the Red Sox being a team that had started the day fifteen games out of first place. She ate the main course, braised lamb, quickly, but lingered over the apple cobbler. She could run it off in Central Park tomorrow.

The day, which fell on an unspeakable and horrible anniversary, was destined to end terribly, Ginny felt. As she paid the check, she stopped at the door, certain that she smelled a cologne from her youth, and turned around in the lobby, startled. But there was no one there. She shook her head at the smell, smiled, and said to herself, "God, who even wears Ice Blue Aqua Velva anymore?"

At around nine P.M., she emerged into the huge parking lot the hotel shared with the Jordan Marsh department store. On a Sunday night in August, with the department store closed, the lot was empty, an eery, apocalyptic tribute to mall America. She shook the memory off as she stepped outside and saw the front tire of the Volvo. It was flat. Ginny cursed for the first time all day: "*Shit.*"

She was not going to miss the plane. In New Hampshire, she knew it could take at least an hour to get a tow truck. So Ginny opened the trunk and retrieved the jack herself and fitted it into the slot beneath the right-passenger door panel. It was quick, easy work for a professional athlete. She was just letting the tire down when she heard footsteps.

"Can I help you with that, Ginny?" Blinky Hammond asked.

It was the most artificial offer of help she had ever heard. The umpire was absolutely breathless, and sweating beyond all humidity and season. Helping was a physical impossibility for this man. She realized that she hadn't heard his car. That meant he had watched her change the tire. He had been sitting in the car, afraid to get out and afraid to turn on the air-conditioning.

"Once again today, you've stayed in your chair too late to help me," Ginny said. "Laziness will be the death of you, Blinky."

She tightened the last lug nut. "I needed your help five hours ago."

He began to stammer again. "I couldn't help you. Evv . . . vry . . . one in the stadddd . . . ddddium saaaaa . . . www . . . that ball was out."

Ginny tapped the aluminum hubcap back on. "You didn't see the ball, Blinky. Admit it. And instead of pulling your rather ample behind out of that high chair and climbing down to check the ball mark yourself, you let the crowd make the call."

Blinky Hammond grabbed his swollen cantaloupe head with both hands and screamed, "You arrogant cunt. You missed the fucking shot. It was out, bitch. O-U-T. You lost the fucking match, Miss Prissy Fucking Pants."

Blinky coughed in mid-howl, and doubled over, wheezing. A glob of green phlegm hit Ginny on the right shoulder. She saw the shot immediately and she wouldn't miss it this time either. She swung the tire iron at the umpire's head harder than she had ever swung her graphite Yonex racquet. She took a full backswing and hit a perfect backhand, striking the umpire neatly in the center of his forehead. It was an outright winner, as clean a shot as she had ever landed. Hammond was blind to this shot, too. He blinked once and fell at her feet.

Struck with an absurd realization, Ginny Glade actually cackled. Blinky Hammond represented her first two-fisted backhand. But then she felt the pressure. It was not unlike a big match. The whole world was watching but she was not afraid. Ginny felt for a pulse. She couldn't find one and looked around the parking lot. It was a blackened tundra. No witnesses. Calmly, Ginny reached into Hammond's back pocket and tugged on his wallet. She grabbed the tire iron and got into her car. As she was pulling out, a car was pulling in.

"Jesus." She ducked and sped out.

A moment later she was barreling down 93 South, crossing the Merrimack River. She tossed the empty wallet out the window, into the water. Then the incriminating tire iron. As she headed farther south, and cleared the New Hampshire border, she began to laugh at her madness. Steadily, Ginny felt her quiet rage evaporate. She felt absolutely electrified. This was better than escaping a triple match point. Once she had done that against Martina Navratilova, during an exhibition match in Florida. There were no witnesses then either.

Murder was better than winning. She could live with being a sore loser after all. But then she noticed, or imagined, the smell of the cheap cologne again and began to cry.

Once her taillights had faded from the parking lot, the spectator stepped from out of the shadows. Ginny's swing and the umpire's collapse had surprised him. This was more of a mess than he had figured on. But it was easily fixed. Especially for her.

As Ginny raced south, she remembered having grown up in a state free of reality and sales tax. New Hampshire was an islandlike state of loners. Indeed, if they had had a state card game to go with the state flower, the purple lilac, it would have been solitaire.

"Damn," Ginny said aloud. "They've got the death penalty in New Hampshire." That was about all New Hampshire shared with Florida, a state she hated. The tennis brats grew up in Florida. She hated Colorado, too. Colorado was sown with skiers. The kids were good enough in either sport now to quit grammar school and turn pro. Occasionally, the young tennis prodigies were tutored. Mostly they traveled with coaches who doubled as fathers and fathers who posed as coaches. Some girls quit the world tour for the crack pipe.

Ginny was different. She read books, not comics. Some said she had the genes for greatness. The only child of teachers, she had attended Molly Stark High School where she had been taught by Burton Bunyon, who eventually went on to win a Pulitzer Prize in literature. Ginny learned that beauty was thicker than tan, and knowledge deeper than snow. She had attended a frosty school, Syracuse University, on a tennis scholarship. The upstate New York campus had less sunshine and more snow than New England, but she still stayed the full four years.

High school had ended for her with a terrible pain. In her town, the big event was the overnight senior bash following graduation. She had had a young lover named Steve Hill. He had lived in Dunbarton, a neighboring town. He had been an enchanting mix of attitude and aptitude. Most teenagers were either jocks or hippies. Steve had had shoulder-length hair but could dunk a basketball with either hand. He had had a full scholarship to play basketball at Keene State College.

Steve Hill had been Ginny's first *real* boyfriend—they had had sex in the state senator's hayloft during the New Boston Fourth of July party. Steve had been a big beer drinker. Occasionally, he carried a .357 magnum. Once, when they had been parking on the Uncannunac Mountains—Native American for ladies breasts—some of their friends had sneaked up on the parked car. Jim Beckman had been the culprit. The young lovers had just finished their lovemaking when Ginny heard someone giggle. Hill had jumped out and fired his revolver. His friends had scattered. The danger had excited Ginny. On the night of the graduation party, Ginny's boyfriend had been riding in the open back of a pickup when, coming down Mountain Road, the driver had rolled the truck. Steve Hill had hit a stone wall on the fly, and had splattered and died on the first night of the rest of his life. The senior class had held their first high school reunion in Goffstown that weekend in the French and Rising Funeral Home.

Ginny had begun her college days as a widow, which was kind of perfect.

The cell phone rang. She fumbled in her jacket for it.

"Hello, Ginny. Are you still suicidal?"

It was her best friend, Hanna. She was calling from her town house on Beacon Street in Boston's Back Bay.

"No. You get used to it."

"I never did, doll. I would have gutted the fatty and dumped him in a lake like those kids did in Central Park."

"He'll get his," Ginny said coolly. "Look, I was hoping to see you before I got to the airport. But I'm just crossing the border. I'm still an hour out. So I'll call you tomorrow."

"Okay, hon. I just wanted to make sure you weren't out testing air bags."

"Hanna?"

"Yeah?"

"I could use a bag of McDonald's hamburgers right now."

"Me, too. But we're past that point, love. Our carnivore days are behind us."

"Bye."

"One more thing."

"Yeah?"

"The ball was in."

Ginny cursed and hung up. She thought back to 1975. That was the summer she'd met Hanna Ottoman. Hanna had been fourteen years old and newly arrived from Transilvania, Hungary. All of the Europeans travel the world with huge entourages now, but when Hanna had arrived, all she'd brought was an appetite. She'd been one of the last players to escape Cold War Europe, and though the sophomoric tennis writers were always asking her what it was like to grow up in Dracula's home town, she did prefer a good, raw, Romanian steak over pale chicken. Young Hanna had been an unbeatable player and an unstoppable eater. Her real weakness was American food. She'd had a serve like Roscoe Tanner and a backhand like Arthur Ashe, the experts had said. But Hanna had put away stacks of hamburgers and pancakes like Haystack Calhoun. Specifically, she had had the worst kind of teenaged girl's weakness—junk food. Whenever Hanna had won a match, she'd closed the local McDonald's. As she was winning matches as many as four times a week that summer, Hanna had seemed to inflate by the hour. And, God forbid if Hanna lost a match. After a loss, Hanna had always rushed straight to McDonald's, then moved on to Burger King and White Castle, where they tended to never close. The young outsider had had heartbreaking acne, too. Ginny could not imagine the pain of being a newcomer in a foreign land with no real friends, a weight problem, and killer zits. One day Ginny had walked into the locker room and found Hanna pressing white pads against her enraged skin. Ginny had smiled at the poor, lonely, swollen teenager. Then she'd noticed the bottle Hanna was using, and stopped dead. The other girls had all been snickering.

Ginny had been furious. She'd walked over and placed a gentle hand on the teenager's shoulder. It was late May, the prom season.

"Hanna, give me those, they aren't good for your face."

Hanna had recoiled. She'd held the pads against her bosom. "Proper H good," Hanna had said in her best broken English. "Better than Oxy Five."

Ginny had not laughed. She'd held the bottle up. "You are right, Hanna," she'd said. "Proper H is very good. But this is Preparation H. This is for hemorrhoids."

"What?"

"For here," Ginny had said, touching her own behind. "Not your face."

Hanna had understood immediately. "Ass pimples," she'd said.

Hanna had turned on the girls, enraged. Then she'd begun to cry. Ginny had hugged her and they'd both begun to laugh. Hanna's body odor, Ginny remembered, was overwhelming. She'd smelled like a New York City taxi driver locked in his car on a ninety-degree day with a pint of curried rice. Then Hanna had gotten dressed, gone out, and beaten, love and love, one of the girls who had been laughing at her. When they'd met at the net after the match, Hanna had handed the girl the opened Preparation H. "You need now, bitch," Hanna had said.

Ginny stepped on the gas, and sped through the realization that her innocent days were over.

THREE

Midnight, FDR Drive Southbound, Manhattan

Flashes of heat lightning lit the way home.

As the taxi crossed the Triborough Bridge into Manhattan, it started to rain in spits and blasts. Within twenty minutes, FDR Drive was a collection of puddles and stalled cars. Ginny called the reception desk from two blocks north of her apartment building on Second Avenue. Victor the doorman, stood with an umbrella in the chopping wind and met Ginny Glade's cab outside the East Wind Towers on East Eighty-first Street. It was just after midnight. A perfectly starched, continental Italian from Milan, about forty, Victor opened her taxi door and brought a white-gloved hand to his mouth. A small, practiced gasp escaped him. He stumbled backward a half step and shook his perfect head. Victor stared with mock horror into the cab.

"Oh, dear," he said.

Ginny Glade was certain he had discovered an overlooked remnant from the murder dangling from her jacket. Or perhaps she had missed a smudge of homicide on her Calvins. The umpire's blood must have splashed across her bosom. She had been too blinded by rage to see it herself. She had been found out. Victor the doorman knew.

"I am sorry, Ms. Glade," Victor said with choreographed delicacy. "It must have been dreadful, dear. There must be some explanation. Please. Escape this way."

Startled, Ginny flattened a racquet against her chest with both hands, trying to cover the evidence that was so obvious to Victor but invisible to her.

"Sorry for what, Victor?" she said. Ginny was surprised by her piercing tone. "Why would I need to escape?"

Victor cocked his head in amazement. He had been opening taxi doors for the tennis player, with the same mannerly greeting, for ten years. Ginny Glade always came home a loser. And she frequently tipped him twenty dollars for his empathy. So why was this hysterical shrew jumping down his throat now? Had she forgotten how many times he had poured that coarse Yankee outfielder out of a cab for her? Or every time he had told Solomon Brothers Boy when he'd come looking for her after last call on Second Avenue that he had the wrong building?

"I caught the last couple of minutes of your match in the country, dear," Victor said in an anesthetized voice. "It was on television. I watched it with Julio, Caesar, and Black Irish at the lobby desk. We wanted you to win, honest."

With a cackle, Ginny Glade climbed out of the cab. She was laughing at her own idiocy. How did one get away with murder anyway? On the shuttle flight she'd thrown back two Johnny Walker Blacks. A moment later, she'd thrown them up just as fast in the lavatory. She might be a killer, but she was never going to make it as a sot. She had switched to peppermint tea, and her hand had steadied.

She snickered and grabbed her racquets off the seat. Ginny Glade, the ice princess turned murderess, was almost broken by the doorman. She might even have confessed.

Victor began to laugh, too, missing the joke. "I thought the ball was in myself, madam."

"It was, Victor."

"Then may I speak candidly, Ms. Glade?"

"Of course."

"We weren't all pulling for you. Black Irish preferred the blonde teenager. And I think Julio desired her father."

"Well, Victor, for some, policy is policy."

Victor grabbed her two Louis Vuitton bags, loaded them on his handcart, and followed her inside to the elevator. On the way up to her apartment, 17 F, she inquired about news of the building.

"Straight news, Ms. Glade, or the usual slander?"

"Victor, I've been watching bulls hump cows in a field for a week. Spare me no grotesque detail."

"Well, the worst of it is probably Mrs. Newton in 18 C. She walked into the men's sauna last Wednesday, unannounced, and discovered Mr. Newton rather forcefully entangled with Mr. Weiss."

"Sex in our sauna? Hideous. But, given Mr. Weiss's attraction to the new village bathhouse, not entirely unpredictable. Mr. Newton was pitching, no doubt."

"Precisely. Anyway, pitcher and catcher moved out together on Thursday morning. The other battery remains. Mrs. Newton and the ever dangerous Mrs. Weiss have since moved in together. They are said to be severely entangled, too, madam. Bottom line: We have one new condo on the market."

"Hold on, Victor. Didn't you catch Mr. Newton boffing Mrs. Weiss in our laundry room last year?"

"Yes, I did. Then they were spotted in the whirlpool." Victor lowered his eyes and sighed. "This kind of marriage swap is a New York tradition," he continued. "I believe two Yankees' pitchers completed a similar trade in the seventies."

"Actually, Victor, those guys swapped their wives."

"Whatever, dear girl. Some of us, remember, never liked baseball players."

"Touché."

Victor pressed on. "And your sport, Ms. Glade, how are entanglements these days on the ladies' tour?" Victor was a professional rumormonger. Like Liz Smith and the oldest of the newspaper gossip columnists, he always gave an item to get an item.

"Oh, Victor, we're all wife swappers," Ginny said, skillfully parrying his crude thrust. "Damn, now I can't use the whirlpool or the sauna. The East Wind is becoming a regular Christopher Street bathhouse."

"I will bring your bags up promptly, Ms. Glade."

She pressed a hundred-dollar bill, one she had removed from the fallen umpire's wallet, into Victor's palm.

———

Ginny listened to her messages as she ran the bath and unwrapped a bar of glycerin soap: Her mortgage was due. Forest Hills wanted her to play in a Celebrity Pro Am mixed-doubles tournament. Her college roommate, Babe Policano, had met a new cop. The Solomon Brothers Boy wanted to know if she was the same Ginny he'd met at the China Club bar. Joey from Yonex wanted to know how she was set for racquets, which he continued to insist on calling wands. Hanna said she heard a Saudi sheik was going to sponsor the women's tour next year. The water would be turned off for an hour two days ago. Forest Hills was offering a $3,000 appearance fee. Babe said good luck in the Volvo semifinals. Ginny's husband, the Yankee right fielder, had joined Alcoholics Anonymous. Her lawyer, Eddie Smith, said the divorce was one signature away. Babe wished her luck in Sunday's final. Forest Hills would team her with the mayor. Hanna called to say all the ESPN replays showed the ball was clearly on the line. Babe said it was a Jewish conspiracy. Blinky Hammond apologized, but the ball was out.

She almost toppled into the bathtub when she heard his voice. He was calling from a car phone. She heard the static. It was surreal. Ginny replayed it twice before erasing it and retrieving her see-through bar of soap. "Hello, Ginny, this is Blinky. I know today was tough. But the ball was out. You're a pro. I'm a pro. We have to live with the consequences. See you at the Open."

She decided for the second time in six hours that Hammond deserved to be dead. She erased the tape as easily as his life and climbed into the tub. She sank down to her neck in the oily, fragrant water, letting the voice of Annie Lennox wash over her. Then Tracy Chapman. Finally, The Cranberries. She stayed in the tub a good hour, and when she finally pulled the plug, fear drained with the water. She was getting stronger by the minute, inflated by an enormous sense of prerogative. Murder was empowering. She felt bathed in accomplishment. So what if the police found a record of the umpire's cellular phone call to her house from the road? It was his conscience, Blinky just being nice to the most decent woman on the tour.

For the first time since she was seventeen years old, Ginny went to bed feeling unscarred. The power of the secret made her horny.

She slept beneath white silk sheets and masturbated. Occasionally she heard a siren. But the strident wailing was not for her. After all those nights of learning to lose well, Ginny dreamed of getting dressed alongside seeded players and former champions in the main ladies' locker room at Wimbledon. Ginny was finally free of the caste system. Murder, like winning, was thrilling stuff.

Around Midnight, East Village, Manhattan

"The Wraith," as the others called him, did not want to be recognized. He was dressed in an oversize black turtleneck, charcoal jeans, and black high-top Chuck Taylor Converse sneakers. He wore a black "No Fear" baseball cap pulled down over his penetrating blue eyes and marble face. He had a sharp nose, broken repeatedly as a kid while trying to make the Golden Gloves final in Brooklyn North. Even sleeping, he looked like a predatory bird. His jaw was equally sharp and the men joked that he should have been a stone carving. The only thing easy about him was a set of freckles sprayed across his nose and a dimple in his left check. The dimple on his right cheek was man-made, pierced by the tip of a sharpened coat hanger. The ghastly, unshaven Wraith looked fiercely East Village tonight.

He studied the street over the lid of his paper coffee container. He was no stranger to Avenue C and didn't mind looking like a fiend. He knew what he wanted.

The Wraith had the stone body of a marathon runner, which he had been. He had a light step and a poppy rear end. His wife used to joke that he bounced like Jimmy Cagney when he smelled trouble. In mind-set and physique, the cop was like a coiled spring. A radio car from the Ninth precinct pulled in behind his navy blue Toyota Camry station wagon, and as he checked the car in his rearview mirror, the other cop intentionally tapped his bumper.

"Aw, shit," the Wraith said, closing the plastic lid on his container. "Not tonight."

They were parked outside a bar on East Ninth Street, just across the street from Tompkins Square Park. The brick dive, a hippie-dippy place, was called Horsepower. Several years ago, when he had been working a narcotics detail, the Wraith had bought a kilo of smack in the place over the bar. And this was ten years before heroin chic. Models overran the neighborhood now, and tonight he was looking for a girl: his daughter.

The uniformed cop directly behind him, in the driver's seat, hit the siren and then shouted over the loudspeaker, "Yo, shithead. Yeah, you in the black. Move the car."

The Wraith balled his hands into fists but steeled his anger. He did not move. The uniformed officer came up to the driver's window and tapped the glass with his flashlight.

"Out of the fucking car, night crawler. You hit my RMP."

The cop was careless. He came too far down the door.

"I said move it, shithead. Or catch a beating."

The silver nameplate said ABRUS. His partner, a black cop, was smart enough to have his own name covered with a black mourning band. He was already on the passenger side of the car, looking in through the window, as he came around. The alert partner spotted the NYPD radio on the passenger seat and thought he recognized the driver's face.

"Hey, uh, partner," the second cop said. "Just a second."

But Officer John Abrus was already at the driver's door. "Hey, stepdaddy. You won't be getting a leg over any teenaged runaway whores tonight. Get the fuck out of the car. I'm going to kick your skinny ass right now."

Just then, the Wraith sprang the driver's-side door open, slamming two hundred pounds across the cop's legs and wedging them against the curb. The cop shrieked and doubled over. They had taught the move at the police academy. The Wraith unfurled from the car. There was a gold shield in a wallet hanging from a metal chain around his neck.

"I'm sorry, Officer Abrus," the Wraith said. "You're going to kick my ass?"

"Shoot the fuck," Abrus wheezed. "Cap this prick . . . Shit, Dave . . . Partner, where are you?"

The Wraith shot a look across the hood of the car.

David Gaines, the partner, froze. He recognized the Wraith as DI Mickey Donovan, and raised his hands in resignation. "I'm not really with him."

Mickey Donovan grabbed Abrus by the shoulders, pinned his arms to his side, and made it impossible for the cop to draw his nine-millimeter service revolver. He grabbed the cop's gun with his left hand and looked into the cop's eyes.

"Bang," he said. "You're dead, Officer. It's that easy."

The inspector shot another look across the car hood, pinning Abrus's partner, Officer Gaines, also. His gold shield dangled directly over Arbus's face, letting the cop know he had fucked up big time. By then, Gaines had calmly placed his own service revolver on the car hood. "Jesus, the guys were right. The Wraith is the last thing you see before the end. You want my shield, too?"

Donovan removed the club from the now complacent cop's utility belt. He thumped it against his own hand. "Officer Abrus, I don't believe intentionally bumping the suspect vehicle during a routine car stop is proper police procedure," Mickey Donovan said. "Haven't you read rule thirty-one on car stops? And your language violates every tenant of the NYPD's CPR program—courtesy, politeness, and respect."

Mickey slammed the black club across the cop's bullet-proof vest, knocking the air out of him. "How about Section twenty-one B of the uniformed patrol guide on etiquette? Or twenty-one C on pro-fanity?" In response, the cop coughed.

"You are a walking civilian complaint, Officer. And in case you haven't figured it out yet, my name is Mickey Donovan. I'm your inspector."

"Oh, shit, the Wraith," the cop said. "We heard about you at the academy. I didn't mean nothing, sir."

Abrus. Mickey Donovan knew the guy's father. He was a patrol captain with Brooklyn North homicide. The partner, who had dis-creetly removed a black mourning band from his badge, came around the car. Mickey let the cop go, brushing off his uniform.

"It is very easy to die out here," Donovan said. "Your old man deserves better."

"He is my steady midnight partner, sir," Gaines said. "He is pull-ing this crap all the time. I can't control him."

Mickey put an arm around each cop. "Come on, you two, let's walk and talk."

They began walking down Avenue C. It was the hour when the neighborhood seemed on the make, people passing each other with excitement and dangerous expectations.

"When I was in the four-four," Donovan began, "I worked steady midnights with Johnnie Magee. He was a hearty, handsome cop. But he had a mouth and a temper not unlike yours. He believed that shield gave him the right to rule the precinct. At his worst, he was a one-man occupational army. We called him Nutsy."

"I've heard of him. My father knew him."

"Your father hated him, and every cop like him. But don't get ahead of the tale, young Abrus. Nutsy Magee was a fiercely active cop. But he couldn't run that fast. And so whenever he caught a suspect who tried to run away from him, he broke one of their feet. I wouldn't stand for beating prisoners, and eventually stopped making collars with him. He just beat prisoners. If you wanted your prisoner beat, you called Nutsy."

"Every precinct got a psycho cop," Gaines said. "We don't just got guys who want to stick plungers up every prisoner's ass anymore, now we got guys who want to stick them up the mayor's ass until he gives us a raise."

"Yeah, well, one night, when I was off, Nutsy got shot at through a door. He crashed through a side window and wrestled the suspect to the ground. It was a grand arrest. If Nutsy had stopped there, he would have been awarded the Combat Cross. But he didn't. He beat his handcuffed prisoner in the radio car all the way back to the precinct. Nutsy was in and out of the holding cell all night long, stomping his prisoner. There were a half dozen cops in the squad room. They watched, winced, but never said, 'Stop.' Nutsy beat the man to death."

"That isn't right, sir," Officer Gaines said. "Only cowards beat handcuffed prisoners."

"Or call citizens 'shithead' over the police loudspeaker in front of a whole neighborhood. Gentlemen, out here on the street, if you want respect, you have to give respect. Nutsy went to jail. All of the cops who were in the squad room that night were fired. But if I had been there, it wouldn't have happened. Every time I see Nutsy Magee—he's out now—I tell him the same thing: 'If I had come to work that night, you'd still be a cop. I would have kicked your ass and saved your life.' Keeping him away from the prisoner that night would have saved two lives—the prisoner's and my partner's."

"I saw Nutsy at a PBA racket at The Harborside in the Bronx," Gaines said. "He's not the PBA poster boy anymore."

"I saw him at last summer's PBA convention in the Catskills, too," Abrus added. "He's a bankrupt, miserable drunk now."

"The cop died with his prisoner," Donovan said. "Officer John Magee never got an inspector's funeral or even a plastic-covered Mass card issued in his name, but perished in the Four-Four holding cell that night."

Inspector Donovan looked past Abrus to his partner, Gaines. "When you see a crime happening, stop it."

Then the inspector turned to face Abrus. "Even if the criminal is your partner."

The inspector walked away, and got lost in the crowd of dykes, spikes, and leather, searching the crowd for a familiar face. But he never found her that night. He was still searching when his beeper went off. The message flashed across the miniature green screen: Call the command center. Forthwith.

This was the great thing about the job. At any second in New York City, anything could happen. Murder. Disaster. Terrorism. Assassination. Everything was possible in New York City at any hour of the day or night. He called from a corner pay phone.

"What you got, Casey?"

"A major shit storm at the mayor's residence, sir. Mayor Caruso just called down here himself from the mansion and said to get you on the phone, now. He's got the early edition of the *Times*. He was screaming about some quote you gave them about why crime was down on the Upper East Side."

"Right; I said we put more cops on foot patrol. I believe I told the *Times*, 'Crime is down because Police Commissioner William Flynn freed us to police the city again.' "

"Mayor Caruso read me the quote, sir," Casey said. "I saw the paper myself ten minutes before the mayor called. We were expecting the call."

"How bad?"

"Caruso screamed, 'I hired that out-of-state cowboy when no one else would let him near a gun. And this is the thanks I get for saving this city? Get your Inspector Puke up here right now. Tell him to come around to the back door, alone. I'll wait up and fire him myself.' "

"I'm on the way to Gracie Mansion now," Donovan said.

He walked back to the car. He had met the mayor for the first time a month earlier. There had been huge shootout in a parking garage in Queens, the greatest firefight in the modern history of the NYPD: seven hundred bullets fired. By the end of the police action, on Queens Boulevard in Kew Gardens, the bad guy was fully aerated, head to toe. The *Daily News* reporter noted that the deceased had "soaked up 20." The "Boulevard of Broken Dreams," as Jimmy Breslin had called it in his newspaper column, was filled with broken glass. The cops had even shot up a Chinese diner where a local congressman was soaking up a quart of wonton soup.

Unfortunately, the cops had also killed an innocent bystander, a hardworking Nigerian immigrant who had left his wife and kid in a restaurant while he fetched the family car. The papers called it a "Friendly Fire" case, but it was really a case about ammunition. Most of the bullets the police officers had fired ripped right through the perp's flesh and kept on going. A couple of them went through doors and walls. One steel-jacketed round had torn clean through the bad guy and killed an unlucky fellow standing twenty yards behind him. He had perished holding a claim check. The department had decided after that shoot-out to issue dumdum bullets. The bullets flattened out when they hit and stopped the guy, usually dead.

Inspector Mickey Donovan, an immigrants' son, had gone to the Bronx wake himself and had told the widow, point-blank, that New York City police officers had accidentally shot her husband to death. He had gone quietly, and had stood in the back of the funeral parlor. Mickey Donovan had expected the widow to slap him. He had figured the NYPD deserved it. Instead, she had hugged him for his honesty. When Inspector Donovan had gotten back to One Police Plaza that afternoon, Mayor Vito Caruso had called him directly. The mayor had wanted to know if Inspector Donovan thought it was a good idea for the mayor of New York City to attend the wake, too. Mickey had told the mayor it was the right thing to do. The papers and television crews had tagged behind the mayor into the funeral home. The next day, the *Daily News* had written an editorial saying, "The NYPD could learn a lesson from the mayor. Why weren't the cops there to pay their respects, too?"

That was the way this mayor worked. No good deed went unpunished. He had to look better, smarter, and more considerate than everyone else.

So now Mayor Vito Caruso wanted to scold Inspector Donovan, the rising star of the police department. The mayor knew Donovan because the detective boss was probably more responsible for reducing the city's murder rate than anyone else in the department. Donovan had come up with the model for attacking crime. He tracked everything by computer and flooded areas with cops. He had also come up with the simple idea of checking turnstile jumpers in the subway for warrants and wanted cards.

"I bet that guys who get on the subway to rob people don't bother paying their fares," Donovan had insisted.

The idea had revolutionized crime fighting. Criminals who expected to be rousted by cops stopped carrying guns. Shoot-outs and murders plummeted in New York City. Maybe the cops had even saved the city. They had certainly saved the mayor, a brilliant but tempestuous tennis-playing womanizer whose propensity for leaving his wig behind in bedrooms around town was legendary. He was also a loud-mouthed bully. At the insistence of his father, a Brooklyn machine politician, who had the good sense to die of a heart attack while walking his pet ferret when a federal corruption unit was closing in on him, Vito had given up a career as a songwriter to become a lawyer. The kid had become a prosecutor and cleaned up his family name by putting some of his father's friends in jail. He had found most of the evidence in the attic of his uncle's house in the Rockaways.

A reasonably handsome man, with dark eyes and a dimple in his right cheek, Vito was championed for office by an obsolete political party, The Jimmies, who held their meetings on East Seventy-second Street only a couple of doors down from where former mayor Jimmy Walker had ended his European exile.

Vito's first job in politics had been Manhattan Public Advocate and he had become hugely popular by personally promoting bills to legalize offshore gambling and register new voters at the state-owned lottery machines. Now, His Honor regularly appeared as the main event at city hall variety shows and boycotted *Letterman* to appear on *Leno* because he believed the California-based show gave him more of a national presence.

Mickey Donovan had just reached the FDR Drive entrance at Houston Street when his second cell phone rang. Only the police commissioner, William Flynn, had the number.

"Inspector Donovan, sir."

"Hello, Mickey," the commissioner said. "I am at The Palm having a late dinner. But I'll meet you in McFadden's in five minutes."

"I can't, sir. The mayor has ordered me to Gracie Mansion to take the loyalty test. I gave an unauthorized quote to the *Times*."

"Oh really? How bad a quote?"

"I didn't put the mayor's name in the same sentence with credit."

"Wow, a death-penalty case. I saw the *Times*, Mickey. Meet me for a drink at McFadden's."

"His Honor doesn't like to wait, sir," Donovan said.

"*We* will be one hour late, Inspector," the commissioner insisted.

"He said to come alone."

"Sorry, but we can't oblige Mayor Caruso tonight, Mickey. Besides, he's only the mayor. It's not as if he has the biggest job in New York City. It's not as if he's the police commissioner."

Mickey hadn't known Flynn until the mayor had hired him as police commissioner two years before. He had interviewed for an inspector's job and had flunked the interview. Asked what he should do with the old guys, Donovan had said, "Keep them, sir. Stability is important in the NYPD."

Later, Donovan had come back and asked, "Can I amend my answer, sir?" Commissioner Flynn had invited the young captain back into his office.

"I would fire them all, sir. All the guys left over from the last administration are ass kissers and yes-men. You can't succeed with men like that, and if I may be so bold, neither can the mayor."

"Be bold. What do I need?"

"You need people to stand up and challenge you every step of the way. Loyalty is great, sir, but ideas are better. You don't want guys dedicated to anything but change. The NYPD is dead with mindless loyalty. You need ideas."

They had become friends and met in McFadden's regularly. Once, when the mayor had felt snubbed by President Bill Clinton on the crime issue, he had ordered his police commissioner and deputies to break protocol and snub the American President's airport arrival. The cops had gone to McFadden's, locked the doors, and hidden out. Hatred between the mayor and his commissioner had begun to grow right then. That night, Mickey had beaten Commissioner Flynn to the bar. They had both retired to a seat in the back under a color poster of Easy Goer, the racehorse. The PC always said the same thing as he studied the muscular animal. "That horse was that fast, and look, not a hoof on the track."

The police commissioner moved through life at the same pace. He switched cities and wives every couple of years. He was not what they called "a commitment guy" in One Police Plaza. He was not unlike the mayor, who only believed in the politics of Vito Caruso. The mayor supported each and every candidate who was good for his career, period. He called himself "an independent" to disguise his disloyalty and argued that after Bill Clinton, politicians no longer needed views or positions to get elected.

"Americans won't tolerate leaders anymore," Vito joked. "They want poll watchers." Vito could hold a finger to the political wind with the best of them. Steadily, he had filled his administration with sycophants and butt kissers who practically wandered the city hall rotunda in knee pads so as to best serve Vito Caruso. Like the mayor, the police commissioner believed in nothing so much as himself. They were both flawed men, neither one believing in any political ideology beyond the last poll.

The police commissioner told his bodyguard to come in from the car, too. Unlike the mayor, who bought his clothes off the rack at a Syms store in midtown, the police commissioner shopped at Barney's. He dreamed of someday being able to afford hand-tailored English suits. As a professional, the cop wanted to make two lists. He wanted to make the GQ best-dressed list the same year he was named Time magazine's top crime fighter. Some people thought he was physically afraid of the mayor, but he wasn't. Like the mayor, the police commissioner just didn't like confrontation.

Flynn ordered one Irish coffee, and then after twenty minutes, a second. He never once looked at his watch. Mickey had a glass of Perrier. Then he ordered an iced potato vodka.

"No fruit," Mickey said.

The waitress, from Belfast, had recently won her immigration status in a lottery. Unlike Mickey, the commissioner was a hopeless flirt.

"Hello, Bernadette, what are the odds tonight?" Flynn asked.

"On what, Commissioner?"

"On me and you, of course."

"A bridge jumper's, sir. Maybe two hundred to one."

"For or against?"

"That is the question, isn't it? You want to take your chances?" And then she turned on a spiked heel and clicked off.

They both liked her because she wanted to be a cop.

"She doesn't wait on the table," Flynn said, sighing. "She stakes it out."

An hour and a half later, the police commissioner strode to the side door of Gracie Mansion and knocked. Mayor Vito Caruso, wearing a silk red-paisley bathrobe, opened the door.

"Police Commissioner Flynn! Oh, what a surprise. Come in."

They walked into the side sitting room. The mayor's keepers were all around, the next day's papers spread out. There was a hole in the paper where the quote should have been.

"I only expected to see Inspector Donovan at this hour," the mayor said. "I wanted to discuss the morning operation against the East Village squatters. Then I saw that he had been talking behind my back to the newspapers again. I want to squash this now."

"Of course you do, sir. But we're all in this together, right, Mr. Mayor? And you are the boss, despite that silliness in the paper. The inspector called me before he spoke to the *Times* and I told him what he could say. Blame me."

"Maybe I will."

The rage went out of the mayor. He had the quote clipped out, in his silk pocket. He crumpled it.

"You are the greatest mayor since La Guardia," the mayor's head cheerleader, Benny Youngblood, said.

"You won the city back, Mr. Mayor," his first deputy head inflater, Dick Concerto, added. "The city doesn't deserve you. You should be our next president, sir."

The mayor could not, and would not, disagree.

"We're winning, aren't we, Commissioner?"

"No, sir," Commissioner Flynn said, smiling. "Actually, there is no *we* here. *You* are winning, Mr. Mayor."

The mayor walked to a humidor and pulled out two cigars. "Castro left these beneath his seat when I had him thrown out of Lincoln Center," the mayor said. The mayor handed one to his police commissioner, and then the second to Mickey Donovan, who stuffed it inside his jacket.

"You have to be up early, boys."

"Good night, sir."

As they reached the door, the mayor whispered to Police Commissioner Flynn. No one saw, or heard. "If you ever show up here uninvited again, Flynn, I'll have you arrested. I *am* the mayor."

"Then stop acting like the police commissioner," Flynn snapped. The commissioner got close and did not flinch. He hoped the mayor could smell his breath. "Don't ever pull this divide and conquer crap again, sir."

All any of the aides could see was the two men, Mayor Vito Caruso and his police commissioner, smiling at each other and shaking hands.

The cops laughed all the way downtown. The mayor was a megalomaniac, but the easiest kind to deal with. He could be neutered with a compliment. He also wasn't much of a knife fighter. For all his bluster, he hated confrontation. He liked people to think that his balls clanked when he walked down the street, but the truth was that he shivered when anyone dared to confront him directly.

"He'll kill me one day, Mickey," the commissioner said. "Just shoot me in the head. Don't forget that."

"No, boss, he won't do it himself. He'll get some lawyer from the corporation council to stab you while he's at the opera."

The PC chuckled. The inspector was right, of course. Before he got out of the car, Mickey Donovan said, "You didn't have to come, sir. I know how to handle him when he gets in one of these fratricidal rages. I could have given him a blow job myself."

"Of course you could have, Mickey," the PC said. "But that sicko only likes it when I do it in front of his staff. Humiliation builds character. Last year people were saying New York was over. If we can last the year, we can win the city a second chance. So let me handle this one bad guy, Inspector. You go out and get the rest of them."

"Character is fate, boss," Mickey said. "Just remember that. So our mayor is doomed."

After Mickey dropped the commissioner off at his Central Park West apartment, his regular cell phone rang. It was nearly four in the morning.

"Casey here, Inspector. We had a suicide on the F train in the Rockefeller Center station. Not much, really, but we can't open the uptown track because they can't find the rest of the body. Chief Higgins says the rush hour will be totally fucked if we don't get the trains moving within an hour."

"I'm on my way."

Five minutes later Mickey Donovan walked into the station. Detectives from the crime scene unit were on the tracks, carrying white plastic bags. A couple of them saw Donovan and quickened their pace.

"Lieutenant Bailey is on his way in," one of the cops said.

"Why? This isn't a murder."

"He says he won't know that until we find all the pieces."

Donovan groaned. "And what exactly are you missing?"

"The right leg."

Donovan wheeled around and surveyed the platform. There was a woman in a Knicks jacket at the end of the platform. She was sobbing on the arm of the transit sergeant. Donovan walked over and hung his head, then offered his hand. The transit cop nodded and took a couple of steps away so he could speak to the inspector without being overhead. "That woman is Evelyn Acevedo," he said. "The sister. She was standing with John Carlos Jiminez when the train started to pull in. He just lost his job with Con Ed. Drinking hard since noon. He jumps right in front of the southbound F train. At first we thought he was a twist-tie job, but he's quite dead."

"Twist-tie job?"

Mike McAlary

"Sorry, I forgot you're not a regular down here," the cop continued. "It's a freaky train thing, Inspector, one of our terrible transit secrets. When the train rolls over a jumper, they don't always die right away. Many times they fall in the gutter between the rails and the passing train crushes them and then twists their legs up into a tourniquet. When we lift the train off the victim with air bags, they untwist and die. We can't do squat to save them. Usually, I got to climb down next to the poor shit and tell him, 'Look, I know you feel great, but you're dead. As soon as we lift the train with the air bags, you're gonna die.' I explain the twist-tie phenomena and then get the poor schmuck's wife down there so he can say good-bye."

"You have a shitty job, Sergeant."

"Yeah, the worst duty on the Job. If I've had one twist-tie job, I must have had fifty of them over the last twenty years. This guy here was killed instantly."

Mickey shuddered and walked over to the sister. "I am sorry," he said.

"Juan ain't no crazy," she explained. "He just got desperate."

"Indeed."

The sergeant took him a step away and whispered, "The guys can't find his leg. They been at it a full hour. The MTA says they got IND trains backed up to the middle of Queens."

Donovan turned back to the track and studied the activity. It was a delicate matter, but suddenly he thought of something and approached the sister.

"I am sorry about your brother. I can see you were close."

"I loved him. We were together all the time."

"Yes, that just makes it harder. You had parties and dances— family reunions, right?"

"Yeah, but what you mean?"

"Oh, nothing. I had a sister, too, but not as pretty as you. When my family got together for the holidays, she always insisted on dancing with me. I lost her a couple of years ago in a car accident. It's very embarrassing, but I love the memory."

"Well, I ain't had that stuff with Juan Carlos. He wasn't one for no dancing."

"Oh, really? Why?"

"Mister, my brother, Juan Carlos, ain't got but one leg. He got hit by a city bus as a kid."

48

Inspector Donovan bowed and tipped his cap, backing away slowly. "I am sorry to intrude on your grief, miss."

He was twenty yards away, his back to the sister, smiling when he gave the order. "Everybody out of the hole," Mickey Donovan said. "We are done here, gentlemen. Move the train."

FOUR

Dawn, East Village, Manhattan

The police commander didn't trust cops not to hurt people. Especially today, in this situation.

Hell, he didn't even like cops carrying guns on days like this one. So as Deputy Inspector John Michael Donovan, the commander of the special investigations unit, stared down at the wall of helmeted cops on East Fifteenth Street in Alphabet City, he was sure his cops would kill someone, probably some drug-crazed juvenile.

Maybe his daughter.

The city was at war again with the surly squatters in the East Village. It happened every spring. They were like college kids headed for the Bahamas for spring break. As soon as the temperature hit sixty, they came out. There were about a hundred squatters living illegally in a row of brick four-story walk-ups on East Fifteen Street between Avenues A and B. Little kids who had squatted in the place their whole lives scurried, like cockroaches, through the rotted floors.

Five buildings were ignitable today. The city's Department of Housing Preservation and Development wanted to gut them for low-income housing. The squatters, insisting they were in the buildings first, refused to move. Fathers named Justice and mothers named

Freedom raised kids named Thor and Rogue. Squatters promised to strap the kids to doors when the cops arrived with their battering rams. Some revolutionary had nailed green-and-white New Hampshire license plates over their mail slots. The state motto was entirely appropriate: "Live Free or Die."

At dawn, only a few hours after saving the morning rush hour for thousands of strap hangers, Mickey Donovan stared through a pair of binoculars down on to East Thirteenth Street from the roof of a sixteen-floor apartment building. As he studied the gathering rabble, he realized that the squatters were but a variation on a theme. If you cut their hair and deloused them, gave them guns and put them in Montana, they would be every bit as dangerous as the Freemen. Or the freshman class in the police academy.

The sons of squatters would probably grow up to join the militia movement. They wrote their own laws. They were an impossible congregation of communists, fascists, political agitators, artists, anarchists, families, rappers, deadheads, pot smokers, felons, computer hackers, and heroin addicts.

The East Village had become a fetid catch basin for failure and featured a wanton crew of would-be revolutionaries led by a disgraced former cop, Peter Herod, aka St. Peter Heroin. The ex-cop had gotten the nickname in 1982, after he'd shot a dealer who'd sold him a beat bag of dope. Based on the off-duty cop's version of events, the Manhattan district attorney had arrested the dealer. He was later convicted of attempted murder and shipped off to Attica. Only five years later did Herod come forward to a newspaper reporter and admit the frame-up. He had said he believed the truth would free him. He sat the reporter down on a bench and said, "Yeah, I shot him right there. He turned at the last minute and lived. Then I framed him."

The cop, who was in psych services by then, had switched places with the framed dealer, who had died of a heroin overdose two weeks after he'd gotten out. Peter Herod had pled guilty, done two years, and written a couple of prison letters on the manifest corruption of police power. They had been pasted over every mailbox and street pole in the East Village. Peter Heroin emerged from jail as downtown's anarchist hero. He reigned today as St. Peter Heroin, the apostle of junk.

Inspector Donovan looked to Francisco Nunez Camacho, a sergeant from his twenty-man Manhattan-based detail, and smiled. "This would be a good time to transfer to the DA's squad. We're looking at a very shitty day."

"Maybe you should have left us for that UN job in Bosnia, boss," Camacho shot back.

The tank was Mickey's idea. If it worked, the mayor would take credit, but if it failed, the inspector would crash and burn. (Although he led a shadowy life as the Wraith, Mickey could be a tank, too— a weapon the police commissioner used to handle matters both loud and delicate. You just pointed Mickey in the right direction and he rumbled, routinely solving the city's most fantastic murders as he protected his city and department from public embarrassment, rebellion, calamity, riot, and assorted other terrors.) Startled citizens ran as the mechanized vehicle rumbled through the East Village. It was armor-plated, seventeen feet long and ten feet high. Mickey Donovan had first seen it used in 1973 when a cop was killed trying to save some hostages. The NYPD had borrowed it from the National Guard to rescue the pinned hostages by crashing through the front door of a warehouse. Mickey had found it in a garage on a Manhattan pier next to a couple of shot-up cars being stored as evidence. They had painted the tank blue and named it *Real Brave One* just to piss off the city firemen. The FDNY had been calling itself "New York's Bravest" soon after cops began calling themselves "New York's Finest." Neither side tired of the intramural war.

Two helicopters roared low over the squats. Donovan ordered them into the sky just to scare the hell out of people. He was betting on a total surrender—hoping the loudmouths were as weak-kneed as a former mayor who had given the village up to them.

Since the embarrassment of a police riot in Tompkins Square Park ten years earlier, the department had simply quit policing the homesteaders. A homemade videotape of the cops clubbing unarmed women had cost a dozen men above the rank of lieutenant their jobs. But now, the NYPD was back, this time with a tank and helicopters to combat the scum. "The Mad Mick," as cops in the gym at One Police Plaza jokingly called the passionate inspector, wanted a win. A couple of days before, the New York State Court of Appeals had given New York City permission to move anyone, and everyone, off East Thirteenth Street.

Mickey had commanded uniformed cops for a year before returning to the detectives bureau. He paced the roof as he considered "Operation Roach Motel" again. The cops stood below in formation, in powder-blue riot gear. The submachine guns were there, but hidden. Cops held black nightsticks against bullet-proof vests. On a humid August morning, law and order looked like a thousand sweaty, flexed biceps.

Inspector Donovan was in plainclothes because the blue bag only infuriated the young anarchists. Uniforms fed rage. Hell, he would wear a tie-dyed uniform and come disguised as Jerry Garcia if they would just go quietly.

Operation Clean Sweep was city hall's official name for the event. It was a test of wills for the new mayor and his new police department. The mayor was your typical morning-after warrior. Historically, he didn't engage people when it mattered. When the Vietnam War had begun, Caruso had enlisted in the college opera club. As a young lawyer, he had been a loud, colorful figure who believed in histrionics over facts. And though Vito might have been all opening argument and no cross-examination, he had won some popular cases. He had proved that a former school board head actually owned a construction firm that had filled a hundred public schools with asbestos before joining a joint state and federal task force that uncovered massive corruption in the region's nursing homes. Then, in a move that put him on the La Guardia track, a cable show had given him a job dissecting the Sunday newspapers.

By the time he ran for mayor, no one could compete with his televised credibility.

"The newspapers don't like me because I was paid by a television station to point out newspaper lies," Vito Caruso explained on election night. "But New York TV stations are just as bad. If some newspaper wants to give me a column to point out their fibs, I'll do that, too."

By the time he was sworn in as mayor, Vito Caruso had signed writing deals with both tabloids. And, by the end of his administration's first 100 days, it seemed as if the only television and newspaper journalist in the media capital of the world with any access to Mayor Vito Caruso was a newly syndicated columnist and television commentator named Vito Caruso. The sour and suddenly obsolete city hall reporters in room nine began calling him Mayor Pravda, not that the insult was ever heard on a broadcast or printed in a newspaper. Vito Caruso, you see, disapproved.

The mayor's principal professional worrier was Benny Young-blood, a kind of human suppository. He dated back to the mayor's days as a prosecutor. Once he had told the police commissioner that he'd better phone the mayor directly to report a rather benign double homicide in Bedford Stuyvesant. When Flynn had asked why the mayor would care at 2:00 A.M. about an anonymous drug murder, Youngblood's face had grown ashen.

"Mayor Vito won't care, Flynn. But if His Honor finds out we knew, and didn't call him, he'll cut our balls off."

So the detective squad commander who hadn't called city hall with the news of a big murder arrest was on public display by noon the next day, guarding the mayor's car in the city hall parking lot. If a press conference started without him, the mayor went into a frenzy. Crime was *his* freaking issue. The NYPD belonged to Vito. Any cop who asked for a raise was disloyal. So what if cops died cheaper in New York City than anywhere else in the Northeast? The troops had to survive the intrusive behavior of a mayor who wanted to be police commissioner and a police commissioner who wanted to be mayor.

Inspector Donovan was on the front lines of city hall's new get-tough policy this morning. He had to prove that this mayor and his police force could preserve the city. He sighed and picked up his binoculars. By 7:00 A.M. the men were ready. Suddenly the rebels pushed a wrecked car into the street and turned it over. They cheered and then retreated behind their barricades. The ambulances were ready, but parked out of sight, under the FDR Drive. Helmeted city housing workers in disposable white paper suits formed a cleanup brigade two blocks away. They stood behind trucks loaded with cement blocks and hissing cement mixers, carrying sledgehammers and shovels. Their job was to seal a building as soon as the cops emptied it. The inspector watched a protestor, about his kid's age, light a match to a wicked bottle. One mother dangled her kid out a third-story window.

"This is Inspector Donovan," Mickey announced into his portable radio. "Advance. Repeat. Advance. Operation Roach Motel is in full effect."

There was a scurrying sound on the sandy roof behind him. The old Bronx cop in Donovan made out the sound of claws, a large ferret perhaps. He turned and came face-to-face with Benny Youngblood.

"But Mayor Caruso is still two minutes out."

The gasoline bomb exploded on the wreck below them. Real Brave One splintered through the first plywood barricade.

The demonstrators broke and ran. The rout was on.

"Oh, really? Well, I hope you gave the mayor a helmet."

Youngblood began to tremble. "But the mayor wanted to order the tank into action himself . . ."

Inspector Donovan smiled, then put his arm around the mayor's special assistant. "I'm sure he did, too. But, Youngblood, only you know, and I know, that the mayor didn't give that order. You can tell those leaden city hall reporters anything you want. You can tell them Mayor Vito Caruso called in an air strike, too, for all I care. They won't know any better. They followed him around for a year in a vehicle you stole from the feds and they never even ran the plate. They are world-class nitwits. They still think the mayor chased crime out of town by going after the big, bad, squeegee men."

"The mayor attacked quality of life crimes. Everything stems from the first order."

The inspector released the mayor's man, saying, "Winning the crack war didn't hurt either. So what if the last mayor did that? Let him prove it. Vito runs the city now. You control the reporters. The narrative and government of New York City is yours to run."

Donovan turned and pointed to the pitched battle below. "My job is to get those people out without hurting our guys. We can handle the surrender. You do what you do. Get your press-office posse in here and rustle up some news. But please keep His Honor off the set until I give the all clear."

He handed Errand Boy his binoculars. "Keep an eye on the vultures. They got camcorders all over the block. We're live, as they say, all the way live."

"Shit. If the mayor sees the tank moving . . ."

Donovan pointed to a box where the press was barricaded behind blue sawhorses. "And look, sport. Those damn reporters are taking notes on their own. No one is spinning them. The mayor won't like that. You can't allow that."

Youngblood studied the mob of unescorted reporters and

moaned. "Jesus. The *Times* actually has two Metro section reporters on the street at this hour. Shit. The story is getting away."

Youngblood fled the roof. Within an hour, "The Battle of Alphabet City" was over. They surrendered from every building—man, woman, child, and dog. Ten city-owned building were freed, with thirty-five arrests and no injuries. By noon, the mayor was doing live interviews against the backdrop of the idling tank.

"I ordered the tank in myself. We won this neighborhood back without firing a shot."

Inspector Donovan watched the event on a tiny portable television. The mayor wore a red-and-white FDNY cap on his toupee throughout the entire television episode. On the roof, the offended cops screamed.

"What is that ungrateful hairpiece doing?"

"This scumbag would wear a Mets cap to game seven at Yankee Stadium."

John Mason, the deputy police commissioner for public communications, groaned. The former television reporter had run an NYPD hat down to the mayor himself. Vito had handed it to a subordinate and had pulled an FDNY hat out of his glove compartment.

"Oh shit," Deputy Commissioner Mason said to Mickey Donovan. "This maniac doesn't do anything by accident. Wearing the FDNY cap to an NYPD operation is a message: 'Eat shit and die.' He is being as subtle as an ice pick in the eye. He won't be happy until we all quit."

One of the angry patrolmen spoke. "Commissioner Mason, is the mayor really that much of a hard-on?"

"Vito tells me where to eat and, excuse my rudeness, even who I can eat. I can't dine in Elaine's on the Upper East Side and I can't be seen with blonde supermodels. Vito was voted into office by Brooklyn and Queens—solid brunette country."

Anger made them braver. Another cop spoke. "A guy who married his sister is telling you who to date?"

"Careful now, boys," Donovan said. "It was only his first cousin."

"And how did that work, exactly, fellas?" Mason said, easing into a stand-up routine he had perfected in Elaine's. "I always imagined a bouquet of flowers arrived at their home one morning, signed 'Love, Cousin Valentino.' Mrs. Caruso says, 'Great. My cousin Valentino never forgets me.' And our boy, the mayor, Sherlock Holmes that he is, says 'What do you mean *your* cousin Valentino? He is *my* cousin Valentino.' Turn up the *Chinatown* screams. 'Oh God. Are we brother and sister?' " Mason was laughing so hard he had tears in his eyes. The cop posted as lookout Detective Sergeant Francisco Camacho, kept making coughing noises.

"Right. And finally I hear the wife says, 'Thank God we never had sex, Vito.' "

"So that was it?"

"No," Mason continued. "After ten years the Catholic Church annulled Vito's marriage. The cardinal gave him a freaking do-over."

There was a scratching sound on the roof again. The deputy commissioner turned and faced Benny Youngblood, who was absolutely bloodless.

"The mayor will get a full report directly, Commissioner."

Mason, a former television golden boy, did some quick math. He was thirty-seven years old. He had quit a $400,000 job at WNYC the year before to make $80,000 as a deputy mayor. "The Buff Life," as he called his new police career—guns, sirens, and radios—was getting kind of old. He was getting tired of being pushed around by the mayor. He could retire today and sign a six-figure contract with any network tomorrow. He could not be bullied.

"Get lost, you walking come stain. And if anything happens to me, the newspaper will get a full report on your boss, Mayor Fidelity. As it turns out, he isn't just sleeping with his relatives anymore. He's also humping his welfare commissioner, who is not related to His Honor by either blood or marriage."

Mickey Donovan pretended not to be listening. The inspector wanted to give Youngblood room to fall.

"It was the mayor's plan, the whole way," Donovan said.

"Nice work, Inspector."

The quivering bureaucrat descended the stairs. A moment later, Deputy Commissioner Mason followed, winking at the horrified patrolmen.

"What's the matter, boys? Don't tell me none of you ever witnessed a suicide before? See you around, Donovan."

Mickey Donovan had survived six mayors. And he would probably survive this one, too. The inspector looked back over the side of the roof again. She was out there, somewhere

Detective Sergeant Francisco Camacho knew what his boss was thinking. Mickey's most trusted subordinate stepped to the parapet.

"Did you find her last night, boss?" Camacho asked, looking straight ahead. "I heard you were down here. Captain Abrus called the parish to say you met his son."

"I checked these five buildings, Francisco. She wasn't in this squat. I just had to be sure first."

They turned and descended the stairs in the dark.

"Boss," Camacho whispered, "you can't go out looking for her again until it gets dark. You'll be on the front page of the *Daily News*."

Mickey owed his fealty to cops, not politicians. He studied Camacho, his regular driver, as they got into the car and rolled south to their secret office in a church basement on West Forty-second Street. Sergeant Francisco Camacho was a constant, dedicated man. He never said much. But last year, when Camacho's father died, the sergeant had delivered the old man's eulogy in St. Jerome's Church on Newkirk Avenue in East Flatbush.

Camacho had been born in the Dominican Republic, like his mother and father. In the eulogy Francisco had called his father his only hero. Inspector Donovan, the son of an immigrant himself, had cried when he'd heard that because his father was not a hero. Sean Michael Donovan was a doorman in Washington Heights who'd left most of his family behind in a Dublin neighborhood called The Liberties, a slum surrounding St. Patrick's Church where outlaws found sanctuary. Sean Junior had come to America with the old man. In a twisted battle to seem more American, Sean Junior had changed his name from Sean Michael to John Michael. Still tormented by the decision twenty years later, the inspector had named his own son Sean. Permanently separated from his wife by the time his son entered grade school, he had other relatives in South Jersey and Philadelphia but saw them only once a year when they held a family reunion in the Irish Catskills. He had never lost his brogue completely. They called him Mickey, he knew, because he was a Mick.

"Let's get going, Sergeant."

Mickey climbed into the front seat of the black Ford LTD. The inspector had achieved a lot in his life, but his daughter was probably a victim of his success. He was forty-one years old, the youngest inspector in the history of the NYPD. He had begun by walking a beat in Fort Apache, the Bronx, and had graduated from Fordham. He'd gotten two graduate degrees from John Jay and Hunter colleges while working his way up through the narcotics and detectives' bureaus. His younger brother, Ryan, was a full inspector assigned to the narcotics bureau.

"I found an unused hypo in her schoolbag."

Camacho said nothing.

"An ecstasy pill, too."

The Inspector was a trim, athletic man just over six feet, with blond hair and a high-tooth smile. He never smoked and he had stopped drinking four years before after he'd seen a videotape of himself at a police racket dancing with a topless hooker. He joked with his old buddies that he might have quit "The Drinking Life," as Pete Hamill called it, but that he, too, got out while the getting was good. Murder and wanton violence permitting, Mickey tried to run ten miles three times a week. Last year, he had run the New York marathon in four hours. He wanted to run Boston this year. He liked running because it gave him time to think. The cop lived by the motto: "Good guys can scheme, too." On his day off, he tutored cops studying for the lieutenancy exam.

"We'll find her, sir."

The unmarked sedan stopped on East Thirty-eighth Street in East Flatbush. Mickey got out and walked up the brick stoop. His was the only white face on the block.

"Hey, Inspector, I saw you on Channel One this morning. We could sure use your tank against the base heads we got in Farragut Park. I'd like to see the Van De Veer Houses *blowed* away, too."

"We're working on it."

He went inside. His mother, Bridget, was still working in the parish rectory, making breakfast and lunch for the priests in the Little Flower parish on Avenue D. He stayed with his mom a couple of days a week. It was a good place for hiding from the world. He called his brother in the narcotics bureau, and then his confessor, Father Pete Hood, at Holy Cross Church in Manhattan. The police inspector fell asleep on the couch with a vision of *Real Brave One* crashing through his home.

East Wind Towers, Upper East Side, Manhattan

The phone call woke Ginny up at eleven A.M. just as Mickey Donovan was falling asleep on the other side of the city. It was Babe Policano, her college roommate from Syracuse. Babe was Ginny Glade's best non-tennis friend, an athlete in name only. She sold advertising for Nickelodeon television but hated Jell-O and fourteen-year-old kids. Babe would walk through a pit of hot coals for Ginny Glade, especially if there was an unmarried cop on the other side. She had one small but insurmountable character flaw: She had a weakness for cops, especially bad ones.

"Quick, Gin. Turn on Channel One."

Ginny switched on the remote in time to watch a tank rumble through a street downtown. She cringed at the thought of Babe in the role of Tank Girl.

"Yeah, so? The marines have landed in the East Village?"

"No. Wait until they run the sports segment again. They got tape of your last shot. Virginia Glade, are you sitting down?"

"Babe, I'm flat on my back in bed."

"You know that overgrown polypeptide umpire Blinky Hammond? Well, he got murdered last night. Struck in the head and robbed, they said. They found him in a deserted parking lot."

"Oh, no." Ginny felt a wave of dread rise in her throat but it quickly subsided.

"It was a New Hampshire car-jacking. The dopes stole his wallet, but not his car."

Babe was expecting the diva act. Ginny did not disappoint. "Blinky made a lot of bad calls, Babe, but no one deserves to be murdered."

"Ginny, snap out of the self-involved mode for ten seconds,

please. This wasn't a tennis thing. It doesn't involve you. The news said he was stabbed in his pukey heart. Blinky Hammond wasn't killed anywhere near the stadium."

Stabbed? Ginny hadn't stabbed the fat fuck.

"With a knife?" Ginny asked.

"They didn't say, actually."

Channel One played the tape of the match point. Ginny again saw the ball hit the tape. Hammond again stayed in the chair. Then the cameras focused on his swollen face under a straw hat. Finally, they cut to a clip of the swollen body bag being removed from the parking lot.

"Good-bye, Babe."

Stabbed? There wasn't anything about the umpire's death in either the *Post Standard* or the *Times.* She moved to her laptop—compliments of another tournament that had bounced checks—and logged on to America Online. She found the story on the Reuters sports wire and printed it out. Even when delivered at 300 megahertz, the news story was short and sweet: "Umpire Found Murdered." It was a bigger story than the two-paragraph blurb on the Volvo tournament final on the sports' agate page. Murder was bigger than sport in America. The story said he'd been stabbed, too. But that was just the cops trying to trick people, Ginny figured. Cops lied to reporters all the time. Tennis players held something back from them, too. Big deal. Ginny didn't feel guilty. She wasn't consumed with dread or worry. She felt no remorse either. When Ginny closed her eyes, she saw herself hitting Blinky Hammond in the head. She'd cracked him perfectly with a two-fisted backhand. At the memory, Ginny smiled.

There was no mention of a tire iron in the news story. And that was important. She was hoping it would take the cops a while to figure out exactly what weapon had caused what they were calling "blunt head trauma." She wanted the car-rental agency to forget she had returned their Volvo without one. Nobody had recognized her in the restaurant. What had seemed then like a slight was now a blessing. She'd paid for dinner with cash, so there was no AmEx receipt with her name on it, to be discovered by cops in the cashier's drawer. The idea of disappearing Hammond's wallet to make it look like a robbery now looked huge.

She had taken two hundred-dollar bills from his wallet. She'd broken the first at Logan Airport, and had used the change to pay the cabbie. She'd tipped Victor the doorman with the second one. She'd liked the symmetry.

As the hour and day wore on, Ginny became more and more intoxicated by her secret. She took an inventory of her desperate life. She had no family in New York. She had no husband and no steady lover. She had no children. If she were to die in her sleep tonight, no one would ever know she had committed a crime. She began to rage with the remembrance of her husband and the ruined quest for a baby. She was back in the abortion clinic, listening to the clock. As she lay on the bed, she spotted a paperback book on her nightstand. She had picked it up, *1,001 Baby Names*, in a bookstore on her way home from the pharmacy with the pregnancy kit. She had been that kind of optimist. Ginny hurled the book at her wastepaper basket but then walked over and picked it up. She had no baby and no husband, but she still couldn't discard the souvenir or the desire. In some dreadful way, God must be paying her back for discarding a life. She didn't believe that, but she said it to herself sometimes. She placed the book on her desk next to an open scrapbook, which was open to a story clipped from the *Post Standard* about an umpire shot last year from a moving train.

"Oh, Melanie," Ginny said. "You unlucky girl."

Ginny spent the better part of the day in her postwar apartment, which was colorful and traditional. When the *Times* had done an "At Home with Ginny Glade" piece on her two years before, the writer had called her bedroom "a sultry place." The blockhead had been hoping for a sleep-over and she had been surprised, frankly, that any man so keen on interior decorating liked women at all. The floor in Ginny's living room was covered with an eleven-by-nine-antique kilim rug. The dominant wall color was mauve, but she was going to change it to mint green. The other color reminded her too much of the abortionist's office.

She had two oil paintings she'd won in Europe. One was a jagged seascape by John Marin. A ship, the sea, and the shore gathered at a small point in Maine she barely recognized from her youth. Now, she reasoned, the wicked, torn place was her future. She also owned a painting by Oscar Bluhm of a lady in a rocker. She'd always liked the cherry-cheeked happiness of the woman. Today the woman looked worn, sallow, and alone.

Ginny's living room furniture included two tufted-back armless chairs in hunter green and a cream-colored sofa. In a fit of fury, she threw a Versace pillow against a gold-framed photograph of her preposterous Yankee right fielder.

The phone rang again. This time it was Hanna.

"Did you hear?"

"I just saw it on America Online."

"He probably choked on a ham sandwich."

"No, they said he was stabbed, Hanna. His wallet was missing."

"I'm not so sorry."

"I am," Ginny said. "It looks bad for my home state. He should have died in Taxachusetts."

"Don't blame this on us. It's fun being married to a cop, especially since he got promoted to homicide with the state police. He just went up there to take a look. The New Hampshire dicks want to see some of his mug shots."

"Why?"

"Apparently, they got a witness."

"Oh really."

The blood ran out of Ginny. She gripped the phone with both hands.

"Yeah. And more good news. That shitbird husband of yours went zero for ten with five strikeouts in a doubleheader against the Red Sox yesterday. *Ciao.*"

And then Hanna was gone.

For a couple of nights after the baby had been aborted, Ginny had put on sunglasses and a floppy hat and had sat in the Yankee Stadium bleachers. She'd booed her husband lustily.

"You impotent sissy boy," she'd screamed. She only sat down when fans heckled her. Still, she'd stood and cheered when her husband looked at a called third strike with the bases loaded. "Way to go, *Jerk Off,*" Ginny had yelled. Then she'd pulled the floppy hat down over her face. Public hate was so tawdry and common.

———

Murderers, unlike fans, had to stay hidden. Unlike the harsh memory of her morning in the clinic, her murderous secret gave her a feeling of completeness. On the way down to the dry cleaner, Ginny suddenly realized that she had concealed power. Killers saw life more completely, she decided. She measured the lady in front of her in line. She was a stewardess. Could she kill, too? And if she did, could she live as easily with the memory? Or would she sink under the burden? Ginny had always been consumed with self-awareness before she'd moved around New York. She could feel every set of eyes on her. But now she could see through people. She felt as if she could spot a murderer. She thought she saw one at the deli, in line to get a bagel. When she heard him instruct the Arab, "No butter either, pal," she knew he wasn't to be trifled with. She stepped in behind him and demanded, "The same for me, pal."

On television, in the early afternoon, she saw an old tape of Blinky Hammond umpiring a match involving Billie Jean King and Rosie Casals. They were winning another doubles match. King had the granny glasses on. Casals was dark and attractive despite her oak-tree thighs. When a spectator screamed a foul remark, Rosie stopped the loudmouth with a wintry stare. Rosie could kill if she had to.

For one brief moment, Ginny turned off the television and wondered, out loud, "Am I going mad?" She sent Victor to the corner video store and spent the afternoon watching movies. First she watched *Pulp Fiction*, then *Reservoir Dogs*. After ordering in Chinese for dinner, she switched from hit men to serial killers. She studied *Copycat* and *The Silence of the Lambs*. By bedtime, after six hours of videotaped slaughter, Ginny was sure she could smell blood in her apartment. She was the heroine of *La Femme Nikita* come to the ladies' tour. And she liked it. She realized with a shudder that she wasn't watching murder movies to be entertained. She was studying the art of shooting, stabbing, beheading, and death by gluttony for technique—dissecting the movies the way she'd broken down the backhand of Evonne Goolagong.

The greatest female tennis player in Manhattan drifted off to sleep feeling contentedly demented. Maybe she would swing a tennis racquet in the morning. Or maybe a tire iron. She was unstoppable.

FIVE

Early Evening, the Donovan Residence, East Flatbush, Brooklyn

Mickey's mother woke him up around dinnertime to get him ready for midnight duty. He was sleeping in the cool, wood-covered room that had been his when he was growing up. The wallpaper showed a fox hunt. Horses and dogs seemed to chase each other. It was a very British scene, and he always thought that was odd. He hated the Brits. So at night he went to bed cheering the foxes.

"Wake up, Sean. Public enemy number one is on the loose again."

"What do you mean?"

"Your daughter came home, changed her clothes, and then left again."

"Oh, Mom, I need a whole division just to watch that girl."

"I don't know where she gets it from."

"She is you, Mom."

"Well, we can always hope, Inspector. The eggs and blood sausage are on the table. Mr. Coffee awaits your appearance as well. I'm off to the rectory. We got the bingo game."

"Have a good evening, Mom."

"Find your daughter, son."

"Was she high?"

"I can never tell."

A moment later he heard the dead bolt slide and the screen door slam. The white widow was the pride of her block in the heart of black Brooklyn. The entire neighborhood was West Indian now, but crime never came knocking on his mother's door. Ordinarily kids announced the arrival of cops on their block by shouting, "Five-oh." Bridget Donovan drove an ancient car, a 1969 white Ford Corona, back and forth to the church rectory every day. As soon as kids on the block saw it, they whistled, "Here comes Eight-oh," as in Bridget's age. Instead of scattering, the kids drew around Bridget. They quit their raps and card games to see Bridget home throughout the 1990s. Bridget and her neighbors were bigger than racial politics. Their relationship was one of the secret, impossible stories that made New York City great.

Whenever Bridget heard a terrible story about a kid turned crackhead, or even killer, she could talk to grieving parents of her own failure.

"We got *pugamahons* in my family, too," Bridget explained, using the Gaelic word for asshole. Her own sons, Mickey—whom she still called Sean when they were alone—and Ryan were grand, even glorious achievements. Mickey had gone to Fordham and then gotten his masters' from John Jay and Hunter. He was unlucky in love, though. One night he'd met a tall redheaded girl during a church dance in the St. Jerome's gym. Her name was Colleen, and she was the daughter of a police captain from Park Slope. Mickey had married the girl after a short courtship but The Job had quickly come between them. They had been married for ten years, which meant two kids, a girl and a boy. The girl was him and the boy was her. They had never divorced officially, because the Irish Catholics, especially the Brooklyn ones, didn't do that. They had just stopped living together. Sean Francis, the boy, went to boarding school on Long Island, the LaSalle Military Academy. He liked the marines and the Islanders, in that order. He was a careful, considerate child yet he had a side that was unrelenting and tough. The girl, three years older, was absolutely fearless, especially when it came to adventures, boys, booze, and drugs.

Mickey and Collen's daughter, Mary Dillon Donovan, was a senior at Stuyvesant High. She was every bit as bright as her old man had been at twice that age, but three times the rebel that her father ever was. Mickey had no control over the child. Her uncle, Ryan Donovan, wanted no piece of the kid either.

"She is tougher than any undercover detective I have working for me right now," said Ryan, who ran an outstanding undercover task force of narcotics cops. "She is fearless and daring. I wish I had ten cops like her. But I won't have her in my home. I won't survive her. None of us will."

Mary Dillon Donovan, or Dill, as they called her, was a comely young woman, as striking as her mother, even with dyed, chopped hair. But beauty only sharpened her edge. Mickey never saw danger coming until she was too close to scream. And when pain came, Mary Dillon was a stiletto in her father's heart. Sometimes he thought she was her mother's revenge. He could not talk to her. Only Bridget could.

"She is an assassin," Bridget had announced one night. "And you are the target."

On his way into Manhattan, Mickey was going to check up on some detectives when he decided to call home. The kid did surveillance, too, he had learned. Sometimes she'd wait until he left the house to go in. He might have doubled back, but he didn't want a screaming scene. She answered on the eighth ring.

"Sorry I missed you, Dill," he said. "Whatcha doing?"

"Anything I want."

"Oh, come on. Don't be like that. Stay home until I get there."

"What, and sit around like a Velvetta cheese head watching VH-One kids with real lives? Screw that, I'm going out."

"Stay home. Jesus, honey, I got a dead priest."

"Then you won't be coming home. Do you realize I'm seventeen and I don't even own a diaphragm?"

"Please."

"I am not your prisoner."

"Stay home."

"Make me."

Click.

Midnight, Brooklyn Bridge, Borough of Churches

As murders went, this wasn't a pretty case. The victim, Father Fred Strang, was a rather rotund young white priest who headed a parish in Far Rockaway, Queens, near John F. Kennedy Airport. The shepherd of St. Vito's—whom Father Fred described to his parishioners as the patron saint of broken kneecaps—also on occasion drove the auxiliary bishop of Brooklyn, which brought him regularly to his boss's home in Brooklyn Heights. But as the detectives quickly learned after Father Fred was found murdered, the priest also liked to cruise under the Brooklyn Bridge looking for male prostitutes. He'd picked up the wrong one, the cops figured, about two weeks ago.

Father Fred was found shot once in the head with his wallet gone and his pants down to his knees. The tabloids went wild with it for a week. It was the worst story in the city for the Catholic Church since the *Times* had broken the story about a black bishop who had secretly died of AIDS. The cardinal had wanted everyone to believe that the dead priest had had a drug problem, but he, too, liked his altar boys a little too much.

The detectives were still canvassing boy toys under the Brooklyn Bridge on a Sunday night, questioning disease-ridden crackheads about their knowledge of a sweaty priest. The prostitutes didn't like cops much and weren't in any hurry to return to their stroll among the gray-and-brick warehouses facing the Manhattan skyline. The detectives sat in the car watching, and waiting.

"I want to go back to the precinct and get my nylon uniform jacket," the older detective said. "I haven't worn any part of my uniform since I made detective in 1985, but this duty is some cold shit."

"They all know we're out here anyway," the younger cop said.

"Yeah, two guys sitting in a car at this hour got to be one of two things," the older cop said. "Customers or cops."

"Or cops posing as customers."

They both laughed.

"And you don't do this no more, right?" the older cop said.

"Fuck you."

The detectives sitting in the silver Grand Fury under the Brooklyn Bridge had spent the last three hours talking about fishing, security work, and landscaping. Richie Sacha, a first-grade detective on loan to the Special Investigations Unit (SIU) from Queens homicide, was looking forward to the summer and the chance to chase bluefish through Jamaica Bay. The other detective, Sandy Cosgrove, was one of two openly gay detectives assigned to investigate Brooklyn Sex Crimes. Although he was the case detective on the dead priest, he specialized in rich Manhattan pedophiles who trolled the Bushwick section of Brooklyn. Cosgrove moonlighted as the assistant head of security each summer at the U.S. Open at the Flushing tennis center. Sacha wasn't much for security work and Cosgrove wasn't much for fishing. Eventually they moved conversation to their common love— landscaping. When they had finished discussing blue firs and roses, they moved to the only thing left, sex.

"Do other cops give you a hard time about the gay thing?" Sacha wondered.

"Only the ones I catch," Sandy replied, sipping his coffee.

"Meaning?"

"I'm working on this case now that involves the brother of a political bigwig," Sandy said. "I had to go see him to ask him to surrender his brother. I got six ten-year-old boys who say he pays them each a hundred bucks to suck each other's weenies. An extra fifty bucks to suck his."

"And?"

"The guy tipped his brother off to the investigation and now the sex fiend is in the wind. And this is a guy who is investigating cops for brutality and corruption. I go to him because he's a boss, and he warns his brother."

"Every cop in the city is going to love you when that breaks," Sacha said. "It's better than catching the head of IA stealing from dead bodies."

"Yeah, well, that's not why I'm doing it. The guy passes around the kids in his man-boy crew. Six kids contracted AIDS. God knows how many people they infected. The Brooklyn DA wants to grab the brother for attempted murder."

"That will be bigger than our gay priest."

The back door opened and both men turned, their guns in their hands.

"What the fuck?" Sacha said.

Mickey Donovan slid in behind them. They both recognized the Wraith and relaxed.

"Good evening, gentlemen," Mickey said. "You two fellows working or dating?"

"Not funny, sir," Sacha said. "I might have shot you."

"I haven't parked in this neighborhood socially since I was sixteen, sir," Detective Cosgrove said.

"I was on my way into the city and I just wanted to see where we are on this one, gentlemen."

"You can't sneak up on people like that, sir."

"Oh sure I can," Donovan replied. "The church and the mayor don't want you to solve this one. A confession from a gay priest killer is going to embarrass them."

"You'll handle the publicity, boss," Cosgrove replied. "But I am gonna find this guy."

"That's just what I wanted to hear. Carry on."

The Wraith started to get out of the car as the central dispatcher sounded a system-wide alarm. The message was heard by 200,000 police band radios throughout the city. Three beeps preceded the announcement.

"Shots fired. Clark and Remsen. Caller says driver is dead. Anonymous and unconfirmed."

Cosgrove picked up his radio. The scene was four blocks away. Donovan was already gone. "Brooklyn sex crimes responding."

Sacha pushed the accelerator to the floor and shot out from under the bridge. He made a left onto Clark and saw a muddy-brown GMC van parked on the corner. Donovan was already standing at the passenger door shining a light. Sacha could see a pink mist on the window inside the car. The grisly paint job was evenly coated. There was a man in the driver's seat, the top of his head missing.

"Slow it down," Sacha said. "Send a bus to Clark and Remsen, forthwith."

"Anything further?" the dispatcher asked.

Sacha was already out of his car. The driver's-side window was partially shattered. "White male victim. Deputy Inspector Donovan on the scene. Will advise shortly."

The victim, wearing a green trench coat, was sitting in an upright position with his head tilted to the right. His face was covered with blood. A portion of his skull was missing. Donovan reached through the window and felt the man's wrist. No pulse, cold to the touch.

"Didn't die here," Donovan said. He opened the car door and the rest of the glass fell into the dead man's lap. Donovan reached around and shined his light on the man. There was another jagged wound on the right side of his neck.

"Okay," Donovan said. "Detective Sacha, take a look at this. The guy was stabbed in the neck well in advance of being shot. The blood is dry there. Probably killed in another location. He is shot in the head, after the fact, through the window."

Mickey felt the deceased right-hip pocket. There was a wallet, which meant no robbery. The dome light was on and there was a miniature television hanging from the rearview mirror.

Sacha stepped closer to the window and studied the face, then looked away. "I know this guy, boss. He's with us. Former detective named Sal Nesto, retired ten years out of Manhattan North narcotics. Works on a part-time basis with the Port Authority. Drugs, mostly. He was in the DEA until one of their informants came forward and said one guy in the unit was hitting the places he gave them for cash."

"I remember," Mickey said. "Use a land line to advise the PC's detail about this but wait on the feds."

Mickey looked around. It was about three A.M. on a Monday morning, perhaps the quietest hour of the week. No lights were on.

"In this neighborhood, that means the guy used a silencer," Mickey said. "So the shots-fired call is bogus. No one else could have heard. The caller is our shooter. Why does he even shoot a guy who's already dead?"

"To show off," Sacha said.

"I bet he's watching us right now," Mickey said. "Get a dump on these pay phones."

Sandy Cosgrove noticed a woman standing under the awning of a closed topless joint—the Club Phoenix—down the block. She waved to him.

"Amber," Cosgrove said.

"She better not be a friend, Detective."

"She's one of my victims, Inspector," Cosgrove said before walking across the street. "I collect them."

Club Phoenix was a mob joint, they all knew, and the site of the ongoing fight to ban topless joints in the brownstone community. Amber was about forty and shivering. She was still cute, the cops agreed, in a raw, beery kind of way. She had washed off her makeup.

"Hello, Amber," the detective said. "Any more problems?"

"None I can't handle."

She had been raped after leaving the club a couple of years before. Cosgrove had handled the case but had never made a collar, mostly because once Amber had realized that her attackers were mob friends of the club's owner, she had decided to trade her silence for a job as Club Phoenix's day manager.

"Is that Sal over there, you know, the former narc?"

"Used to be. What did you hear, Amber?"

"I didn't hear shit, Sandy. But Sal was in here all afternoon. We close around midnight on Sunday."

"By himself?"

"Most of the time. But he was also with this stone-crazy-looking severely white guy with stringy hair, about forty. Yankees cap pulled over his eyes. Didn't say much. But he was a pig. Grabbed my ass twice. Then he said something about being from upstate."

"So he was a con?"

"Uh-huh."

"Hear a name?"

"Sal called him Sy."

"What else?"

"Sal was okay. He brought his clients in a lot."

"So, Amber, why you helping?"

"Because when the nasty fuck snuck out with Sal, he stiffed me on two lap dances and a tip."

"Bad business move."

"Yeah. Sal left this. It's his black book. Found it under the table. Must have dropped it on the way out."

"Equally bad business move," Cosgrove said as he opened the book.

"It's the only thing they dropped on me. That ain't like Sal either."

Cosgrove was walking back toward the van thumbing through the book when he froze on seeing an entry on a piece of yellow paper folded in the book.

Father Johnson.

The detective recognized Father Fred's beeper number from his investigation and the parish rectory phone numbers next to the name. He showed it to his partner and explained the significance to Inspector Donovan.

"Just follow the erect penis," Mickey suggested. "Now you have probable cause to get a dump on the priest's phone, too."

SIX

Morning, East Flatbush, Brooklyn

When Mickey got back to his mother's home, he discovered a note on the kitchen table from his daughter. It was addressed to Bridget, but left for him to see.

> Bridget,
> I am going to stay with my friend Regina in the city. She's cool, but don't tell Daddy. I'll be back for breakfast. Up the rebels.
>
> > Love,
> > Dillon

Dillon Donovan ran away every once in a while, especially once she'd started smoking blunts. There was nothing Mickey could do about it. When he grounded her, she could sit in her room, lights out, for five hours. The kid was a born terrorist in search of a cause. If his daughter was on the lam, Mickey imagined her sitting in a tiny safe house for ten years. Or lying in the tall grass with a knife for ten years waiting for a blood enemy to wander past. Once, after Mickey had taken the TV, stereo, and books out of her room, she had memorized Bridget's Bible. Another time, after she'd stayed out all night, Mickey had threatened to move her to a different school. She'd gone on a hunger strike, which lasted five days, until her father broke.

"You think you're so tough, Dad?" she said. "Well, I'm not afraid of dying. And don't forget that."

Dillon didn't like malls, or movies, or anything invented after 1969. Bridget understood that sentiment, and recognized the girl's rebellious heart. At some point, Dillon added the phrase "up the rebels" to her slacker jargon. She fit it in right between "whatever" and "That's phatt." Ireland and "the troubles" had no meaning for the kid, so when she said "Up the rebels" what she really meant was "Up yours."

And whenever Mickey punished her, she cried and asked for more. She was a complete riddle to him. Even her sexuality was confusing to him. Dillon didn't seem to like boys, or even girls. "You and Mom cured me of love," she'd announced one day.

As Mickey was finishing the coffee, his beeper began to vibrate. Mickey's only brother, Ryan, was calling from narcotics headquarters. The message read: "Dangerous sighting. Please call."

Ryan answered on the first ring. "John, has Dill gone missing again?"

"Yes."

"Well, an undercover just saw her copping a bag near Tompkins Square Park."

"I'm on my way."

He stopped to pick up Francisco Camacho at One Police Plaza and within minutes they were driving down East Third Street. They were wearing dark pants and sweatshirts and riding in the inspector's personal car, the navy blue Toyota Camry station wagon. This was not police business. You never knew what rat had called what newspaper to give them dirt. Only Mickey and Francisco knew they were out here tonight, looking.

And, frankly, Mickey didn't care if he wound up on the front page of the tabloids. "I just want her back before she gets sick."

"Give me your gun," Camacho said.

It was the smart move. Francisco was doing the job Mickey had taught him. He always ran through the worst possible scenario before he ever entered a dangerous situation.

"Right. If I walked into a room and found her nodded out with a needle in her arm, I'd probably shoot everyone."

"No you wouldn't, man," Camacho said coolly as they got out of the car and walked through Tompkins Square Park. He stuffed the inspector's gun in the small of his back. They climbed through a hole in the wall and down a ladder. They smelled candles and strawberry incense. Camacho dropped into the room first and landed in about six inches of wood shavings. There were about ten people in a room that smelled like the inside of a hamster cage. They looked to be skin poppers.

"Who goes there, man? What's the password?"

The inspector snapped on his flashlight and two kids scurried, like cockroaches, free of his beam.

"The password is Kurt Cobain," Francisco replied.

"No it isn't."

"Chris Farley?"

"*Nada,* man."

"How about River Phoenix then?"

"No."

"Then Jimi Hendrix," the cop yelled. "How come you scumbags always use dead white guys' names?"

"They're cops, dude."

This was an older voice, a voice on parole, Donovan figured. He shined a beam into brown eyes and recognized a face.

"You got a warrant, cop?"

"You got a lease, junkie?" Francisco replied.

The inspector turned to Camacho, and said, "We're done here, Sergeant."

They climbed the ladder back into their world, then walked to the Camry and sat silently for a few moments. A man followed them out of the building and walked around the corner. They followed, made a right on Avenue A, and killed the lights. The man from the building opened the door and got in the backseat.

"Hello, Inspector."

"Good evening, Peter."

"What brings you out here so often now? Or can we expect another tank raid in the morning?"

"No. The tank is on loan to Albania. Besides, I am here on another matter entirely."

"Oh, really?"

"Yeah. So cut the bullshit. Back in the old days, Peter, you were well on your way to a gold shield. So let me test your investigative skills. Why am I down here?"

"That's very good, Inspector. Flatter your informants. Test them. Give them confidence in themselves. That's what you taught us in the academy, too."

"Well, it didn't work for you in East New York, Peter. You guys used our intelligence on drug dealers and conducted your own raids. A lot of thieves left the department as rich men. Only you were stupid enough to use the stuff and get caught trying to whack a rival drug dealer."

"The department is just a big money grab, Inspector. Patrolmen steal drugs. Bosses steal disability pensions. The bosses pay off their lawyers and doctors. Get the right one, Inspector, and you get a full tax-free disability, one hundred twenty-five thousand per.

"You're right, Peter. Stealing is stealing."

"How gracious of you, Inspector. You are in a perfectly giving mood."

Peter Heroin blew cigarette smoke across the seat. "I knew Sal Nesto, Mickey. We went through a lot of hairy shit together in the Seven-Five."

"That may be the worst thing I've heard about him."

"Piss off," Heroin said and reached for the door.

"We got his black book," Mickey said. "Why did Sal have your number on him? You still play together?"

"Fuck off, Donovan. Sal was straight."

"He didn't like priests?"

"You are mixing your cases, Donovan. But even if Sal was doing the Brooklyn priest, too, what business is it of yours?"

"Getting dead piques my interest. But anyway, I'm not down here on police business, Peter."

"Yeah, so let's see what we do have. We have a sudden appearance of the Wraith. You are here, Deputy Inspector Mickey Donovan, because your daughter is down here with the Undeadheads. They're slinging major horse. And you want to get the pretty lady back before she becomes too much of a pincushion."

Inspector Donovan turned and faced the disgraced former cop. Years before, Donovan had commanded a squad of active officers in what the white police-union cops called a sewer precinct—meaning only that it was poor, drug-ridden, and black. Peter hadn't been using smack when they'd met. And if you had to go through a door, you wanted Peter with you.

"Like I said, this is not NYPD business, Peter, either official or unofficial."

Heroin opened the door, climbed out, and turned back to ask, "How did you know I'd come out here to see you, anyway, Inspector?"

"I was betting you wouldn't pass up the chance to gloat."

Heroin actually giggled. "And that's the only reason I'm gonna help you find her, *Sergeant*. Three minutes."

Donovan winced at the demotion, but coolly watched Peter Heroin walk off. "Look at me, Camacho. My credibility is burning down. I have been reduced to this."

"If we get the girl, be happy with the win. You won't owe this guy shit, man."

Years before Mickey had watched Peter Heroin, too. The inspector had been Heroin's sergeant at a Brooklyn precinct, the infamous Seventy-seventh. Mickey had been the night supervisor in a station house where the cops *were* the robbers. Peter Heroin's work was notorious. The case was important because crack had changed police corruption in New York City.

Before crack, internal affairs only had to worry about detectives in elite narcotics units stealing money and drugs. Street cops didn't have a shot at stealing. You had to be around drugs to be tempted. But crack had changed all that. The little rocks were available on every corner in every charred urban neighborhood. Every uniformed cop had to make the decision: Am I with *us* or *them*? Peter Heroin was with them. Unfortunately for then Sergeant Donovan, two of the most corrupt cops in the city had been working for him in the heart of Crown Heights. These guys careened from crack house to crack house holding dealers up at gunpoint. In one place they'd even stood behind an oak door and exchanged crack vials for crumpled ten-dollar bills through a mail slot.

By the time Donovan heard about Herod and his partner, the cops were running out of bad guys to steal from in their sector. Internal affairs had no chance of catching them. And Donovan would not put up with it. This wasn't tattletale stuff. This wasn't even "blue wall of silence" crap. No one was lying or smacking a prisoner here. This was lowlife drug dealers disguising themselves as cops and getting dressed in your precinct's locker room.

They had to go.

Donovan knew that corrupt cops never again went back to being good cops. Once a meat eater, he warned, never again a vegetarian. Mickey would have to be twice as ruthless and cunning as the dirty cops he was chasing.

One night, while responding to a call of a burglary in progress, the suspected thieves had been called to an apartment on Eastern Parkway. The cops called the Seventy-seventh precinct the Alamo, which really only meant that it was the lone white outpost on Utica Avenue. The station was filled with a division of cops from the Long Island suburbs who spent their days as an army of occupation in the heart of the city's largest geographic ghetto. Peter Herod and his partner were met by an old lady in the doorway to her apartment The shaken victim had explained that she had come home to find the door ajar and jewelry missing from her top drawer.

"I ran out of the apartment," she had explained. "I was scared the burglar might still be in there. I think he got everything, but I'm not sure."

Suddenly, Officer Herod was interested.

"What do you mean, you 'think he got everything'?"

"Well, I keep a lot of money in the closet, but I didn't dare open it," she had said. After looking both ways, she had whispered, "No one knows this, but I keep a tin box hidden under my Sunday hat boxes. I just don't trust banks. Could one of you two nice officers go in and check to see if it's still there?"

Herod had nodded to his younger partner and had placed a reassuring hand on her shoulder.

"I'll stay here," Herod had said, pulling his pistol. "Just to keep her safe. You go check it out."

The younger cop had walked into the apartment, stridden directly to the closet, opened the box, and removed five hundred dollars in fives, tens, and twenties. The low denominations spoke to the woman's poverty and pain. The cop had put the money in his pocket and had walked back out of the apartment, winking at Herod.

"Yep, lady," the cop had announced. "They got it all."

By the time the cops got downstairs, Donovan had been waiting with the chief of the internal affairs bureau. The old lady was a grand actress and a first-grade detective. The apartment had been wired for sight and sound.

"No, you're wrong, Peter," Mickey Donovan had announced as IA had handcuffed the two cops. "You didn't get it all. But we did."

Peter Herod, the heroin addict, turned rat and took down the whole precinct. Mickey Donovan, the greatest police hero since Serpico, got a job in One Police Plaza the very next day. But even though he had an office in One Police Plaza—or the Purple Plaza as cops liked to call it—Mickey was also allowed to set up a second secret office in the basement rectory at Holy Cross Church on West Forty-second Street. His childhood friend, Father Peter Hood, was the parish priest. They were perfect together, and at times Mickey even worked as the parish altar boy. On some days, the father heard confessions, on others, Mickey heard them. The cop and the priest poured through cases of blood and wine in rooms beneath and behind the sacristy. They each had their informants. Only a few people knew about the secret setup. Certainly not the mayor. Or the cardinal. Sure, Mickey had been on the NYPD fast track ever since turning Peter Herod. Or at least he had been until his daughter had become a junkie.

True to his word, Peter Heroin was back in three minutes. Along with a blonde teenager, he came walking down the block, out of 1960. Dillon Donovan looked like Peggy from *The Mod Squad*. She was barefoot, and wearing black bell-bottoms and an orange tie-dyed shirt. She was high. They could both see the needle marks from ten yards away. Camacho put his hand on the inspector's left shoulder. It was a clamp. "Easy, boss."

"My God, Frisco. She's flying at thirty thousand feet."

Heroin walked her to the door and placed Dillon in the backseat, protecting her head. Camacho released the inspector, then spun around in his seat. He did a quick inspection of the girl's vital signs—pulse and pupil dilation.

"She's pretty high. But she's not gonna die."

"Hey, man," Dillon shouted blindly. "My father is a big-ass cop, mister. Don't try and rip me off, cabbie." And then she passed out.

Inspector Donovan, the Manhattan commander, opened his door, got out, and offered his hand. Peter Heroin wouldn't touch it.

"I owe you."

Heroin laughed, and turned to walk away as Inspector John Michael Donovan got back in the car.

"You don't owe me, Inspector. We ain't never gonna be even. And not for nothing, but I hear Sal and the priest used to go hang at Club Phoenix in Brooklyn. Sal liked tits and the priest liked seeing guys get excited over tits. Word is, the priest used to pay kids for sex with dope."

"He was getting dope from Sal?"

"Nope. The airport. Sal was working the priest. Totally legitimate case."

"Thanks."

"Your daughter already thanked me."

Mickey couldn't figure out what Heroin meant by that. Once they got back in the car, Mickey found a set of Polaroid photographs in his daughter's back pocket. In most of the photographs, Peter Heroin was kissing his daughter. In the last one, Mary Dillon Donovan was naked and kissing Peter Heroin. Mickey stuffed the photographs in his shirt.

They had driven a block when Camacho's portable radio sounded, with bells and whistles. "Cop shot. Eighty-first and York. Confines of the Nineteenth Precinct. Several calls via nine-one-one, anonymous and unverified. MOS shot in Paisley's Diner, Eighty-second and Second."

The inspector took his hand off his daughter's shoulder and turned up the volume on the handheld. Camacho had already pulled over.

"Confirmed cop shot over division radio. Eighty-second and Second. Inside Paisley's Diner. Gunmen still inside. Hostages. Sending a bus. ESU ONE, TWO, THREE forthwith. Mayor's detail notified. Chain of command notifications being made. Clear FDR Drive southbound to Bellevue. Blood bank be advised."

The inspector's beeper went off just as his cell phone sounded. "Inspector Donovan. Yeah, I heard. Have a radio car pick me up at East Fourteenth and First. Now." He snapped the phone shut and started to speak, but Camacho spoke first.

"I'll put her in your apartment, boss, and have my wife rush over from Brooklyn. I'm on the horn with her now. Meet you at the scene."

"Thanks."

Mickey was starting to walk away.

"Your gun, sir."

"I should eat the fucking thing. And if this cop was killed by a junkie, I might just do it."

"Easy, sir."

"I am fucking compromised, Sergeant."

"No you aren't, sir. You are just saving your daughter."

Camacho handed the gun through the window, punched the gas, and left Mickey Donovan on the corner. He checked the inspector's kid in the backseat again. It wasn't the worst possible scenario, but close.

The sergeant had been fully prepared, too, for the daughter of Inspector John Michael Donovan to die of a heroin overdose in the backseat.

SEVEN

Evening, East Wind Towers, Manhattan

Around midnight Ginny Glade was hungry. She was out of videotaped mayhem but still wide awake. Ordinarily, Ginny was one of those orderly souls who actually rewound videotapes before returning them to the video store. She could not bear the idea of being that unkind. But after the last murder splashed across her RCA home theater, she just popped the tape out and put it back in its plastic cover. Slayers, she imagined, returned unwound tapes to Blockbuster. *Had* to be so.

She also considered herself the recycle queen of the East Wind Towers. She meticulously separated her bottles from her cans after running them though the pot-scrubber cycle on her dishwasher. If only the world were still separated by color and weight. Most citizens just dumped them all—plastics, glasses, and metal—into a blue plastic bucket. Ginny separated her newspapers and magazines by intellectual weightiness. She would not stack the *Post Standard* and the *Times* any more than she would put the *Daily News* with *The New York Observer*. Their reporters and editors would never be seen together, so why integrate their products in history's ash heap? *Screw* magazine and *The Village Voice*, she felt, had an indubitable sexual simpatico. So she bound them together—one last S & M ritual—with a laugh, and added them to Mr. Heath's sordid pile. The only time Ginny had wound up with a copy of *Screw* in her apartment, incidentally, had been when the Yankee outfielder had forgotten to take his copy to the clubhouse. He had insisted that he'd only bought the magazine to read Al Goldstein's editorials. That *couldn't* be.

So after stacking her unwound movies, Ginny threw everything in one pile. All the papers were tied together. She threw all the bottles, cans, and plastic into the plastic bin. They were one great, unwashed mass. She was an executioner, Ginny decided, and should start acting like one. What was it the marines said? Oh, yes. "Kill them all and let God sort them out." This would be her recycling rule from now on.

She decided her vegetarian days were over, too. She longed for a juicy—perhaps even fleshy—slab of meat. She pined for a souvlaki sandwich from the Greek diner across the street. Paisley's was on the corner of Eighty-second Street and Second Avenue. No one knew where the name had come from. The Greek, Gus, always wore severely striped ties. Anyway, just like that, Ginny lost her religion: The salad days were over.

She was on the Homicide Diet.

Ginny Glade liked Gus. She had never walked into the place and not discovered him there. His wife, chewing a toothpick, was usually at the old manual register by the door. And sometimes their daughter worked the counter. She was twenty and had been named Venus, but she preferred being called Venita. The girl was frighteningly beautiful, with a ripe bosom and a head-turning ass. The kid usually wore some kind of flinty lace, but she never wore a bra. She also usually wore bell-bottoms and kept a pearl-handled dagger tucked in the waistband of her pants. The cops who flocked to the place said the girl's blade only added to her sexual attraction.

"I didn't realize you were gypsies," Ginny had said to Gus one day.

"We're not. My brother is in the shipping business. This year, though, Venita is a gypsy. Last year she was Dennis Rodman *and* Madonna. Before that it was Prince *and* Vanity. She is whatever guest Barbara Walters had on last week."

This year, The Venita Package, as she sometimes called herself, rarely shaved her armpits. The combination drew the occasional transsexual customer. But Venita, a hopeless flirt, was prepared for that, too. "What do you desire, honey?" she would ask: "The boneless chicken or the boneless fish?"

Venita reminded Ginny of those Israeli soldiers in Day-Glo bikinis who carried submachine guns slung over their shoulders at the beach in Tel Aviv. Once the owner's daughter had worked Ginny's table while she was eating lunch in a back booth with Babe. Everyone in the diner had been happy. Babe had been ogling the cops, who were panting over Venita. As the waitress had passed them, a musky smell had wafted over the table. It was almost as if a wave from the Aegean Sea had crashed across them.

"Holy shit," Babe had said. "I'd jump Venita myself today, and I'm not even like that. Hell, I mean Venita isn't even a *female* cop."

Venita had a crazy boyfriend from Long Island City, Demetrius. Didn't they all? Dee, as this one liked to be called, worked teaching English to taxi drivers at the taxi and limousine commission's training center. Unfortunately, Dee had a problem teaching. He spoke the king's English as if there was a meter attached. He made ten dollars an hour teaching drivers to place the word "no" in front of each of their thirteen words: Left. Right. Go. Stop. Uptown. Downtown. Brooklyn. Queens. Bronx. Manhattan. Airport. Receipt. Change. By the time he'd finished with them, they were ready for talk radio.

Dee had reduced his own life to two beliefs. One, he believed that every man who set foot in Paisley's Diner wanted to have sex, right then and there, with his exquisite Venita. Two, he believed that Venita wanted to screw every male customer over the age of fifteen. Unfortunately, Dee was right on both counts. In between orgasms, the goddess of love and the god of fertility were a bomb waiting to explode.

"Can I have a souvlaki, no onion, extra tomato?" Ginny asked.

"You want chicken, doll?" Venita said. She had added a diamond stud to her nose, to match her navel ring.

"I want beef," Ginny gushed breathlessly.

Venita raised her eyebrows and leaned over the counter, which was empty save for one uniformed cop. She did not read the newspapers.

"They got cowboys in New *Haven*?"

"It was New Hampshire, Venita. And the only man worth talking about from there was named Daniel Webster. He died over a hundred years ago."

Venita was wearing a black lace tank top and hipster skirt. Ginny thought she looked particularly dangerous. "You and this Webster's devil might have worked a deal."

Kaboom!

There was a crashing, crunching, splintering sound at the door. By the time Ginny turned to the sound, the door had disappeared. Dee had smashed through the plate-glass window in a black Harley-Davidson motorcycle. He was wearing sunglasses at midnight, Ginny noticed. He was also holding an impossibly large pistol.

"Bitch, you should have learned the word 'no'!" Dee screamed. "If I can't have you, Venita, nobody else can either."

He calmly pulled the motorcycle onto its kickstand. Venita stumbled even as the uniformed cop, Arjune, started to get up. Dee pointed the gun at him. Then there was a tremendous explosion. Dee had clipped the cop in the right shoulder. The shot hit his bulletproof vest, but the blow knocked him over. His gun scattered across the floor. Technically, Ginny realized, it was time to die.

"Hello, Ginny," Dee said evenly. "Why you here this late?"

She said nothing. His voice exploded into the silence.

"You fucking cops now, too, bitch?"

"I just wanted some beef," Ginny managed. Dee thought she said "beefcake."

The cop was groaning. Venita peed in her lace panties. Her father came out of the back room. "What the hell . . ." Gus stammered. "Dee, what you doing?"

Those were his last words. There was a second explosion and Gus toppled forward into the syrupy baklava, mortally wounded. There were sirens now. Venita began to wail like an Irish banshee. Dee leveled his silver-plated .45 at her. Ginny was surprised to hear her own panicked voice.

"Hey, Dee," Ginny said shakily. "This isn't what you want." As he hesitated, she shouted, surprised that she would care about Dee's safety by this point, "Look out behind you."

Someone had suddenly appeared behind Dee.

Ginny thought, for a brief instant, that she recognized something in the stranger's face, but he wore a navy blue Yankees cap down to his dark eyebrows and it made his face impossible to identify. He was holding a gun in his right hand.

"Who the fuck are you?" Dee said.

"Learn some manners, boy," the stranger growled. He then fired his automatic relentlessly into Dee's chest. Dee fell beside his bike, a broken mass.

The stranger, with a twisted, almost painful smile on his face, nodded slightly to Ginny before turning and walking out the door.

In the aftermath, Ginny realized that she had been grazed by a bullet. She stood and faced Venita, who was ashen and staring at the ground. Dee's forehead was a sopping trench. He gasped one last sucking sound, then fell quiet.

"I saw his face," Ginny said. "I know his face."

Then she was silent.

Within minutes, there were cops all over the place.

As soon as Mickey Donovan arrived on the scene, he saw Detective First Grade Richie Lasak walking out of the diner shaking his head. Donovan stopped and turned the headlight off on the motorcycle. Lasak had just talked to the wounded cop, who was placed in a waiting ambulance and rushed down to Bellevue, lights and sirens wailing. There was a sheet over Gus. Venita was still sobbing quietly at the counter, her shoulders heaving up and down. She knew all the cops by their first names and they couldn't wait to console her. A couple of them waited in line to hug her.

"Whaddaya got?" Mickey asked.

"We got shit," Lasak commented. "Bottom line: We got a white male vigilante who gets away."

Donovan barked, "Establish the crime scene, fellas. Separate the witnesses. And take the young woman into the ladies' bathroom."

A female sergeant arrived to pry Venita loose of her adoring male mourners.

"We also got a bona-fide heroine, boss," Lasak added, nodding at his partner.

Lasak's partner, Timmy McCann, another first grader from Manhattan North Homicide, was debriefing the heroine, a thirty-five-year-old professional tennis player named Virginia Glade.

"How's the cop, Timmy?" Inspector Mickey Donovan asked. Family always came first.

"He's fine. He got a dent in his vest. The owner is the older fellow on the floor. His vest is cotton. He probably died instantly. I knew him. Very good to us. The girl in the bathroom is his daughter, Venita. Very good to us, too."

McCann flipped open his spiral reporter's notebook.

"This piece of shit lying here is one Demetrius Thelmadolas, twenty-three, of Ely Avenue, Queens. He is an extremely former boyfriend and our first shooter." The detective held up the bagged Smith & Wesson .45.

"A second guy comes in after the shooting starts and proceeds to perforate Mr. Thelmadolas here. Says something about bad manners and just knocks him. Guy wearing a Yankees cap. Then our Bronx bomber fan backs out, nods, and disappears."

He turned and pointed to Ginny Glade. "She's the only one who gets a clear look at him. Describes a white male, athletic, fortyish."

"Anything else?"

"Yeah. Maybe Italian. The girl says he was wearing a Fila warm-up jacket and tennis shoes."

"What?"

"Yeah, and not from the factory outlet either. This is the stuff they sell only in Italy."

"Oh, come on."

"No. She's in the tennis business."

"Who is she?" The inspector studied the woman. She was a smoky, poised brunette. She looked vaguely familiar. Perhaps he had seen her on television. It was hard to picture her in a tennis dress.

"Do I know her?" Mickey Donovan asked.

"Maybe. That lady makes this story page one for a week. She isn't just any witness. She is the top-ranked professional women's tennis player in New York."

"Ginny Glade," Mickey said. "I saw her on TV the other day. Some fat ump was killed after one of her matches. Does she live around here?"

"Right across the street. She distracted the gunman as he was about to execute his girlfriend—the PBA playmate of the decade. The mayor is going to fucking love her."

The inspector whistled, then said, "She isn't even sweating. Where's Deputy Commissioner Mason?"

"I'm right here, Inspector," Mason said, surveying the bloody stage. "I ran over from Elaine's. I've been on the phone with the network morning news shows ever since."

Mason's cell phone rang and he walked off singing. Donovan stepped over the broken glass, then walked to the back of the diner. The police commissioner was five minutes out. The mayor was ten minutes out. Donovan slipped into the booth with Detective Mc-Cann, across from Ginny Glade.

"Good morning," Donovan said. "You've had some evening, Ms. Glade. I'm Deputy Inspector John Michael Donovan. But please call me Mickey."

She was ice, but her hands were surprisingly warm.

"You want any coffee or maybe a shot of something?"

"I usually prefer tea in these moments."

The inspector was surprised by the woman's odd choice of words.

" 'In these moments,' " he said. "I'm sorry. This has happened before?"

"I dispatch people myself with some regularity on the tennis court, Inspector."

"Yes, of course you do."

"We have a saying for this kind of thing on the Tour, Inspector. 'Fortune favors the daring.' "

"Indeed it does," Mickey said. "Do you want to go to the hospital? This has been a traumatic experience."

"Not really. I didn't have time to be afraid."

"Okay, Ms. Glade," Mickey said. "My sergeant, Francisco Camacho, will see you home and protect you from the TV mutts."

"Could you do it? I live right across the street."

"Certainly." The inspector started to wave a cop over but then raised his hand as if he had suddenly remembered something. The cheap *Columbo* move was practiced.

"Uh, just one more thing, Ms. Glade."

"Yes?"

"I thought the ball was in. I saw a replay on the news the other night. Those are the breaks, I guess."

"Are you a tennis fan, Inspector?"

"No, I'm a murder fan. Sorry about your friend Blinky Hammond."

"He was no friend of mine, Inspector," Ginny snapped. "As you saw yourself, the ball was in." Revealing her anger so easily was a mistake. She wondered if she would get away with it.

"Good night, Ms. Glade. And congratulations."

"But the ball was called out. You saw."

"Not the tennis match," Mickey said. "Your win here tonight in the diner. It took a fair amount of courage and mettle to distract this fellow. The newspapers will go crazy with this."

The inspector stood up and led Glade by the elbow through the broken glass and back through the kitchen. The television reporters, who hadn't spotted the side door yet, missed their exit completely. Victor met them at the door of Ginny's building but said nothing. On the elevator up to her apartment, Ginny spoke first, "I will never forget his face."

"Whose face?"

"The man who shot Venita's boyfriend. I think I've seen him before."

"Where?"

"I can't remember. But I know him from somewhere."

The elevator door opened and they walked down the hall to her apartment. At her door, Mickey nodded his head and pressed his business card into her hands.

"Good night, Ms. Glade. Get some rest."

Ginny handed Mickey her keys. "Could you just go in and make sure the apartment is safe? I'm pretty spooked."

Mickey walked in and switched on the lights. He noticed a scrapbook on a table, a pair of scissors, and some newspaper clips. The place was immaculate. He saw a few copies of *Vogue* on a coffee table and some videotapes near the machine.

"I'm surprised by your taste," Mickey said.

Ginny blew past him and closed the bedroom door. She smelled faintly of roses. He hadn't noticed that in the diner.

"Oh, I know," Ginny said. "I hate this furniture. I was going through a traditional phase."

"Not the furniture, Miss Glade," Mickey said, smiling. "I mean your taste in film. Look at those videotapes. No wonder you're so scared."

Mickey picked one up and read the copy on the back of the box.

"Oh, I just love thrillers," Ginny gushed. "They actually help me control fear."

Mickey walked to the window and looked down on Second Avenue. The morgue wagon was gone. The television trucks were leaving. Ginny stood a step behind him. Mickey could see that the girl was still afraid of something.

"Would you like some tea?" she asked.

"Yes, but let me make it, the Irish way," Mickey said.

In the kitchen, Mickey turned the kettle on and pulled out two cups from the cupboard above the sink. He stood silently measuring every detail in the apartment until the water boiled. He poured hot water into each cup and then emptied the cups into the sink.

"You have to get the chill out of the cup," Mickey explained. Then he placed two bags in each cup and poured in the boiling water. Ginny was surprised that a man could make tea so interesting.

"I like that," she said. "It's not as strong as I would have imagined."

"Or as weak as you're used to, probably."

They walked back toward the living room. Mickey stopped to study the newspaper clip in Ginny's open scrapbook. He stiffened as he recognized the headline. "Bronx Umpire Shot from Train." It was a *Post Standard* story about the murder of Melanie Morgan four months earlier. Now Mickey was spooked. He pointed to the page.

"Did you know her?"

"Yes," Ginny said. "We used to play some tennis together but I hadn't seen her for years. I was very upset they didn't solve the case."

"So was I," Mickey said, gulping his tea. "It's my unsolved case."

"Oh, I'm sorry," Ginny said, touching the cop's hand.

Mickey stood up, rattled. He liked her touch. The danger of being caught with her aroused him. He finished his tea wordlessly and walked to the door.

"Good night, then," Mickey Donovan said.

———

On the elevator, he felt his mind reeling. He had put his daughter's condition out of his mind, but now he needed to find out how she was doing. He was also thinking about throttling Peter Heroin. But mostly he was thinking about Ginny Glade, and that made him mad. It wasn't right. He could still smell her and he liked that. Why had she touched his hand? When he was younger, women had sometimes jumped his bones when he'd walked them back to their apartments. He'd always hated that then, but he was touched by loneliness to-night, and the thought of some female company appealed to him.

As he reached the street and turned the corner, still thinking about the way Ginny Glade had smelled, he bumped shoulders with a passerby. Mickey was instantly apologetic but the man just grunted and continued on his way. The guy was small but more muscled than Mickey had expected.

"Sorry, sir," Mickey said.

"Whatever," the guy replied. He didn't even look up.

Mickey was embarrassed. Cops never bumped into people on the street unless they wanted to search them. Mickey took another couple of steps toward Second Avenue, then refocused on the man. He was built like a rock.

"Oh shit," Mickey said out loud. "Prison muscles."

He turned to ask the guy a question but the street behind him was empty. And they call me the Wraith, Mickey thought.

He found Camacho waiting across the street, with the car. He slid onto the passenger seat, still spooked.

"My wife, Felicia, is on your couch, Inspector. Dillon will be fine. But you better get to Bellevue before the mayor does."

"Doesn't our Florence Nightingale ever sleep?"

"Not if he knows even a single photographer is awake."

"Okay, I'll take a radio car to the hospital. You park outside Glade's apartment and keep your eyes open. I'll call Commissioner Mason to get Ginny out of here. The reporters will find her in an-other hour. Outside, I just bumped into a guy she described as our shooter. Tell her to pack a bag and have Mason bury her in a mid-town hotel, preferably an older one. The Warwick Hotel, on West Fifty-fourth, has only one entrance. Sit on her, and keep the reporters away."

"Got it."

"This woman just won the Wimbledon of crime—imagine Billie Jean King on the subway with Bernie Goetz. That's what we got here."

"Anything else?"

"Yeah, tell Mason to keep his dick in his pants."

"Okay, man. But that sounds like mission impossible. And we better bring Bridget up to date. You're gonna need your ex-wife back, at some point."

Twenty minutes later Camacho led Ginny down to Mason's car. They drove away, oblivious to the man in the shadows wearing a Yankees baseball cap.

After Midnight, Bellevue Hospital, Manhattan

As soon as the mayor heard about the diner shooting he was on his way to the hospital. Oh, the cop was going to be fine. Cops get shot all the time. And if the truth be known, it was quite hard to kill a cop now since they had started wearing bullet-proof vests. The hospitals were getting better, too. Part of the reason the murder rate was dropping in Brooklyn was because the best emergency rooms didn't lose as many shooting victims as they had five years before. The trauma teams were improving by the tour, it seemed. So as long as you weren't dead too long, you could be saved.

Bellevue had a terrible reputation, dating back to the turn of the century. It was known chiefly as America's insane asylum. But the trauma teams were the best in the world. Whenever an American president visited the city, Bellevue was put on red alert. Now, they could handle any disaster, from a terrorist bombing to a crazed gunman on the Empire State Building. It was kind of disturbing seeing all these young men and women running through the emergency room in blood-spattered Nikes and Reeboks until you realized that those people *were* the doctors. Trauma was a young man's business. And while everyone loved to watch the organized chaos of a hit television show named after an emergency room, the truth was that no one shouted or screamed anymore in the country's most famous emergency room.

The mayor roared through the doors of Bellevue quite regularly. His pollsters said that voters liked a mayor who chased ambulances. They liked *caring* politicians. So the mayor rolled on every major shooting, consoling every known victim. So what if all the hugging and hand-holding was just for the cameras? He didn't mind being called Mayor Florence Nightingale if it would get him reelected. The mayor had bolted from a dinner party at Elio's on the Upper East Side to get to Bellevue for another reason entirely.

"Where is Ginny Glade?" the mayor demanded as soon as he burst through the door. "I must meet her, immediately."

Benny Youngblood, who had arrived first, quickly surveyed the situation and sounded the all clear. "The cop is fine, Mr. Mayor," he said. "His wife is on the way."

"Later for the cop," the mayor whispered. "I'm not here for him. Where's Ginny Glade?"

Youngblood had misjudged this situation. He had often heard the mayor talk about Glade. Once they'd met at an AIDS benefit for Arthur Ashe at St. Luke's Hospital. The mayor had clearly been smitten. But Ginny had brushed past him as if he were another demented fan. Now, Mayor Caruso wanted to hug her. Wanted to console her. Hell, the mayor simply *wanted* Ginny Glade. He wanted to give her the key to the city *and* Gracie Mansion.

"Miss Glade wasn't really injured, Mr. Mayor. She went home."

The politician punted a metal bedpan across the tiled floor. Everyone turned to the clatter. Suddenly, a crowd began to gather around the mayor. The nurses and doctors were stunned. They looked at each other, and asked, "What's with him?"

"BUT SHE HAS TO BE HERE," the mayor screamed. "I have to console, don't you see? These people are all idiots, anyway."

"Operations says Inspector Donovan walked her home."

"Donovan? Not that asshole. Beep him and get him here."

This was not going well. The *Daily News* and the *Post Standard* had the place wired for sound. One columnist's mother worked in the emergency room. The mayor was still trying to live down his last Bellevue outrage. Back then, the mayor had insisted on bringing a white cop and a black cop together after the white cop had mistaken the black cop for a thug, in the subway, and had shot him four times in the back. It was a very nice photograph and had probably quelled a race riot. But within two weeks, the black cop and his lawyer had insisted that the photo session had been a sham. They claimed that the mayor had personally drugged the black cop and had forced him to pose for a photograph. He was suing the city for $12 million.

So Youngblood, the mayor's paid worrier, had to take control. "We're getting the officer's *wife*, Mr. Mayor," he announced to the gathering crowd. He blinked twice urgently at his boss, who quickly realized he was being watched and put his libido on hold.

"The poor thing must be terrified," Caruso said in a dead voice. "Cops' wives are heroes, too. Every one." And with that he turned on a leather-shod heel and stormed out the back entrance of the emergency room. He made a beeline for a bank of cameras, determined to meet Ginny Glade. Mickey was behind him by then.

"Our police officer is going to be fine," the mayor began. "Thank God he was wearing his bullet-proof vest. But consider for a moment the actions of one daring citizen tonight. Her name is Ginny Glade. She is a professional tennis player, one of those delicate secrets that make New York City great. Ginny isn't the player she used to be. She has never won the U.S. Open or Wimbledon. Probably never will, either. And yet when she saw New Yorkers in trouble tonight and heard people begging for their lives, she acted. She distracted a killer. In one desperate moment, Ginny Glade reached out and saved a diner full of people."

The mayor paused a full beat, then offered his best whimsical look. Voters loved humility, even when it was false. "You know, I don't care if Ginny Glade ever wins another tennis match. The police will find the Good Samaritan with the gun. Until then, let New York City celebrate the tennis heroine. I love Ginny Glade and I want all of New York to love her, too. Tonight, that single brave woman has won the heart of New York City. This is for you, Ginny Glade."

And then the mayor stepped back from the bank of microphones and began to applaud, his eyes misty. The mayor continued to clap as the cameras continued to roll. He just stood there smiling, one man applauding. He looked like your typical Bellevue lunatic. But just as suddenly, people began to cheer. Everyone behind him in the hospital began to applaud. Doctors and nurses, patients and visitors, cops and firemen. This was *magic* television.

After the camera lights were turned off, the mayor stepped quietly to his car, a royal blue Land Rover. Youngblood touched his shoulder, saying, "So let me guess, sir," he said. *"Brian's Song?* You were doing Gale Sayers and his Brian Piccolo speech?"

"So where the hell is she, anyway?" Caruso said.

"The cops have her."

As the executive Land Rover pulled away, the mayor put on his FDNY hat. That night, all across the city, cops howled against the slight once again. So the mayor preferred firemen; let *them* save the city.

"Ginny is one of the *bravest*," the mayor said as he got into the car. "She dove right into the line of fire."

The mayor's use of the word "bravest" was designed to piss off the cops and his police commissioner. The cops' contract with the city had expired twelve months earlier. The mayor had settled with the firefighters two years ago.

"Let One Police Plaza swallow that slight, too," he said.

His driver checked him in the rearview mirror and said, "That tennis player has to be happy, sir."

"Well," the mayor said, "if this doesn't get me laid, nothing will."

Once the mayor had departed and things had started returning to whatever semblance of "normal" there was at Bellevue, Mickey found the injured patrolman's wife sitting, red-eyed, in the lounge.

"My husband almost gets killed, and the mayor leaves in a fireman's hat? I'll kill him."

"You cannot threaten the mayor, ma'am," Inspector Donovan said, seething.

EIGHT

Midnight, the Deputy Commissioner's Car, Midtown Manhattan

John Mason had died and gone to heaven. During the ride over to the hotel, Ginny Glade, wearing a black Donna Karen sheath, had sat in the front seat of his buffmobile, a black Lincoln, and had asked, "Could you turn the police scanner up. I've never heard one before."

The deputy commissioner for public information was in command now. It was amazing how easily women fell for the radio stuff. It never failed him, thank God. Any one of a dozen famous models had sat in that same seat and quivered as soon as he snapped the radio on.

Shots fired.

Man with a gun.

MOS down.

Women liked the police radio more than the gun. On more than one occasion, he had managed to get a hum job in the car. The cop talk, he'd discovered, really excited girls. He'd drawn the line at firing his gun for them, however. Once, when he'd been parked under the Brooklyn Bridge with a German model, the young lady had insisted on firing his gun before they had sex. He had refused and she'd taken a cab home. That would never happen again. Now the deputy commissioner carried a starter pistol under his front seat.

"Are those real cops?" Ginny Glade asked.

"Yes, they are," Mason replied, turning up the volume. The front dash was awash in blinking red lights. The deputy commissioner was monitoring the emergency services unit band, the detective band, and the ambulance band. His car was a rolling disaster.

"They sound so calm," Ginny said. "I expected them to sound more, well, frantic."

"Well, we train our heroes to be calm."

Ginny had great legs, even in this light. Mason had been in this kind of situation before. A lot of times, cops liked to brag, after they saved a woman's life, the woman wanted to have sex with them. Immediately. But this situation was different. Ginny Glade had saved a cop's life.

"You can hear the control in their voices," Ginny said. "It's all so exciting. Can you imagine the way their spouses must worry? I can't imagine sitting at home listening to the radio transmissions, waiting and wondering if my partner is going to make it home again."

Mason pulled up to the Warwick Hotel on West Fifty-fourth Street. After making the right turn off Sixth Avenue and parking in front of the place, Mason turned and faced the city's newest heroine. He liked the idea of screwing a woman who had just survived a shoot-out. He was a pig, but at least he knew it.

"Well, some women feel that way about cops and other men of action," he said.

Ginny smiled, but then saw the hotel's golden awning and re-membered something. "I've been here before," she said, groaning. "When my former husband got called up by the Yankees the first time; it was obscene."

"Who?"

"The despicable one."

"Your husband?"

"No. The other one. The old Yankees manager."

She had met Billy Martin, the broken Yankees manager in the Warwick Hotel bar just before he'd killed himself in a drunken car crash. He had been drinking green crème de menthe for three hours by the time Ginny had been introduced to him at midday. The man-ager's tobacco-stained teeth were tinted green. He had become even more hideous when he spoke. Mostly, Billy Martin had spent the time talking about how much better a lover he was than Reggie Jackson.

"Did you ever have sex on an airplane, in the lavatory?" Martin had wanted to know. "I can't get a hard-on now unless I'm at thirty thousand feet."

Then, the drunken manager had whistled at her through grassy teeth. She had begun to hate baseball players right then and there.

"Actually, I imagine the cop glamour would fade fast, too," Ginny said. "Sort of like listening to Phil Rizzuto announcing your husband's name and at bat on the car radio. I honk the horn whenever the turd strikes out now."

"I'm not a fan of your husband, either," Mason said.

"Yeah, well, cops probably aren't much different than ballplayers. I have a friend, Babe, who collects cops. It doesn't seem possible, but she says cops are bigger degenerates than baseball players. So if I was married to a cop who was cheating on me, I'd probably be cheering for the big strikeout."

"The what?" Mason asked.

"Cheering for him to get shot," Ginny said.

It was time for him to play cop. "I was wondering, Ginny," Mason said. "You don't actually have a gun, do you?"

"No," she said, "not anymore. I have a carry permit, though. I got rid of the gun because I was afraid someone would break into my place, steal it, and shoot me."

"Yes, that is a worry," Mason said, satisfied.

"I learned to shoot in New Hampshire," Ginny continued. "Turkey shoots, mostly. But some pistols and a black-powder musket, too."

Mason decided to sleep alone that night. He was reminded of Officer Johnny Rizzo's recent passing. On the night he had been shot two years before, the police chaplain had knocked on his door in Starrett City. A gunshot had sounded and a bullet had whizzed through the door, nearly killing the priest who was there to notify the cop's wife that she was now a widow. The old lady was sitting in the chair holding a .357 magnum. She was half drunk and waiting for her old man. She was going to kill him as soon as he walked through the door. She had mistaken the chaplain for her loutish husband.

"Die, you scum!" she had screamed.

Upon hearing that she was the NYPD's newest widow, Mrs. Rizzo had sobered right up. The life insurance policy alone was worth

$200,000. She had smiled and laughed through an inspector's funeral, complete with riderless horse and a helicopter flying over. On this occasion, the widow wore white.

"I'm a little rich," she had explained. "And back in the game."

Mason walked Ginny to the front desk and checked her into a business suite. He let the maroon-and-gray bellman carry her over-night bag up and then positioned a uniformed cop near the elevator bank.

"You know, a lot of the old Yankees used to stay here," Mason said. "Billy Martin wasn't the only one. He liked it because it was within staggering distance of the Hilton, where visiting teams usually stayed if the Hyatt Regency on Forty-second Street was booked. He could also snoop around without being seen. The place was built for surveillance. William Randolph Hearst built the place for his wife in 1927. She wanted to be a Broadway star, and this was as close as he could get her to the Ziegfeld Theater, which was across the street."

"Oh really?"

"Yeah. The place was quite a hit with the jet-set people, even before there were airlines. They would float over slowly on the *Queen Mary* and send their steamer trunks ahead on a faster boat. Later, Paramount Pictures used to put all their stars here. Private detectives watched them around the clock. The place is quiet, private, and el-egant. The rooms are too small, but all of the big stars stayed here. James Dean, Jane Russell, Cary Grant, Elizabeth Taylor, and even the Beatles."

"You missed your calling as a tour guide, Commissioner."

"Yeah, well, Elvis has clearly left the building. And I am right behind him."

"Imagine. I'm hiding from tabloids in a building built by the father of yellow journalism."

"Indeed. Good night, Miss Glade."

"Pleasant dreams, Commissioner Mason."

After becoming "the Diner Diva," as the *Post Standard* nicknamed her, Ginny Glade became one of the greatest tabloid characters in the history of New York City. That week, anyway. The mayor came to see her in the morning with a breakfast tray. She took it at the door and sent him away. The *New York Post Standard* couldn't get enough of her. They retold the tale of her boorish husband, Shane Heath, a seldom-used Yankee outfielder who hung out in the topless bar Scores so often they'd named a lap dance after him: The Yankee Stripper.

The *Daily News* hired a team of window washers to take pictures of her through a telephoto lens as they cleaned the Hilton Hotel windows across the street. Even the *Times* was impressed with the heroic performance in the diner. But instead of just admitting that Ginny was a great New York story, they covered the tabloids covering the New York story. The shooting made Ginny a bigger international star than tennis alone had ever done.

But no matter how hard the mayor tried to get an introduction, Ginny wasn't interested. She didn't tell His Honor the truth, which was that the self-centered mayor reminded her of her contemptible husband. Steadily, "Ginny Mania," as the *Post Standard* referred to it, died down. Mason made another lame run at her, and even got Ginny to meet him for dinner at Elaine's. But there was a Yankees game on and Ginny pouted through veal chops with her back to the television. Mostly they gossiped about the welfare commissioner. The deputy police commissioner was also said to have had a romantic link with the lady. Mason denied this as best he could. "Listen, Ginny," he explained, "anyone who wants to get anything accomplished in city hall has to go through that dreadful woman. So, if I did anything, and I'm not admitting I did, at least I had to do it. I did it for the NYPD. The mayor did it for himself."

Ginny didn't move out of the hotel. She could hide from the newspapers there. The Warwick was so happy to have her on the premises that they stopped billing the city $159 a night for her room. They ate the bill. August came and went, taking the U.S. Open with it. Ginny again lost in the second round to Rory Bliss, adding insult to injury. The Jackster replaced Deputy Commissioner Mason as her grotesque would-be suitor. But neither the father nor the cop from hell could piss Ginny off as much as her husband could.

Mickey got a report from some of his Bronx friends that Miss Glade was going to some Yankees games disguised. He went to see her one night and slipped into a seat beside her after she'd bellowed at her husband's strikeout.

"Miss Glade," he said. "Is that you?"

She fell back into the seat.

"You caught me," she said. "I am so embarrassed."

"Don't be. I hear the guy is a real wanker."

"He is."

"Well, discretion is the better part of valor, Ginny, and revenge. You don't want to wind up on Page Six acting like this."

She touched his hand again. He let it linger. She removed it only to boo her former husband as he took the field.

"I can't stay," Mickey said. "But could we have dinner next week?"

"I would love that," Ginny said.

"Maybe even take in a Mets game," Mickey said, laughing.

He got up and shook her hand, saying, "I'll call you."

Mickey started to walk away, but then stopped. He reached into his pocket and came out with a small plastic ladybug. There was a button in the middle of the bug's back.

"This is an alarm," Mickey said. "It is our newest weapon in the war against domestic abuse. This one is tied in directly to my beeper. Press it if you get in trouble."

"I need this?" Ginny said.

"No, I need it," Mickey said. "I think I bumped into our suspect outside your building. He may just live around there or he may be a stalker. So protect my career, Ginny, please, and wear this."

"Hold it, Donovan. You came up here to see me."

"I'm not following you, but I make it my business to know where you are. Actually, I have you on my mind a lot lately."

"Which side of your brain? The business side or the personal side?"

"Truthfully, Ginny, you command attention in both spheres," Mickey said. "But I don't want a business dinner."

"Maybe I'll reach out and touch you."

"Don't cry wolf, Ginny. I'll call you."

Ginny laughed and said, "I could use a wolf."

Her husband went on a hitting streak and got his average above 200—the so-called Mendoza line. To make matters worse, the Yankees played tremendous late September baseball and passed the

Baltimore Orioles to win their division on the last day of the season. They also crushed both a wild card team and the Seattle Mariners on their way to the World Series. Then things got god-awful. Bernie Winters, the Yankee right fielder, tripped on the same outfield drain that had ruined Mickey Mantle's wheels, tore up his knee, and was lost for the World Series. This had the net effect of making Shane Heath the starting Yankee right fielder for the fall classic. Ginny quit reading the newspapers entirely for fear of finding something nice written about him. After six games in the error-marred series, Shane Heath was in a zero for twenty hole.

"Good, let the whole country see what a fraud he is," Ginny told Mickey.

"Careful," Mickey counseled. "Cheering against the Yankees right now is like cheering for the iceberg against the *Titanic*."

And if the truth be known, sometimes Ginny fantasized about killing her husband. She had killed before. She could do it again. But the World Series collapse of Shane Heath was better than murder, more immutable.

And then Game Seven happened.

NINE

World Series, Game Seven, Yankee Stadium

The right-field umpire was Al Lisker Jr. Everyone called him Blackie because he had wrestled at Northern Idaho State under that name. He claimed to be part Comanche Indian and part Cleveland Indian. He was all baseball, the son of a baseball writer from the *Newark Star Ledger*.

Blackie Lisker dressed in the umpire's room under the stands to the right of the Yankees' clubhouse and quietly jogged out to right field for the game all of New York would be watching. He had worked third base in Game Six, and had even made a couple of good calls on bang-bang plays. By comparison, the outfield job was boring. And that was fine because after game six, Lisker had pulled a calf muscle getting onto a bar stool in Greenwich Village.

Yankee Stadium had been made safe for the World Series and national television. The park, including some bare patches in center field, gleamed with fresh paint. At game time, tickets were selling for a thousand dollars a pop. Every television in every bar throughout the city was tuned to the game. The streets were eerily empty of traffic and had the look and feel of Thanksgiving at dinnertime. Police records indicated that no one had been shot in New York City in the two hours leading up to the game. New York was pacified and happy, but a little apprehensive. They were playing the Colorado Rockies, a team coached by a former Yankee.

After decades of despair, New York was back. The city wasn't over. It was back, loud and proud, too. Every piece of litter along the Major Deegan and Cross Bronx Expressway had been picked up. The highways and byways of New York City hadn't been cleaned so thoroughly since Mikhail Gorbachev had come to town in 1991.

The mayor was passionately distressed about his national image, convinced that he would be considered as a vice-presidential candidate for either party in the next presidential race. He was terrified that some lunatic would run onto his field, start a riot, and ruin his reputation as America's toughest politician, the greatest law and order candidate since Thomas Dewey. "No maniac running on the field is going to keep me from becoming president," he'd told his aides during a five-hour pregame meeting at city hall.

So the city cops were everywhere. There were uniformed cops in the stands, dugouts, and parking lots. The narcotics bureau had undercover cops posing as popcorn vendors, ushers, and bullpen catchers. The guys from the warrant squad were selling programs. One detective from the Safe and Loft squad helped warm up the opposing starter for the Colorado Rockies. A team from the parking violations bureau was running the license plates on every car that exited the Deegan at 161st Street. As a white guy who had been elected over a black mayor he had dared to refer to as a bathroom attendant, Caruso now had the cops passing out towels in public rest rooms.

"Just keep the cops away from the bathroom plungers," the mayor warned. He then held a rather remarkable press conference behind home plate an hour before game time.

"I promise New York City and America a new standard," the mayor began. "Any fan who runs on the field tonight will be arrested, charged, tried, convicted, and jailed until the Yankees open their next spring-training camp."

A couple of reporters snickered.

Police nightsticks, riot helmets, motorcycle helmets, and horses were standard ninth-inning drama at World Series games now. The mayor wanted something new. So he had police paratroopers readied at Floyd Bennett Field in Queens and a helicopter gunship hovering over the center-field bleachers. The entire stadium gasped when a fan ran onto the field in the first inning. He was wearing a sign that read: "Vito, Kiss My A—."

The center-field gates opened to reveal the police department's half-track tank, Real Brave One, the star of the squatters' rebellion in the East Village. It was freshly pin-striped and outfitted with turf-friendly rubberized tracks. The drunken fan heard the roar, turned, and gave up the fight. He stood in front of the tank, offering his best Tiananmen Square pose, mute and humbled. He was just as quickly hit with a shoulder-launched stun gun. He wobbled, jiggled, and then fell, losing control of his bowels. He was wrapped in a new NYPD blue tarp by the grounds crew and rushed off to Bronx Central booking. Only a couple of fans still had to be chased down by the tank, frozen and tarped as the game progressed.

By the seventh inning, the Yankees and Rockies were tied two to two. An autumn-night wind began to swirl. By the time Shane Heath came to the plate with two out in the bottom of the ninth, the wind was blowing to right center, toward the Bronx criminal court. And then the felony happened—grand-theft championship.

Falling behind in the count, zero and two, Heath slapped a lazy fly ball to the right corner. Later, everyone would admit they had been surprised that the ball even made it to the ten-foot wall. The padded blue barrier was 310 feet from home plate and in the shallowest part of the park. The right fielder set up under the ball on the warning track, tapped his glove, and waited for the ball to drop. But at the last moment, a fan reached over the fence and snatched the dropping ball, turning a certain out into a Shane Heath home run.

The umpire, Blackie Lisker, completely missed the play. Blackie had been too slow to get down the foul line. Even worse, NBC had ten cameras working the game. Although every American could see the fan interference from every angle, the ump raised his right arm and made a circle: *home run.*

Yankee Stadium exploded, and with it New York City.

Instead of the third out in the inning and extra innings, the Yankees won the World Series. The Rockies manager became enraged. The Yankee players began to ride around the park on horseback. Dozens of people who tried to run on the field were stunned and tarped by the mayor's police. It wasn't just the greatest blown baseball call in a decade. The fan-aided home run stood as the difference in a three to two Yankees' win. Sure, they were world champions with an asterisk. The network people were thrilled, too. So were Republicans, including Newt Gingrich. Suddenly, there was another reason to hate New York City. They stole from the rest of us.

At least one New Yorker was suicidal.

The umpire's blown call had turned Ginny's ex-husband, Shane Heath, into a national sports hero. He could always be traded, waived, or sent back to Columbus next year, but he belonged to Yankees history now. The umpire had transformed a Yankees klutz into a Yankees immortal. Shane Heath had hit the most preposterous pop fly in the Yankees' annals—even more unlikely than Bucky Dent's home run against the Red Sox in 1978.

No one cared that Heath was the progeny of an umpire's mistake. All that mattered to fans was that the Yankees were world champions again. But the fable got better for a mayor who wanted to be known throughout the world as a crime fighter and Yankees fan. It turned out that the fan who'd reached on the wall to make the catch, Frankie Johnson, was wanted for jumping bail on a wife-beating charge in Queens County. His battered wife had called the cops as soon as she'd seen him on the replay.

"He never wore a glove when he was beating me," Mrs. Johnson said. "And he ain't ever bought a baseball bat or glove for any of his six kids."

Frankie Johnson, the Yankees' savior, was arrested at the stadium as soon as *Hard Copy* finished interviewing him. The mayor was deliriously happy. Not only had the Yankees won, but his cops had gotten to arrest the star of the show. A Yankees' win was a victory for the city against domestic abuse, too.

Ginny was despondent by the time Yankee Stadium emptied. Her lecherous husband was right about his place in sports: The miserable cad really did belong to America. The tabloids were insane with stories about the unlikely New York hero, especially after Shane Heath offered to bail the guy out of jail and buy all of his kids balls, bats, gloves, and Yankees uniforms. The failed marriage to Ginny was back in the news. Hell, the *New York Post Standard* joked that they were going to name a sperm bank after Shane Heath at New York University Hospital.

Ginny wanted to die, or at least kill someone again. "Why couldn't the Yankees have given us his and hers shotguns?" Ginny said when Babe called in the middle of the celebration.

The other umpires in the crew didn't say anything to Lisker in the tiny dressing room. They got dressed and left. The crew chief was the first one out. So he knew he was dead. He could hear the reporters outside. Ordinarily, you could just wait them out. They all worked for morning newspapers and had early deadlines. Most times, they just quit the stakeout. But not tonight. Not after this call, in this game. The baseball writers were waiting on history tonight.

After about an hour, the man from the baseball commissioner's office burst through the door. He came in holding a videotape. The reporters were barking questions from behind the barred door.

"You have to get that ump out here, chief. America wants to know."

"Is the commissioner's office investigating?"

"Kill the umpire. He just ruined the national pastime."

The flack's name was Henry Ignoble, a 350-pounder who fit in well with the rotund umpires. Ignoble waddled into the umpires' room and punched the videotape into a TV. The screen came alive. Shane Heath swung and launched a tame, looping drive to right. The fly ball was heading for the right-field corner again. The fan reached again. And the ump, Blackie Lisker, was slow to get down the line, again. The ump watched himself missing the play. He signaled a home run.

"Well?"

"Well what, Ignoble? I blew the play."

"And what are you going to say to the reporters?"

"That I'll get it right next year."

"Wrong. The commissioner sent me down here to tell you to resign immediately."

"Show me that quote in your notebook, dickhead."

"Excuse me?"

"Go hump the foul pole. Your man, *the acting commissioner*, let that maniac from the Mariners pick his nose and flick it at me. We agreed to do the series anyway. So piss off, grocery boy. I just talked to my union. We got a *situation*."

Blackie Lister stood and kicked the television stand over. Then he walked to the door and stepped out into the swirling frenzy of reporters. The ump was going live from coast to coast. He was a set of blue eyes in a blue uniform.

"I made a mistake," Blackie said. "But it was an honest one. This entire shortened season was a mistake. We came from a players' strike, following an owners' strike. And honestly, we're all out of shape and practice. You are cheering triple-A talents who spit at us. America is cheering fakes, frauds, and major-league pretenders. But tonight, I screwed up. Still, mistakes and lucky breaks are as American as the national pastime. But don't blame the umpires. Blame the baseball commissioner. He's the one passing this minor-league crap off as the real deal. Good night."

And then the umpire turned on his rubber cleats and flopped off to the stairwell. He didn't even bother to change out of his uniform. He walked straight out the door and across Babe Ruth Way to the Yankee players' parking lot, which was an armed camp. It was absolute bedlam by then. Helmeted cops were loading a police bus with handcuffed prisoners. The blue line was shoulder to shoulder, billy club to billy club. This was not going to be like Detroit, where fans rioted after the Tigers won a championship. This mayor would arrest the whole town if need be. His prisoners already included the bail jumper from Queens who had caught the ball. The police horses the Yankee players had ridden around the stadium in their victory celebration were being loaded into their trailers. Boss Glassbrenner's limousine was still in its parking spot. The Scooter was long gone.

The cops let the umpire pass quietly. They all seemed to know who he was, but no one said anything until he reached his car. Then he heard it.

"Thanks."

The ump reeled at the sound and searched the parking lot. Shane Heath was standing by the gate, signing autographs. He waved an autographed ball at him.

"Thanks again, man," Heath said. "You should get a full player's share. Maybe even a World Series ring, too."

The umpire just balled his fists and silently got into his car. He screeched past the guard at the gate and made a right turn to get on the Major Deegan Expressway. The cops scattered, laughing.

Blackie never saw the car get in behind him as he got on the ramp leading to the Triboro Bridge.

TEN

Evening, Methadone Clinic, Park Slope, Brooklyn

Mickey Donovan was back in the junkie world. He sat in his car watching the front door of the methadone clinic, waiting for his daughter. His life had become an absurd *Crime and Punishment*. After all those years of arresting junkies, he was now sitting outside the methadone clinic hoping his daughter could be saved.

The cop was back on the Bronx foot post again. Many years before, he had worked outside a new methadone clinic at the Forty-fourth Precinct in the Bronx. It was a rough and tumble place. He had been young sergeant then, teaching a history class at a P.S. 124 in Brooklyn. This was years before anyone in the country started to talk about community policing or zero tolerance. It was a year before Officer Friendly had started visiting grade schools, too.

Mickey Donovan, then twenty-five, wasn't sure he wanted to work as a cop anymore. So he had taken the job as a substitute teacher on the side. Most precinct commanders would have fired him. But Mickey had had a boss, Captain Sean Cotter, who thought it was great that he had a cop who wanted to open a book. The captain had even hosted a reading group for cops. After a week of busting heads in the Bronx, they had gathered to read *Crime and*

Punishment. They had read a great novel every week and had then discussed it before retiring to Maquires' on Second Avenue. They had been an unlikely group—chaired by Cotter, a rummy who loved Graham Greene and regularly vacationed at the Olafson, with its stagnant swimming pool, in Port au Prince, Haiti. He drank dark rum from the bottle and recited passages from *The Power and the Glory.* Hell, Captain Cotter had known lines from the novelist's parables of the damned better than most cops knew the *Miranda* warning. He had stopped drinking several years ago, after two stickup men had walked into his bar and announced a holdup. He had been at the opposite end of the door facing the masked gunmen. He had calmly placed his glass on the bar with his left hand and had come up firing. Two head shots. The robbers had both hit the floor, dead. Cotter had left with the glass in his pocket, never refilling it.

"Why did you quit drinking?" the younger guys would ask him.

"Because I can't remember the seventies," he'd said, truthfully. "A whole decade is blank."

Sometimes, "the Men," as he'd called cops, would kid him about the drink. They were always trying to get him to run off on a bender.

"Yeah, I retired from drinking," Cotter would say. "But just remember one thing boys. *I retired with the title.*"

Mickey Donovan was a rarity, a thinking man's cop. And when he'd knocked out a mugger on his way to a reading one night with a hardcover copy of *The New Centurions*, all of the other cops had known he wasn't a closet liberal. So rather than banish or snub Mickey, they had made room for his decency, toughness, and smarts. They had allowed him to work what they called the "MD chart," meaning whenever Mickey was free from school, he worked as a cop.

The cop had had to work hard everywhere they'd sent him. By that year, the nasty precinct had been up to its elbows in heroin junkies. Most of them had descended on methadone clinics at Morrisana Hospital. The place had been filled with them. And they had all been lying blood clots, the cops said. It was amazing, but if you walked into the Morrisana Diner at any hour of the day, the place would be filled, with four junkies to a booth. And they would all be talking about the cop who had beaten them or the junkie who had beaten them out of a high. They had had tales of scam, scheme, and strategy. Mickey and the cops he'd worked with had also used the diner. It was amazing how the junkies had lied. No event so small or so insignificant that it couldn't be twisted or exaggerated into a huge social injustice. They had always been conniving and sticking up for each other and trying to get over on someone or something. Mostly the cops just sat in the back of the place, listening. And then one day Mickey had stood up and shouted, "Cut the bullshit. You are all weak men chasing the bag. Stop making excuses. Just shut up."

The other cops had all begun to laugh at Mickey's almost naive outburst.

"Shut up or what? You'll give them detention?"

Mickey had hated junkies ever since. None of the real, hard ones ever came back. It was just one long ride to the cemetery.

After a few minutes, he picked up his cell phone and called the clinic, asking for Dillon.

"I ain't seen her, but I'll look," the guy said.

"She should be done."

"Well, I don't see her. She may be in the ladies' room."

He snapped the phone shut. He couldn't go in and check himself because he would be recognized. The mayor would hear from the city-owned clinic within five minutes. But he didn't trust anyone else to bring her to the clinic. She would bolt on them. Dillion had once jumped out of Camacho's car and ditched his wife, who was a major-league detective, in a movie theater at King's Plaza. She had been gone for two days. They had found her nodded out in Tompkins' Square Park. Mickey had taken her to a methadone clinic associated with Methodist Hospital in Park Slope, Brooklyn. They had been dispensing little plastic cups with the pink liquid inside. The block had been filled with junkies who moved through the neighborhood like zombies.

And his daughter was one of them.

Mickey watched a couple of guys struggle on the stairs with the weight of a dirty laundry cart. He watched them load it into a truck. The inspector picked up his phone and called the Warwick Hotel to check on Ginny Glade again.

"Boss, she gave me the slip," the cop in the lobby reported. "There was bedlam here last night after the Yankees game. I went up a couple of hours later and she was extremely pissed off. She kept screaming about how some umpire had ruined her life. She asked if I could walk her to the Stage Deli to get a brisket sandwich. While I ordered, Miss Glade slipped out. She hasn't returned."

"Great. I'll have somebody check her apartment. She probably just went home."

Mickey snapped off the radio as he replayed the conversation in his mind. *Damn*. As he watched the door and waited, he began to think about his daughter. How did she get this far from him? She was becoming a terrible memory. He visited some of these memories again as he waited.

The only thing she adored was danger. She worshiped adventure, slam-dancing, Kerouac, Janis Joplin, The Doors, Amnesty International, and lost causes. She hated authority, politics, and uniforms and badges. Aerosmith and Alice Cooper were mixed in there somewhere, though she talked dreamily of shoving a live cat down the throats of Ozzy Osbourne and Marilyn Manson.

"You know what, Dad?" she'd said one day. "You know what emotion I live to feel? Revenge."

The cop's daughter had lost her virginity when she was thirteen, beneath the Coney Island boardwalk, to a fireman's son, no less, just to spite her father. Mary Dillon Donovan was a born squatter. She liked to drink malt liquor by the quart at Foster Avenue Park but she also drank with friends after dark in Prospect Park. She was every bit as reckless and wanton as her father had been. Once the cops had been called to the park after Dillon had threatened an old man playing chess with his grandson. The kids were playing something called slapboxing, and whacking each other in the arm as hard as they could. The old man had taken exception to Dillon's cursing. "Are you looking for trouble, young lady?" the old man had asked.

Dillon had jumped onto the bench and had leaned her twisted face into the old man's. "Listen, Doughboy," she'd said, sneering, leaning in so close the old man had sworn he could taste the Colt 45 on her breath. "I *am* trouble."

She certainly was.

Mickey Donovan kept a two-bedroom apartment in Manhattan's Stuyvesant Town in the East village, near FDR Drive, but usually stayed with his mother two nights a week. One day last summer Dillon had come home and announced, "I am going to follow Phish this summer."

Mickey had thought his daughter meant she was going to chase salmon in Alaska. He could be that old.

"I didn't even know you liked fishing," Mickey had said.

She'd laughed, then said, "Not 'fish,' Peter Frampton Breath *Phish*. They are a band from Vermont. Very funky."

"I've never seen you with their CD's."

"No one buys their albums, Dad. That's, like, so uncool. But they're, like, the greatest concert since The Dead. One of their anthem songs, 'Fluffhead,' wasn't meant for dunderhead cops, though I suspect 'Theme from the Bottom' was. Very spicy hyperfunk, but they have very flashy guitar riffs, too."

The cop had brightened. He had come of age with Eric Clapton and The Doors.

"Oh, sure," Mickey had tried. "Something like the old Steely Dan."

"Your whole life is unplugged, Dad," Dill had replied, blowing a wisp of her bangs over her right eye. "Are you going to sleep through the next couple of decades, too?"

But in the morning, Bridget's car had been gone—just vanished, along with Dillon's best friend, Dred Mercedes. Mickey had reported it stolen, thinking that it might do Dillon some good. But she'd been gone one day, then one week. The inspector had followed the tour in the paper, and had died with each dispatch. One teenager dead of an overdose in Maryland. Five OD's in Ohio. Three in Colorado. Two in California. He'd sent Camacho, on the sly, to find Dill in Minneapolis. She'd made the undercover from a block away.

"This is so uncool," she'd said. "Tell Dad I'll be home in a week."

In Oregon, Mickey had quickly learned, they'd run out of money. An FBI agent following the tour, looking for a serial killer, had spotted Dillon's car, had run the plate and called the New York office. The New York director of the bureau, a personal friend, had called Mickey Donovan directly.

"What the hell is this, Mick?"

"Please give her some room."

Two days later, in Washington, an alert patrolman had watched Dillon and Dred panhandling outside a Burger King in Seattle. The cop had followed them back to the tiny, odd, white car and had run the New York plate. It had come back as stolen from East Thirty-eighth Street, Brooklyn, New York. He'd arrested Dillon, Dred, and two local hopheads. That same day Inspector Donovan had stood with the mayor in the blue room at city hall as Mayor Caruso had announced a complete victory over New York City panhandlers and squeegee pests. After it was over, Mickey had driven directly to the airport and flown to Seattle. When Mickey reached her holding cell, Dillon had started to cry.

"I love you, Daddy." The cop's anger had evaporated. His daughter hadn't called him "Daddy" in ten years. They'd flown back together and shipped the car home. On the plane ride back, he'd sat with a manicured, middle-aged man who had introduced himself as a father who was following the tour, looking for his son.

"Did you go to the concert?"

"No, I picked her up in the jail."

"You're lucky to get her back this soon."

He was a big movie agent who had lived in Manhattan but had moved to Montana with the other Hollywood types two years ago. His son, then twenty-one and a Colgate graduate, had stayed in New York. He'd quit his job and joined the Deadhead/Phish tour at The Meadowlands. After a year, the father had gone to look for him. He'd found him in a San Francisco shooting gallery with a needle in his arm and had brought him home.

"There are usually about thirty parents following the show in every venue," the guy had said, sighing. "We're all looking for runaways. We call ourselves 'the Satellite Tour.' "

The father with the lost son had checked Dillon's arms, then whispered, "Do you know about the heroin?"

Mickey Donovan had looked at his daughter. She was sleeping next to Dred. Mickey had spent five years in narcotics. He had given her arms the once-over, too. He would have known a track mark from across the room. She hadn't had any visible ones.

"I heard heroin was back," Mickey had said. "The kids following these bands are heavy users." Under the circumstances, the cop had not been afraid to be indelicate. He had continued, "And your son?"

"By the time I got him back, he was HIV positive."

"I'm so sorry."

"So is he. But he is back out there again."

She was back in the shit again, too. Mickey was suddenly afraid again. *What was she doing in there?* His daughter was taking too long. On average, a visit to the methadone clinic took about ten minutes. Sign in, gulp the juice, and out. Dillon had been in the place for an hour now. He called the front desk again and got the same recovering addict.

"Oh, like, Dill already left, man. She hitched a ride with some Manhattan dudes."

"Impossible. I'm parked right outside. The only thing to come out of there in the last ten minutes was two guys pushing a laundry cart from Don Budge Laundry."

"Well, she is quite gone."

"Oh shit," Mickey said, realizing that his daughter had been *inside* the laundry cart. Never underestimate the craving.

"Hey, dude, is everything copacetic, man?" the guy on the phone wanted to know.

That junkie word took him back. He was back with Cotter, hearing him say, "Junkies don't ever make it back."

The seventeen-year-old daughter of the most highly regarded cop in the city was fast on her way to becoming a stone junkie. Some detective, too, incidentally. The kid had given her old man the slip. Again. He was just pulling out when the homicide dispatcher called.

"Did you see the Yankees game last night, Inspector?"

"Of course."

"Well, Sergeant Francisco Camacho just called in, sir. He said you better get over to Sheridan Square."

Early Morning, Sheridan Square, Greenwich Village

The umpire was on a green bench inside Stonewall Jackson Park. His blood was pooled at the foot of the dead Confederate general's statue. There was always something odd about every crime scene, and there were two interesting things about this one. First, it looked like the Civil War hero was leaking blood. Years ago, when Greenwich Village had been becoming the political center of the gay universe, rioting cops had beaten the hell out of some residents. It wouldn't take long for *The Village Voice* to say that Stonewall Jackson was still bleeding for gay men and women all these years later.

The second thing Mickey Donovan noticed was the shoes. The dead ump still had on his rubber cleats. Mickey's sergeant from Manhattan South, Francisco Camacho, was standing over the body when Mickey arrived.

"Yeah, he came right down here from the stadium," Camacho said. "He died in his uniform." Camacho had been born in San Francisco de Macoris, a town in the Dominican Republic, and he was fiercely proud of his heritage. The ancient town cemetery was filled with young crack dealers who had died on a tour of duty while slinging the product in Washington Heights. The dealers who'd made it home had built, in the middle of town, pastel mansions with huge satellite dishes. Last year, another kid from his town who'd grown up to become a New York City cop had been arrested for robbing drug dealers in the latest police corruption scandal. The stereotype was killing the reputation of his people. Dominicans weren't all drug dealers, any more than all Irishmen were drunks. But to read the newspapers, you wouldn't know that.

"Please tell me this is a simple gay sex murder," Mickey said.

"It's not," Francisco said.

"Why not?"

"He was across the street, in The Triplex, about three hours after the Yankees game. That was his second stop. He went to The Lion's Head first, but everyone knew who he was and insisted on buying him drinks."

Mickey studied Christopher Street. The Lion's Head was the fabled writers' bar. It was a regular stop on the literary tour. *Is this the place where writers with drinking problems hang out? No, this is the place where drunks with writing problems hang out.* The place had gone to hell after writers had stopped drinking. The book covers on the wall had yellowed along with the livers of the customers. Nobody who wrote chapters drank in the place anymore. The Triplex was located next door, on the corner. It was a piano bar mostly, but a gay one. After the Broadway shows emptied, many world-class performers gathered there to sing and play piano before retiring. The Triplex was one of the city's most exciting last-call stops. It was not a sports joint. They didn't even have a television in the bar.

"So if he's not gay, why is he in The Triplex?"

"Two reasons. First, no one in the place cares about the Yankees. And second, the bartender, who says she is not currently gay, is his girlfriend. The deceased lived right across the street. He told our bartender friend he was going home to wait for her."

"And?"

"He gets this in the neck." Francisco held up a twelve-inch shiv with a primitive look. It was standard prison cutlery. "It's probably a soup ladle. The cup is snapped off and the end sharpened. The weapon is crude, but effective. It went right through his neck."

Mickey held the shiv in a gloved hand. "The brand name is Cutco. My neighbor Jay used to sell this stuff door-to-door. He was always bugging me about buying some ridiculous boxed set. I think they're out of business now. Find out if that's right and when they stopped making this. It looks industrial, so see if you can find out where they shipped this kind of thing."

"Done."

Mickey made a face, "I don't mean to be so obvious, but why isn't this a gay murder, again?"

"Someone saw a woman running from the park."

"Maybe a transvestite, then."

"Nope. We got this, too." In his gloved hand, the detective held up a piece of paper in a plastic bag. "Typewritten. Short and sweet. It says: 'Going, going, GONE. You blew the call. America demands justice.' "

"Oh shit."

"Right. Someone followed our umpire here with that note and weapon. Definitely premeditated. Like some bullshit ESPN sportscaster's rant. Our murderer was lying in wait. I'd say he or she even opened the park gate so Mr. Lisker could take a shortcut home. Probably jumped out from behind the Confederate soldier's statue with this Riker's Island sword. So I figure we either got a very pissed-off gambler, like those guys in Colombia who killed that soccer player after the World Cup, or the sports revenge killing of all time."

"Where's our girl?"

"Ginny?"

"Yeah. Was she up at the stadium again?"

"Ginny Glade sure has motive, boss. But this would be some cold-hearted shit."

"I want to know where she is."

Camacho dialed his phone as Mickey Donovan studied the crime scene. He was impressed by the detective's logic. He knew Camacho had worked as a cave cop in the subway before transit was merged with the rest of the NYPD. Mickey had spotted his talent then. Camacho was also one of the toughest cops Mickey had ever worked with. Even though transit cops were tough guys, their boxing team was a joke. They wore bathrobes taken from Brooklyn by-the-hour hotels. The NYPD cops had a real team. They were guys who had boxed in the air force and navy. They wore powder-blue satin robes. Donovan remembered a time years ago when the two police forces had fought a smoker in a Brooklyn high school gym. Camacho had gotten in the ring against a PBA fighter who came within a hair of making the Olympic team. He was the real deal. During the bloody bout, the transit cop hadn't run and hadn't fallen. He'd been beaten to a pulp after three rounds, but had made it. It was clear that pride had been the only thing keeping Camacho up.

"You still got dimples in your knees, Camacho?" Mickey asked.

"Probably, sir. But I never hit the deck." The cop laughed as he watched the inspector measuring the crime scene.

"Of course I could be completely wrong," Camacho said. "This could be a savage gay killing made to look like an attack on our national pastime."

"That would be even more unlikely than the dead ump's mistaken home-run call," Mickey said.

"Here, take a look at this." Camacho walked him to the steel gate. Ordinarily the gate on the park was locked at night. But the padlock had been snipped in half.

"That would take a decent amount of hand strength," Camacho said.

"You do a canvass?" asked Mickey.

"Uniform is doing a door-to-door right now. And these residents are not happy. They think this is just a new cop roust to find out who's sleeping with whom."

Mickey Donovan smiled. So did Francisco.

"And what did you tell them?"

"I told them, 'Be discreet. But for God's sake let me know if you catch my boyfriend up there.' One of the younger cops actually said, 'Don't tell me you're a fudge packer, too, Sarge.' I swear, Inspector, we're hiring cops now from the Howard Stern audience. Anyway, I told him, 'Officer, that is precisely the kind of question you can't ask people when you knock on their doors.' "

Mickey Donovan snickered. It was a good management technique.

"Roll this guy over," the inspector said, looking down on the dead ump.

Francisco rolled Blackie on his side. The holes on either side of his neck oozed. You could see his face now. It was a mask of blood.

"The right eye is gone," Francisco said.

"So the killer has a knife, too."

Mickey pointed to the note Francisco held. "What else?"

Francisco held it up to the streetlight, then turned it over. There was writing on the back. It was some sort of receipt.

"I don't know what to think of the paper it was written on," Francisco said. "And it was written with a red crayon. It could be just a piece of trash the killer picked up in the park."

The detective sergeant studied it for a moment. "Let's see. They paid cash. No credit card number. Not dated, either. That isn't going to help."

"What's the name of the place?"

"Some place called The Falls. At the Sheraton Wanderer. Let's see. Out of state. Bedford, New Hampshire."

Mickey Donovan fell silent as a sudden truth hit him. "That's the place they found the tennis umpire in the parking lot."

"Ginny answered her home phone, boss. We're about done here. Where do you want to go?

"Elaine's. I want to visit the Count before we do another thing."

"The Count?"

"Count Smirnoff."

Last Call, Elaine's, Upper East Side

An hour later, at four A.M., they were pounding shots of vodka in the back of the restaurant with the last of the boorish, drunken Yankees fans. By then, Elaine Kaufman, the owner, had even packed the Yankees' owner into a cab. Mickey was in a hateful mood. His daughter was chasing needles. The woman he liked was a murder suspect, and that was unsettling to say the least. And the mayor wanted to kill him. As if fate had arranged the tables, Mickey recognized a couple of gangsters sitting at a table behind him.

Francisco tried to eavesdrop on their conversation but Mickey got madder and madder. He knew the guys were members of the Gambino crime family, who operated Club Phoenix in Brooklyn. The gangsters were loudmouths and dangerous fools. They didn't recognize the cops and began waxing nostalgic about their heady crime days and lost leaders. Mickey saw a chance to make a point and get some useful information.

"Oh, yeah," Mickey said, turning and interrupting their conversation loudly. "It's really too bad about your capo. Didn't he hang out at those gay bars in Queens? In fact, didn't he run nozzle night himself?"

"Who the fuck are you?" one gangster demanded, picking up his steak knife. "I should cut you right here."

Mickey placed his palms on the table and smiled. When these guys weren't selling horse to kids like his daughter, they were committing fashion crimes. One of the guys, Mickey noticed, was wearing a striped oxford button-down with a gray double-breasted suit.

"Your capo is a scumbag piece of shit," Mickey said by way of introduction. One of the guys at the table offered to settle the debate in the bathroom.

"Oh, well, you wouldn't enjoy me," Mickey replied. "You're used to those guys with really big drills." Gay humor was sophomoric, Mickey knew, but it was as deep as gangsters got.

"Me and you right now, right here, fucko," the gangster said.

"There's nothing holding you back," Mickey replied. "But before we get started, I want you to know how this is gonna go. I'm a detective and my friend here is holding a gun on you under the table." Camacho nodded at the gentleman. "First I am going to bitch-slap you in front of all these people. And when I'm finished, I'm going to arrest you and personally drive you to the Nineteenth Precinct, where you'll spend the whole weekend in the hole. Maybe you'd like that."

"We don't want any trouble, Officer," the smaller gangster said, quickly changing his attitude with the shifting terrain. "We're leaving now."

Mickey leaned over the table. "Not so fast, gentlemen. I want to know where the dead priest who used to hang out in Club Phoenix was getting his horse."

"Fuck you, cop," the loud gangster said. "He was getting it from one of yours. You know, what's his name?"

"Peter Heroin," the smaller gangster said.

Finally, Elaine came over to the table and demanded to know what was going on. The larger Mafioso, afraid of a life banishment, pointed at Mickey Donovan and whined, "Hey, he started it."

John Mason, the deputy commissioner, had been listening at the bar, half-hiding behind a pay phone with a hand on his Glock. He stepped forward and announced, "Hey now, come on, boys. You aren't supposed to rat."

At dawn, after breakfast at a diner on East Seventy-ninth Street, Donovan went to see Ginny Glade.

Victor the Doorman was a careful fellow. The newest thing in New York City that season was home-invasion robberies where crooks using fake ID's broke into the apartments of rich people.

"Miss Glade is upstairs now," he said. "She came in early this morning. Is she expecting you, Inspector? I'll have to announce you."

"You will do no such thing. And if you call up to her on the phone while I'm on the elevator, we're going to have a personality conflict. In fact, ride with me."

They rode up silently. Mickey Donovan crushed the man with a look. "What shape was she in?"

"Miss Glade is always in perfect shape, sir."

The cop got off the elevator and dismissed Victor with a wave of his hand. He had to knock several times before Ginny answered. She had to speak over Diana Ross and the Supremes playing in the background. It was Ross's *Greatest Hits*. "Run, Run, Run" was playing. Ginny opened the door wearing sweatpants and lugging a duffle bag full of laundry.

"Hi, it's Mickey Donovan," he said. "We got to talk."

There was a flicker of doubt in her face. Then anger. "I couldn't stay at the hotel anymore, Mickey. I had to get out. I needed to do my own laundry."

"Yeah, Ginny. I just wanted to ask you a few questions. Could I come in?"

"Yes. Excuse the mess. I'll make some coffee."

"Only if you want some."

"I always want some."

Ginny sniffed the air. "You've been drinking."

"It's been a long night."

The *Daily News* was on the floor. The front page screamed, "Top of the World," and featured a photograph of Ginny's husband riding a horse around Yankee Stadium. Donovan noticed that his eyes had been circled, then gouged out. That was disturbing, but no more so than his phone call to the New Hampshire State Police had been twenty minutes earlier as he sat in traffic on the West Side Highway. Blinky Hammond had been stabbed in the neck, too, Mickey had learned. And his right eye had been missing. Neither detail had ever been published. The cops up there were nowhere with their homicide investigation. Someone had found Hammond's wallet floating in the river. It looked like a vicious robbery. They were still going over calls he'd made from a cell phone. There had been only one in the hour before his murder. He'd called a Miss Virginia Glade of East Eighty-first Street in Manhattan but the call hadn't lasted long enough to show that a conversation had taken place.

Mickey pointed to the newspaper. "Yeah, I figured this would be a rough morning for you."

Ginny sighed. "The night was rougher. I wasn't even watching the game. I just couldn't. Then my friend Babe called me, and screamed, 'Turn on the television. That prick is a national hero now.' They were carrying Shane off the field. It was an insufferable scene."

"Yeah, well the city will be crazy with him for a while. But they'll get over it."

"I keep telling myself I don't care, that I'm better off without him. And I am. But I don't need to be reminded of my failure every time I turn on the television. It's all, so, *withering*."

"Legacy and infamy are hard to survive."

"The only person who feels worse than I do has to be that umpire."

The detective froze. There hadn't been a word about the murder yet. "What do you mean, Ginny?"

"That he has to live with his error in judgment. He can't go to a clinic somewhere and have his blunder erased. Videotape lives forever. Absolution won't save him, Inspector. He can't terminate his problem."

"Murder and television are permanent conditions."

The song had changed. Now Diana was singing "Baby Love." Mickey could see that Ginny was a beautiful woman, even at this hour. There was no denying it. He looked into her bedroom and saw that the bed had been slept in. The bathroom was still wet with moisture. Mickey Donovan was kind of afraid. She *could* be a murderer. He didn't like the idea of her washing away evidence.

"I have to get to practice over at Columbia University," Ginny said. "I haven't hit a ball in two days. And I need to get my laundry done."

"Okay, come on, I'll walk you down. We can have coffee, later."

Ginny stood up, then froze.

"Just a minute, *Inspector*. Why are you here?"

Mickey Donovan smiled tightly. The papers were all over the story. Her phone rang. He put his hand over the receiver, hoping it wasn't her lawyer.

"Before you answer that, Ginny, I want to tell you something. The umpire who made that bad call last night was murdered after he left Yankee Stadium. We found him a couple of hours ago. The newspapers are gonna want to talk to you about it. So am I, actually."

"Why?"

"Because it's the second one," Mickey said, releasing his grip on the phone.

"What do you mean? Who was the first?"

"Blinky Hammond."

The answering machine answered on the fourth ring. The *New York Post Standard* was calling.

"Can we talk over a cup of tea, Ginny?"

"Am I being arrested, Mickey?"

"Not unless the tea really sucks," he said.

As they left, the cop was humming "Stop! In the Name Of Love."

He was afraid again as she touched his hand.

ELEVEN

Two Toms Jazz Club, Lower East Side, Manhattan

Francisco Camacho walked into the barroom on the Lower East Side and saw the dead body immediately. He did a quick count and stood back, smiling. He counted ten holes.

The bartender was still behind the stick, smiling, too. He was a huge black man with two miniature anvils for hands. Some years ago, when the Delancey Street bar was beginning to change clientele, he had suffered a stroke. His left foot was partially numb and his arm was permanently cocked. So, as he lurched around the place, he was just all the more intimidating. They called him Tommy Tom Tom because he would bang you like a drum if you tried to beat him on a check. Years ago the Two Toms Jazz Club had been a jazz hangout. But when the music had died, some of the tough guys had stayed and turned it into a hustlers' joint.

Mostly the place was a hangout for stickup men. Everyone in the neighborhood knew that. It was the last stop in Manhattan before the Williamsburg Bridge, just down the street from Ratner's the oldest continually owned restaurant in the city. Kosher deli had died along with the jazz business on the Lower East Side.

Camacho leaned over New York's newest homicide, a white fellow who looked to be about twenty years old. He was wearing a short-sleeved shirt that showed off his track marks, lots of them.

"The big mosquito got him," Camacho said.

"That fellow there is the dumbest, ahem, customer I ever met," Tommy Tom Tom said. He didn't even bother to look up as he rinsed the glasses. "His name was Martin Forbes. That's his college ID on the corner of the bar. Apparently he used to be a student at Long Island University. I would guess he must have been majoring in stupidity."

"How did Joe College here get so well punctured?"

"He came in and asked for a beer. He was a glass of milk just waiting to be spilled. Half the black gangsters on the other side of my bar—legitimate stars of our stickup society—were already grumbling. As you can see, the kid is barefoot now. But he thudded in here wearing maroon-and-green Timberland boots. Some of my customers wanted to rob him for the nifty footwear as soon as they saw him."

"So someone shot a college puke for his boots. Tommy, that is not going to be good for business at all. Shit. The mayor wanted to close your place after the last time."

"That was not my fault, either. That guy deserved my ice pick. But don't get ahead of the narrative, Detective."

"Go on."

"So your man there orders a pint of Budweiser, takes one sip, smiles, and then pulls out a knife and announces, 'This is a stickup. Empty the register now.' The guys hear this and all of a sudden your would-be stickup man is facing ten real stickup men with guns."

"Stupid kid. He brings a knife to a gunfight."

"Right. Only now the guys are furious. They're professionally insulted. Big Green was the maddest. He stands up and screams, 'You can't stick us up, white boy. *We do this shit for a living.* Who the fuck do you think you are coming in here and trying to rob stickup men with a knife anyway?' "

"What does the kid do?"

"He yells, 'Don't shoot. I don't even have a heater.' That was the word he used. 'Heater.' It was like some kid out of a time warp. Big Green slid a gun down the bar. The kid went for it."

"He dies an amateur," Francisco said.

"On their way out, the guys took his boots and the knife. Some of them are still out there laughing."

"And Big Green?"

"He's in the wind. But you have better homicide cases against him anyway. This matter today was self-defense."

"Yeah, or professional honor at the very least."

"Exactly. If somebody was allowed to stick up a stickup joint, I'd be finished."

"You may be anyway."

"I don't think so."

"How's that?"

"Mr. Numbnuts here came in with a girl."

"An accomplice?"

"Ask her yourself. She's a junkie and too young for me, but a bit of a looker. I locked her in the bathroom just to keep the boys away from her. She went in to take a pee before all this started. Big Green wanted her, too. But, luckily, Peter Heroin, your old cop friend, was sitting in the back when this whole thing broke. He talked them out of hurting the girl and left."

"So where is she?"

Tommy Tom Tom walked over to the door, pulled the key out of his pocket, and unlocked the door.

"Come on out, Annie Oakley, the DT's are here."

Francisco Camacho switched on the light. A bare sixty-watt bulb hanging from the ceiling revealed a girl sitting on the toilet bowl. The teenager squinted against the intrusion. She wore a glorious, curly red wig. The detective had to look twice before he recognized her.

"Come on out, Dill. I'll call your father."

Same Day, City Hall, Manhattan

The mayor had just finished his press conference in the blue room. He strode through the back of city hall to his office. There were only two entrances. The front door led out to a waist-level gate and the lobby. Sometimes he would stand by a stone pillar there and chat with reporters on his way out. Most of the reporters worked across the lobby in room nine. Only a few of them knew that the mayor had poked a hole in his floor to build a stairway to sexual heaven. Mayor Caruso didn't need to go out for a rendezvous anymore. He could get laid at work, which is why he worked late hours and seven days a week. His mayoralty was one big sleep-over.

The gilded stairwell led to his welfare commissioner's office. She had a tiny desk and a large couch. And the furniture fit her job requirements perfectly. In the beginning, Nicole Nesbitt didn't have a desk. But then the mayor's wife came down to the office and spotted the couch. She understood the commissioner's job requirements perfectly and announced, "Well, well. I thought you were doing away with welfare queens." Vito had been married when she'd met him, too. She'd had a couch installed in her office, too. That's how she'd landed him.

And so it went. No one really cared about the affair. He was a good mayor who kept crime down and didn't screw too much with the city's booming economy. Who cared if he was getting laid? Besides, after the intern and the President, no one cared about politicians who fooled around.

"There is a difference between fucking and fucking up," Vito quipped.

Mostly, the reporters liked to share rumors about the mayor's affair, so the mayor had steered clear of Room Nine—the press office—before he slipped into the welfare commissioner's office. When the mayor came down the back stairs to see his in-house lover, he was surprised to see Mike Berger, the chief of the NYPD traffic division, already sitting on Nicole's couch. Berger was from Brooklyn South and a well-known back-door visitor to city hall. He was a tattletale and hopelessly ambitious, so the mayor would never trust him to be police commissioner or even first deputy police commissioner. But he pulled a lot of weight in Brooklyn's Hasidic community if only because he was always fixing parking tickets and funeral marches. The mayor was happy. Brooklyn Jews were a big piece of his political base. Berger was hoping to become Chief of Patrol. An obsequious man, Berger was comfortable with betrayal. He served no man but himself.

Mike McAlary

"I got some information for you, Mr. Mayor," he announced. "I got it from a friend of the department. It is a matter of some delicacy. No one in the NYPD wants you to know this."

"Except you, of course."

"I serve the greatest mayor of this century."

"Okay, cut the crap. Let's hear it."

The queen of welfare, Nicole Nesbitt, the mayor's constant companion, added, "No, this time he's really got something to offer. He isn't just ratting out his friends for smoking dope and slamming hookers. This time he has material."

"Oh, really? Then spill."

"I know you have been looking to hang Inspector Mickey Donovan. We all hate him too, sir. At the Compstat meetings, he embarrasses us."

"He embarrasses you because you lie to him about your crime stats. You are always inflating your arrest totals. I like him torturing you lying oafs. It may be the only thing I like about him."

"Whenever I get up to talk about how we're improving traffic conditions in the city, he flashes a cartoon character onto the projector screen behind me."

"Oh, really? Which one?"

"Pinocchio, sir. When everyone starts laughing, he shouts, 'Your nose is growing again, Berger.' "

The mayor had to grab his jaw to keep from laughing. Nicole snickered.

"Funny, I always saw you as 'Casper, the Friendly Ghost,' " the mayor said.

"Or Mister Magoo," the welfare commissioner added.

The chief was red with embarrassment. He had expected to be treated better.

"The inspector is living a lie with all this zero tolerance crap, sir."

"What do you mean, Casper?"

"Zero tolerance doesn't apply to his own family?"

The mayor leaned forward. Now he was interested.

"He has a junkie for a daughter, sir. We know where she buys heroin on the Lower East Side."

Second Avenue, Upper East Side, Manhattan

Inspector Mickey Donovan was standing at the counter of the Ching Tau Laundry on Second Avenue with his prime suspect in the murders of Blinky Hammond and Blackie Lisker. Ginny Glade lifted her bag of clothes and plopped it on the scale. This was an uptown place. They charged you four dollars a pound to wash, dry, and fold your clothes. Mickey eyed the cloth bag suspiciously. He was deathly afraid that Ginny was going to wash away blood, fiber, and hair evidence from a murder in Stonewall Park. If that happened, he would be the laughingstock of The Department.

Ordinarily, Ginny did her own laundry in her apartment building's basement, but today, she explained, after weeks in the hotel, she had too much stuff to do herself. If Ginny was covering something up, she was quite cool.

"I'm going to get a bagel and coffee from across the street," she said. "You want anything? You can wait in the car."

"Black, no sugar."

Mickey walked her out and opened the car door. As she walked across the street to the deli he took the cell phone out of his pocket and called the laundry.

"Yes, this is Deputy Inspector Mickey Donovan from the NYPD. Ginny Glade just dropped some clothes off. Do not open the bag. I will have a uniformed police officer from the Nineteenth Precinct coming over to guard the clothes until a judge signs a warrant to search the bag. Understood?"

"I set aside now. Any trouble, Officer?"

"No. Someone has been threatening her. She left a letter from him in her pocket. Don't touch the bag."

"Yes, sir. Anything to help Miss Glade. She our best customer."

Ginny stuck her head out of the diner and yelled to him, "Give me ten minutes, please. Venita wants to have breakfast with me. Please, Mickey. I can't be rude."

"I understand. I've got some calls to make, anyway. I'll be right here."

As Ginny disappeared into the diner, Mickey spotted a store

across the street: Silver Screen Video. He got back out of the car, and walked into the store, showing his badge and identification. He had just remembered something from Ginny's apartment.

"I want to see your files, the names of movies customers take out."

"You'll need a warrant."

"Oh, really?"

Mickey walked to the back of the store, where he knew the porno section would be found. He pulled back the curtain and exposed two boys who looked to be about fourteen years old drooling over a triple-X-rated selection.

"Now are you going to help me or do I make a federal case over our *young* friends here?"

"Okay, okay. What name you want?"

"So you can tell them? No thanks."

"Then just come around here and scroll. Alphabetical. Very easy."

Mickey walked over to the monitor but noticed that the guy was looking over his shoulder. "I'll stay here. Why don't you visit your X-rated movie section and ask if those boys wouldn't be happier with Disney instead."

Mickey found what he was looking for in about thirty seconds. Ginny liked to watch dramas and love stories. *Kramer vs. Kramer* was a favorite. She also liked *The War of the Roses, An Unmarried Woman,* and *Sophie's Choice.* The more recent stuff she'd rented was *The First Wives' Club, The Bridges of Madison County,* and *The English Patient.* No adventure films. No mindless violence. No Stallone or Arnold. Until the night Mickey had met her at the diner. Then the murder, mayhem, and slashing films. Four of them.

"Curious," Mickey said. "Why would she lie to me?"

Mickey walked out of the store and called Camacho's cell phone. Ginny was on her way back to the car and the two reached it simultaneously.

"Where you been, Francisco?" Mickey asked, waving to Ginny.

"Get to a land line, boss. We got a difficulty. I'm headed for the Central Park Precinct."

"Give me two minutes."

As Mickey Donovan drove down Second Avenue, he shared his

problem with Ginny. "Pardon me, but I need to stop and use a pay phone."

"Is your battery dead? Here, Mickey, you're welcome to use my cell phone."

"Sorry. I need a secure line."

He stopped the car and walked to the phone booth, then punched in the number. Francisco answered on the second ring.

"We found your daughter, boss. She's fine. A little strung out, but fine. I came here because I know the squad room is a safe one, and usually empty. The men think she's an informant, helping us identify some kids who mugged a Japanese tourist. She's showered and clean, but I don't know where to take her."

"What happened?"

"She was in Two Toms, on Delancey Street. She came in with some hophead looking to make a score. He died trying to rob the place. Tommy hid her in the bathroom. So he knows."

"Who else knows?"

"Peter Heroin was there."

"Anybody else?"

"Chief Berger responded because crime scene was screwing up traffic on the approach to the Williamsburg Bridge."

"Did he see her?"

"Worst possible scenario? Assume he did."

"Then the mayor knows."

"My friend in the mayor's detail just called to say they saw the cockroach leave city hall ten minutes ago, boss."

Francisco paused. Dillon was sitting at the desk, handcuffed to a metal chair. Once, the teenaged rapists in the Central Park jogger case had sat in the same room and had sung about how they had brutalized a female stockbroker out for an evening run.

Francisco was careful with his words. "She can't stay here, boss. And I got to get moving on the umpire thing. Where's Ginny Glade?"

"I've got her in my car. Her alibi for last night seems to stand up. The doorman sees her arrive at home an hour before the ump gets whacked. You get my daughter and bring her out in front of the precinct. I'll pick you both up. We can talk while Glade practices at Columbia."

Francisco was careful again. He wasn't sure how to play this one at all. "Do you want your daughter in handcuffs?"

Mickey did not hesitate. "Shackle the prisoner's ankles, too. I don't want her running off."

"What if she tries to say something to Glade?"

"Gag her."

TWELVE

Newsroom, Manchester Union Guardian, *Manchester, New Hampshire*

Arlon Kettles didn't do much work for the *Manchester Union Guardian* once the tournament was over. The state house in Concord was closed for the summer. He wrote a column for the paper on national politics. Mostly this meant watching CNN and ripping stories off the wire. His life was pretty simple. He was either in favor of something he read on the wire or against it. There was no reporting in his column, just opinion and criticism. But he was a news buff. He read all the wires and all the papers. The Internet was his friend. He could read every paper in every city as well as Reuters, AP, UPI, and Gannett News Service. The reference material was incredibly liberating. He would never be a hick again. Unlike the old days, he knew everything there was to know about every presidential candidate as soon as he landed at the airport. There was no hiding anything from him anymore. Pierre Salinger was right about the TWA missile, he believed. The militia had a point about the ATF in Montana. The UN really did have black helicopters hovering over the Midwest.

There is a reason to be so paranoid. Just look at the Web sites.

He read everything, even on his day off. So as soon as he saw the news about the murdered umpire in New York City, he knew he had a scoop. He called a friend, Nigel Scrum, the most recent Fleet Streeter to try his hand as city editor at the *New York Post Standard*. They had met years ago while Scrum was vacationing—or "on holiday," as the editor explained—on Horace Lake in Weare, New Hampshire. Scrum had stolen a story from Kettles every couple of years, but always threw him a bonus check during the presidential primary season.

"You aren't gonna do to me this time what you did with that murderous schoolteacher, Pamela Smart?"

"We won't."

"Fuck *To Die For*, Nigel. I gave you quotes to come for."

"Admitted."

"Well, this one is the real deal. I got the big one for you, Nigel. You write the New York part and I'll write the New Hampshire part. We have to share notes. We run it in both papers with double bylines the same day. No byline, no deal. And one more thing, you story stealer, you have to promise me that Global will buy the rights, too."

"Film rights? Aren't we going a little fast?"

"I got the big one."

"Okay. I can't promise anything, but I can try. But don't dither, Arlon."

"This story marries murder and sport. It's bigger than O. J."

"Listen, you country cocksucker, nothing is bigger than O. J."

"Do we have a deal or do I call the *Daily News*?"

"Deal."

"What stories sell the most newspapers?"

Nigel sighed. "Baseball pennant race. Then celebrity sex. Celebrity murder is third."

"Right. Remember that time we got drunk at the Salty Dog during the 1992 primary and fell out of the bar singing zydeco?"

"Please, Arlon. I don't have time for this. I've got wars to start, bigots to inflame, Kennedys to chase, and readers to scare."

"You told me the best story would be discovering that the Yankee right fielder was a serial killer."

"Oh, Arlon, Bernie Winters couldn't even hit Doc Gooden this year. I can't imagine him challenging Dr. Hannibal Lecter."

Arlon didn't laugh. "What would you say, mate, if I told you someone was murdering American umpires?"

The editor heard the same excitement in his head as when the twin towers had exploded down the street. He bit his lip against the thrill.

"Meaning?"

"Meaning, you got a dead ump in Greenwich Village, Nigel. I saw it on the news wire. We got a dead tennis umpire up here. He was stabbed in the neck. His right eye was cut out, too. Very nasty business. How was your baseball umpire killed?"

"Holy shit. The cop's haven't confirmed the details yet, but I spoke to a friend at One Police Plaza who says the ump was stabbed in the neck, too. His right eye is missing."

"We got serial killer in sports, fucko. The dream story of all time."

"Send me an E-mail with everything on your murder, Arlon. I'll call our brothers at Global and have a television crew dispatched from Boston straightaway. I'll send you the skinny on our ump. We break the link in our papers first, then have the Global network run with it all night long. Get ready for 'The Umpire Killer,' America. We're going to scare the *bejesus* out of this country."

"I'll have my notes ready to dump to you by ten."

"That's too late. We'll miss the first edition."

"Sorry, Nigel. But I don't trust you not to rob me."

"Save something for the second-day story."

"I already have. I'll give it to you tomorrow. I have somebody who saw something. And a suspect who will blow you away."

"Just give me a taste, please."

"Don't fuck with me this time, Nigel."

"Why don't we just hire you?"

"Because you can't afford me."

And then he was gone.

Parking Lot, Central Park Police Precinct, Manhattan

Dillon got into the car wordlessly. She sat in the backseat, the cuffs tight on her hands. Mickey studied her in the rearview mirror. She tried to smile, but the play at innocence only angered him. He gripped the steering wheel tightly. Ginny was sitting beside him in the front seat. She was kind of surprised to see someone so young in handcuffs.

"What did she do?" Ginny asked.

"She's a witness in a murder case," Francisco said.

"Then why the handcuffs? I'm a witness. You have me in a hotel room."

"She's also a junkie," Mickey said. He froze his daughter with a glance in the rearview mirror. "We have to get her into detox before anyone hurts her."

Dillon yawned, bored. "Yeah, like, whatever."

Ginny turned back and faced the front of the car. "So what happened to the umpire? Or can't we talk about that?"

"We can talk. This here is Detective Sergeant Francisco Camacho. He caught that case."

"Nice to meet you, Miss Glade," Camacho said, smiling through perfect teeth. "Your courage in the diner that night was remarkable."

Mickey had a plan. The uniformed cops were already with Ginny's laundry. They would have a warrant to search her apartment in an hour. She was a very pretty woman, perhaps the best-looking murderer he had ever seen. She also had a great mind. He wasn't going to trick her into anything. He didn't want her getting a lawyer just yet either.

"Ginny I'm going to be straight with you," Mickey began. "We got a problem. There are too many people who have affected your life being murdered. First the tennis umpire. Then the baseball umpire. Apparently, they were both followed by a killer, then struck down. It may be nothing. But you begin homicide investigations looking for common threads. The most obvious connection is you. Two men who made your life difficult are dead, horribly killed. So step one in this investigation is you, Ginny."

"I didn't even know the baseball umpire," Ginny protested.

"Look, you aren't a suspect, Ginny. We're just being cautious. We need to know that we can scratch you off our list. This is very basic, functionary, detective work. So, where were you last night?"

"Oh, this is absurd, dime-store detective-novel stuff. Why don't you shine the light in my eyes?"

Dillon had been listening quietly with practiced disinterest. Now she giggled, and chimed in with, "Oh, no. Don't you read the papers? Cops don't pull that lame stuff anymore. Now they stick a toilet plunger up your butt."

Mickey checked the rearview mirror. Francisco was taking notes in a little pad. He had no choice. He had to show a firm but predictable coplike response.

"Young lady, would you be so kind as to shut your sewer mouth?" Mickey asked through gritted teeth.

The girl in the backseat had cut her hair to within an inch of her scalp and had dyed it orange. She had a hole in her tongue, Ginny noticed, but was missing the rivet she saw teenagers on the tour wearing.

"Oh, leave the kid alone," Ginny said. "She's having a bad-hair year."

Four blocks later, Mickey's daughter was nodded out, sleeping the sleep of innocence.

"I just want to eliminate you as a suspect," Mickey continued.

"Like I told you before, I was in the hotel until Babe called me about the game. Then I wanted a sandwich. One of your cops walked me over to the Stage Deli. I got really pissed off at the situation and bolted. I went to Babe's house on East Eightieth Street, by the park. We drank a couple of bottles of Merlot. I dozed off and then came home. Victor saw me come in."

"That's very good. See, Ginny, that was easy."

"And after the tournament in New Hampshire, what did you do then?" Camacho asked from the backseat.

"I returned the courtesy car to Logan Airport and then caught the Delta shuttle to LaGuardia. Then took a taxi home. I have the receipt. Pretty tame stuff. Victor met me at the door."

"So you drove from North Conway to Boston by yourself?"

"Yes. I wasn't in the mood for company."

"Did you stop along the way for food?"

Ginny paused. "No. It was a straight shot."

Mickey smiled, then laughed lightly. "Whew, that was easy. I'm sorry to have asked anything at all. But you know, it's like practice, you don't want to do it, but you're a professional."

He turned in his seat and jerked his head at Detective Sergeant Camacho. "Anything else, Francisco?"

They worked together. This was Francisco's cue to play the bad cop to Mickey's good cop. "Yeah," he growled. "So if someone said they saw you around where Blinky Hammond got murdered, they would be lying, right?"

Ginny was back in her frozen zone. She was ice. If he was asking if the ball was in, she didn't know. "Correct."

"Oh, come on, Francisco," Mickey said. "Ginny is our friend."

"Ginny, why did Blinky Hammond call you the night he was killed?"

"He called to say business is business. No hard feelings."

"Now you tell her the same thing, Francisco. Apologize to Miss Glade right now."

"Sorry, ma'am," Francisco Camacho said on cue. "Some habits die hard. Suspicion is my big weakness."

"Well, maybe you should work on you hair, too, Sergeant Camacho."

"What's wrong with my hair?"

"It's too long and undisciplined. It makes you seem disjointed and gives you a very undetectivelike quality."

"Yeah, well, sometimes I am all over the place. For example, I don't understand why you took out all those crazy murder movies on the night you intervened in the diner. Your taste in movies isn't that severe. You lead a very Disney life, lady. Why were you watching all that mayhem?"

Ginny made a grinding sound with her teeth, then said, "Are you kidding me? You guys studied my movie rentals? That's a total invasion of privacy."

"Actually, no, Miss Glade."

"Pathetic. Are you going to check my library card out, too? Mickey, how could you?"

"I didn't know *Underworld* wasn't about the mob," Francisco laughed. "I haven't read that many pages in a decade."

"Jesus, Mickey. I feel violated."

"Camacho is a detective, Ginny," Mickey said. "You have to give him room to detect."

"What's next, Mickey? My underwear drawer?"

Mickey just let the question hang there as they pulled up to the Columbia courts, overlooking the Hudson River. It was a beautiful morning. Francisco stayed in the car with Dillon. Donovan lingered, too.

"We'll wait for you, Ginny," Mickey said.

"Don't bother. I'll catch a cab. Your friend gives me the creeps."

"Francisco takes some getting used to. He's just concerned about me. He knows I like you and he doesn't want to see me hurt."

Ginny started to walk away, but then stopped. "The girl in the car is cute. Someone should save her. She reminds me of half the mixed-up kids on the tour."

"If it helps, Ginny, we're on our way to search her underwear drawer."

"Well, as long as you don't show up in my apartment wearing it."

"I promise," Mickey said. "No Marv thing."

Ginny giggled. Mickey was surprised by her laughter and her compassion for his daughter. It didn't fit.

"Can I call you later, Ginny?"

"Do I need a lawyer, Inspector?"

"For dinner at the Supreme Macaroni Company? I would think not."

Mickey watched Ginny Glade disappear into the clubhouse. He then turned on his heel and walked back to the car. His daughter was still sleeping. Francisco was in the driver's seat now. The inspector slid in beside his daughter.

"What did you think?"

"I think I am not letting Dillon out of my sight. In the meantime, you and I are going to New Hampshire," Mickey said, groaning. "What kind of father am I? How did I let her get this far gone? I'm solving all these bullshit cases and my own daughter is a mystery to me. She's the one case I can't crack."

"We're gonna make it, man."

"How about the kid who was shot?"

"Just some college puke turned doper. He was living in the park. She met him there last night for the first time. The robbery was his idea. She was too smashed to say no to the caper. Thank God she was drinking. If she hadn't had to empty her bladder, she'd have gotten whacked, too."

Mickey hugged his sleeping daughter. He was starting to get misty. Francisco tilted the rearview mirror. He did not want to see his idol crying.

"Did she tell you about her friend Linda, the kid from East Flatbush?" Mickey asked.

"No."

"Last week, Dillon ran away from Bridget, in Brooklyn. She knows this Linda from the Van de Veer houses. So they take the subway into Manhattan and begin looking around for a fix in Alphabet City. They hook up with this very debonair black guy who says he knows where they can score. They follow him into an empty building. He grabs Linda and drags her into this basement, then rapes the shit out of her. Dillon smacks him in the head with a beer bottle and they both run. A sergeant I know from down there, Duke Herman, just happens to be riding past. The rapist is chasing them down the block with a knife. Herman stops, saves them, and arrests their new friend. This creep has eighteen collars dating back to 1985, including two rapes and a manslaughter conviction. Herman likes me, so he pretends Dillon was never there."

"Jesus."

"Six months ago she was taking her SAT's. We were picking out prom dresses. Now we're taking an AIDS test. I can't get either of us out."

"Easy."

"I think she was screwing Peter Heroin, who is right in the middle of our cases involving a dead priest and a retired cop."

"Okay, so here's what we have, Mickey. Your daughter is here and she's alive. We just have to get her clean."

"One of the best detox centers in the country is in Dublin, New Hampshire. I already called. She goes there, directly. It's on the way to Bedford. You and I are going to the Sheraton Wanderer. We'll put her in the Central Park cell until we're ready to go. Okay, Frisco?"

The inspector was snapping. Francisco Nunez Camacho, like inhabitants of the city of San Francisco, got angry when anyone shortened his name to "Cisco," "Fran," or worst of all, "Frisco." He allowed only one man to get away with abbreviating his name—Mickey Donovan, who only did it when he was disconnected. The sergeant closed his notebook and started the car.

"What did you think of Ginny Glade, boss?"

"She's like my daughter, Francisco. A beautiful girl. And a bullshit liar."

THIRTEEN

The Big Rub Store, West Thirty-fourth Street, Manhattan

Ginny wanted a rubdown. She was crumpling, one lie at a time.

Fibs were like slight injuries, she sensed. They could hobble you. It was dangerous to deny she had stopped to eat at the Sheraton near Bedford, New Hampshire, after the tournament. It could easily be disproved. Maybe someone would remember her. She'd read about detectives and lies in a Joseph Wambaugh novel once. What was it he'd said? "The biggest crime is cracked with the smallest lie," she said out loud.

It was like the new opponent who ran around a backhand to hit her forehand. The lie was a mistake. Just as invention revealed a weakness in your tennis game, lies revealed a deficiency in your alibi.

How did the lie help her?

She was married to the lie now. But maybe the cops would believe her if she said she'd just forgotten about the meal.

She went to see her masseur, Jocko, on the West Side of Manhattan, near the Jacob Javits Center. She enjoyed being rubbed, snapped, baked, and rolled as the kids from the nearby St. Lawrence Catholic grammar school shrieked in the playground. It was relaxing.

"What happened to you?" Jocko asked as Ginny reached his second-floor office on West Thirty-fourth Street. "I got customers who used to work in the foulest Times Square peep shows who look better than you."

"Really?"

"No."

"They don't look worse?" Ginny asked.

"No, they aren't my customers," Jocko said. "I was just joking with you. They're my girlfriends. I'm their client. But, hey, I still read the newspapers. Notoriety doesn't agree with you."

Jocko was from Poland, and a friend to athletes the world over. For years he had worked on the great Yankees in the bowels of the stadium. He had been at it so long that he always smelled of heat balm. He got drunk one day in between games of a doubleheader and started to rub down Thurman Munson, the Yankees' catcher, with gin instead of rubbing alcohol. Munson did not complain but that mistake got Jocko fired and landed him on the fringes of Times Square.

"Did you see our new neighbors? Once I moved in, they all came. Disney. Hercules. I remember when *Snow White and the Seven Dwarfs* was a gang-bang movie just up the block. Now all the 'toons are neighbors. But you know, I saved the neighborhood."

He had a great, firm touch. The players said Jocko had steel pistons for fingers. The Yankees used to sneak into Manhattan to see him. The tennis players hired him to work at the U.S. Open for a month and whenever there were tournaments at the Garden.

"My hip is acting up again, Jocko," Ginny said. "The shoulder, too."

Ginny had had hip surgery in December 1991, after she'd fallen at the French Open and pinched a nerve in her femoral joint. She'd needed nine months of rehab at the Rusk Institute on the East Side and didn't play again until the U.S. Open in August. She'd come back too soon and had developed tendinitis in her shoulder; she had had to continue her rehab for another three months. Most people had figured Ginny was finished.

By the winter of 1992, she had fallen completely out of the computer rankings. Ginny came back on at 610 in February 1993, and had climbed to 60 by September of that year.

There wasn't an ounce of quit in Ginny. She began riding a mountain bike that year and hiked the White Mountains. In a weak moment, the former country girl had bought a cow, Wiggles, and had threatened to bring it to New York City. She had wanted to give it to a zoo but quit the idea after reading that some Brooklyn kids had shot up a polar bear in the Prospect Park Zoo.

"How's the Holstein, Ginny?"

"She's feeling worse than me."

"How's that?"

"She broke her leg on the ice this winter, Jocko. She fills a meat locker now. It's disquieting when your best friend becomes hamburger."

"Oh, I know what you mean, dear. Mickey Mantle had the mobility of a meat patty in the end."

"Well, at least the Mick was well marinated."

As he worked on Ginny's muscles, Jocko's gaze drifted to the window, to the pedestrians on the street. He saw a man standing by the sign for the bus. He was about five-ten, and chewing on something furiously. Jocko watched the man reach into his pocket and pull out a red-and-green bag.

"Don't choke on your chaw," Jocko said, recognizing Red Mars chewing tobacco. He sighed and rubbed harder as he watched. Seeing the foil of chewing tobacco made him miss the baseball clubhouse again.

Thousands of people walked under Jocko's window every day on their way over to the Garden and Penn Station. The escape hatch to suburbia—the Long Island Rail Road—opened below them in the subterranean world beneath Madison Square Garden. Only a few commuters noticed Jocko's building. This guy was staring up into his window, mashing his chaw.

"Curious," Jocko announced as he kneaded and chopped the three muscles in each gluteus maximus.

"My butt is funny-looking?"

"No, this hard-chewing fellow outside."

The only reason Jocko even noticed him was because the young man was still standing at the bus stop, after the crosstown bus had departed, and was peering up at his window.

"What about him, Jocko?"

Ginny was flat on her stomach and oiled with liniment. She was in heat and calm.

"This guy across the street. He looks like a young Don Mattingly. Yankees cap. Mustache. Sloped shoulders. Standing slightly pigeon-toed. I would bet he has an inside-out swing. Must have been a minor leaguer at one time. He's got half a pouch in his right cheek."

"What?"

"Tobacco. Our admirer is a chewer."

"A dreadful habit. My ex-husband puked when he tried it."

Jocko gave Ginny a pat on her back to announce that he was finished with the rubdown. He handed her a white robe.

"Get dressed and take a look."

"I don't really care, Jocko."

"Just take a look. He can't sneak up on me. I know what he looks like. And you're the only one here. He seems to be waiting for one of us."

"Oh, Jocko. Don't be so paranoid."

She pulled on her terry-cloth robe and walked over to the window. She peered out at the bus stop below, spotted him immediately, and fell back with a gasp.

"It's him."

The Diner Vigilante was back, in his Fila outfit.

"Jocko, hand me my bag and your phone."

"Who is he?"

"The guy with the gun in the diner."

She stepped back and dialed the number. Jocko stepped to the window and waved.

"I can't really see his face."

"Jesus, Jocko, why are you waving?"

"In my book, he's a hero."

Ginny held the phone closer.

"Yeah, go ahead. Inspector Donovan here."

Mickey and Francisco were alone in the car again and headed down to Mickey's Forty-second Street "office" for a few hours. They had just placed Dillon in a cell for safekeeping.

"That man is outside. The guy from the diner."

"Ginny Glade?"

"Yes, sorry, Mickey. I'm at 440 West Thirty-fourth. Between Eighth and Ninth. He's in the middle of the block, south side of the street. He must have followed me here."

"Don't move, Ginny. And stay away from the window. I'm three minutes' away. Stay on the line. Talk to Sergeant Camacho."

As they turned left from the highway past the Jacob Javits Center, Francisco Camacho held the phone and cursed.

"Dead spot. Lost her."

Mickey Donovan called for a sector car from Midtown South to come in from the East Side. No lights and sirens. He was at the bus stop thirty seconds after Francisco had lost phone contact. By then, the stop was empty and Francisco got Ginny on the phone again.

"She says he just disappeared, boss, maybe down into the train station."

"And the guy she's with?"

"His name is Jocko. He don't see too good anymore. He saw a slope-shouldered man in a baseball cap."

"I don't like this. I don't give two shits about the diner shooting. The killing that matters is the dead umpire. Go upstairs and get her."

He pointed to the radio. It was tuned to a sports radio station. Some guy who compared unfavorably to a snarling Doberman was growling. The host, who called himself "the Mad Mongrel," was howling again. The story of the murdered umpire, blasted across the world by the *Post Standard* and an AP story out of New Hampshire, was like a drug, the entire nation getting its fix. Francisco sprinted for the door as Mickey Donovan waited in the car and turned up the volume.

"Can you believe this, Mongrel? A dead tennis umpire in a parking lot and the guy in the Village? They're killing umpires who make calls favoring the Yankees. It's outrageous. This is worse than that thing out in Washington last year, remember? There was this guy, Bob West, a referee with twenty years' experience. He disqualified a high school wrestler in Spokane. And the kid head-butted the ref so hard he knocked him unconscious. Think of it, Mike. If they're going to kill every ump who rules in favor of the Yankees, we're doomed. We'll never win another World Series. Killing the umpire is no longer a joke. It's happening."

Five minutes later, Ginny limped across the street. Her hip still bothered her.

Mickey lowered the volume as Sal from Bensonhurst called in. "This may be a racial thing, like that murder in Springfield Gardens a couple of years ago," Sal said. "Remember? These black kids were playing a tournament game. Drug dealers owned two teams. There was major money on the game. Anthony Mason used to play in that park. Anyway, this ref makes a bad call and the guy just caps him at half-court. The ref's name was Shorty Black. Remember?"

"Yeah. And Shortly Black was black. It wasn't racial. It was gangster fever," Mongrel replied.

"Are you sure?" Sal from Bensonhurst continued. " 'Cause shooting a black ref, well, that's different."

"Good-bye, knucklehead." And Mongrel signed off on the caller. He punched another lit phone on his bank of lights, cursing the imbeciles who spent their days listening to him.

"Hey, bow wow, first time, long time. There was a junior varsity game in Wisconsin last winter, Mongrel. Some guy ran on the court after his son fouled out, and knocked the offending ref down. The father happened to be the district attorney. And last summer in Loveland, Texas, a group of teenaged baseball players who had just been ejected from a recreation-league game came back and pummeled the umpire. He suffered bruised ribs and needed four stitches to close a gash in his mouth. And how about that kid who had to be arrested in Philly for punching the ref? We're way past spitting. We're becoming a trash-talk nation of Dennis Rodmans. It started when Rodman butted the ref at The Meadowlands. In Texas, you got two hundred coaches a year being thrown out of school games. In Florida, you got five hundred kids a year being thrown out of football games. What ump is going to dare call this bum, Shane Heath, out now? Sorry, Mongrel, but to pick up a whistle in America today is to take a chance on dying."

"Maybe that's true," Mongrel said. He promised to have an umpire in the kennel as his guest, within the hour. Ginny Glade listened to the tirade as she slid into the backseat. Francisco Camacho eyed her suspiciously.

"Ginny," Mickey said in his sweetest voice. "Forget dinner in the city. I know another place. I would like to put you in protective custody. I don't know what we have here. But until I get some answers from up in New Hampshire this weekend, I want to put you on ice."

"I'll go to New Hampshire with you," Ginny said.

"Not so fast. I have to do some detective work up there. I need some space."

"So drop me off at my mother's."

Mickey looked at Francisco, who looked away.

"Francisco is going up with me. It could be kind of crowded."

"And don't forget our prisoner," Francisco said.

"If somebody is stalking me, I'm leaving Manhattan, sergeant."

"What about your exhibition match in Arthur Ashe Stadium?"

"I withdrew this morning," Ginny said. "I may wear Versace, but I don't want to *be* him."

Mickey headed across town and then up First Avenue. They continued to listen to the radio, magnetized by the interest in the case. There were hundreds of callers and they just seemed confused.

"Yeah, hello. My screen says this is 'Shooter' from West Fourth Street. Go ahead."

A woman's voice surprised them. "I stuck that fat ump like a pig. And I'll do it again."

Click.

First Avenue, Upper East Side, Manhattan

Mickey pulled over next to a cabstand in the Seventies to let Francisco out. The inspector still had to fetch his daughter. He had told the guys with the warrant for Ginny's apartment to wait until they'd left town to hit the place.

"Okay," Mickey said. "Francisco, I'll let you out here. Go retrieve our prisoner from Central Park. I'll meet you in an hour outside the precinct. Be standing on Madison at Seventy-eighth Street and I'll pick you both up."

"Where are you going?"

"I'm going to drive Ginny to her apartment so she can get an overnight bag."

Ginny looked at the cops, then said, "What about stuff for your prisoner, Dillon? She'll be a bit gamy, gentlemen."

"We'll survive. Just go get her, Francisco."

"She looks to be my size," Ginny said. "I'm going to pack her a few things—a sweatshirt and a toothbrush at least. You can't be Ne-anderthals, and I'm sure by now you guys know I can spare the underwear."

"Francisco," Mickey said. "Please explain the transportation rules to our prisoner, again."

"Yeah, boss," Francisco said, his eyes hardening. "But don't forget Stoney Rivers, either."

"Duly noted, Sergeant."

Mickey smiled as Francisco backed onto the curb.

"Could you get in the front seat, Ginny?"

"Why?"

"Departmental policy, Ms. Glade."

Mickey had to laugh at Francisco's paranoia. Every cop knew the legend of the policy. Ten years ago, two second-grade homicide detectives had been transporting a woman to Rikers Island, along the Grand Central Parkway from Queens Central booking on Queens Boulevard in Kew Gardens. She was seated in the back of the detectives' car. No one had searched the rear-cuffed prisoner, a young mother who had been arrested for credit-card fraud, before they put her in the car. And she had been left alone to go to the bathroom in the squad room. She had picked a combination lock and had stuffed a revolver down the back of her pants. She had pulled it out as the detectives slowed near LaGuardia Airport. Turning sideways in the backseat to aim the gun, the young mother had shot both unsuspecting cops in the backs of their heads, then grabbed their handcuff key. She'd fled the car, never to be seen again.

There were still floral arrangements hanging on the chain-link fence that separated the highway and the airport runway.

"Careful, boss," Francisco said as the inspector and his witness/murder suspect sped away.

Twenty-ninth Precinct, 125th Street, Manhattan

Francisco Camacho climbed the stairs of the Twenty-ninth Precinct and entered the squad room. Two guys, one grayer than the other, were working a quadruple homicide from that morning in The Polo Grounds Housing project. The witness looked like a kindergarten kid.

"How old are you, big fellow?" Francisco asked.

"Nine."

"How old?"

The kid held up seven fingers.

"Did you ever hear of Willie Mays, son? He used to play in your backyard."

One of the detectives coughed, then said, "We tried that, boss. He never heard of Jackie Robinson either."

"But I seen everything," the kid interrupted. "The Power Rangers did it."

"What's your name?"

"My mom calls me Alias Alias."

"Okay, son. Did the detectives get you something to eat?"

"I had a cherry blow pop."

Francisco motioned to the older detective. They walked to the back of the room, by the holding cell.

"What you got?"

"We got a seven-year-old witness that the Manhattan DA doesn't want to hear about. Remember about ten years ago when every city kid believed in this mythical gang called the Septicons? Then the little hoodlums started calling themselves the Transformers and Bebe's Kids. Two seconds after Hollywood makes a cartoon, you got kids calling themselves Rouge, Storm, and Wolverine. Mutant Ninja Turtles have come and gone. For a couple of years there, one teen-aged perp called himself Michelangelo. And we'd collar these kids, the worst part, they had no idea who the sculptor was. Last year we were up to our asses in X-Men and Power Rangers. This year it's something called Spawn."

"So?"

"So the kid is right. The new team working the polo grounds this year call themselves the Power Rangers. His older brother, Jerome, aka Major Minor, is skimming crack vials and money from his crew. So the kids come to the house looking for the money. They don't get shit. So they shoot his mother, father, and both sisters. Gas silencer on a nine millimeter. They leave Alias Alias where they found him, bathing in the tub. When his bubble bath goes flat, and the water gets cold, Alias Alias wanders out and finds the bodies. He thinks it's a cartoon show."

"He's too young to make solid identifications."

"I know. But he knows all the players. Any advice, Mr. Sergeant? I feel like that novelist, Joseph Heller."

"Yeah. The bad guys don't know Alias squared is too young to be used as a witness against them at trial. Call Larry Seals, the police reporter, at the *Post Standard*. Give him the whole case. Names, ages, and bits of the kid's statement. Ten to one, the bad guys read it and rush in to rat each other out. This is felony murder, a death-penalty case."

"Will this reporter, Seals, realize our kid is too young to make the identification?"

"Maybe. If he does, let him in on the trap. Later, the newspaper can say they helped grab the bad guys. And if that doesn't work, let the kid talk to the *Daily News* over the phone tomorrow."

"Thanks, boss."

They were standing at the back desk. The detective started to walk to the phone, then stopped.

"Your prisoner in the cell woke up about half an hour ago. She said some amazing shit, Sarge. She said she was Inspector Donovan's daughter."

Francisco managed to smile. "You're shitting me," he replied, laughing. "She said that?"

"Yeah. We didn't believe her though. She has tracks on her arms."

"Yeah, well, she's my stoolie on a gang doing push-in robberies in the East Village. She heard me mention Inspector Donovan's name on the way up here."

"That it?"

"Shouldn't you be calling Seals, Detective?"

Francisco stepped to the cage and unlocked the door. "Get the fuck up, Cinderella," he said. "And shut the fuck up."

The two detectives smiled, contented. The foul language put them at ease. No cop, especially Francisco Camacho, would speak to the Wraith's daughter that way. They turned back to their own business as Camacho entered the cell and put handcuffs on Dillon.

She was eighteen years old and a version of every screwed-up teen Francisco had ever interviewed. Francisco briefly spotted the hole in Dillon's tongue when she yawned.

"Isn't that like chewing on a pair of blue dungarees?"

"They *are* called jeans now," she whispered. "I don't really like it, Francisco. But when Dad said I couldn't get one, I decided to get two. Will you hold my tongue while I put this one back in?"

"I will not," the cop whispered back.

Francisco handcuffed the prisoner and walked her out the door.

"Good night, gentlemen. Happy hunting."

As soon as he got Dillon down to the car, Francisco turned to her, saying, "I didn't mean to talk to you like that, kid, but I had to put on a show for those detectives. Are you completely insane, Dillon? You can't tell cops who you are. You're putting a gun to your father's head."

"Yeah, like, whatever. He's, like, more of a father to you than me."

"That's not right, Dill. He loves you. But can I be straight?"

"There's always a first time."

"He's afraid of you, kid. He knows he can't break your will. And as hard as he pushes, he knows you are going to push back. You're tougher than he is, Dill. And if you repeat that, I will call you a liar."

"I don't, like, want to be a junkie, Francisco. I don't want to be, you know, a liar. I'm not, like, a slacker, either. I don't even like half the guys I screw. I do it because it makes him mad. I have a bright side that can't shine through my dark side. I want to do, like, great things. Just my own way."

"Well, we got a ways to go, kid," Francisco said.

"You hate me, don't you?"

She was a child, still. He recognized the toddler in the teenager.

"No, no. I actually like the hair."

"Really?"

"Well, I don't like the color. But I like the length."

"Would you prefer purple?"

"Maybe red."

She laughed. Francisco walked her to the car and sat her down. "Okay, we have a more immediate problem. We have a dead umpire in Greenwich Village and a prime suspect. You met her. Miss Glade. We're taking her to New Hampshire in a car with you. You are going to rehab. She is staying with us."

"She has a racquet stuck up her ass."

"Well, then why is she up in her apartment getting you clothes and a toothbrush?"

"She knows who I am?"

"Absolutely not. You are not going to say one damn thing to her. You sleep in the backseat and I promise, Dillon Donovan, if you say a word, I will put you in the trunk."

"Who is the woman, really?"

"Our prime suspect in two murders. Very classy. Very dangerous."

"Really?"

"No bullshit, Dill. One word and I put a gag in your mouth."

"Do I have to wear, you know, the handcuffs?"

"Not if you behave. I will be in the seat beside you the whole way. It's a five-hour trip."

"Can we, like, stop at Roy Rogers?"

"Sure, kid, whatever. We'll find one on the way."

The kid began to sulk again. "I bet she brings me some really stupid old-people clothes. Like Levi's or something. Something very lame and Wrangler, I bet."

"Junkie beggars can't be choosers. But I have to ask you one more thing. No bullshit. Are you screwing Peter Heroin?"

"Ooohhh, no. He's grosser than my father." Dillon pretended to stick a finger down her throat.

"Thank God for small miracles of taste," Camacho said, sighing.

"I got one question for you, Francisco. Do you think, like, I'm fat or something?"

"Oh, stop it."

FOURTEEN

Notorious Ray's Pizzeria, Elm Street, Manchester, New Hampshire

Arlon Kettles slid into the back booth of Notorious Ray's Pizzeria, on Elm Street in Manchester, New Hampshire. The newspaper office on Amherst Street was a half dozen blocks away. Once, Ed Muskie had stood outside the paper and cried. His presidential bid had died before his tears hit the sidewalk.

There should be a plaque in the street, Arlon always said. Maybe even a little teardrop. "William Loeb killed him with a sentence about his wife," Arlon said. "Bill Clinton we couldn't kill with ten girlfriends and a hell of a lot more rumors. Newspapers are dead."

But Kettles didn't really believe that. So long as you had the story, you had the reader by the throat. And he had one now. This was better than when he'd caught a former governor's daughter with a horse.

His source came in, and removed his red Nike coat and black Nike hat. He crossed one red Nike sweatpants leg over the other and tied his Air Jordans.

"Am I going to get paid for this?" he asked.

"It depends on what you have," Kettles replied.

"I saw someone in the parking lot that night."

"Anyone I know?"

"I have a name, too."

The waitress came over. She was attractive in a smokey, last-call sort of way. But they were ten hours away from closing. Kettles was in his crime-reporter, androgynous mode. He rubbed his spiked hair.

"Oh my goodness," his lunch guest said upon seeing the waitress. "What a coincidence. My name is Jack, and I'm doing a commercial for Nike. I'm looking for someone with rugged good looks, a sort of washed-out beauty, to promote a hiking show. Could you do a screen test for us? Here's my hotel number, the Marriott in Nashua. What time do you get off?" Then he flicked his tongue, lizardlike, at her.

"Down boy," she said effortlessly. "I wear Keds to outrun people like you. Arlon, where do you find these hideous people? Remember when that turd Don Bevus was up here, doing his talk show during the primary? Even he wasn't this much of an insufferable prick. And the other pin-striped hog, Bill Clinton? At least he had the sense to have an aide ask me to come by his hotel."

"This gentleman is Jack Bliss," Arlon said. "His daughter won the Volvo Classic in North Conway last month."

"Oh yeah. I saw it on TV. That was the one where the dead ump blew the call. Tell me, Jack, did you make him the Nike offer, too? Anyway, gentlemen, we got no specials today and no soup. I made the pizza this morning."

"Just coffee," Arlon said.

"Do you have any herbal tea?" Jack asked. "Maybe some caffeine-free Earl Grey perhaps? No, no. I'd rather have some Vita Calming Tea."

"Get a life, pal. Let me guess, Jack is short for Jackass. Or maybe Jackoff? I'll be back with two leaded coffees. You can fight over the Sweet'n Low."

She padded off, and Arlon smiled.

"How do I even know you were at the Wanderer that night?"

Jack pushed an American Express credit-card receipt at him. "Same date. Look at the time. I was there at nine P.M. The monkfish was a little dry."

"Okay. What did you see?"

Jack held out an open palm. It was a soft, uncalloused hand. "I didn't hear a purchase price."

"I can't give you squat. But I have a friend connected to one of the networks. A Brit. They pay. I'll put you on with him now."

"Okay."

Kettles dialed the *New York Post Standard*. He had called Nigel Scrum an hour earlier and explained, "This may cost you."

"Yeah, Nigel, old boy," Kettles now said. "This is your friend in the north country. I have that package. I'm going to put him on."

He handed Jack the phone.

"Duncan Morgan will pay five thousand dollars. First and last offer. You talk to our buzz-cut friend. He dumps to me and we have a TV crew meet you at the hotel in two hours. You will be on the cable channel tonight. Book deal to follow."

"Deal," the Jackster said. "I want the whole Newt slash Sammy the Bull treatment."

"One step at a time, Mr. Bliss," Scrum said. "First the *Post Standard* and the *Herald*."

"Then Lippo Collums Publishing. Finally, Global Film and Television," the Jackster chimed in. He giggled as he hung up. He hadn't expected any money. No one had ever paid before. He waited until the coffee arrived to tell his tale.

"Wait till the end for the name. I just happened to see her on Ninety-three South after I left the hotel in North Conway. She was pretty steamed. Talking to herself in her car. I lost sight of her at the toll booths in Concord. She had exact change. So I stopped at the state liquor store in Concord to get a case of Crystal champagne. I saved a couple hundred on the sales tax alone. I was in the mood to celebrate. Then I got hungry. As I pulled into the Sheraton Wanderer around nine-thirty that night, I almost got rammed by a taupe-colored Volvo courtesy car. I recognized the driver. I waved and blinked the lights, but she didn't see me. She looked kind of, well, disconnected. I parked on the far side of the lot and went in to eat. When I came out an hour later, about ten-thirty, the paramedics had a sheet over the body. Blinky was doing the big one-eyed stare. They closed his remaining eye, and I got out of there, pronto."

"Why?"

"Cops ain't my thing. I got some child-support problems in Florida."

"So who was the woman?"

"Ginny Glade. I didn't put it together until I reached Boston that night. What is it the cops say? She has it all—motive, opportunity, and rage. Don't you see? The Morgue Girl snapped like an icicle and stabbed the umpire."

"She struck me as more controlled."

"Oh, that is an act, Kettles. When she's alone, she's an animal. The rage is just beneath the skin."

"Did you talk to the cops?"

"No way. I didn't speak to *anybody* about this."

"We're done. I'll call you later."

Kettles paid the check and left. The Jackster rushed off to his hotel in his daughter's new car. Kettles walked to the paper. And as he passed Muskie corner, he wiped a tear of joy from his cold newspaper eye.

The Ride from the City into the North Country

As they crossed the Manius Bridge into Greenwich, Connecticut, on U.S. 95, the prisoner in the backseat of the car spoke. "This bridge fell into the water once," she said. "Just disappeared. One car went over and another one just braked safely. One carload saved. One carload dead. I read about it."

No one said a word. The cops had cautioned Ginny not to speak to their prisoner. Francisco kept his eyes on the road. Donovan, sitting next to his daughter, gripped her knee tightly and smiled menacingly. He was petrified of the kid.

"Several cars went over," Ginny said, staring out the window. "I was driving to Hartford that day for an exhibition match at Trinity College. The traffic was backed up for days."

"Really?" Dillon said. "What could you see?"

Like most kids, she was fascinated with tragedy. And who could blame her, really? The America she knew—from movies to television shows—was just one big disaster in surround sound. Her favorite film anthems were from *Scream* and *Scream II*. The movies were about speed, volcanoes, tornadoes, dinosaurs, and star wars involving convicts on planes and aliens on spaceships. Life was just one special effect after another. And the heroin helped.

"Can you imagine being the car that stopped in time?" Dillon said. "The guy in front of you is dead, and you're not. That would be so fucking cool."

"You never know when your time is going to come," Francisco said.

"It would be bitchin'," she continued. "I'm telling you."

Donovan coughed loudly. Dillon watched the bridge disappear in the rearview mirror and fell back in the seat. She sighed and returned to her sullen, aloof act.

"Hey, Francisco, did you bring my bag with my Nirvana *Unplugged* tape?" Dillon asked. "Silence is boring."

That was the sound track to the kid's life. *Silence is boring and boring is death*. Mickey coughed again. The Wraith could see that this was not going well. His daughter was a live grenade on the seat beside him.

"The driver is a New York City homicide detective, young lady," he snapped. "He is not Casey Casem. And this is not 'America's Most Wanted,' the sound track. You will be quiet or I will strap you to the hood."

"Whatever," she replied.

Francisco held up the tape.

"Music soothes the savage beast, boss," he said.

"Go ahead, Sergeant," Ginny said, lightening the mood. "I won't tell anyone I was kidnapped by MTV cops."

First he had to remove the tape in the deck. Francisco placed it on the seat. It was a new tape of an old voice: Maria Callas. Ginny was surprised. A lot of people listened to Pavarotti now. But Callas meant more of a scratchy commitment to opera.

"I figured you for more of a Doors fan, Inspector," Ginny said. "You know, like this is the brutal end, a murder, my pal the ending. Something like that. This is the end, my only friend the end. Maybe even the whole *Apocalypse Now* sound track."

"I, like, love that one," Dillon said. "He has it."

"The prisoner will shut up," Mickey ordered. Ginny flinched, and Mickey immediately regretted saying anything. The Morgue Girl noted the slip and wondered how Dillon knew what was in Mickey Donovan's music collection.

But it was too late. Kurt Cobain was already singing "About a Girl." A couple of years before, the song had been big in the tennis locker room. The tumbleweed kids who blew through the satellite tour loved Cobain. Especially the California girls, who liked to call themselves wannabes. Ginny played with them while she was working her way back from a knee injury. They were surfer types who loved the sun and pot. The tour was just something to do after college, before you became a teaching pro in Florida.

Ginny had learned the words. She sang them softly, almost absently, as she remembered that soft, easy time with other knuckle-headed kids.

"I guess we could all use an easy friend," Ginny murmured.

Dillon suddenly sat up. She had remembered a detail. "Did you say you played tennis, or something?" Dillon asked in her best Alicia Silverstone/*Clueless* voice. "Like, what's that about?"

"A silent and boring life, mostly," Ginny said. And then *she* remembered something. "I brought you some clothes. I've never worn them. They never fit me. Baggy stuff. Jenko jeans. One pair is black corduroy, the other is denim with a gold stripe. And some matching shirts that could fit all four of us comfortably."

"Way cool," Dillon said. "I figured you were, like, a dried-up Gap lady."

"I like to surprise people," Ginny Glade said, smiling.

As the girls nodded off, Francisco felt free to speak. "I heard from Bailey over at Crime Scene," he said. "He has a bit of a coincidence. Forensics told him they got a bullet match."

"A confusing one?" Mickey asked.

"The guy shot in the diner by our mystery man. Remember, he fired a nine? We found the shell casing on the cash register."

"Yeah?"

"Well, the bullet from his nine matches the one we took out of Sal Nesto."

"Shit. The guy stalking Ginny Glade killed an ex-detective in Brooklyn?"

"Maybe the same guy didn't, Mickey, but the same gun did."

Green Garlic Tavern, Granite Street, Manchester, New Hampshire

The cop was at the bar when the reporter walked in. The cop was an old-timer, maybe the last careful man. He wasn't going to be fooled by some reporter. He had been in the place for half an hour before Arlon Kettles arrived. He took a seat near the jukebox and loaded it with ten dollars' worth of quarters. He knew he couldn't be recorded secretly over the din.

Kettles walked in and took a seat at the cop's table. "Hello," the reporter said.

"Put your jacket on a chair at the bar," the cop said.

"Why?"

"Policy is policy. I talk to you, not a tape."

The reporter removed his jacket. He was wearing a short-sleeved shirt. "I'm not even insulted, Bobby," Kettles said. "Honest. I've known you too long. You're a quirky bastard."

"Safety first," Bobby Winkle said. "No wires."

You could understand the guy's peculiarities. His father had been the chief of police in neighboring Pinardville. In the old days it had been a three-cop, one-stop-sign town. Chief Winkle's favorite thing had been to park near the elementary school on Main Street and stop speeders with out-of-state plates. One time he'd followed a guy to the town border and pulled him over. He'd demanded twenty dollars for the widows' and orphans' fund in a town where, thankfully, no cop had ever suffered a catastrophic injury in the line of duty. The guy had fumbled around for a while, but had finally paid up. He'd even asked for a receipt. Chief Winkle couldn't see the tape recorder under the front seat. The driver had been a New York judge. When the transcript had shown up, Bobby Winkle's father had quit the job and fled to Florida.

"Bartender," Bobby Winkle yelled. "Turn up this song. I love Van Morrison." The music roared as Morrison searched for a brown-eyed girl.

"Why don't we just meet in a jail cell?" Kettles said.

"Good idea," the cop said. "I'll put you in right now. Come to see you after the weekend."

"What have you got on this thing, Chief?"

"I'll tell you, but you'll owe me again. I need help getting money for new cars out of the city council."

"I'll co-sign the car loans, Chief."

"Sure. Have I told you lately, Arlon, that you are an obsequious kiss-ass when you want something?"

"So are you, Chief. Remember the rush last summer when you needed a dozen bullet-proof vests? My story on the mad tourists from Taxachusetts made you invincible in front of the council. Remember Kaptain Kevlar?" Kettles said.

"Well, we don't have much." Winkle got down to business. "The umpire was stabbed with some kind of sharpened instrument. The wallet and money were taken but recovered nearby in the Merrimack River. He has a nasty bruise on the forehead. But that didn't end him. A neat stab wound to the neck killed him."

"And what about the eye?"

"Just popped out of his head with the point of the shiv, I imagine."

"Motive?"

"Robbery. An unthinking crime. The stab wound in the neck just above the right collarbone shows a lucky kill. The guy grabbed the wallet, dropped the shiv, and ran."

"Why do you think, guy?"

"Ladies don't hide eighteen-inch shivs in their tights, not even the old mill-yard hookers."

"What about Ginny Glade? I heard you have a witness who puts her in the parking lot that night."

"Well, well, Inspector Kettles. We do come to the table prepared."

"Is she a suspect?" Kettles asked.

"We got her in the restaurant," Winkle said. "She ate and left. Maybe she's a witness."

"The ump blew the call."

"So?"

"He cost her fifty grand," Kettles said. "You have guys who would kill for fifty cents."

"There's something else. I can't go into it with you right now, but maybe later."

"What about this thing in New York City? An umpire was killed there after the World Series."

"So what?" Winkle said. "The Yankees win on a bad call. Big deal. Is this 'the Revenge of the Red Sox'? Or maybe voodoo and the ghost of Mike Torrez come back to seek his revenge?" Winkle sneered.

"No, Detective Dickhead. The guy who hit the absurd, quote, 'home run,' unquote, is Ginny Glade's ex-husband. She hates him and the world knows it."

"Maybe a coincidence."

"Oh yeah, well here's another one," Kettles said. "He was stabbed with a shiv. Don't let these New York cops play you for a hayseed. This could be the sore-loser story of all time."

"Yeah, well, your theory is great for the tabloids but I've already talked to the New York dicks. Besides, our killer is a male."

"How do you know that?"

"Does Ginny Glade chew tobacco?" Winkle asked.

Marriott Hotel, Daniel Webster Highway, Nashua, New Hampshire

The Jackster sat in his hotel room at the Marriott overlooking the Nashua tollbooths on the Everett Turnpike. There was a state liquor store in the distance.

"Vice is big business in New Hampshire," the Jackster said, closing the venetian blinds. "Maybe bigger than snow."

"I got a case of Jack Daniel's and five cartons of Newports," said the Jackster's guest, a muscular young man in a Global TV tank top. "The crew is stationed in Boston, but we can't get them up here fast enough."

"If these people would just allow some porn," the Jackster said, sighing, "they would be able to build a golden highway from here to the top of Mt. Washington."

"Yeah, well forget that, mister. The good rock-head people of the granite state hate any mention of sex."

"They should make porn a First Amendment issue," the Jackster said. " 'Live naked or die.' "

"New Hampshirites hate people who wear condoms as much as

they hate people who wear seat belts and motorcycle helmets," the field producer said. "You can't teach either subject, safe sex or safe driving, in their public schools."

"Okay," the Jackster said impatiently, pointing to the Minicam television camera on the coffee table. "How does this go?"

"We're on live at noon," the field producer said. "We put a bug in your ear. You'll hear the studio questions from our anchor in New York."

"Okay," the Jackster said.

"Be brief. We're live, all the way live. You just tell what you saw. *Capish?*"

"What about the other arrangements? The book deal?"

"The powers that be at Global can do it all. Newspaper. Book. TV show. Movie," the field producer said. "If they arrest Ginny Glade, you win the multimedia lottery."

They fitted the microphone to the Jackster's shirt and sat him in the corner of the room under the white light. They plugged his ear and then tested the device. He could hear New York. He was wearing his best red Nike cap. The Jackster couldn't wait to talk to the world.

"New York says to lose the hat," the field producer said. "You're not Tiger Woods. And this is not the Nike network."

"I will not," the Jackster said. "I'm having a bad-hair decade."

"Wear this if you're worried about your chrome dome." The producer handed him a Global network hat, saying, "You're our boy."

"Thirty seconds out," someone yelled. "Ready on the set."

The Jackster still had on his periwinkle Nike shirt. Maybe they would see that.

"Tight on his face," the stage manager yelled.

And then they were live.

"And with us now in Bedford, New Hampshire, is the father of a young tennis professional. His daughter, Rory, won a tournament up here earlier this summer, on the day another umpire was horribly murdered. You saw something that night, Mr. Bliss?"

"I was pulling into the Sheraton Wanderer parking lot that night. I was headed to a Nike banquet in Boston to celebrate my daughter Rory's stunning victory. As I pulled in, I saw someone pulling out. A high-ranking person on the women's tour."

"Who was that, Mr. Bliss?"

"Ginny Glade. I saw her as plain as day. I even beeped my horn at her. We've called her 'the Morgue Girl' for years, and now it looks like she fits the title because she's filling refrigerators with umps. She sped past me out of that parking lot like a bat out of hell. I walked in and had dinner. After I came out, I saw the body."

"Did the cops tell you she was their main suspect?"

"I told them she was the only person leaving the parking lot."

"Anything else, sir?"

"Yes. We used to see her husband around the tour, Shane Heath, the journeyman outfielder for the Yankees. They had a bad marriage. Ginny told me she had to get an abortion. She despised the man."

"I'm sorry, Mr. Bliss," the female anchor interrupted. "Are you saying Ms. Glade told you about an abortion? You were that close?"

"Sorry. Actually, Ginny told a friend about it, who told me. But I saw Ginny Glade running from the murder scene."

Then the Jackster actually sneered. "Look, maybe I wasn't supposed to tell you about the abortion. But it seems to me, Miss Anchor Lady, that I just gave you two scoops."

The anchor looked as if she had just been made to swallow acid. For viewers, this was like watching one of those cop chases where the suspect's car is walloped by a passing train. She had been sideswiped by a manipulator in ten million homes.

"Thank you, Mr. Bliss."

"Don't thank me. Thank Nike. If they hadn't scheduled a sports banquet, I would never have been there to witness anything."

"Somebody unplug that man."

And then the nation was gone. The Jackster was alone in a motel room with the shaken field producer. The young man was beet red as the New York producer shouted expletives in his ear. "Where the fuck did you get that disaster guest? He sandwiched slander between sneaker commercials."

The Jackster heard and stood up. He grabbed a handful of cheese and crackers and stuffed them in his pocket. He seemed particularly obscene in that moment. He dropped the Global hat to the floor.

"Don't try and bullshit a bullshitter, young fellow. Now, give me my hat back."

Mike McAlary

Room 2007, World Trade Center, Manhattan

They'd never expected visitors. The cop, a member of the mayors' security detail, had just been trying to get laid. He'd met the lady, Babe Policano, a pretty good looker and an obvious cop buff, during a ceremony at One Police Plaza to raise money for a police museum. He'd caught her eye and she'd winked at him. He was thirty, with blond hair and a mustache, and while protecting the mayor was a great assignment, you couldn't have any healthy relationship if you had this job. This mayor didn't allow married men to work his city hall detail. He didn't like bumping into morals.

"I would like to write a screenplay about cops who protect politicians," Babe had told the cop, who looked like a lifeguard. "Maybe a thriller."

He hadn't heard that one before. For about a week there, he had been assigned to guard this room in the trade center. It was the mayor's secret bunker. He'd invited the girl over with the idea of screwing her on the mayor's secret couch.

"Can I bring my tape recorder so we can do some work?" Babe had asked.

"Hell, you can bring a video camera," the cop had joked. "We could make a porno movie. We got the whole day alone."

They had been on the couch together, the tape recorder between them, when they got the call. They were half dressed by then.

"Mayor is on the floor. One minute out."

Babe barely had time to get dressed. The cop had spotted the bag at the last moment and had shoved it under the couch. Then, he'd hidden Babe in a back bathroom, in the shower stall.

"You'll be okay," the cop had said. "But don't move. He's never here more than twenty minutes and he never uses this bathroom."

A moment later she heard the mayor being buzzed in. She heard ice in a glass so she knew he was serving himself a drink.

"Do I smell perfume?" the mayor asked.

"Probably," the cop admitted. "I met this lady on my lunch break. She damn near raped me at lunch. Her perfume is all over my coat. Sorry, Mr. Mayor."

"Thank God you're not married," Mayor Caruso said. "I had this mistress who almost got me killed. I had to demand she wear no lipstick or perfume. Wives can smell the other lady on you. I even tried buying them both—wife and girlfriend—the same perfume for a while."

There was a buzz at the door. Another detective announced the guest, federal judge James Parnell. The judge, about fifty-five, wore a black-and-white Brooks Brothers suit. He was perfectly manicured and coiffed, and doubled as Brooklyn's unofficial conservative leader.

"Thank you for coming, Judge," Mayor Caruso said. "Wait outside, boys."

The judge and the mayor sat on the couch. After pouring the judge a drink, the mayor spoke. "I need a favor," Caruso said. "Actually, more than a favor. We have a contract we have to deliver on."

The judge scowled, then said, "Please, Mr. Mayor. I can't really get involved in this stuff anymore."

Mayor Vito Caruso placed his glass on the coffee table and then balled his hands into fists before he spoke again. "Oh, really, who the fuck are you now?" Caruso said. "Big federal judge, huh? Well, I just got off the phone with New York's senior senator. He said the next appointment to the federal bench is his. And he is giving that appointment to me. So if you want a lifetime job, fucko, listen closely. I should have put you in jail years ago, when I caught you fucking around with the parking violations bureau. Now it's payback time."

"Is it something illegal? How do I know this isn't some kind of Abscam-type sting?"

The mayor laughed, then said, "Oh, that's precious. You should be so lucky. I was the last federal prosecutor to pull off that kind of stuff in New York City. Welcome to the new Tammany Hall, Judge. The old politics is the new politics. Of course, the newspaper would call this corruption. But it isn't about money. It's about power."

"I heard rumors that you did this for that Hamas guy we freed last year and the Lubavitcher kidnapper the year before."

"Consequently, I am the only thing Brooklyn Arabs and Jews agree on," the mayor said. "Now we add the Irish."

"What's your scheme?"

"There is a guy who is going to come up in front of you for a bail-reduction hearing next week. It's an extradition case. Michael McPhee. He's from Sligo, Ireland, but our British friends want him for a bombing."

"Yeah," the judge said, "I've already denied him bail twice. He killed a schoolbus full of kids. Scottish children, for damn sake. They have nothing to do with the war. McPhee should be returned for execution."

"Well, that's not going to happen," the mayor said. "You are going to order him released. As you know, my support among the Irish has suffered because I won't be held up for a raise by that fucking police union."

"Jesus, Vito," the judge said. "You made your reputation as a prosecutor putting these guys in jail. He killed twenty innocent kids with a bomb."

"McPhee's friends have already combined to donate one million to my reelection campaign," Caruso said. "You cut this prick loose, now. There's peace now. What the fuck do I care?"

"It's corrupt," the judge stammered. "I won't do it."

"Then you're one dead judge." The mayor sighed and opened a manila envelop he had been holding.

"I don't care if this fuck blew up a kindergarten in Brooklyn," Caruso said. "By the way, Judge, this cash that you're accepting in this photograph. Does it happen to show up on your income tax? Probably not."

"Oh my god," the judge said. He dropped his glass.

"I imagine the IRS will have fun with this," Caruso said.

The mayor got up and poured himself a second drink. The judge continued to shake.

"This is the deal," Caruso continued. "You free this guy and my campaign gets the cash. It isn't really so bad. I'm not taking drug money; hell, I'm just getting reelected. And you're not going to jail for tax evasion and fraud. Instead, you are getting a lifetime gig on the federal bench."

"Jesus, Vito, you're sicker than I am."

The mayor took the photographs off the couch.

"That's all, Judge. Don't fuck it up."

An hour later, after the judge, the mayor, and all the mayor's detectives had left the apartment, Babe Policano tiptoed out of the bathroom. She hadn't heard all of the conversation and that was fine with her. She just wanted out.

Only during the cab ride uptown did she discover that the tape recorder in her bag had been on during the entire clandestine meeting.

WZEA Media Center, Rockefeller Center, Manhattan

Shane Heath was happy to hear from the television crew. It didn't really matter to him that they didn't want to talk about his home run, or even the dead umpire in Greenwich Village. It fit with his torpid view of the universe to see Ginny as a bad guy. It was also good to be on television.

"I don't know what she was doing up there in the parking lot with the tennis umpire. But I know she hated umps. Ginny really hid this from people. But she was a sore loser. She was angry, obviously, when we broke up. She could not live with not being the star of our household. She resented me for making it to the big leagues."

"Really?"

"She's a hater, like I said."

"Are you saying your ex-wife was capable of killing an umpire?"

"I am saying that the only people she hated more than me were umpires," Shane continued. "Anything is possible with Ginny. She got an abortion without ever telling me she was pregnant. Long before the umpires, she killed our child."

The utility outfielder handled the microphone like many a fly ball and dropped it with a thunk. The talk-show host, Mongrel Man, began to laugh.

"That's you, Heath, good hit, no field. You are like the heroic version of that old Met Marvelous Marvin Throneberry, the antihero of the worst team ever."

"How so?" Heath asked. He was embarrassed, almost whimpering.

"You get the biggest hit of your life and all people want to talk about a week later is whether your wife killed the ump who made you an American hero. It's pathetic."

"I hit the home run that saved the Yankees," Shane insisted.

"You are a walking baseball asterisk, a bonehead call come to life. Like I said, you remind me of Throneberry."

"Why?"

"He dropped everything, too," Mongrel said. "When the general manager of the Mets called him into his office to cut him from the team, finally, they say Marvin walked to the door and turned the knob. It came off in his hand. That's as sadly perfect as you dropping the microphone. You're a lummox, Heath. But you're our lummox."

"Well, thank you very much, I guess," the sports hero said.

"Will you take a call?"

"Uh-huh."

"Mike from Brooklyn," Mongrel said, punching a lighted key on his board. "Go ahead, Mike."

"I like the lady, Mongrel. But I think she'd be better off dancing on tables at Scores than hanging out with you, Heath. We all heard that guy on Global and the truth about Ginny's abortion. What about that, Mr. Big?"

Heath said, "Like I said, Ginny is a sore loser."

Northbound Interstate

"Can you turn the radio on?"

Francisco checked the inspector with a glance in the rearview mirror. They had passed Hartford and were heading northeast on U.S. 81, barreling toward Sturbridge and the Massachusetts Turnpike. The car was a rolling cage.

Donovan grimaced. He was losing order, he was playing Good Cop/Bad Cop with Francisco to music. His life was ridiculous. He shook his head.

"Maybe a little later," Francisco said.

"Yo, Tennis Lady," Dillon said. "What do your friends call you?"

"Ginny, or Gin, which I hate."

"That's a lame name. If that was my name, my friends would call me Countess Tanqueray or Lady Gordon. You know, some hideous gin joke. The name isn't very phat."

"The real name is probably worse. Virginia."

"Are you, like, a really famous player or something? Or do you just teach?"

"I used to do better," Ginny said with a sigh. "But I got slower and the kids got faster."

"Oh, like, the age thing happened?"

"Yes."

"Well, you still have a sexy body," Dillon said. "Doesn't she, Francisco?"

Donovan grabbed his head with both hands. "I will not have this talk-show banter in the car," Donovan said. "Francisco, isn't it time to feed the prisoner?"

"Yeah, boss. There's a Roy Rogers coming up soon, on the other side of the Mass Pike tollbooths."

They continued in silence for another couple of miles, then pulled into the Roy Rogers and parked near the front of the lot.

"Francisco, go ahead. I'll meet you with Dillon here inside."

Donovan watched them go and waited to speak to his daughter until after the detective and his prime suspect were inside.

"Dad, you're, like, being a total donkey," Dillon said. "What's the big deal? I embarrass you, don't I?"

"No, of course not, Dill. I mean, well, yes, a policeman shouldn't have a junkie for a daughter."

"You hate me, don't you, Dad?"

"I love you, Dill, but hate what you've become."

The cop remembered then the first time he'd heard the question. She had been about four then, and the girl had told him, "I hate you." They were just words, he knew. And every kid said that to his parent at some point. But they had been a dagger in his heart then, and were a dagger now.

"I just want you to get better."

"I want to be better."

He hugged his daughter. Ginny Glade was inside; she glanced

over her shoulder and watched the two people talking with great animation. She was surprised to see the cop hugging his prisoner.

"Hey, Detective," she said, turning back to the salad bar. "Is hugging the bad guy part of this new community-policing thing?"

Francisco turned and saw the hug, then said, "No, he's just consoling her. She has some severe personal problems. And we need her as a witness. So you comfort."

"Well, it doesn't look right."

Roy Roger's Restaurant, Massachusetts Turnpike, Sturbridge, Massachusetts

A moment later, Donovan and Dillon came in together. The girl's eyes were red. She had been crying. But food seemed to brighten her spirits. She filled her plate with fried chicken and a giant container of Coke and joined Francisco and Ginny at a plastic table.

"Scrumptious fare," she said. "But I have to go wee-wee."

Francisco looked at the inspector, who rolled his eyes.

"I'll go," Francisco said. "I'll empty the room and then guard the door."

Ginny made a face, then said, "Oh, come on. This is all, so, unnecessary. You gentlemen are worse than hockey players. I'll take her. Where is she going to go?"

"I can't allow it," Mickey said. Ginny saw an uneasiness in his eyes. Had the cop been crying, too? Ginny got up and took the teenager's hand.

"We'll be right back."

"You better be, Dillon. No funny stuff or you have to wear the handcuffs."

They walked off holding hands. The inspector watched them go. They were easy together. He felt a jab of melancholy as they disappeared into the women's room. His wife had always taken the girl to the bathroom in rest stops. That was all gone now.

"We got something from the lab boys on that soup ladle," Francisco said. "They called just before I met you. I didn't want to talk about it in the car. The ladle was made by Cutco, ten years ago. The company just makes knives now. The ladles were only made for a couple of months in 1975. We got lucky there. Only a couple of hundred of them. We're tracing the shipments. They keep good records because when a salesman goes door-to-door, he collects names and addresses for a mailing list. We may even get luckier, boss."

"I like that. What else?"

"A strange thing. It may be nothing. It may not even be from our killer. But we believe our killer sat on a bench in the park, watching and waiting. That meant he knew where the ump lived. We're checking with motor vehicles to see if anyone accessed the license directory that night. But he may have just followed the guy home from the stadium in his car. Anyway, there is some stuff on the ground under the bench. Quite a bit of it. We will definitely get DNA evidence. It makes our guy a male."

"What? He jerked off in the park or something?"

"No. Not that good. If our guy waited on the bench, the lab guys say he had a chaw in his mouth. Tobacco, boss. He was chewing tobacco and spitting it on the ground. Then I remembered something the old massage guy told us."

"About the guy he saw in the street, watching."

"Right. The guy Ginny said she recognized as our mystery man in the diner."

"Yeah?"

"The old man said he had a chaw of tobacco in his mouth."

"And?"

"We found tobacco juice on the passenger-side floorboard in Nesto's van. We're doing DNA."

Ginny came running around the corner. She looked frantic.

"She's gone, Mickey. I gave her a quarter for a video game while I used the bathroom, and when I came out, she was gone."

Mike McAlary

Daisy Buchanan Restaurant, Newbury Street, Boston, Massachusetts

Hanna Ottoman was scared for her friend. Ginny was expected at her mother's house in New Boston the following day. But Hanna's husband, the Adonislike cop, had bad news. Because he knew tennis society, the cops had called him in when they'd questioned Jack Bliss in Boston. Hanna's husband was afraid for Ginny Glade.

"She isn't a killer," Hanna said. "Jeez, if Ginny was going to kill someone, she would have killed that insufferable man Jack Bliss."

Then, as she remembered, again, her battle with the hamburgers, all those years ago, Hanna began to cry. "What am I going to say to her? Ginny has a temper, but not like this."

"I don't want you talking to her about this."

"Screw that, she has to know she's a suspect. It's all over the news. Her former husband, one of nature's real noblemen, is on the TV saying she was always talking about killing umps."

"It's just that jerk's opinion."

"Ginny wanted to choke her husband. I'll castrate him myself if he calls my friend a sore loser again."

"Easy, Hanna."

"Easy for you to say."

"We have two problems. But it doesn't mean they'll find her guilty. One, Ginny was at the murder scene. Two—and I shouldn't even tell you this—when Ginny returned the car, it had one of those emergency tires on the front-right rim."

"Big deal. Ginny got a flat. She changed it. So what? That makes her a killer?"

"No. This is the curious part. The flat tire was in the trunk. But there was no tire iron."

"So she left it by the road somewhere."

"Hanna, we're not having this conversation. But that better be Ginny's answer to the tire-iron question when the New Hampshire cops ask her about it."

"Why?"

"Because I've seen the autopsy photographs, Hanna. Blinky

Hammond was conked on the head with something remarkably similar to a tire iron."

Roy Rogers Restaurant, Massachusetts Turnpike, Sturbridge, Massachusetts

Inspector Donovan was going to check the video game first. He steeled himself against his fear, as he had done as a young cop in the Bronx when entering an apartment with a crazed gunman inside. He went boldly around the corner, but the games blinked in an empty, dull room. There was an OUT OF ORDER sign over the featured game, Lethal Weapon II. His mind quickly moved from the best possible scenario to the worst.

"Francisco, check that line of tractor trailers first. Stop every rig. Check every cab."

Francisco was out the door, his gold shield hanging over the front of his shirt on a silver chain.

"Get in the car, Ginny, and block the front rig in line."

The cop ran to the trucks with his badge out in his left hand and his right hand on the gun on his waistband.

Inside the rest station, Donovan walked to the bank of phones. He checked them all. Nothing. The manager, having spotted the man with the badge in his parking lot, walked over to Donovan, who also wore his gold shield.

"Do we have a problem, sir?" he asked. "Should I dial nine-one-one?"

"Don't panic. We just misplaced a package. No need for more police just yet. Thanks." Mickey even managed a smile despite his cold worry. He backed out the door, into the parking lot, and saw his car parked in a position to bar escape. Francisco had put a flashing red bulb on the roof.

"What's this about?" asked the first trucker, a huge man with a frayed face. "I got a load of fish here that I have to get to Faneuil

Hall in ninety minutes. I came straight from the Fulton Street fish market in New York. It's a madhouse. I had time for one coffee."

"Just hold on, mister, we're looking for a girl."

"Ain't we all, *paco*? I could use a little lady right now." The trucker pointed at Ginny Glade. "Is she a cop, too?"

Inspector Donovan strode right up to the man. His gun was still holstered. "This missing person is my teenaged daughter. And no one is leaving until I find her."

"Okay, boss," the trucker said, holding up the palms of his hands. "Search my truck. The only thing I got that smells like a fish is fish."

"I'll check your cab. Open the trailer for Detective Camacho."

"Your daughter . . ." Ginny Glade said. "I had no idea."

"Later," Donovan snapped. He began to climb up into the black cab. He poked his head into a black velour cab that reeked of cigarette smoke, Chinese food, and dirty underwear.

"Jesus, you're ripe."

"It covers the fish smell."

Just then, Francisco turned to his right; wide-eyed, he stared at the girl at the door. Dillon was smiling, until she saw the flashing red light. Then she measured the activity near the trucks, saw the fear on her father's face, and understood.

"You thought I ran," Dillon said aloud. She held a vanilla ice cream cone in her right hand. It dripped to the pavement as she watched.

Francisco leaned into the car and snapped off the light. Inspector Donovan turned and saw, too. He ran over. He was embarrassed by his fear. Once, many years before, when the girl had been about three, they had gone to a friend's house. He had been talking on the phone for about five minutes before he'd noticed the open door.

"Oh, God," he'd said.

He'd run outside and called her name, but had gotten no response. He'd decided to go to the worst place and work backward. The neighbor had a pool. He'd run across the cul-de-sac and found Dillon standing at the edge of the pool, pointing to a rubber duck in the water.

"Nice ducky," she'd said.

Somehow, Dillon had opened the locked gate. He had the same helpless feeling now.

"Where did you go?"

"I went outside to use a pay phone because there were too many creeps inside. I called Mom. Told her I was going away to get better. Then I came back in the side door and got a Mister Softee."

"We thought you—"

"Dad, you have no faith in me."

"Jesus, Dill, we've been at war. You sticking diseased spikes in your own arms—"

Ginny stepped between them. She had spotted the tracks in the kid's arms earlier. Now she understood the fear and the hugs. Ginny put her arm around the kid and smiled. "Why don't we take a time-out and go to the bathroom? Now that I know who you are, I'll take a chance on lending you some real clothes. Also, it turns out that I haven't scared myself shitless. I could use the potty."

Dillon laughed but followed Ginny into the bathroom, the tennis player carrying a bag of clothes and Dillon wearing fetid jeans and a stained sweatshirt. They came out a few minutes later. Dill was now wearing a sky-blue warmup suit. No athlete had ever looked like this. The pants were unzipped up to the knees. She had on a tiny jacket that was zipped from the navel only to her black bra.

"Aw, shit," Mickey mumbled.

"I offered a T-shirt but she wasn't interested," Ginny said.

A truck driver walked past and said, in a low voice, without breaking stride, "Frankly, I'm not interested in seeing a T-shirt either."

The cops and the girls laughed. The situation had become painfully absurd.

Ginny hugged Dillon, who smiled.

"If I was my dad, I'd shoot me," Dillon said.

"Your dad is just a lug, Dillon. How about we sit in the back together the rest of the way? Boys in the front. Girls in the back."

The police inspector said nothing. He was still trying to get the image of a greasy truck driver mauling his trapped daughter out of his head. He didn't even feel like a cop anymore. Mickey Donovan was the Wraith no longer. He was just another wounded victim, a casualty of his daughter.

FIFTEEN

Glade Family Farm, Page Hill Road, New Boston, New Hampshire

That night as she slept in her childhood bed, Ginny Glade dreamed of Arthur Ashe again. She had been nine years old when she'd met him. Professional tennis players, led by Ashe, had just formed a union. Players were striking Wimbledon that summer. Most of the best players had simply refused to go. An average Czechoslovakian grass-court player, Jan Kodes, had won the tournament. He'd beaten Nastase, as Ginny recalled.

The best players in the world had descended upon New Hampshire that summer and had played their own tournament in Mount Washington Valley in Bretton Woods, New Hampshire. They had advertised the tournament as "Instead of Wimbledon."

It had been the summer of 1972. She would never forget it. She had still been a barnyard kid in so many ways. She remembered having been amazed when they'd had lunch in the ballroom at the Mount Washington Hotel. Stalin and Roosevelt had once met in the same room. They had given her a plate of fruit. Another human being had taken the time to spoon the vaguely orange cantaloupe and soft green honeydew melon into balls. She had not thought such a delicate delight was possible. She'd never really understood money before she'd looked in the silver fruit bowl.

And then a loudspeaker had crackled.

"Attention, please. The president of the United States, Richard M. Nixon, has just resigned."

A low growl had rolled across the room. And just as suddenly, a tall ponytailed player who attended UCLA had begun to unfold from his seat. He had been angry, lean, and bearded. Almost Christlike. His name was Jeff Boran.

"Who gives a shit?" Boran had said. And then he'd grabbed his wooden Jack Kramer racquets off the table, wrapped them in the white tablecloth, and said, "Let's play tennis. Let's do something for our players' association."

They had played the final. She'd met Arthur Ashe as he sat near the center court, his back against a chain-link fence. He studied the commotion near the entrance to the ballroom.

"What happened in there?" Ashe had asked.

"Nixon resigned," she'd said.

"Oh, really?"

"Yes, sir."

He had been a little surprised to be addressed as "sir." He'd turned and studied the mountain. She could still remember his words and gaze all these years later.

"What are you doing, Mr. Ashe?"

"Focusing," he'd said.

"On the president?"

"Not yet. First comes the match. There's plenty of time for other things. You can't be distracted."

"What do you mean?"

"I mean, tennis is what makes me matter. No one would listen to a losing tennis player."

"Huh?" Ginny had asked. It had been a confusing morning.

"I see you are wearing a tennis skirt. Do you play?"

"Yes. But not very well, yet."

"It's a lot of work," Ashe had continued. "But in America, being the best at something makes you vital, young lady."

"I want to be great, like you."

"Being a great person is more important than being a great tennis player."

"I want to do great things," Ginny had said, almost bursting. "Like you with South Africa."

"Being a tennis player isn't enough," Ashe had said. "Winners are allowed to have voices. You can't talk about politics and the world if you lose."

"I think I know what you mean. In school this year we learned about legacy and that your legacy isn't just money and power, the toys you collect. Your legacy should be the people you help."

"What a smart young lady. Let me see, is that written on your wrist?"

She'd held up her hands so Ashe could inspect them. Then Ginny Glade had tapped her head with her index finger and said, "Most of my writing is in here."

"Then write to me in care of the Association of Tennis Professionals, New York, New York."

"I will."

Ginny had been afraid. She hadn't wanted the moment to end. She had been noticed. Someone had offered her adult conversation.

"You aren't wearing glasses," Ginny had said. "How come?"

"I wear contact lenses now," Ashe had said.

"You are very cool," she had said.

"Thank you."

"Can I touch your hair?" Ginny had asked. "I've never touched an Afro before."

Ginny hadn't unknowingly been a racist and would have made the same request of John Lennon. To a young girl like Ginny, celebrity had been equated with hair.

Arthur Ashe had swallowed a laugh. It was a delicate chuckle, as soft and precise as the melon balls. "I have to get ready for a match, young lady," he'd said. "I don't mean to be rude, but what's your name?"

"Glade. Ginny Glade."

"Well, Ginny, I need to focus on work."

"Okay, I'll write."

Ginny Glade had stood up and started to walk away. She'd turned when she'd gone a few feet and had watched Arthur Ashe focusing on the mountains again. She hadn't asked him for an autograph, but Ginny Glade had carried the tennis immortal's signature on her life across all the years.

Hampshire Glen Detox Center, Route 101, Dublin, New
Hampshire

Ginny parked her car beside a perfect lawn outside a soft white
building in Dublin, New Hampshire, and walked to the front door.
The place reeked of antiseptic and control. Outside, a man seemed
obsessed with his job. He was cutting the single leaves of a hedge
with his penknife scissors. He may even have slept in his plastic safety
goggles. "Like, hi, man," he said. He was wearing a Smashing Pump-
kins sweatshirt that suggested everyone get smashed.

Ginny nodded and was met by the rehabilitation center's official
greeter, a woman in a paisley Laura Ashley dress. The woman
seemed too happy with the ordinary moment.

"Hello," Ginny said.

"And what a grand day it is, ma'am," she replied. Scissorhands
and Ms. Sunshine were clearly recovering dopers.

"Yes. I'm here to see Mary Dillon Donovan. She's a new patient."

"Oh yes. She came in last night. Is she expecting you?"

"Yes. Please tell her Ginny Glade would like to see her."

"Please step through here," the greeter said, "and wait in the
garden."

Then the greeter leaned over and whispered, "Oh, I love your
tennis. You are great. I am so jealous of you."

Ginny was still a hero in her home state. They used her name in
the same sentence with Carlton Fisk and Mike Flanagan when they
were talking about New Hampshire's greatest athletes. Ginny looked
at the kids and tried to remember how confused she had been. She
had Ashe in her head, again.

"There are greater things than tennis," Ginny said. "I would prefer to help people reclaim their lives."

Dillon had removed her rivets and earrings. Spiked and thin, she was
a cactus in the New Hampshire woods. She was in visual conflict
with both the bright, drying leaves and the soft evergreens.

"Hey there, Tennis Mom," Dillon said. "What gives?"

"I just wanted to see you," Ginny said. "My parents have a home a couple of towns over."

"Came out to water the junkie, huh?"

"No, Dillon. You can grow yourself."

"So why are you here?"

"I could use a friend. You remind me of someone."

"Yeah, like who?"

"Me," Ginny said.

"I could use a friend with a spike," Dillon said.

"Well, I can't help you with the Kurt Cobain act," Ginny replied.

"It isn't an act."

"Sure it is," Ginny insisted.

"Did you ever do heroin?"

"Once, in Amsterdam. I snorted on a dare to prove I wasn't a prissy pants."

"And?" Dillon wanted to know.

"It was wasted on me," Ginny said. "I vomited and fell asleep."

"How about angel dust?" Dillon wanted to know.

"No," Ginny said. "I missed that one."

"Were you a coke head?"

"We all dabbled in it," Ginny said. "And I smoked a joint a day in college. I only quit because I gained twenty pounds on Cheez Doodles and Big Macs. There was this place called Hungry Charlie's at the end of my block. On most nights, I fell asleep in their kitchen."

"Can I tell you something?" Dillon asked.

"Of course."

Dillon leaned forward. Ginny could smell Ivory soap. "I'm afraid," Dillon said. "They got the shit in here, too. This morning, the dishwasher asked me if I wanted to score an envelope."

"You have to be strong, girl," Ginny said. As soon as she'd said it, she knew it was a mistake. She sounded like Nancy Reagan.

"Oh, that is lame, Tennis Mom. Heroin is the only friend I need."

"It's a false friend," Ginny continued. "And if you want, I can make you bigger than the drug."

"Oh, stop. This is like a bad script. It's a hack version of that Brit film we were talking about in group this morning, *Trainspotting*."

"I can show you other things, Dillon. You are a fearless kid but you have to overcome things. I can teach you that."

"Sorry. I don't see it."

Ginny now said something publicly for the first time in twenty years. She was surprised by the evenness of her voice.

"You know, Dillon, I was raped when I was about your age. I wasn't as tough as you in the beginning, but you can grow courage. Now everyone says I have survived because of my toughness. But you're tougher than me, Dillon. The only thing stopping you is you."

"Being raped is no big thing."

"Really? Maybe you can beat the memory with drugs. I tried that, too, with alcohol for a while. But you let the rapist win if you let it destroy you."

"I'm sorry you got slammed, but what does that have to do with me?"

"I know your problem, too."

"Oh yeah? And what is it?"

"Boredom."

"Oh fuck this, Tennis Mom. You ain't gonna be around long anyway."

Ginny froze. She had imagined that this would be easier.

"Oh, come on," Dillon continued, "don't be such a cheesehead. You haven't figured it out yet?"

"Figured what out, Dillon?"

"My father is afraid you're his killer."

Ginny was ice.

"This time next year, hell, I'll be taking a bus upstate to visit you on Jean Harris's old cell block in Bedford Hills."

"What do you mean? Your dad drove me up here."

"Maybe I don't know squat about tennis," Dillon said, "but you don't know dick about police surveillance. It's the oldest trick in the world. The good cops don't tail you. They get in front of you and wait. They learn your routine. But my old man has done something better. He's tricked you into following him."

"Why are you telling me this?"

"Because it will screw my father up pretty good," Dillon said. "Besides, I like your *cojones*."

"*Cojones?*"

"Yeah, you got balls. It's like Francisco told my father before you got in the car. 'Watch her, boss. Her ovaries clank when she walks.'"

"How much do they know?" Ginny asked.

"I heard them say they got you identified in a case up here. Some umpire. Blind Melon Something."

"Blinky Hammond," Ginny said.

"Yeah, that's it."

Ginny stood and smiled. She liked the kid even more than she might have imagined.

Dillon grabbed her head with both hands, then said, "Do you know why I'm, like, really fucked up this time?" Dillon asked. "I hate to admit it after what you told me."

Ginny sat back down. "Why?" she asked. She touched the girl's hands, on the table.

"I saw my girlfriend get raped," Dillon said. "And then the guy came for me. He didn't screw me or anything. I got away. But I was, like, had. I wake up every night feeling helpless."

"I know what you must be going through, Dillon," Ginny said gently. "You can't escape the cold."

They were done. Ginny stood up again. She had discovered something.

"I'll be back to get you out of here this afternoon," Ginny Glade said.

"What, like, a breakout or something?"

"Maybe we can rescue each other," the tennis player said.

SIXTEEN

Players' Parking Lot, Yankee Stadium, the Bronx

Bugout Newby had a case he needed to work off. He was wanted in Queens for dealing ten vials of crack in the Forties houses. It wasn't major weight and he wouldn't have to do a major bit. But cases cost him time and money and he didn't have time for either.

So he hadn't been hanging out much in South Jamaica. He was living with his friend Darius Griffin in the Bronx, near Yankee Stadium. He couldn't sell in the Bronx, so mostly he slept until noon. Then he would go down to the park, where he played basketball at the entrance to the Stadium Club. It was a good park, built and maintained by the Yankees with double-reinforced steel rims. Bugout couldn't shoot or dribble but he could jump through the sky. He wanted to be nicknamed Helicopter Legs or Thrust, but he screwed up too many dunks. So they called him Bugout.

Most of the kids hustled the Yankee players as they arrived for off-season workouts and walked across the parking lot to the locker-room entrance. You couldn't do it during games because there were too many cops protecting the players. But you could make a dollar in the off days.

"Yo, Yankeeman, you got change?" Bugout asked the severely tanned player he recognized from television as Shane Heath.

"How about an autograph?"
"Unless it's on a check it don't be much help to me, Yankeeman."
"You work?"
"You hiring?"
"Maybe. I'll catch you on the way out."

Bugout was still waiting about an hour later when the Yankee player came out with his gear-packed duffle bag. They spoke briefly, at the gate.

"Take the train into Manhattan and meet me outside the Second Avenue Deli. Four o'clock. Don't be late."

Shane Heath handed Bugout half a torn hundred-dollar bill. "You get the other half when you do the job."

Bugout took the bill, then smiled. "This ain't, like, no nasty sex thing, right?" Bugout said. " 'Cause homey don't play that shit."

"Don't flatter yourself, jerkoff," Shane Heath said. "I just need you to clean out an apartment."

"Burglary be extra."
"I have a key."
"Then we be partners."

Newsroom, Manchester Union Guardian, *Manchester, New Hampshire*

When Arlon Kettles got back to his office, there was a letter on his desk. The mail clerk had just dropped it off. The letter, written on *Yankee Magazine* stationery, had been mailed in Dublin, New Hampshire, postmarked the previous day. The return address read *"F. Hammond. Sheraton Wanderer Parking Lot."* The reporter tore it open. The letter, which included Al Lisker's blood-smudged Yankees' lineup card from game seven, was written with block letters torn from newspapers and magazines. It was a very simple message: "KILL THE UMPIRE."

In the late afternoon, the cops sat in the hundred-year-old Manchester police station on Granite Street, an anonymous gray building. The television trucks were parked outside. Their satellite dishes were raised forty feet over the building.

America was electric with the story of "The Great American Umpire Killer." If Ginny Glade had tuned into Global before she'd entered the garden at the rehab center in Dublin, she would have recognized herself as the prime suspect. The Jackster was coast-to-coast.

The city cops and the country cops were seated across from each other just outside the gray holding cells in a grayer room filled with even grayer chairs. The New Hampshire cop, Bobby Winkle, whose red face was the only color in the bloodless room, spoke first. Chief Winkle, an uncomfortably thin man, rose and pointed an accusing, bony, Ichabod Crane index finger at Inspector Mickey Donovan. No one believed the divergent police departments could trust each other enough to conduct a quality joint investigation. They never had before.

"This isn't going to be like that subway vigilante Frankel," Winkle said. He was quivering, his skeleton almost rattling. "I was up there ten years ago in Concord on that. We took your subway gunman's statement. The guy was a stone psycho. And do you know something? If we'd tried Frankel for attempted murder up here, he would never have beaten the case. That white boy went hunting black kids. We'd have him sitting in jail right now."

"The videotape was first-rate, sir," Francisco Camacho said. "A major-league confession."

"And you are?"

"Detective Sergeant Francisco Camacho, sir. I was a transit detective before I moved to Manhattan homicide. I was up here on Frankel, too."

"Well, your people screwed us on that," Winkle said. "Called us country bumpkins. How dare you blame us for losing that case? We even got a videotaped confession."

"That was wrong, sir," Francisco continued. "But that wasn't us. That was the Manhattan District Attorney's office."

"It was bullshit, Detective Frisco," Winkle said.

"Granted," Francisco replied. "We're not in disagreement here. But please, sir, don't call me Frisco."

Donovan coughed hard, then said, "Oh stop the brown-nose waiter act, Francisco. If this guy doesn't want to talk to us, screw them; they can deal with the FBI."

Winkle did not back down. He wasn't going to allow the city cops to play their good-cop/bad-cop routine on him.

"I know you glory boys from New York think you invented detective work," Winkle said. "And, hell, while we may not have a TV show—'Queen City Blue' or some shit—we still know what we're doing."

"With all due respect, Chief. Stop whining. You sound like an old washerwoman, or worse, a fireman. This one is bigger than Bernie Frankel. And if sport is bigger than race, then maybe bigger than the Super Bowl. The nation awaits. You're a detective. Start detecting."

Winkle measured the city cop for weakness. His hand was steady, his breathing even. He did not want to play poker with Mickey Donovan. He would not call his bluff, if it was a bluff. "Okay," Winkle said. "Then let's set the ground rules. It will be like kindergarten."

"Go ahead," Mickey said.

"Rule number one: sharing," Winkle said. "I'll give, if I get. Share the facts and share the credit. No press conferences. No leaks."

"Agreed," Donovan said. "Anything else?"

"Yeah, another kindergarten rule: no hitting. None of that, 'We're working with bumpkins' shit from you and we'll stay away from the dumb city-slicker crap."

"Fine," Donovan said, then smiled. "But are you guys still riding cows on patrol? And how is your father doing? Does he write to the guys he met in prison?"

Winkle stood up and closed his manila file, the one marked, "Investigate DOA. Blinky Hammond."

"We're done," the chief said. "What is it the city boys call you? Oh yeah, the Wraith. Ghosts don't scare us bumpkins, pal."

"Oh calm down, Sheriff Billy Crystal," Donovan said. "That was a joke. So is this conversation. Stop the sanctimonious bullshit. You're a pro. And we're pros. Let's get to work."

Donovan studied him for a moment, then offered his hand over the case file. Winkle shook it. Then Mickey opened a file he'd carried into the room and began to read from detective document one aloud. "Okay, starting with our DD5's. We have a white male, forty-five, stabbed with a sharpened soup ladle in Stonewall Park in the West Village. You fellows would hate the neighborhood. Most cops do. The dead man's right eye was removed after he was killed. Just plucked out and removed from the crime scene. We also have a note written on a dinner receipt from the Sheraton Wanderer. It's dated August seventeenth. Cash. Lamb. One glass of Merlot. Twenty-three dollars. That means a legitimate meal, probably one person."

"That puts your killer at our murder scene," Winkle said.

"Go ahead," Donovan said.

"Hammond was stabbed in the heart with a sharpened shiv. Left near the body but first used to pluck the right eye out of the head. The ump had a nasty bruise on his forehead. So he was clubbed before he died, because blood was still flowing after he got smacked. The lab says it would take about five minutes to hemorrhage that badly."

"Anything else?" Donovan asked.

"You first," Winkle replied, and almost regretted sounding juvenile.

"Does your shiv have any brand name on it?" the city cop wanted to know.

"Yes. Cutco," the chief cop replied.

"Our brand name is Cutco, too."

Donovan turned to his second and asked, "Francisco, anything more on that?"

"Not yet," the detective sergeant replied. "We're checking with the company's shipping records."

"We did the same thing," Winkle said. "They traced it to a warehouse in Rochester, New York. Ten years ago. Just disappeared."

"Thank you," Donovan said. He was genuinely impressed.

"Do you have any witnesses in New York?" Winkle asked.

"Not yet. And you, Chief?"

"We have one," Winkle continued. "Jack Bliss, single white male, fifty-three, of Hialeah, Florida, and Saratoga, New York. He is the father of the kid who won the tournament up here that day. The ump blew the call that gave her the match. Even Bliss admits the ump screwed Ginny Glade. Anyway, as characters go, this one is a pink flamingo. Half carney and half gigolo. Alias 'the Jackster.' A cartoon character."

"Yeah. I just saw him on television. He's a world-class shithead, but so what? What did he see, and how's his vision?" Donovan asked.

"He sees a lady rushing from the parking lot in a car."

"Who?"

"Ginny Glade."

"Ah shit, I heard him say that on television but I was hoping you'd tell me something else."

"Why?" Winkle asked.

"She is known to our department," Mickey said. "You know the umpire who got killed in the Village? He fucked up a call in game seven and made Ginny Glade's former husband a national hero."

"Even this hayseed department is aware of the World Series result, Inspector. We even have television up here now. Have you questioned her?"

"No, Chief, but we're following her."

"Well, be careful, Inspector."

"Why? She was there that night, at the very least, and maybe played a role in this."

"The car she returns to Boston has one of those doughnut tires on it, Inspector. Ginny Glade says she got a flat. But when the service guy checks the trunk, there is a flat back there but no tire iron."

Mickey sighed. "So what, Chief? She left it on the road."

"Unlikely, Inspector. We have some pretty good forensic evidence. There are microscopic paint chips in Hammond's head wound. Volvo paints its tire irons. He was struck by a black object. We tested her car. There are paint chips on the lug nuts. Fresh paint."

Mickey was catching on. He whistled and asked, "Have you checked the paint from the lug nuts and the head wound?"

"We have, Inspector. Perfect match."

"Okay, Chief. So we have a suspect."

"Where was she the other night when you lost your umpire?"

"Out and about," Mickey realized. "But she seems to have an alibi."

"One more thing, Donovan. As I told you, we checked Hammond's cell-phone records. He called Ginny's home just half an hour before he died. We dialed the number ourselves. Message machine. Maybe you guys can get a warrant for the tape."

"Okay. Slow down just a second. Ms. Glade is there. She is changing her tire. Maybe she left the tire iron behind and the bad guy smacked Hammond."

Chief Winkle shook his head once and asked, "Then what's the motive?"

"Robbery," Donovan replied. "Detective Camacho tells me the dead man's wallet is gone."

"No wallet, but probably no robbery either," Winkle said. "Blinky Hammond had a five-thousand-dollar diamond ring on his pinky and a ruby worth a couple of grand in his left ear."

"Jesus," Francisco said.

"Yeah," Winkle continued. "The murder was made to look like a robbery. Anyone who hangs around long enough to grab an eye would have checked the pants, too."

"How can you be sure they didn't?"

"Because Blinky had five large folded in a Day-Timer in his jacket and another five hundred in his front pants pocket."

"So the robbery is a red herring," Mickey said.

"Our umpire has his wallet," Francisco said.

"What do you make of the missing eyes?" Winkle asked.

"Kill the blind umpires," Donovan suggested. "Tear their eyes out."

"Maybe," Chief Winkle said. "I've screamed the same thing at Fenway Park when the Yankees were playing the Red Sox."

Francisco got chesty. He suddenly remembered the "Boston Sucks" button of his Bronx youth. "I done it at Yankee Stadium when Looie Tiant was pitching. I may like you well enough, Chief, but if I have to like Bill Lee and Carlton Fisk for us to get along, this is not going to work out."

"Fuck Bucky Dent."

"Hey, I hate the Mets, too, but how could Bill Buckner miss that ball?"

"Hey," Winkler replied. "I've seen you guys misplay ground balls, too."

"The Yankees?" Francisco asked.

"No, I mean the NYPD," Winkle snapped. "You still haven't solved your last Central Park jogger murder."

The homicide investigation was degenerating into a sports-radio talk show.

"Gentlemen," Donovan said, and clapped his hands together. "Let's get back to *our* game."

"Sorry."

Francisco was taking notes in a blue memo book. He exhaled and refocused on his list. "Let me ask you something else, Chief," Francisco said. "We found something on our guy's shirt. The lab is doing a DNA test on it."

"What was it, blood or saliva?"

"Tobacco juice," the city cop said. "Somebody may have spit on him at the park. Maybe a player. Maybe a fan."

"Well, that's interesting," the county cop said.

"Why?"

"Because we have tobacco juice at our crime scene, too."

"Well," Mickey said, "that can't be Ginny Glade."

"Right," the country cop said. "So we're thinking that, at the very least, she had an accomplice."

IRT Subway, Times Square Police Substation, Manhattan

The cops caught him riding on the Number Seven train between Grand Central Station and Times Square. He claimed he was going to take the F train to Brooklyn, where he was supposed to meet Shane Heath in the Borough Hall station. The cops listened to the story and wired the suspect up, but Shane Heath never came to meet Emory, alias Bugout, Newby.

The cops were surprised because they believed the story and because Bugout had a key to Ginny Glade's apartment. They couldn't understand why the kid had only stolen a triple-A all-star trophy when he could have taken a computer or a stereo.

"Shane Heath hired me to steal this trophy for him," Bugout said. "He said his wife wouldn't give it back to him."

"Anything more?"

"Yeah, he said his wife wouldn't be home, but he said I could smack her if she came in unexpected."

"Lovely," said the detective.

The cops from the Manhattan burglary squad found Shane Heath watching a television game in his Fort Lee, New Jersey, apartment. He invited them in for a beer. When they asked if he knew anybody named Bugout, Heath asked them to leave and suggested they call his lawyer. They were leaving when he asked an odd question.

"What happens to my trophy now?"

"It's evidence. We keep it until your wife tells us what to do with it."

"Motherfuckers."

"What?"

"My old neighbors tell me Ginny is screwing cops now. Good night."

Heath wasn't much of a suspect. Bugout wasn't so hot either. And the assistant DA laughed out loud when the burglary suspect asked to make a deal on his Queens drug case.

"Ain't this some weak-ass shit?" Bugout complained. "All I got is half a Ben Franklin."

"What else you got?"

"Nothing, unless you promise me I gets a deal."

"For what?" the assistant DA asked, about to give up on the punk.

"How about if I knew a murderer?"

"Who?"

"This guy who says he killed a Brooklyn clergyman who tried to beat him on a kilo of coke."

"What kind of clergyman, Mr. Bugout?"

"You know, that gay priest I seen on *Eyewitness News* a couple of weeks ago."

The cops took Bugout's handcuffs off and called the Brooklyn DA.

Mike McAlary

City Room, New York Post Standard, *Manhattan*

"We got a dame, a good-looking one, as a suspect," Nigel Scrum, the editor of the *New York Post Standard*, told his ace police/court reporter, Mike Bangle. "Jesus, just think of the possibilities," he continued. "The girl as the bad guy. Who knows where this could go?"

"It goes on the front page, boss," replied Bangle, who averaged three byline stories a day. "If someone started killing people to get The Mayflower Madam's black book, it wouldn't be as good."

"What was that phrase you old hot-type guys had for the front page?" Scrum asked.

"We called it 'The Wood,'" Bangle said. "They used to hammer the type in place on a piece of wood."

"This is the wood for a week."

The umpire murders made the front page of the news section, and the sports section. The paper even printed an extra edition with a photograph atop the guest column of Arlon Kettles, their man on the scene in New Hampshire.

"The prime suspect is no lady," he began. "To cross her is to take a chance on dying. She is a brooding, dusky killer, the police believe. She learned the art of survival on the great green lawns of Wimbledon and Forest Hills. And now she is stalking the sporting world, stabbing and butchering the great umpires. The cops have already nicknamed the frosty suspect. They're not fooled by the treacherous legs or pouty lips. In county and city police stations, homicide detectives have nicknamed Ginny Glade, 'the Sore-Loser Slayer.'"

The *Post Standard* sold 700,000 papers the first day. On day two, the *Daily News* broke a million in circulation for a weekday paper for the first time since the Gulf War. Even the *Times* allowed the news to grace the front page, with the headline, "Gracious Tennis Champion Is Focus of Murder Investigation That Jars Sporting World."

Just after deadline on the first day, Arlon Kettle called from Manchester. "Have I got a job or what?" Arlon asked Scrum.

"The starting salary is a hundred and twenty-five thousand. Two years."

"Three years with a fifty-thousand raise over the term of the contract. I want the same medical plan you have."

"Okay. What's next, mate?"

"Go check out your office fax machine. I got a letter."

"From whom?"

"Our killer. Hold it until tomorrow."

Over the next week, some remarkable events occurred. The Yankees were playing an exhibition game in Puerto Rico. A couple of triple-A umpires had traveled south to do the game. The tabloid's crack baseball writer had traveled south to do a story on Ginny's former husband. But when he got there, he discovered a greater story. The Puerto Rican pitcher, no matter how he tried, could not throw a strike to Shane Heath. And after the second at bat, Heath had walked the first two times up. He was grooving Little League strikes. Heath, who'd flown to San Juan after Bugout's arrest, wouldn't swing and the petrified ump wouldn't call a strike. Ginny's former husband caught on quickly. When Heath stole second base, the rifle-armed catcher threw him out by ten feet.

"Safe," yelled the terrified ump.

The coach of the Puerto Rican national team rushed onto the field. "Are you fucking blind?" he asked.

"Not ordinarily," the umpire yelled. "Mr. Heath was safe. And I'm safer."

The coach protested, as he was almost certainly entitled to. They showed a tape of the play on the center-field television. Fans threw batteries on the field. The coach continued to scream.

"You are out of here," the ump yelled. "And I am right behind you."

As far as the *Post Standard* could tell, the ump was the first to throw himself out of a game. Under the stadium, the ump explained. "I can't work under these conditions. I just suspended myself for sixty days."

It was absurd, sure, but the sporting world was just getting rolling.

Midway through the game, the *Post Standard* writer stood and said, "Hold it now, guys. I just realized something. If I say Heath was out and the ump blew the call, what happens to me? What if this psychopath reads the sports pages? The way I see it, we're all in danger if we tell our readers what happened here today. Who's safe if they tell the truth?"

"Oh, that's bullshit," the gentleman from the *Times* said. "Even your least-deranged reader knows you can't be trusted with a fact. Hell, I've seen you get the wrong score on a Word Series game."

"Maybe the story has some holes," the *Post Standard* fellow replied, "but that's the way I'm writing it."

"Well, of course you will. You abandoned truth years ago."

The cancer quickly spread to other sports. The previous night, during a Rangers game in Madison Square Garden, fans began throwing rubber knives and water pistols on the ice after a referee disallowed a first-period goal. The city seemed to be in a rush to make good on the old bleacher bum cheer, "Kill the umpire." Someone suggested to the Madison Square Garden management that they allow the police to check a list of season ticketholders for arrest records.

"The killer is a season-ticket holder," said a mystery caller. "Mezzanine seat 7 K. I heard him plotting his revenge last year."

The cops followed him for a while. It looked interesting.

Almost overnight, it seemed, kids were spitting at and slugging umpires the country over. At a high school football game in Bellport, Long Island, a ref ruled that a winning field goal was wide to the right. The call probably cost the team a state championship. During overtime the crowd began to chant, "We want Ginny. We want Ginny." In Florida, several college-aged gentlemen came dressed for a game between Miami and Florida State University as female tennis players. These pranksters sat at the fifty-yard line under a banner that read, "Screw the 'Canes and Virginia Slim will get you."

Suddenly, rage was the national rage.

The killings quickly became a part of the twisted, American sports culture. Jets fans were particularly ripe. When the ref called back a Jets' kickoff return for a touchdown in the Meadowlands that weekend, the team's first in three seasons, the crowd began to pelt the ump with bubblegum eyeballs and shout, "You're next. You're next."

The *Post Standard* managing editor, Nigel Scrum, called his sports staff into his office. He was a Brit, and all he really knew was soccer. To be heard, he had to turn down a Manchester United game he had been watching on television. The American editors he hired were world-class brownnoses.

"Oh, please, leave that on," said one servile fellow who lived near the Ebbets Field housing project in Brooklyn. "I like their boots."

As the morning news meeting began, it was explained that the paper's reporters had been on the phone all night, making telephone calls the world over. The "Hunt for the Umpire Killer" had captured the wild imagination of the country. By noon of the first day, it was a national obsession. There were ten Web sites. The nation was frantic with the realization that some maniac was killing referees and umpires. Every game in every city was a version of Black Sunday.

The talk shows reeked of conspiracy. No one believed the easy story, that the killings were the sick work of one woman, a leggy tennis player no less. Everyone was scared. Umpires were afraid of making a ruling against any New York team. Callers to the sports talk-show host complained, "How can we be expected to beat the New York creeps and their referees?"

"We have become a nation of homer calls," quipped Phil Kruger, the paper's bemused and hairy sports television columnist. "I just checked with Las Vegas. They're carrying a line on the next umpire to be killed. Dizzy Meltzer, the NFL ref who blew a call against the Dallas Cowboys in the NFL championship game in each of the last two years is being carried as a two to one favorite to be carried out of the Super Bowl on a stretcher."

"And where is Ginny Glade?"

"Our man on the ground in New Hampshire says the cops got her hidden away. They're not sure if she is the suspect or the target. But she is in the middle, somehow."

"No shit."

"Anyway, they got a crazy story up there," another reporter began. "The head linesman in a Bruins game against the New Jersey Devils was found dead three hours after the game at a gin mill in

Mike McAlary

the Back Bay. A place called Crossroads, at the intersection of Mass Avenue and Beacon. We were there last year after the Yankees series. I don't remember anyone ever saying the place was safe to eat in. Anyway, the ump was found dead, sitting in a booth in the back. Witnesses said he just took a headlong divorce into his Buffalo chicken wings. The Boston newspapers speculated that he was poisoned."

"Was he?" the boss asked.

"No. The fat prick pulled a Mama Cass. He choked to death on a chicken bone."

"So what have we got, really?"

"Well, if the cops don't solve this soon," said the paper's genius sports columnist P. J. Moran, "every call by every referee in every American sport will be suspect. Don't you see? We've become a nation of sore losers."

The Jackster became a subject briefly after Camacho developed the information that America's tennis dad was seen in The Triplex, drinking. Some said he was there the night the umpire was killed outside. Mickey didn't like the coincidence.

Mickey Donovan, just back from New Hampshire, went right over to the Jackster's. As the leaves swirled at his feet, Mickey watched a woman come out of her apartment with Chinese food cartons and walk to the garbage room. She was wearing a bright-red Nike outfit. The cop followed the woman back to her apartment, put his ear to the closed door, and heard the Jackster bellowing on the phone. He went downstairs and got the phone number for the apartment, then called the number and said he was a lawyer for Jack's ex-wife.

Jack bolted out of the apartment and right into the inspector's arms. Mickey confronted Jack with the warrants and said he was going back to Florida in handcuffs. The Jackster began to cry. He was dating two women in the same building. One was a fashion designer. The other was a bartender at The Triplex. She was his alibi.

Driving South from New Hampshire to New York City

They were only a couple of hours' free of the rehabilitation center when the policeman's daughter made the request. By then they had already stopped at a little country jewelry store in Milford, New Hampshire. The store was called Oz and featured a collection of Dorothy plates and Tin Man pins. The place was wall-to-wall cheap silver, a pile of freaky bracelets and tie-dyed shirts. By the time Dillon left there, she jingled out of the place. She was covered with silver rings, bracelets, and beads. She had a collection of cassette tapes, too. They included the Grateful Dead standards "Suagree" and "Momma Tried."

"Can you take me to Forest Hills?" Dillon asked.

The child was in a time warp, aided by the abundance of hemp-worn, hemp-soaked, and tie-dyed clothing. Ginny had been a hippie girl for a summer, and had even tasted chocolate mescaline once at a three-day festival in New Boston, but the hippie stuff had really been before her time. Dillon was a throwback, and Ginny liked that because it reminded her of being a teenager again. She didn't even mind that the kid reeked of patchouli oil.

"You don't even play tennis," Ginny said. "I'd love to take you to Forest Hills, but why would you want to go there? To see the Arthur Ashe exhibit?"

"Who?"

"Arthur Ashe. The great tennis champion. He died of AIDS. A man full of grace and courage."

"He rode the white horse, too?" Dillon asked hopefully.

"What?"

Ginny was totally confused. She'd always thought she was hip until she'd met this kid.

"Sorry," Dillon said, playfully slapping her right hand against her left forearm. "You know, my friend. Heroin."

"Oh, God no," Ginny said, her foot absently touching the brake. "He got it in a blood transfusion at a New York hospital after he suffered a heart attack."

"Sure, like, that's what all the junkies say, man," Dillon replied with a sigh. "Blame your virus on bad blood."

Dillon rubbed her head. It was freshly sheared. She was wearing an earring in her left cheek. "What did my dad say about us going back?"

"He said he trusted you not to get high and trusted me not to allow you to get high," Ginny said.

"That's my dad," Dillon replied. "Dueling surveillance. He has me watching you and you watching me."

They weren't sure where they were going or even for how long. Ginny had parked her car a half mile away and waited. Dillon rambled down the road about half an hour later. Ginny's picture was on the front page of every newspaper by then. Dillon's father had called her five times in one hour at her mother's home in New Boston. Hanna had called to say she could smuggle Ginny into Canada.

It looked bad. But Dillon didn't seem to mind. Ginny could bring her back in a day. It was fun to be impetuous. Running away was the first spontaneous thing she had done in years. It was liberating to be young, footloose, and dangerous.

"Look at us," Dillon said. "Thelma and Louise on steroids."

When they had stopped to fill the car with gas in Amherst, a tattooed kid with a rugged voice and shoulder-length chestnut hair tied back in a ponytail spotted Dillon and asked, "You like The Black Crows?" Dillon responded, "They're wannabes." The boy then said, "They're playing tonight in Brattleboro. I got room in my van. You'd have to sleep in my bag, of course."

Dillon said, laughing, "Nah, but thanks for freakin' tryin'."

Ginny was impressed. The rawness of the kid's sexuality excited her.

"Arthur Ashe really was exposed to AIDS in a hospital," Ginny said. "But he never asked, 'Why me?' He once said that if he asked why he had been chosen to die, he'd have to ask why he had been chosen to live."

"Everyone with the virus blames somebody," Dillon said. "If I jumped that kid's bones back in the station, he'd blame me in a month."

Ginny hit the brakes again. She was afraid to speak, but she found her voice. "Have you even been tested?" she asked.

"Yeah, Tennis Mom," Dillon said. "I'm clean. But I got hepatitis last year. I was way sick. My liver was major-league fucked up."

Dillon rubbed her head roughly until her wrists jingled. "You think I like this hair?" Dillon asked.

Ginny replied, "It seems popular."

"When I got hep, my hair fell out," Dillon said. "It doesn't grow back right. I had to go skin."

"Well, the do—if that's what you call bristle—works," Ginny said. "It takes courage to be different. And that was Arthur Ashe. Anyway, the last time I saw Ashe was at a rally for racial peace at the St. John the Divine Cathedral in Manhattan. He was saying, 'Hey, sometimes life throws you a curve.' I know it's a cliché, but coming from that man, under those circumstances, well, his courage was empowering."

"Yeah, well, like, whatever," Dillon said and shrugged. "Lots of people die of the virus. Why shouldn't tennis have one? Is this supposed to be one of those meaningful conversations? 'Cause I'm lost."

So was Ginny, although she delighted in conversation that could veer off crazily in any direction at any point.

"So, again," Ginny said, "why this sudden interest in tennis and Forest Hills?"

"What does Forest Hills have to do with tennis, anyway?"

"You're kidding me, right?"

"No."

"Forest Hills used to be the capital of the American tennis world. Forest Hills Gardens, where the club is situated, is a neat, hidden neighborhood in Queens filled with Tudor homes and chestnut trees. Almost no crime. The United States tennis championships were played there before they moved them off grass and built the Arthur Ashe Stadium for the U.S. Open near Shea Stadium about twenty years ago."

"Well, I don't know about that. I just heard it was a good place to hear bands."

"What?"

"They have the Further Festival every year in Forest Hills Stadium," Dillon said. "It's named after the destination plaque on one of the first acid tripper's license plates. You know, further, like, as far out as you can go."

"Oh."

"Didn't you ever hear of Ken Kesey and the Merry Pranksters's chartreuse Volkswagen microbus?" Dillon asked. "This was before vans and four by fours. Back when a Jeep was still a Jeep and not a Cherokee. It was in the old eight-track life."

"Yeah," Ginny said, "but that was twenty years before *my* time."

"Yeah, well, whatever," Dillon said. "I went there last year and heard Mickey Hart jamming with Planet Drum. The long, strange trip continues every year. Jerry's dead but a lot of the guys from his band still play. Bob Weir. Hart. You get pretty stoned. It's the only sane moment in New York City."

"It sounds like a time warp," Ginny decided.

"Yeah, but the sounds are vibrant, and pretty Deadlike," Dillon said. "It can be a searing day, Tennis Mom."

"God, it's almost sacrilegious," Ginny said. "Forest Hills Stadium has come to this."

"You should be happy anyone even knows the place exists."

"I could take you," Ginny said. "But you have to let me show you around the whole place, the clubhouse, the grass courts, everything."

"Cool," the kid said.

"Just a little test, Dillon, okay?"

"Uh-huh."

"Did you ever hear of Rosewall, Laver, Goolagong, and Billie Jean King?"

"Not really," Dillon admitted, bored. "I think I heard of Rosewall, though. That's the place in Arizona where the UFO ship crashed."

"Scary," Ginny said. "The town is named *Roswell*, not *Rosewall*, Dillon."

"Fine," Dillon said, pouting. "Don't like my answer. Well, let me give *you* the culture test. Who's Jorma Kaukonen? Who does he play for?"

"I have no idea," Ginny said. "Sounds like a doubles player from Hungary I used to know."

"ZZZZZZZZZ!" Dillon said in an annoying buzzerlike voice. "He used to sing with Grace Slick in The Jefferson Airplane."

"Oh, that is even before my time, Dillon," Ginny said. "They were Jefferson Starship by the time I caught them."

"How about Arlo Guthrie?" Dillon asked.

"You can't know him. He was singing 'Alice's Restaurant' before Kenny Rosewall, Rod Laver, and Arthur Ashe became household names."

"They were never names in my household," Dillon said.

"Further," Ginny said and sighed. "That license plate makes more sense all the time."

Morning, Holiday Inn Motel, Manchester, New Hampshire

The major called Mickey Donovan in the morning. The cop was shaving and getting ready for the trip back to the city. Francisco was sipping coffee at a table. The phone rang and Mickey could tell by the way Francisco handled the call that they were in trouble.

"I'm sorry, sir, this is his assistant. I'll put the inspector right on the phone."

Francisco walked to the bathroom and pointed to the extension on the wall. He held his hand over the phone, saying, "It's Himself," Francisco said.

"The commissioner?"

"No, Mister Himself."

Mickey dropped the razor and picked up the phone. "Yes, Your Honor."

"Game, set, and match," Mayor Caruso said. "I was just getting set to play my morning match against Judge Green from Queens out at Forest Hills this morning when I realized I have already won my greatest match."

"Excuse me, sir?"

"Oh come on, Inspector," the mayor said. "You and that power-crazed police commissioner have lost. I know everything. Everything about your daughter, Inspector. I had hoped to be delicate about this, but there is really no chance of that now, is there?"

"Go ahead, sir."

"The daughter of the commissioner's supercop is a junkie," the mayor gushed. "I had hoped to be a better sport about this, really I had. But I am not a man for the indelicate. We have a photograph of her buying heroin in the village. I also know she was at a homicide scene. And now she's on the run."

"I have her in a detoxification unit in New England, sir," Donovan said. "We're going to get through this."

"Check again, Inspector," Caruso said. "She flew the coop, as the cops say. And believe me, they're all talking about it."

"I think not, sir. I gave her permission to go back to the city for a couple of days with a friend."

"Don't you mean she ran off with your prime murder suspect?"

"Your information is wrong on both counts, sir. Ginny Glade is not our bad guy."

"Forget Glade, Inspector," the mayor continued. "Your problem is your dirtbag kid. The *Post Standard* called me about the girl an hour ago. They want to know how the cops are going to clean up the drug problem in their city when they can't even clean up their own families."

Mickey was biting his lip. He had a white-gripped hold on the phone. He would not breathe for fear of telling the mayor to go fuck himself. And that was obviously what the mayor wanted. "I'm just trying to save my kid, your honor," Donovan said. He paused a full beat. "Are you done, sir? I'd better go check on her."

"No, Inspector, I'm not," the mayor said. "The New Hampshire cops report that they are going to put out an arrest-on-sight order for Glade, their chief suspect in their umpire murders, and Miss Dillon Donovan. They were seen together in a car just twenty minutes from the state border."

"Shit."

"Oh yes, big shit, Inspector. I am sending my detectives from the department of investigation up to look for them. They work in tandem with some federal agents."

"Good-bye, sir," Mickey said.

"Stay tuned, Inspector. By the time *Nightline* comes on tomorrow, you and the commissioner will both be trying to teach zero tolerance techniques in Mexico."

"Mr. Mayor," Mickey said, "I say this with all due respect, sir."

"What's that, Inspector?"

"Piss off, Mr. Mayor."

Heading South

They stopped listening to the radio because the news made them uncomfortable. Ginny found it almost surreal to hear her name without hearing a sports score attached. Although technically the cops were looking for them, Ginny called Camacho every couple of hours to give them their location. Once they cleared the Mass Pike in their rented car, they didn't have to worry about being spotted by the cops. They'd rented the car from Jalopy Inc. on the west side of Manchester. The salesgirl, a gum snapper wearing a T-shirt celebrating Marilyn Manson (Ginny hoped it wasn't a cult, and Dillon assured her that it was a band) apologized between bubbles for the computer being down the whole Labor Day weekend.

"That's cool," Dillon said. "I'm down for the weekend, too."

Dillon used her license to get the car, a Ford LTD, and Ginny used a tennis-company credit card to pay.

They would be invisible on the road.

"I have one of my dad's Visa cards, too," Dillon said. "I only used it once, when I was on the road following the Dead. My dad told me, 'If you are ever on the road and you want to get help, use the card. I can find you.'"

"Gee, that's smart."

"I started to float and forgot," Dillon said. "Coming out of a daze, I used to buy pancakes at a Howard Johnson's in Seattle. He showed up the next day."

Dillon was the better fugitive. When Ginny started to use an ATM machine at a rest stop near the Connecticut border, Dillon stopped her.

"If they're watching a database in New York, the cops can be here in five minutes," Dillon said.

"But we need gas."

"Pay with this Exxon card."

Ginny looked at it. She did not recognize the name—Bridget McCarthy.

"Who is that?"

"My grandmother Bridget," Dillon said, smiling. "That's her

maiden name. She taught me half of the bad stuff I know. She was married to The Troubles. Up the rebels and all that. Now fill up the tank."

"God, you are a walking revolution," Ginny said, laughing. She kissed her on the cheek.

Ginny had a little surprise of her own. They had just walked through the line when Ginny spotted her. Hanna waved them over to the back table. She had a half-eaten Roy Rogers hamburger in front of her.

"Oh, no," Ginny said.

"Just for old times' sake," Hanna said. "I had two while I was waiting. You said you'd be here by two P.M. You're two hours late. I was just starting to think about having a couple of chocolate shakes. My God, Ginny, remember that McDonald's by the Nickerson Field House in Boston where we practiced?"

"It's not a happy memory," Ginny said. "I thought you'd develop colon cancer in one sitting."

"You saved my career," Hanna said, "gave me a life."

Ginny and Hanna had become forever friends as kids. Or as she explained to Dillon, Ginny had taught her hygiene and Hanna had taught Ginny ground strokes.

"One winter we both played doubles for a world tennis team named the Boston Lobsters," Ginny said. "Hanna's uniform was the only seafood she ever touched. At night, she dreamed of playing for the golden arches and became a San Diego Padres fan."

"Didn't McDonalds own them?" Dillon asked.

"Exactly."

As Ginny explained, Hanna had been the only seventeen-year-old in the world who still burst into laughter at the sight of The Hamburgler. One night as they had traversed the Massachusetts Turnpike, Ginny had taken Hanna to her first fast-food salad bar. Hanna had eventually lost the weight, but had kept her hug-a-bear attitude. By the time she was twenty-one, she was the number three player in the world. On the way there, she'd taught her friend Ginny a new wrist snap to her backhand. Occasionally, Hanna had refused to play in tournaments unless Ginny was added to the draw. That was friendship. And loyalty. They still played doubles together. But after ten years, Hanna had made $10 million in prize money. At twenty-seven, Hanna had decided to retire from the tennis life. Beating teenaged kids had put her in touch with something.

"She wanted her own kids," Ginny explained with a far-off look.

Hanna had married a motorcycle cop from Boston. Ginny had been with her when they'd played Boston that week and met the cop in Filene's Basement. He was handsome and slightly bowlegged. He had watched them walk down the street, then had parked his bike and followed the women into the store. Ginny had been there buying shirts when the leathery, tanned Adonis walked up to them. She had been desperate to find a size-sixteen neck.

"Is that what size your boyfriend wears?" the cop had asked Ginny.

"We don't have boyfriends," Hanna had replied. And then she'd eyed his abundant leather look and gotten scared. "Do you?"

"No," the cop had said. "And I ain't looking."

Hanna had been electric. "My friend buys size-sixteen necks because every man she ever liked is a size sixteen. She is just stocking up for love."

"Aren't we all?" the cop had replied.

They'd left together, and Ginny had whispered to the cop, "By the way, Officer, what is your neck size?"

"Seventeen. Sorry."

He was a suitable fellow. Ginny could sense his decency as they'd pawed the shirt bin. The next morning Hanna had arrived for a match at the starched Longwood Cricket Club in Chestnut Hill on the back of the cop's motorcycle. He had driven her to the clubhouse, blue lights and sirens wailing. The members had been aghast. Play had stopped on the grass courts.

Hanna had gone straight to the locker room, dressed, and then bolted out to her match on the stadium court. She'd won the match in forty-five minutes and had laughed out loud during her own service games during whole game. Hanna had rushed straight to the locker room after winning. She'd appeared briefly on the public-television station and had publicly thanked the Boston Police Department.

"For what?" the startled announcer had asked. "This is Chestnut Hill."

"Their *endurance*," Hanna had said, laughing. The interview had ended there. Back in the clubhouse, Hanna had squealed when she saw Ginny, and had jumped nude off the massage table.

"Did you know that cops get to take their handcuffs home at night?" Hanna had gushed breathlessly.

Ginny had begun to giggle. It had been the only time anyone on the women's tour had ever seen her laugh.

"I love you, Hanna," Ginny had said.

The cop and the tennis player were married the next summer. Hanna announced that they were going to circle the world on matching Harley-Davidson Sportsters. As a going-away gift, Ginny had given Hanna a booklet of McDonald's coupons and a matching tube of Preparation H. Husband and wife had roared off, laughing, a pair of silver handcuffs dangling from each of their belts.

Dillon watched them and munched on French fries as they retold the stories. She had changed into all those oversize clothes that Ginny had packed for her. She imagined that she looked like a gray smudge.

She noticed that Hanna was wearing a diamond-studded replica of a cop's badge around her neck.

"You on the job?" Dillon asked.

Hanna laughed. "You must be the cop's daughter," Hanna said. "I used to be married to tennis. Now I'm married to a Boston cop."

"Yeah, I saw the badge. I have one at home. It's a rivet, actually. My father's badge number. My father thought I had it done just to spite him."

"Did you?" Ginny asked.

"No, I thought it was cool," Dillon said. "One of my girlfriends wanted to start a band of NYPD girls and call ourselves The Badge Girls, you know, like The Spice Girls. It would have worked. We could have had plastic guns, had the whole dick thing working."

"And handcuffs?" Hanna asked.

"Definitely," Dillon said.

As they spoke, a state trooper walked into the restaurant. He went to the counter and began talking playfully with the oversexed, underage cashier. He kept one hand on his gun belt. He believed it made him sexier.

"What time you get off tonight?" the cop asked.

Hanna and Ginny put their hands over their mouths to keep from laughing. Dillon was steamed.

"Every time I see or hear that shit, I see my father," Dillon said. "He must have been a piglet all those years with my mother. They all do that Sergeant Ramrod shit."

"Your father doesn't strike me as that sort," Ginny said, perhaps hopefully.

"Oh, they're all led around by the one-eyed dog," Hanna said. "This guy has two perps sitting twenty feet away from him and he can't see anything beyond the length of his prick."

"Yeah," Dillon said. "My father must have been the same way. My mother broke up with him over a blonde patrol assistant," Dillon said. "She wasn't even a cop."

"I'm sorry," Hanna said.

"Oh, fuck her," Dillon said. "She's dead now."

"Your mother?"

"No, the cheater," Dillon explained. "She was cheating with my father on a rookie, who was cheating on his wife. The cop world is just one big gang bang. The rookie walked up to her one day on Queens Boulevard, grabbed her by the face, and just capped the bitch in her peroxided head. Then the rookie swallowed the gun himself."

"Did he have the bag on?" Hanna asked.

"Most certainly," Dillon said. "He was wearing full-metal jacket, his best funeral dress uniform on, right down to his white gloves. He even shined his brass buttons before going to look for her."

"Oh, that's terrible," Ginny said.

"Yeah," Dillon said. "The rookie was hot. He looked like Derek Jeter."

Hanna was unmoved. She leaned forward over her half-eaten burger, checked the cop at the counter, and asked, "Ginny, did you really kill Blinky Hammond?"

Ginny didn't hesitate this time either. She saw the tennis umpire's cantaloupe head and her swing. "I hit him with a perfect, two-fisted backhand," Ginny said. "It was a classic Chris Evert shot."

"Damn," Hanna said. "And why the rest of it?"

"I took the wallet to make it look like a robbery," Ginny said.

"No, I mean the rest of the violence. Why?"

"What rest of it?"

"Adonis was in a meeting with the cops up there," Hanna said. She waited a full beat before asking, "Why did you cut the freaking guy's eye out, anyway?"

Dillon slapped a hand on the table. "Wow, Tennis Mom, that's some real *X-Files* shit. You collecting them? Is it in your pocketbook? Let me see."

"Stop it, both of you," Ginny insisted. "I didn't touch his eyes. Blinky's problem was that he didn't have any eyes."

"Okay," Hanna continued. "Why did you stab him in the chest? Where did you get a shiv, anyway?"

"I didn't stab that fat fuck. I just swatted him in the forehead with the tire iron."

"This is screwed up, girl. Did you have a doubles partner?"

"I was by myself."

"The Jackster was there, Ginny. He puts you in the lot. Adonis heard him."

"I didn't stab him, and I certainly didn't melon-ball his eye."

"Then, okay, you didn't kill him, Ginny. What about this umpire in New York? The one who turned your dickless wonder of a husband into a national hero."

"That wasn't mine."

"That ump's eye was missing, too," Dillon interrupted. "I heard my father say that. Could you have had a blackout and done it? I do some wild shit when I get high."

"I've never been that high," Ginny said.

They discussed the case some more. The first murder was suddenly as mysterious as the second.

Hanna had been to an ATM in Boston. She handed Ginny five thousand dollars and one of her cash cards. "I have about twenty-five thousand in this account," Hanna said. "Adonis doesn't know about it. The password is one of my worst memories. Four digits. The score of our one and only match at the U.S. Open."

"Six-love, seven-six," Ginny said. "Maybe the most psycho score of all time."

"That's us, girl," Hanna said. "I love you. Where will you go?"

"New York, I guess," Ginny said. "But I don't think I can go back to my apartment."

"I know a place," Dillon said.

"Get out of here, then," Hanna said.

"You leave first," Ginny said.

"No, I'll stay and keep on eye on the fellow with the handcuffs," Hanna said. "Maybe have another hamburger for old times' sake."

They parted with a kiss.

SEVENTEEN

Mickey Donovan's apartment, Stuyvesant Town, Manhattan

Francisco was waiting in his car outside the inspector's building when Mickey called in from home. The detective sergeant had a clipboard on his lap. He had beeped the inspector as soon as he'd gotten the news.

"We got lucky, boss," Francisco said. "Could you meet me at the Seventy-fifth Precinct?"

"What's happening in East New York?"

"The room has ears," Francisco said. "And besides, there is somebody I want you to meet."

"Okay, Sergeant, but give me an hour to stop by One Police Plaza first. I haven't been in the office in a week. I want to see if she called."

"They're home safe," Francisco said. "I have forwarded all your calls to my cell phone. I have your messages and mail with me."

The inspector chuckled and said, "Francisco, did I ever tell you that I hate officious little pricks?"

"Yes, sir," Francisco said. "Me, too. But we can talk about this on the phone now."

"Go."

"We got something on that cop killed last week. A kid burglar caught in Manhattan says he had information on the dead priest. He says he got a friend Cookie who says the priest was trying to beat him on a deal when they met under the Brooklyn Bridge. This kid Cookie says he took the priest's pants down after he shot him to make it look like a sex thing."

"I like that. Do you believe him?"

"Yeah, and there's more. I met this Cookie today. He says Peter Heroin is his supplier. Picks his photo out of a drawer."

"So why is the retired detective dead and who is his mystery guest in the topless bar?"

"I've been studying Nesto's phone book. Remember that kid from sex crimes, Cosgrove, who said he heard the nickname Sy? That's not his name, really. It's SI as in CI—confidential informant. The club is using the airport to fly drugs on a small plane upstate. It's the prison run. This guy is giving information about Attica. I found Sal's notes in the tire well of his van. That's all, boss."

"Does the police commissioner's office know?"

"Strange thing about the PC, boss," Camacho said. "I think he's ready to quit on us. He went to Venezuela for a long weekend with a rich friend. Guy owns a couple of car dealerships. The PC goes as his guest. And the mayor's people are sniffing around."

"They are going to argue that he took an unlawful gratuity," Donovan said. "How can the cop on the beat not accept a free cup of coffee when the commissioner is accepting free vacations?"

"Exactly. Only the PC doesn't care. He told guys in his detail he isn't coming back, anyway. He's says he's been offered the chance to do a cable TV show on how to stop crime in your neighborhood. Computers. Detectives. You can hire the guys on his show to crack down on crime. The whole bit."

"Great," Donovan said. "This means we have no backup. See you in an hour."

An Hour Later, Seventy-fifth Precinct, East New York

They met inside the police parking lot at the back gate. This was arguably the worst precinct in the city. For a ten-year period, from 1985 to 1995, the precinct averaged one hundred murders a year. That was more bodies than fell in all of Great Britain each year. The neighborhood high school, Thomas Jefferson, saw an average of three students murdered a year. Morning classes included a mourning class where kids gathered to cry each day over the butchery. The school had better security—pocket scanners, walk-through metal detectors, and radar machines—than most Midwestern airports. Cops were culling the school's yearbook for mug shots until the American Civil Liberties union found out about it.

The place may also have been the most corrupt police precinct on the north side of New Orleans. (That city has the greatest police corruption statistic of all time: three cops on death row.) Only recently in East New York, as the murder rate plummeted, and the police force hired a former New York cop as a deputy commissioner who used zero tolerance techniques, had the situation improved.

It was still a hellhole, Inspector Mickey Donovan felt, but a glorious one.

Francisco was waiting for him in the parking lot, where criminals routinely swiped police officers' personal cars and had even a few weeks ago, stolen back a van filled with fireworks that the police had confiscated. In this same lot, when Mickey had been working on an internal affairs detail years ago, he'd found a getaway car. An off-duty cop had robbed a bodega and had then hightailed it to the precinct, where he'd put on his uniform and hidden from the detectives investigating the caper.

"We got lucky with the blade," Francisco said. "Cutco made only about forty of these ladles. They were part of a giveaway program. But they never gave the things away because the glue sucked and the ladles fell off. According to their records, they shipped a box of them to an Italian guy on Atlantic Avenue years ago, Argent's Silver. I drove past it on the way in. He should be open now."

———

Five minutes later they stood in "the box," as Dominic Argent, the proprietor, called it; he stood on the other side of his Plexiglass cage.

"Police," Mickey Donovan said, pressing his badge to the cage. "Could you open up? We want to talk to you."

Argent, a robust man, was curling a ten-pound weight in his right hand as he spoke. He had a two-shot derringer in his left hand. Only in this neighborhood, where cops were the bad guys, did store owners grab a gun when someone introduced himself as a cop.

"I can hear you right there," Argent said. "Badges mean nothing on Atlantic Avenue after Michael Dowd."

Mickey looked at Francisco, who shrugged his shoulders. It was a fair point.

"Okay. Do you keep shipping records?"

"Do you have a warrant?"

"I can get one."

"Well, it won't help. I don't keep records."

"None?" Francisco said.

"I used to keep records, pawn receipts, but no more," Argent said. "The cops were always dragging my records into court. Screw that. I'm out of the pawnshop business. I buy and sell silver. Period. It's a very good business, a very Latin thing."

"But dangerous."

"I'm licensed to carry. Check your own records. I've shot four people in here in the last five years. One was an off-duty cop."

"Yeah, I know," Mickey said. "We were just looking to find out what you did with one box."

"Call my lawyer."

"Lighten up," Francisco said. "You aren't the bad guy."

"But you may be," Argent replied.

"This was a box of soup ladles," Francisco said. "No silver, not even guns. It's an odd thing. Maybe you would remember."

"Shipped from Cutco," Mickey said.

"Maybe I want a hundred dollars. Cash. Right now."

"What for?" Francisco said. "You don't have records."

"I have memory and information," Argent said. "You are a customer, after all."

Mickey reached into his back pocket. He didn't mind, really. This guy had been around enough cops and crimes to know the routine. He dropped the money into a plastic drawer. Argent put down the weight and pulled the money in. He counted the money, then dropped it into a tube. Francisco was impatient.

"So?" the cop asked.

"I had a son," Argent began. "Angelo, born in December 1957. He got stupid twice in his short life. The first time he pulled a gun while robbing a Pennsylvania Avenue gas station at the foot of the Jackie Robinson Parkway. He pistol-whipped some eggplant. Arrested an hour later. He gets five to fifteen in prison."

The store owner put down his derringer and picked up a cigarette. He smoked unfiltered Luckys. He had some kind of anchor tattooed on his left forearm. Mickey made him for a navy veteran and, judging from his age, maybe World War II.

"He is a good prisoner, they say, and even gets a job as a porter," Argent said, blowing smoke. "He got promoted to kitchen detail. He writes me a letter and says he is gonna make it. I was happy for him. I decided to help him some. He said they had no utensils. The inmates kept stealing them. So I sent the box from Cutco to the prison. It cost me a hundred bucks. The stuff was shit."

"Then what happened, sir?" Francisco said gently.

"Nothing," Argent said. "He got a better job in the kitchen. He was a pretty good athlete, too, the only white guy to play basketball at Thomas Jefferson in the seventies. Then he did the second stupid thing. He got into a fight during a game and punched a referee. It broke some rule they had among inmates. Can you imagine? They found him hanging by his uniform shirt in his cell later that night. Someone had shoved a silver whistle in his mouth for good measure."

"I'm sorry," Mickey said.

"So was his mother."

"One more question, sir," Mickey said quietly. "Where did he do his time upstate?"

"Oh, didn't I tell you?" Argent said, snuffing out his butt. "Attica."

Mickey began to back up. "Thank you, sir," Mickey said.

The old man hit the buzzer, and Francisco opened the door.

"Navy?"

"USS *Missouri*," Argent said. "They signed the treaty about a hundred feet over my head. I never saw the war end. The Japs and MacArthur had come and gone by the time I was allowed to come up."

"Well, you were still there. No one can ever take that away."

"Come on, Inspector. Look around you. I've been belowdecks my whole life." He buzzed them out with his left hand and picked up the derringer again with his right.

East Wind Towers, Upper East Side, Manhattan

Ginny and Dill spent the first night at the Rye Hilton in Westchester just to get their bearings. Ginny paid cash in advance. They spent the second night at Ginny's apartment. Victor gave her a quizzical look as she walked in.

"We had some difficulties while you were gone, Ms. Glade," Victor said, handing her a new set of keys. "The authorities have arrested a young man who claims he was employed by your wretched former husband to steal some of his possessions from your apartment. The fellow gained entry with a key and stole a trophy. We changed the locks."

When they were settled in her apartment, Ginny sat in her bed and she and Dillon watched movies all night. Dillon watched three Brad Pitt movies, one in which he played a cop whose wife was decapitated by a serial killer, one in which he played a horny vampire, and a third in which he played an IRA soldier hiding out in a cop's house.

"When your father checks my rentals this week, he's going to think I'm thirty-five going on fifteen."

"Don't tell me my father checks on the movies you rent, too?"

"Yeah, but for different reasons. You're his daughter. I'm his murder suspect."

"Both classifications suck. You can try what I tried."

"Huh?"

"Just keep renting those police-corruption movies—*Serpico* and *Prince of the City*—over and over. Then ask him, 'Mickey, do you steal, too?' That drives him crazy."

"I wouldn't want to face you on the tennis court," Ginny said.

That night Camacho showed up with his wife to take Dillon out.

"Just her," Camacho said. "We'll be back at midnight."

"And what am I supposed to do?"

"Mickey said he would be over in about an hour."

"Jesus, I'm a kept woman," Ginny said.

Mickey rang the buzzer at around eight P.M. He had a complete Italian dinner from Gazabo's in three neat bags.

"You make it hard to hate you," Ginny said.

"That's the idea."

Mickey placed the bags on the table. When he turned around, Ginny Glade had her hands at her sides, and said, "Should I be scared?"

"Actually, Ginny, I don't think you've ever been afraid of anything in your adult life."

"Oh no. You're wrong, Inspector. In the beginning, I was afraid of men."

"But not anymore."

"Is that what you want?" she asked, moving in closer.

"I think I want dinner." Mickey felt a rush of heat through his body.

"There isn't time for that."

"Oh sure there is. We can't make love for hours straight."

"We can try."

And then she touched him. He pressed against her and her mouth opened. Mickey Donovan actually closed his eyes. The cop hadn't done that around another human being in ten years. She tasted like butterscotch. He wondered if her eyes were open. She slid a hand onto his thigh and then his crotch. He had her blouse off, and was embarrassed as he fumbled with the bra strap. She giggled and took it off herself. He eased her to her carpet and immediately felt like a stupid teenager. They were groping and grabbing. This was the way he feared his daughter acted when she was with a boy. Ginny was on top of him and pinning him to the floor with her hips. And then the cop did not feel alone anymore. He opened his eyes and she was completely naked. He was still pretty much dressed and startled. He had imagined he would be asked to handle the pace of this. She was on him, pressing and pushing him through the floor. She leaned over him and pressed her bosom in his face. And he was afraid, afraid of his passion.

In the end, Ginny had miscalculated slightly. They were exhausted, spent, but finished in three and a half hours. The food was extremely cold. When the buzzer rang, Mickey met his daughter at the door. He was sure the room reeked of sex. Hell, he could taste it. If it did, his daughter had the good grace not to mention it. She gave him an easy smile, and when she noticed that Ginny was wearing a simple T-shirt and an old pair of Calvins she looked from Ginny's bare feet to the uneaten food on the table and offered her a knowing smile.

"Good night, Dad?"

"You two move to my mother's in the morning. Bert can keep an eye on you. I have to go upstate. Ginny, if you hit the buzzer on the key chain I gave you, then Sergeant Camacho will respond."

"Tonight doesn't change how I feel about your sidekick," Ginny said. "He's rude."

"Good night, Ginny."

She pulled him back into the apartment and told him about Babe Policano's tape with the mayor and the judge on it. Mickey smiled hugely. Moments later the cop gave Ginny an open-mouth kiss in front of his daughter and left, embarrassed.

Once he was gone, Dillon turned to face her roommate.

"Jesus, I'm gone one hour and you jump my father."

"It was a mutual lunge."

Dill held up her hand. "Talk to the hand, girl, because the ears ain't listening."

"He is a very passionate man," Ginny said. "A special man."

"Jesus, don't become my mother on me."

"In my state of mind, I'm more than vulnerable. Shit, I'm wheelchair accessible. Maybe it will pass by morning. Maybe I'll like a fireman tomorrow."

"The first new friend I get in a year and she's screwing my father."

"If you don't want me to see him again like this, I won't, Dill."

"Right, right. Let's just get some sleep. I hope you remade the bed."

"Don't just blow me off, Dill. I think you know enough about me by now to know I cherish my misery. So if it will destroy me not to see him again, I might just do it."

Dillon walked over to Ginny and hugged her. She held her tight and began to cry. "Well, at least he can make one of us happy, Ginny. But I'll tell you right now, if you start acting like one of those dopey cop wives, I am going to become the biggest Yankees fan in the city."

"Fair enough, Dill. If you catch me cheering for your father, you can root for my worthless ex husband."

In the morning, over coffee, Ginny seemed more sensible. She didn't quite understand how this could work.

"So we're going to hide from the cops in your grandmother's house," Ginny said. "That doesn't make much sense."

"You don't know my grandmother. She hid her husband in a piano bench when the Black and Tans came looking for him," Dillon said. "She sat on the bench and played 'God Save the Queen' until the soldiers left. No one dared ask her to get up."

"A priceless piece of theater," Ginny said.

"My grandmother is a lethal woman, still," Ginny said. "My hero."

Ginny remained quiet for a moment and tried to remember the odd toughness of the women she'd read about in Frank McCourt's book about his childhood in Limerick. *Angela's Ashes* was all she knew about the Irish. In some ways, she had argued after reading the book, the Irish ladies who first emigrated to New York had been the first women's tour.

"Read about these women and tell me we have it tough," Ginny had told Hanna. Ginny had wanted to set up a readers' group of tennis players. But even the older women preferred magazines. It was sad, but it was her life. Ginny couldn't quite understand why she was even spending time with Dillon. The kid was magnetic, certainly. And she liked the idea of helping her to a greater end than a needle.

"Bridget is kind of protective about her son," Dillon said, smiling.

"So if you don't tell her you're doing the nasty with her precious boy, we could have a slammin' time."

"I'm not sure I don't want to talk to the police in New Hampshire," Ginny said. "I didn't stab that idiot. And I certainly didn't cut out his eye."

"But you hit him in the head," Dillon said. "Life is cheesy, but if you hit the guy in the head, you are going to get busted, Butthead."

They drove into Brooklyn on the Brooklyn-Queens Expressway. It might have been the worst five-mile section of road in America. The only people who ever made decent time crossing the road were marathon runners. Every year, they steamed across the Kosiusko Bridge and down into Queens and across the Fifty-ninth Street bridge. The rest of the year the road was a parking lot. Traffic and construction at any hour. The road was an impossibility.

As they approached the Williamsburg Bridge, Dillon tuned the radio to Mongrel Man's sports-radio talk show. They listened for the same reason that people slow down when they pass a car wreck— terror is captivating.

"Who is Ginny Glade anyway?" Mongrel screamed. "Probably just a bull dagger. All women who play that much golf and tennis are switch-hitters. But a killer? No, I'm not buying. One woman, a freakin' namby-pampy tennis player, can stab American sport in the heart? No. This is bigger. This is some kind of group. One prissy girl can't be doing this. This is a hit team. Maybe even Middle Eastern terrorists—destroy Americans by killing their sports. But a lace-panty killer? No, this homey don't play that. Anyway, we got to make some money. Back in sixty seconds, after these commercials."

"You should kill *him* next," Dillon said, snapping off the radio. "We're dead in this traffic. Let's take the bridge into New York. Kill an hour."

"And do what?"

"I need to get pierced," Dillon said. "I know a needle shop on St. Mark's."

"Forget that," Ginny said. "None of that heroin crap."

"Not that needle, Tennis Mom," Dillon said, laughing. "A piercing needle. Maybe a tattoo."

Ginny was embarrassed again.

"I forget," Dillon said. "I can't bang square people through my round life . . . But you can bang my father?"

Midnight, Gracie Mansion

"Thanks for seeing me, Mr. Mayor," Police Commissioner Flynn said as he entered the mayor's study and closed the door.

"Your timing is very good, Flynn," Mayor Caruso said, tightening his bathrobe before he sat down at the desk, across from his police commissioner. "I was about to summon you up here. Where the fuck have you been? You can't leave town without notifying me, Flynn. Hell, I don't even leave town for more than forty-eight hours."

"Yeah," Commissioner Flynn began, "well, I've come up here to tell you I'm leaving my post. Our computer programs are in place. Stay on autopilot and you'll cut the murder rate in half. You saved New York by hiring me, Mr. Mayor. I'm done here. I have a chance to make big money. And I'm not sure the chance will come again. Worldwide Film is going to hire me to run their global investigations and security operation."

He handed the mayor a letter across his oak desk. Caruso didn't even bother to read the letter before ripping it in half.

"Not so fast," the mayor said. "You have some more pressing legal problems you have to face in New York City first. Frankly, Flynn, I'm going to fire you in the morning. And you are going to take it, too."

"Excuse me?" Flynn said. He was dead calm. He sat back and crossed one leg over the other.

"First of all, we caught your main guy, Inspector Mickey Donovan, covering up for a serial killer. His teenaged daughter is a junkie. We have photographs, witnesses. So Donovan goes. But you go first, Flynn. You are going to admit you have been taking free trips from enemies of the administration for the last year."

"Enemies of the administration?" Flynn said. "You sound like Nixon."

The mayor opened his drawer and shoved a stack of papers at his police commissioner. "Receipts of hotel and airplane tickets. Your name, not your credit card. Japan, the Bahamas, the Virgin Islands. The trips were paid for by Hank Travis, the left-wing publisher and worldwide brewery owner. Look closely. There's one page, dated this month, in there from Interpol. You friend, the one who uses his magazine to belittle my accomplishments, is going to be busted for shipping drugs in the bottom of his beer kegs. Tell me, Commissioner Flynn, did you tell your sugar daddy what days it was safe to deliver his poison to our city?"

"This is rubbish," Flynn said, "a complete crock."

"Maybe," the mayor said. "But you are going, and you are going out this way."

The mayor hit a buzzer. "Johnson, get in here and take our former police commissioner. He is done here."

Flynn smiled. Then he began to laugh. Johnson knocked on the door and entered the room as Mayor Caruso's face reddened.

"You think being fired is funny, Flynn?" he yelled. "You think going out as a crook is laughable? Get out, now."

Flynn didn't move. Then he stood up and said, "Mr. Mayor, do you have a tape recorder in this room?"

"Yes. Why?"

"Because I want you to play this."

The mayor nodded to Johnson, who closed the door. "What is it?"

"A conversation."

"Between who?"

"Between you and Judge Jim Parnell. Recorded last month. The couch you were sitting on was bugged. This is only a copy, but it's very clear. The judge doesn't speak much. You do most of the talking. I like the part where you say you don't care if this Irish terrorist killed a whole kindergarten full of kids. You trade a killer and a corrupt judge for votes. I don't really see you screwing around with me or Mickey Donovan anymore."

"Does he know, too?"

"Nope."

Flynn handed the tape to the now quivering mayor.

"This is the end of you, of course. Or it would be. I'll be in Key West when you want to talk again."

"Get out."

"It was fun saving your city, Mr. Mayor. Don't be bitter. Good night."

Parish Office, Holy Cross Church, Manhattan

Francisco handed Mickey his mail as the inspector opened the door to his cluttered basement office in Holy Cross Church.

"That should be interesting," Francisco said.

It was mostly police stuff. Everything mailed to One Police Plaza was sent through a metal detector now, so no one mailed dangerous surprises anymore. Even internal affairs had an E-mail address, so regular mail that included a nasty anonymous letter from some dirty cop with a sudden burst of conscience about another crooked cop was scarce. Most of the mail, opened by Francisco before Mickey arrived, was boring.

Internal affairs wanted to talk to Mickey about an old Brooklyn case. The commissioner wanted him to attend a medal ceremony. A kid from the Bronx, who'd shot it out with a gang, was getting the Combat Cross. The New York Shield Society wanted him to speak. The publisher of the *Daily News* wanted a NYPD plate for his limo. The PBA president, Louie Baptiste, wanted help from the mayor's office on management. John Mason, deputy commissioner for public information, had resigned and had returned to television. The honor society wanted Mickey's help getting the troops to pay their dues.

This left a manila envelope marked, "FOR INSPECTOR'S EYES ONLY," in block magazine letters and postmarked from East Flatbush, Brooklyn, his mother's neighborhood. It was probably more nut mail.

Mickey sniffed the envelope first. It smelled of Aqua Velva. Then he opened the letter and dumped the contents on his lap. A three-inch-wide, one-inch-long Bausch & Lomb plastic contact lens holder fell out with a letter. The piece of paper contained a message cut from block magazine letters.

TRY THESE ON. THEY'LL HELP YOU SEE ME.
UNTIL NEXT TIME.
THE SORE LOSER.

He dropped the letter on the seat beside him. "Plastic gloves?" he asked.

"Top drawer," Francisco replied. "What have we got?"

"Maybe nothing." Mickey snapped on the disposable plastic gloves. They matted his hairy hands. He smelled the letter again. The cologne covered a dead smell.

"I don't want to spill this," Mickey said, placing the contact lens case on his desk. He unscrewed the hard white plastic cap marked "L"—for left eye—first. He opened it and spotted the tiny yellow fleshy lens. He twisted the cover back on and opened the right lens holder. There was a fleshy lens floating in an eyedrop of Aqua Velva in that tiny well, too. He twisted the cover back on.

"We're in business," Mickey said. "Let's go right to the medical examiner in Queens. I don't want to chance One PP."

"What is it?"

"Well, they sure as hell aren't contact lenses."

"Then what are they?"

"It's only a guess, Francisco, but I'd say two corneas, cut from the dead eyeballs of our two umpires."

"Oh shit," Francisco said. "The price of poker just went up."

EIGHTEEN

Backcourt, Madison Square Garden, Manhattan

The basketball referee, Jonas Witherspoon, age twenty-nine, still lived in Fort Greene, Brooklyn. Last year he'd worked the finals in the East. Next year he might work the NBA Finals. He loved his neighborhood, and his neighbors loved the Witherspoon family.

The neighborhood was coming back. The Witherspoons had never left it. The ref's father, Hap Witherspoon, had run an appliance store on Washington Avenue, near a block of lovely brownstones. The referee's family was bigger than gentrification.

On July 13, 1977, the lights went out all over New York, scaring the hell out of the city. Even the Son of Sam, who was killing white girls with brown hair that summer, stayed home. When the lights went out, the thieves came out to play. The old man stood at his store door with a shotgun that night, talking, and tried to convince looters to leave him alone. They stole everything in his store, and the gun.

The old man stayed, and rebuilt his business. But he never trusted his neighborhood again. His son grew up to become a great basketball player, on the Division III level, at Brooklyn Community College. Jonas grew up suspicious and fast. He hadn't been good enough to become a major-league player but he'd become a referee three years before after a stint in the minor leagues. He was one of the biggest heroes in Fort Greene, after his father, who was bigger than neighborhood spite and petty revenge. No matter how big his kid got, the old man was the first referee in the Witherspoon family.

The basketball players liked Jonas became he wasn't what they called "a star fucker." Jonas could run up and down the court on the fast break with Michael Jordan but wouldn't allow the greatest player of their generation to run his mouth. Jonas had even dared to whistle His Airness for double dribbles. He had made another rare, even daring call, whistling Patrick Ewing for traveling. When Ewing had roared, and the Garden had booed, the ref had just folded his arms and said, "You didn't invent the game, Mr. Ewing. Or the rules. They will be here long after you, and me."

When Spike Lee had stood and screamed, "You are betraying Brooklyn, Ref," after Witherspoon fouled John Starks out of a game, Witherspoon had turned and said, "You're betraying your profession. Study the film before you speak."

Spike Lee sat down.

Jonas usually took the subway to work. He switched from the IRT at Brooklyn's Borough Hall and took the D or F train into Penn Station. Then he walked upstairs to the referee's dressing room and dressed for work in the Garden. On this fall night at the start of the exhibition season, Jonas carried his travel bag with him. His schedule called for him to travel to Philadelphia to referee a 76'er's game against the Boston Celtics the next night.

NBA life was easy. The weekend day game should be over around four. He could catch a 5:30 P.M. Amtrak south from Penn Station.

The game had been remarkably easy. For three quarters, anyway. John Starks had drained three-pointers early and often. The Knicks' opponent, the Indiana Pacers, had played a listless game, and entered the fourth trailing by fifteen points. But then Reggie Miller, the Knick killer, had caught fire. He'd hit ten three-pointers in the last ten minutes of the game. At the buzzer, Jonas had whistled John Starks for hacking Miller as he'd launched his last three-point attempt. Reggie had calmly sunk three at the line to give the Pacers a one-point win with no time on the clock.

"That was an audacious foul, but a magnanimous call," the Knicks television announcer, Walt, "Clyde the Glide," Frazier had explained. "*Bodacious* ending."

The crowd had booed as Jonas left the court. But it might have been the easiest call he had ever made. It was almost as if Starks had been daring him to make a call against New York.

"Damn, Jonas, you could die for this," Miller had said as they left the floor. "That call took world-class courage. I thought you would go dark in the last minute. Especially in this town, in this moment."

"I don't believe in blackouts," the ref had said.

An hour later the referee boarded the train in Penn Station. He had just entered the lavatory when he heard a knock at the door. The conductor had just announced that they were ten minutes from their next stop, Princeton, New Jersey. The train was fairly empty on a Saturday evening, traditionally the deadest hour of the train week.

"Just a second," Jonas said.

There was another knock.

A second later, Jonas cracked open the aluminum door. "Yes?"

The attack was timed to coincide with the train passing an intersection near Princeton University. All the other passengers heard was the train's horn. The powerful man in the Fila jacket pushed his way in and pressed the gun to the referee's face.

"Not a sound, Mr. Witherspoon," the man said. Jonas, recognizing a silencer on the pistol, said nothing.

The stranger brought his gloved left hand up, revealing an unmarked canister. By the time he saw the white spray, and felt the chloroform wet on his face, Jonas Witherspoon was unconscious. His last conscious thought was, Where's the whistle?

In death, the ref had been blind-sided by a moving pick.

Manhattan

Francisco hung up the phone and walked back to the table. He had just been beeped by the department's special operations unit. They were in a Manhattan deli on Second Avenue near the entrance to FDR Drive on Ninety-sixth Street, about to drive to the airport and catch the last USAir flight of the day to Rochester, New York. Attica was another two-hour drive west of the airport. They knew the route. Both men had been there before to talk to informants. Francisco was grim. He was biting his bottom lip and thinking.

"Good news and bad news, boss," Francisco announced. "Your daughter is still with Ginny, but the tennis player is not our killer."

"How do you know that?"

"Because we got another dead whistle-blower at a train station in South Jersey. Jonas Witherspoon. Male, black, twenty-nine. NBA ref from Fort Greene, Brooklyn. Got off the train with a male, white. Found dead an hour later on a wooden commuter bench. Shiv in the chest. Missing his right eye."

"So what do you want to do?"

"Our boys are en route to Princeton, New Jersey. I'll follow them. You go to Attica. Call me when you get to the hotel. The guy is gonna meet you there. Wally Lord. He's the athletic director for the prison. Used to run the kitchen. Knew our guy well."

"Anything else?"

"Yeah, my mole in the mayor's office called. They say Dillon was in New York City an hour after the train left. Ginny was with her."

"Where?"

"They were in the East Village. The DEA has an agent posing as the receptionist in a body-piercing parlor. The guy is working a federal drug case against the club kids. Positive ID on your daughter. Positive alibi for our witness."

"So what's bad about that?"

"Dill got another navel ring. Spent about three hours in the place."

"Okay, so Ginny is home with my mother. After last night, I'm very happy she didn't kill anyone this morning. But she could have done the others. We could have a copycat."

"Unlikely," Francisco said. "We got tobacco juice again. That detail hasn't made the newspapers yet. By the way, boss, what happened last night?"

Mickey didn't answer, but he was glad his life's crimes didn't include having made love to a serial killer.

Brooklyn

Bridget Donovan met them at the door. It was just before midnight. She had come outside and moved her Ford Corona from in front of the house to make room for their car. A couple of homeboys came down from the stoop across the street to watch her, protectively. Ginny took their bags out of the car. She was about to grab the racquets, too, when Bridget held up her hand.

"They should be safe in the car," Bridget said. "I don't think the neighbors need to know what you do for a living just yet, dear."

They climbed the five brick steps into the house. Bridget turned off the green porch light and fastened the metal door with a loud, deliberate click. She turned and pointed to the couch. "Sit," she said. "Don't mind the doilies. I made a spot of tea for you both."

Dillon stood and hugged her grandmother until a tear dripped over her pierced cheek. "The rebels have come home, Nana."

"And a fine mess you made."

The steam whistle on the kettle interrupted them. Bridget clunked off in a pair of black shoes she'd bought from the old nuns in the Little Flower Parish. Ginny silently watched. She remained silent, in awe almost, as Bridget returned with a tray of tea. She had two grapefruit halves in bowls on a white porcelain tray. They had been neatly quartered.

"Sugar?" Bridget asked. "From the look of you, I wouldn't imagine . . ."

"No thank you."

"I'll have hers," Dillon said.

"How long you been straight?" Bridget asked.

"A week, Nana," Dillon said. "But I miss it."

"I don't care piss-all about desire, dear," Bridget said. "But I can't have you running off and leaving me with missy here."

"Don't get your knickers in an uproar, Nana," Dillon said. "I won't go anywhere. Dad says she isn't really wanted anymore. He just needs to know where she is at all times."

Bridget turned to Ginny, narrowed her eyes, and gave the tennis player her best schoolmarm look. The once-over was intended to petrify her visitor.

"I never cared for that husband of yours," Bridget said. "He can't hit the curve *or* the fastball. But it could be worse. That bugger could play for the Mets."

"You prefer the Mets," Ginny said.

"I prefer curling, but you can't get a game," Bridget said. "So, by default, I'm a National Leaguer. That Bobby Valentine cuts a nice figure."

"I prefer the Mets, too," Ginny said. "Incidentally, did you know that Valentine was a champion ballroom dancer in his youth?"

"Well, he has the grace, love," Bridget said. "By the way, you don't seem like much of a serial killer to me."

"How about, like, a spree killer, then?" Dillon asked with a smug smile. "You know, like the guy who whacked Versace. She stalks the umpires in the name of sport . . ."

"No, she is too lovely for all of that," Bridget said, shaking her head. "Would you like a Manhattan, then, dear?"

Bridget clunked off to the kitchen again to pour herself a Manhattan. She could be heard breaking ice and rattling the vermouth bottle over an all-news radio station in the kitchen.

"This just in to the Ten Ten WINS news desk," the announcer said. "A referee from Brooklyn who made a controversial call against the Knicks at Madison Square Garden yesterday has been found dead at a rail station in South Jersey. Our reporter is on the way, but police fear that the Sore Loser Killer has struck again."

Bridget put down her hammer and clutched her glass. "Didn't you ladies come into New York from the other direction?" she called out from the kitchen.

"Yes," Ginny said. "I didn't do that one, either."

"I didn't say you did," Bridget said, smiling.

Mid-span, Triboro Bridge, Between Manhattan and Queens

Mickey met the Bronx detective on his way to LaGuardia Airport. The guy said he had new information about an old case. The cop was from a new outfit called the cold-case squad. The cops parked their cars at the tollbooth and walked part of the bridge, talking. There were so few new homicides over the last few years—the number had been cut to the Woodstock generation totals—that cops now had time to go back and work the old ones.

"Remember the umpire who got shot from the train a while back? We said publicly that it was a random shot."

"Of course. Melanie Morgan, William Tweed Field. But it wasn't a random shot. We had a witness who saw the guy step between the trains, wait, aim, and fire."

"Right. Well, I don't know how we missed this at first but I went back and found out she was a rape victim about twenty years ago at a summer camp near Utica. They made an arrest and she testified. The guy said in open court that he'd kill her when he got out. No one knew her name, of course, because she was a sex-crime victim. But I went deer hunting with a friend near Syracuse over the weekend and he asked what I was working on. My friend works for the state police. He had a piece of the rape case. He knew the victim's name, Inspector."

"Where is the perp? He should be out by now."

"The court files list him as Dustin Stone, but the name seems kind of hinky to me. I know what prison he went to, but I can't find him there. I don't have his inmate number yet. But my friend gave me an old brochure from the summer camp. It lists Melanie Morgan as a softball and field hockey instructor. There's her picture."

As Mickey held the old brochure, his eyes were drawn to another black-and-white picture that showed the camp's staff. The old Camp My-Tee-Na tennis instructor didn't look much like she did in the picture anymore. She looked to be about seventeen then. It was a little whimsical, and he'd never seen the similarity before, but with dyed blonde hair, Ginny Glade even looked a little like his daughter.

"Can I hold onto this, Detective? I'm going to Attica now. I'll look into finding this Dustin."

"Thank you, sir. If we get a good name, I can show the photograph to our witness."

"You have to put yourself in a position to get lucky."

"Yes, sir. You taught us that at the academy, too."

"How did you do deer hunting?"

"The deer threw a shutout at us, Inspector. I bagged the trip as soon as I heard this."

NINETEEN

Lobby, Holiday Inn, Attica, New York.

Attica Correction Captain Walter Lord was waiting near the hotel's front desk just as Francisco Camacho had said he would be, at
around four in the morning. The hotel was about ten miles north of
the prison. The hotel billboard said LIFERS WELCOME.

"Donovan?"

"Thank you for meeting me on such short notice." Mickey then
turned to the clerk.

"Are you in town to see an inmate?" the girl asked. "Do you have
a relative presently incarcerated in Attica? We have a special reduced
rate for visitation. And we have a deeper discount if the inmate you're
visiting is serving a life sentence. Just get us a mimeographed sheet
of your visiting-room pass."

"Happily, no," Mickey said. Attica was a strange town. It was a
homey place, in a western New York State agricultural way. But steel-
gray buses rolled into the town every day. The stores lived on people
buying gifts for the inmates and food for themselves. Everyone in
town knew someone who worked inside the prison. They were still
waiting for another riot. The worry never went away. It was a weird
place.

In the local bar, Donovan met guys who had worked in Attica for twenty years. That meant the guards spent ten years of their life behind prison walls. They did more time than many of the convicts. And though they cursed mother rapers and killers, they were living off crime, like cops. Murder paid the bills.

The hotel lounge had long since closed. Room service had stopped at midnight. Captain Lord, a hard, six-foot man with white hair, measured Mickey as he checked into the hotel. The prison guard had the habit of watching men, trying to read them. Survival depended on it. He walked into a small kitchen off the lobby and poured two cups of coffee. By the time he returned, Mickey Donovan, bleary-eyed but still excited by the chase, was standing at the elevator.

"Good morning, Inspector," Lord said, holding the coffee. "There is nothing open this side of Batavia at this hour. We can't get into my office till they finish the morning lockdown and head count. This is the best we can do. I brought an Entenmann's coffee cake, too."

"Thank you, Captain," Mickey said. "Nice to meet you."

The guard followed him into his room. Mickey threw his bag on the table and pulled a couple of yellow legal pads out of his carry-on bag. He placed them on the table next to his coffee and sat down.

"I could give you small talk, but I don't think we have time for that," Mickey said. "I'm offering all of this on a need-to-know basis. I am working on a serial killer. That's all I can tell you. As we go along, I'll fill in some blanks. I'm not a one-way street like the feds. I just don't have time. Okay?"

"Okay," Lord said, sipping his stale coffee. "Shoot."

"An intimate named Angelo Argent used to work in the kitchen," Mickey began. "He was stabbed and hanged in his cell about three years ago. You remember him?"

"Yes," Lord said. "Popular inmate. Pretty good athlete."

"Well, I don't think I care about that," Mickey continued. "His father is a half-assed pawnbroker in Brooklyn. He sent a box of soup ladles up here. They had to be checked in by Attica security. You would have a record. My sergeant, Francisco Camacho, tells me you might have been in charge then."

"I was," Lord said. "This was before I moved to the gym. I have a specific memory of the ladles. They were junk. Dangerous junk. The cups snapped right off. I sent them to the metal shop to be soldered. They came back a couple of days later. But they were still useless. Inmates wouldn't even have to sharpen them into shivs. They could be snapped off in the cafeteria. One kid did just that and was injured, but lived."

"So where did the ladles wind up?"

"I believe they were destroyed."

"Okay, now what about Argent?" Mickey continued. "Was he close to any other inmates?"

"Yeah," the captain said. "It's a strange story. He was very close to a basketball player here, a transvestite who could shoot the hell out of the basketball. Very tough player. She could dunk wearing those platform sneakers and eyeliner. This was ten years before Dennis Rodman, mind you. This inmate had a nickname, Mother Dearest."

"Go ahead," Mickey said.

"We played a game every year with the Harlem Globetrotters," Lord continued. "They came in here and Mother Dearest matched up with Meadowlark Lemon. Curly Neal, the showboat guard, even wore Mother's blonde wig for a quarter. The inmates were going crazy. Anyway, Mother Dearest killed the Globetrotters. She scored forty points on Meadowlark. This was legendary stuff. And the best part? Mother Dearest did it wearing culottes."

Mickey allowed himself a chuckle. It was a cute story. But it didn't bring him anywhere. "What does this have to do with Argent?"

"Oh, Mother Dearest was keen on Argent, but your boy was straight, a complete homophobe," Lord said. "They became best friends, shared a cell."

"Purely platonic?" Mickey asked.

"Probably as platonic as Attica gets," Lord said, laughing. "That reminds me of a story. Once, when I was a teenager, I was hitchhiking to Hackensack, New Jersey, when I got picked up by this hairy fellow. Five minutes into the ride, he looks me and says, 'Can we make love, son?' I measured the pervert, considered breaking his nose, but really needed the ride. I looked at him and said, "No, sir. We can't. But we can have a platonic relationship as far as the Tappan

Zee Bridge." The corrections guard began to hoot. Mickey laughed politely.

"So you were telling me about Argent and Mr. Mommy Dearest," Mickey said.

"They had a guy in the middle," Lord continued. "This guy was a hillbilly. Vargas.

"Is that his first or last name?"

"His first name was Dusty. As I remember it, he raped and tortured some teenaged girl at a camp near Utica."

"Hello—Melanie Morgan?"

"What?"

"Our first umpire. She testified against the guy. Go ahead."

"Yeah, Vargas was from the South, somewhere. At first we thought his name was Stone, but after he was here, the cops in Tennessee sent our parole boys a birth certificate for him. Anyway, he was the commissioner of our summer softball league. Can you imagine twenty-five Attica inmates with bats? It happens every summer and no one ever gets hurt because if anyone does, everyone knows the league is kaput. I had this wise guy from Mulberry Street who hit a double in his first at bat. He got to second base and asked for the ball as a memento. He yelled, 'This is the first friggin' thing I ever hit with a bat that didn't bleed. Can I keep it?' "

Mickey laughed.

"Yeah, and if an inmate hits it over the wall, everybody volunteers to chase the ball. So Attica has one tough ground rule: Anything over the fence is an automatic out."

"I think the Mets must play by the same rules," Mickey deadpanned. "They hit the fewest home runs in the majors. When I get back to New York, I'm going to run their roster through our computer."

"Yeah, their center fielder looks just like a guy I coached here a couple of years ago."

Mickey sighed. Some of this act was certainly a routine. But the cop liked it. Still, he wasn't here to gain comic material for the next ten-thirty—officer needs assistance—fund-raiser. "So let me guess," Mickey said. "The hillbilly likes Mother Dearest, but she has no interest in him."

"Right," Lord said. "The hillbilly thinks Argent is saying bad things about him. We have a football game that year. This is a good narrative, Inspector, excuse me."

The prison's athletic director sipped his stale coffee again.

"Tell it at your own pace, Captain Lord," Mickey Donovan said.

"You see," Lord continued, "in Attica, hate is a game. For example, inside those walls, we play a lot of sports. Inmates play tackle football with equipment donated by the Buffalo Bills. We play in the same yard where the state troopers were ordered in by Rockefeller. One of the guards that Rocky's boys shot that day was my uncle Eddie."

"It must be kind of eerie," Mickey said.

"Well," Lord said, "I carry a key from the gym to the yard in my belt. No one knows I have it. But I wouldn't work in the place now unless I knew I had a way out."

"I don't think I need to know that kind of detail," Mickey said.

Lord held up the palms of his hands. "Just telling you who I am," he said. "This guard is nobody's fool. After the riot, I trust no man— inmate, guard, cop, or politician."

"Fair enough."

"Traditionally, there are only two inmate teams. The Black Muslims have their squad and the white separatists have theirs. Every sporting event in Attica is a race war. But some stereotypes die hard, even in the joint. The black bigots have only two white guys on their team—the quarterback and their field-goal kicker. In turn, the white supremacists have only two black players—the running back and the wide receiver."

"It sounds like a better script than *The Longest Yard*," Mickey said. "But what has this got to do with my guy?"

"Vargas is a soccer player," Lord said. "He kicks field goals for the black team. Argent is his holder. Mother Dearest plays wide receiver for the white separatists. Anyway, she dropped the ball in the end zone, allowing the supremacists to win. Vargas won Mother Dearest as a prize. The next thing we hear is that Argent is hanged."

"Who's still here?"

"Mother Dearest is still in residence," Lord said. "Her knees are shot. She referees our intramural-league games now. Vargas was paroled two years ago. At the very end, he was involved with in-house drug trade—he had a heroin connection on the outside. He avoided getting caught and got out about eighteen months ago. Just took his bag of Red Man and disappeared."

"What?" Mickey asked. The captain saw goose bumps rising on the inspector's forearm.

"His bag of Red Man," Lord said, warming to the subject. "I told you he was a hillbilly. He was a juicer."

"What?" Mickey said again.

"White inmates chew tobacco, Inspector," Lord said, "just to keep the blow-job demands down. Or that is prison folklore, anyway. You ask me, Dustin Vargas chewed tobacco because he liked spitting on people after he beat them up."

Mickey was feeling like his old ghostly self. The Wraith sipped his god-awful coffee and smiled. He had a suspect and a name.

"You buried the lead, Captain Lord," Inspector Mickey Donovan said.

Elevated Platform, Amtrak train station, Princeton, New Jersey

Francisco eventually saw the note. They hid it from him at first. The locals were saving it for a team, the behavioral sciences division, heading in from Washington's FBI headquarters.

"What—you think the feds are your friends?" Francisco asked. "They're paving the world with one-way streets. The are the vacuum police—they suck, suck, suck."

One of the junior men showed him a photocopy of the letter. It was cobbled together with letters cut out from headlines, a total of three decks of type.

> Are you ready for some football? I am.
> Eye'll be seeing you, Donovan.
> P.S. I like Dillon better than Ginny.

Francisco stuffed the folded sheet in his pocket. This was taking an extremely personal turn. The country sheriff was standing near the New York cop's car. He had worked only on a handful of murders in ten years. The television vans were already beginning to fill the lot, their satellite dishes beginning to scratch the night sky. A half dozen TV commando types were crawling over his crime scene. They zoomed in on the covered body as it was loaded into the morgue wagon.

"Get those people back," the sheriff shouted to a subordinate. "Deputy Johnson, handcuff the next person who steps past the crime-scene tape."

He turned to Francisco and set his jaw. He was too proud to ask for help.

"I would move the body out," Francisco said. "Set up your command center in the middle of the lot. Put two cruisers with sawhorses at the entrance and exit. No one without a badge in or out."

"I'm not much of a public speaker," the sheriff said.

"You'll do fine," Francisco said. "Prepare a statement. Read it, but take no questions. All they want is a talking head. Announce you'll have a press conference at ten A.M. tomorrow."

"Thank you, Sergeant," the sheriff said. "He was stabbed with a shiv."

"Cutco," Francisco said.

"What?"

"That's his brand," Francisco said. "The referee should be missing his right eye."

"He is."

"Any witnesses, sheriff?" Francisco asked. He had not opened his notebook yet.

"The conductor sees a white male, maybe five-ten and forty years of age, help Mr. Witherspoon off the train," the sheriff said. "They're five steps out, with their backs to him. The conductor yells, 'What happened?' and the white guy turns slightly and says, 'He tried to drink the bar car. I'll get him home.' "

"Anything else?"

"He gets back on the train. The conductor thinks he was wearing a black warmup outfit. Fila. Green-and-white Reebok sneakers. American. Maybe Southern. Funny, but he didn't see him on the train."

"The referee is found on the bench," Francisco said. "The killer can see anyone who comes within five hundred yards of the stop. The light is out. He gets lucky."

"One more thing," the sheriff said. "There's a stream of blotchy black stuff on the guy's chest. We're not sure what it is."

"You'll find it's tobacco juice," Francisco said. "Our boy is a chewer. Get swabs from the DNA kit." Francisco excused himself and walked to a pay telephone.

"Get a numbers dump on all these pay phones," Francisco said. "The guy might have been stupid enough to have used one. Dust the bench and the booth."

Francisco walked to his car and sat down. Dawn was just breaking. After a few minutes, a cop walked over and knocked on the window.

"The Bell Atlantic guy says there was only one call after ten P.M. made on this bank of phones. At eleven-sixteen P.M., which is just a few minutes after the conductor sees our guys get off. There's one phone call to Brooklyn, New York. I wrote down the number."

The cop handed Francisco a slip of paper. Francisco read it, but said nothing. The detective was a world-class poker player.

"How long was our guy on with the Brooklyn party?"

"The connection was never made," the cop said. "They just dialed it collect, but hung up after it was answered."

"Thanks."

The cop walked away. Francisco watched him go and counted to ten. He tried not to fumble as he dialed Mickey's cell phone. Mickey Donovan, waiting in the hotel, answered on the second ring.

"I'm on a cell phone," Francisco said. "Two important events. Our friend mentions one relative in the note. When he's through with his business, he calls another relative."

"Whose?" Mickey asked. Francisco was being a little too cryptic.

"Yours," Francisco said. "I'll call you with more as soon as I can get to a land line."

The Donovan House, East Flatbush, Brooklyn

Bridget answered the phone on the first ring.

"Mom, why is my suspect calling you at home before he leaves a crime scene?" Mickey asked.

"What suspect?" Bridget responded.

"One question, Mom." Mickey said. "How is your grapefruit supply?"

"We've had a run on grapefruit," Bridget said. "That's all I'll say. The girls are fine. I won't have you turning me into an informer at this late date."

"Francisco will be there within the hour, Mom," Mickey said. The inspector ended the call. Within a few moments, he approached the Attica gates and towers. The prison was a medieval place, rising in the humidity. Every time he saw it, Mickey heard Al Pacino again. He was playing a bank robber turned street-corner celebrity in *Dog Day Afternoon*. "At-tica, At-tica," Pacino screamed.

Attica indeed. He checked his gun at the door. The guard led him down the long corridors and through the gates called "Times Square." He waited behind the gate as a prisoner detail walked past.

"It started right here," the guard said.

"What?" Mickey asked.

"The riot," the guard said. "When they gained control—of Times Square—we were lost."

Mickey hadn't asked a question. On the way in he had passed a row of orange uniforms, helmets, and nightsticks. The riot squad was only a few feet away, waiting for the call.

Mike McAlary

Athletic Department Office, Attica Prison

Wally Lord was sitting in his office, which was in the middle of the gym. A couple of porters were bench-pressing weights nearby. A young man was in the office, pushing a broom.

"Good morning, Inspector."

"Good morning."

The porter didn't look up. He pushed the broom against the clean tile.

"This is Mother," Wally said. "She's just going to sweep. If Mother gets called down to an interview room, inmates start talking. I've told her what you want. You can face me and take notes. Mother will just drift around and talk."

It was uncomfortable, Mickey realized, but necessary. He didn't want to get Mother Dearest hurt.

"I hear you can play some basketball."

"I used to rule on West Fourth Street in The Village," Mother said.

"You can still get a good run there," Mickey said.

"Not on my knees," Mother said. "My wheels need to be spoked, scoped, filleted, basted, and inflated."

"Well, Attica ain't the NBA," Mickey said.

"Or even the WNBA," Mother said, laughing. "I got to catch one of their games."

"Tell me about the hillbilly," Mickey said.

"Vargas was a punk," Mother said. "I don't do the nasty with punks."

"So how did you get out of the predicament?"

"Can we *conversate*?"

"Sure, talk away."

"I'm incarcerated but emancipated," Mother said. "I'm certainly not a trophy wife."

"Duly noted."

"Besides, Vargas liked booty better than poontang."

"Meaning?"

"He let me buy him off," Mother said. "He was a punk poker.

He just liked stabbing things. So I bought him out with a box of ladles my man Argent had stashed in the metal shop. He took them back here one at a time and stashed them in the metal rods of his bed. He had ten of them, I recall."

"He used one on your friend before he hung him," Mickey guessed.

"Yep. And the punk did the bitch thing of all time with the rest of them," Mother said.

"What?"

"He took them with him when he left," Mother said. "The guards don't check your roll on the way out. Nobody smuggles shit out of the joint. I think the hillbilly did it just to piss everybody off. A good shiv goes for about a hundred dollars on my cell block."

"Like stealing moonshine on your way to a liquor store," Mickey said.

"Some seriously inbred shit."

"Did Vargas like sports?"

"That little country hay bale was crazy for the ball," Mother said. "Baseball. Football. Basketball. He even watched hockey. But the man really loved the only sport you can't even play in Attica."

"Horse racing?" Mickey guessed.

"No," Mother Dearest said. "Hillbilly sure loved him some tennis. Especially women's tennis. He used to yell at me, 'Mother, why can't you dress like Martina? That's my dream girl.' He could name, like, the top fifty players in the world, if you can imagine an inmate knowing such a thing. I learned later that he was in here for raping some junior skirt at a tennis camp. He had an autographed color picture of one young lady. Took it with him. The degenerate used to jerk off in the dayroom watching girls play. He called it 'holding his racquet' and would scream, 'Look at my western grip.' He wasn't even a self-respecting degenerate. A lot of guys liked him 'cause he could get drugs." Mother fell silent then, dropped the broom and picked up the mop.

"I think we're done here," Mickey said.

East Flatbush

That night, Francisco knocked on the door. Ginny opened it and smiled warmly. The cop was crushed. He had hoped to scare the hell out of the Morgue Lady.

"Hello, Detective Camacho," Ginny said. "We've been expecting you. Dillon was going to use her father's Visa card at the corner pharmacy just so you would know we were still here."

"I wouldn't recommend it," Francisco said. "I suspect you've developed a tail."

"Aren't you enough?"

"No, someone a bit harsher than me. We had someone search your apartment tonight. They were going through your underwear drawer about an hour ago and found two bags of heroin. Is Dill clean?"

"Yeah."

"Then someone broke into your apartment and left it there for her. The crime lab says it's cut with rat poison. She would have died on the spot."

"In my bedroom—God, I never thought I'd actually thank you for invading my privacy."

Francisco walked into the house through the tiny living room and dining room, past the china cabinet and into the kitchen, Ginny following him. He dropped a manila file he had been carrying onto the Formica table. As he settled into a chair, Bridget came up out of the basement carrying two grapefruits from the food cellar.

"They were holding me hostage," Bridget said, joking. "They gagged me and made me watch a videotape of Lady Diana's funeral. Then they threatened to make me listen to 'Candle in the Wind.'"

Francisco didn't even smile. He said, flatly, "We got some serious problems, Mrs. Donovan." The detective opened a ten-photo spread across her kitchen table. The office had called the corrections department in Albany and readied the photographs. He handed Ginny the sheets.

"Recognize anyone?" Francisco asked.

Ginny looked at the photographs, only vaguely interested. "That one there," she said, pointing to a man with a weathered, tan face. He had that hard, junkie look, she imagined. "This chain-gang-looking fellow."

"Where do you know him from?" Camacho asked.

"The diner," Ginny said. "He had the gun. And then again, later, outside Jocko's massage parlor."

"You are sure?" the detective said, leaning closer.

"He reached past me to shoot the guy in the diner."

"Thanks."

"I've seen him around before, too," Ginny said, narrowing her eyes. "I just can't place the where and the when."

Francisco closed his book and stood up, saying, "Thanks again."

"That's it?" Ginny said. "Who the hell is he?"

"His name is Dusty Vargas and he's our problem," Francisco said. "If you see him, run the other way."

"I plan on it," Ginny said. "But I should do the same thing the next time you show up, too. You cops are duplicitous bastards. As bad as the tennis writers."

"Oh, come on, Miss Glade," Francisco protested with a smile.

"Miss Glade, crap," Ginny said. "I was your problem before this guy. I was the suspect until last night. Then I see the television."

"She was in your boss's bedroom on the second floor," Bridget said. "I'm her alibi witness."

"Well, you haven't been exactly forthcoming with us," Camacho said.

"What do you mean?"

"The old case," he continued. "Melanie Morgan, the ump killed on the ball field. You worked at a summer camp with her."

"Big deal. I told Mickey I knew her."

"Vargas raped her and threatened to kill her when he got out."

"I didn't know that."

"Did you know Vargas?"

"I may have seen him once or twice."

"Well, he's been obsessed with you for years. Where's Dillon? Still upstairs?"

"Sleeping," Ginny said.

"Well, we're going to have some more problems. The mayor probably knows you're here. We're sunk if he goes to the press."

Ginny Glade, who had only recently learned that she wasn't a murderer, said nothing. She looked out the window and studied Bridget's rosebushes. There were larger burial plots in Greenwood Cemetery.

"The mayor plays tennis, doesn't he?" Ginny said.

"He plays every morning at the West Side Tennis Club in Forest Hills, Queens," Francisco said. "Why?"

"I have an idea."

TWENTY

Baggage Claim, Delta Shuttle, LaGuardia

Hanna caught the shuttle from Boston the next day. Ginny and Dillon met her at the airport. By then the radio and television stations had cleared Ginny as a suspect in the case. Dillon had two banana daiquiris as she waited. By the time the shuttle landed, she was wearing tiny wooden umbrellas as earrings. Ginny watched the television as they interviewed her insufferable husband on the most recent killing.

"I don't even play basketball," he said. "So I have no idea. I was sure my ex-wife was involved."

Then they interviewed the Jackster as he moved outside his mobile-home dealership in Hialeah, Florida. "I saw her there," he insisted, and then held up his hand.

Ginny stormed off. People recognized her in the corridor and started to applaud. That had only happened a couple of times before to Ginny. One couple pushed their plane tickets at her, demanding autographs.

"I was really hoping you were the Sore Loser Killer," one pimple-faced teenager told her.

As they walked away, Ginny turned to Dillon and said, "What a sick country. The only people Americans treasure more than athletes are killers."

Hanna came off the plane and hugged her friend. "I was pretty sure you were a butcher," Hanna said.

"You sound disappointed," Ginny said.

Dillon was getting bored. As they passed the newspaper stand, she clipped a pack of gum. "I'm the only self-respecting criminal in the lot," she said.

"Did you bring the outfit?" Ginny asked.

"Yes," Hanna said, giggling. "Both of them. Do you think he'll go for it?"

"He's worse than Clinton."

When they got out into the lot, Mickey Donovan was waiting for them. "We have to talk," Mickey said. "You come in my car with Francisco. Dillon, you can drive Ginny's friend Hanna back to my Manhattan apartment. There's a media circus at Bridget's. Someone in the mayor's office leaked word you were hiding out there."

Mickey reached over and grabbed Hanna's bag from Ginny. He opened the back door of his car and Ginny got in. He got in beside her. Francisco waited for the other two to get in Bridget's Ford Corona before driving off with Mickey and Ginny.

"I thought about you a lot," Ginny said.

"What did you think?"

"I think you should quit the police department and open a tennis club in New England with me. I do the lessons and you handle the credit applications."

"The cops hate me too much up there. I think most of what we want to do is illegal in New Hampshire, anyway," Donovan said, laughing.

She reached over and held his hand. He felt electric, again.

As they headed toward the Midtown Tunnel, Manhattan rose before them like a three-dimensional postcard. He had an odd thought as he studied the buildings and waited to speak. Someone knew about the case on every floor in every building he could see.

"I think you saved my daughter's life," Mickey began. "She likes being alive. That's a start."

"She's a smart girl," Ginny said. "A bit peculiar, but her dad is a mite eccentric, too."

"Not really," Mickey said. "I'm just a cop. That's all I know. All my relationships are framed by what I know and what I do."

"As your daughter might say, right about now, 'Yeah, whatever.'"

"Okay, on to business." Mickey held up his hand and spread his fingers. "We're not having this conversation," Mickey said.

"Dillon says that's one of your favorite expressions."

Mickey slapped the headrest in mock anger. "Whatever," the cop said, smiling. He held up his hand again and stretched his fingers. "Consider this legal advice. Your lawyer is waiting at the station house. This is a speech I give to police cadets."

She withdrew her hand from his.

"With apologies to Saddam Hussein, 'Homicide is the father of all killing,' " Mickey began. "It has five sons." He spread the fingers on his left hand and pointed at them with his right, one by one. "The first is murder. The second is manslaughter, then criminally negligent, justifiable, and excusable."

"I understand."

"If someone were to strike someone in the head with a tire iron and kill them in a fit of anger for something that person said, that would be manslaughter, at best. Maybe even justifiable."

"You mean excusable."

"Arguably. But the blow has to cause the death. And if the autopsy report says the guy died of a gunshot wound or a crude knife in the heart, then you don't have much of a manslaughter case."

"I understand."

"No, I'm not sure you do, Ginny," Mickey said. "You may have wanted to kill Blinky Hammond. You may even have believed you killed him. You may even have covered up what you believed to be a murder. But unless you make a statement, they have nothing."

"Understood."

"We never had this conversation, Ginny, and we will never have this conversation again." Mickey placed his free palm on his knees and sighed. Helping Ginny was easier than he had imagined. He wondered how he would have handled it if the guy had died of his head wound.

"What about that leathery trailer-park-looking weirdo?" Mickey asked. The cop's face hardened as he continued. "Ever see him before?"

"I may have seen him once or twice at the camp twenty years ago. Then the diner and outside Jocko's. He's stalking me?" Ginny said.

"More of a problem than that," Mickey said. "Because your doorman Victor says he used to come by the building. He was a pizza deliveryman. Then a laundry deliveryman. He thinks he helped the guy carry stuff into your apartment once because he had too much to carry by himself."

"Oh God," Ginny said. "I feel violated."

"Did you ever see this guy around The Tour?"

"Not that I recall."

"Well," Mickey continued, "the New Hampshire people report that he was an employee of the company that loaned cars to the tournaments. He would drive the cars from one tournament site to the next during the summer. Washington, Boston, North Conway, Toronto, Cincinnati, New York."

"Jesus, what do you make of that?"

"He likes you," Mickey said. "Actually, more than likes you. He's probably been around your life for more than a year now. My people checked with Yankee Stadium security this morning. Just a wild hunch. We got a positive ID. Dustin Vargas used to sell beer during Yankees games. Worked the section behind the Yankees' dugout. We've checked tapes of Yankees broadcasts. We have tape of him in a Yankees cap and red bandanna."

"I used to sit in that section."

"We know," Mickey said. "And one more thing. My guys checked with the police in DC. Last summer you filed a burglary report in the James Madison Hotel when you were there for a tournament. You reported that someone stole your underwear. Two pairs."

"Yes."

Mickey opened a paper bag on the seat between them. He took out a pair of rose-colored underwear.

"Those are mine," Ginny said. "Where did you get them?"

"The maniac mailed them to me with a note."

"What did the note say?"

" 'No need for these. Dillon prefers Joe Boxers.' "

"Jesus."

"Yeah, he's been in your room at home and on the road. He wants me to believe he has been in my home. And I believe him."

"Why hasn't he hurt us?"

"He likes you," Mickey said. "I think he killed the basketball referee because he knew we were looking at you as a suspect. He knew you had an alibi, my mother and my daughter."

"Oh, I feel so soiled," Ginny said.

"He's a show-off," Mickey said. "As soon as he killed the basketball referee, he called my mom. He knew we would check phone records. He wants me to know he knows where you guys are every second."

Ginny shuddered as she realized how the earth felt when it thawed. An icy tear welled up in her eye.

"I'm afraid," Ginny said. She reached for him and he held her.

"Me, too," the cop admitted. In that moment, in a battle against an invisible criminal, the Wraith did not feel like a phantom.

City Room, New York Post Standard, *Manhattan*

The story broke in *The New York Times* the following morning. By nine A.M. the tabloids were reeling. They had been hit with a shot to the body. The tabloid story of the year had been taken over by *The New York Times.* They had on-the-record quotes from the inspector handling the case. The *Times* had a name, a pedigree, and a motive.

"This sucks," Arlon Kettles said when he read the *Times* story just before midnight. He got straight to work rewriting it for his last edition. The story stealers at the *New York Post Standard* and the *Daily News* were even more reprehensible. They just stole the *Times* story and pretended *they* had talked to the cops.

"You sports pricks stay in the toy department until further notice," Nigel Scrum yelled across the newsroom. "You're all wankers."

The paper's police staff was called directly into Scrum's glass-walled office. They were all red faced. Too many of them didn't know any cops. They covered the police department's office of public information. They covered police spin, not New York crime. Hell, Scrum had had to listen to the *Times* guy on the radio on the way into the office.

"I have no idea what's going on in One Police Plaza," the reporter had said. "And One Police Plaza can't tell you what's going on in the streets of New York City."

Scrum had nearly driven off the Saw Mill Expressway while driving from Scarsdale to work in the wretched city.

"You can cover the police department with five sources," the reporter had said. "All you need is one detective in each borough to do the job."

In the end, the tabloids had lost the Sore Loser Killer to the *Times* because the new metropolitan editor of the paper had demanded that his reporters make friends with detectives, not public relations agents passing as cops.

On orders from Mickey, Francisco had given the story to a Brooklyn detective who had given it to the *Times* guy. There was a picture of Dusty Vargas on the front page within two hours of Mickey's conversation with Ginny Glade.

"There isn't someone out there killing umpires because he hates them. We have one man who is killing people to impress some woman he doesn't even know. Remember Hinckley and Jodie Foster? That's what's happening between Dusty Vargas and Ginny Glade," Donovan was quoted as saying.

By mid-morning the wires were moving even more complete details. They knew about the shivs and the blades. UPI had the brand name of the shiv: Cutco. Reuters, the international news wire service, had good details on the suspect's Attica life.

"What's the motive, Inspector?" Channel One shouted at Mickey Donovan as he left the Seventeenth Precinct in Manhattan on his way to his office on Forty-second Street in the parish rectory.

"Lust," he said as he got into his car.

People were quoted saying wonderful things about Ginny Glade. The Jackster told the Associated Press in Florida, "I am so happy I was wrong about Ginny Glade. She is a beautiful woman. I hope she will forgive me over dinner."

"What a turd," Dillon said as she and Ginny watched that clip while sitting on Bridget's couch.

The sports-radio talk-show people weren't so sure. On his afternoon drive-time show, Mongrel Man said, "I don't believe a word of it. Let's review the obvious. Umpires are dying. Fact. This woman is in the middle of it. Fact. They know who they're looking for. Big deal. We're still under attack. Especially the New York teams. And I'll tell you something else, boys and girls. The umps, refs, and assorted other whistle-blowers have been scared for a month. Granted, there have been some favorable calls. Even I admit that."

The Mongrel stopped and gulped a glass of water. "But now look at what will happen. The umps are saved. And they're going to come back at New York teams with a vengeance. Mark my words, New York. This city will never get another fair call. We're doomed, doomed . . ."

That night, the Rangers played the Bruins in Boston and the Knicks played the Celtics at home. The Rangers lost five to zip. They had six goals called back on offside calls. The Knicks lost by twenty. Patrick Ewing was whistled for his sixth foul in the third quarter while sitting next to Jeff Van Gundy on the bench.

"I wasn't even on the floor," Ewing protested.

"You never are," the ref responded. "Good-bye, big fella."

Shane Heath was released by the world champions within an hour after a copy of *The New York Times* issue absolving his wife was delivered to the Yankees' front office.

Arlon found another letter when he checked his mail. This one had been mailed from Princeton, New Jersey. The news chase ended for Kettles as soon as he opened the letter. It read: "Your last exclusive will make you immortal. You're next." Arlon read it, understood the death threat, and marched directly into Scrum's office and announced, "That's it. I'm going back to New Hampshire. Let me know how it works out."

TWENTY-ONE

Morning, West Side Tennis Club, Forest Hills, Queens

On cue, Hanna and Ginny burst into the mahogany lobby of the ancient tennis club as the mayor walked through the front set of doors. Ginny was wearing a simple Fred Perry outfit with yellow trim. She was a boring classic. Hanna followed her out of the locker room in a golden Versace outfit. The panties to the outfit were lined with red lace. The chest of the outfit was mesh. From a distance, it looked as if Hanna's breasts had been fenced in.

The attendant at the coat check saw her and began clucking. "You must wear whites," he said. "Your outfit violates clubhouse etiquette."

The mayor, waiting near the desk, recognized Hanna immediately. He never had a chance, which was the idea. Caruso saw Ginny, too, but in the presence of Hanna, in that outfit, he didn't care.

"Oh come on," Caruso said. "Don't be so rude to the lady. Don't you realize who this is?"

"Yes, sir," the attendant said. "My apologies, sir."

Hanna gigged, but extended her hand. "I am so naughty," Hanna said. "I just couldn't help it. I haven't played in a month. I did it just to shame Ginny."

The mayor checked out Ginny Glade, giving her a plastic smile.

In his new view, she was just another club player. "I'm sure Miss Glade could use a dose or two of humor, Hanna," the mayor said. "She has had a rough couple of weeks." He gripped Hanna's hand and she gripped it back.

"I am sorry," she said. "My name is Hanna."

The mayor was amused. The only thing greater than not being recognized was being able to introduce yourself. "I am Vito Caruso," he said. "The mayor of New York City."

Hanna made an animal sound and brought an embarrassed hand to her face. "I am so sorry," she said.

The mayor put his arm around Hanna and pulled her close. "Oh, that's okay," he said. "I can use being humbled. I only belong to the city. You belong to the world."

"Are you here to make a speech?" Hanna asked.

"Oh no," the mayor said. "I play some. I try to hit here every day."

"Really, Mr. Mayor?" Hanna asked. She was giving the Big Tuna plenty of line to run deep.

"Please, Hanna, call me Vito," the mayor said. The mayor sighed and put his hands on his hips tilting his head, studying her like a painting. "I'm your biggest fan," he said. "I thought your Wimbledon final against Andrea Stolle five years ago was the seminal match of our time. You went to her strength—the forehand. You could dictate play and make her run. I never saw a player attack a strength so intelligently. You knew if she got your inside-out forehand, she would probably go cross-court, which she did. That set up your favorite shot—the running forward. Brilliant strategy."

Hanna laughed and turned to Ginny. "Does he know government this well?"

"Not according to the *Times* op-ed page," Ginny dead-panned.

"Very funny," Caruso said. "But can I confide in you, Hanna?"

"Of course, Vito," she said.

"I copied your game plan," Vito said. "In the last election, I mimicked you. I used the same strategy against my Democratic opponent. I attacked his strength. He was frozen in place. He was a liberal, and he never expected a Republican to try and out-nice him. He cried during our last debate."

"It isn't enough to win," Hanna said truthfully. "You have to humiliate them, too."

The mayor smiled and touched his hair. "Gee, Hanna," the mayor said, "would you like to hit some?"

"We could play two on one," Hanna said, pointing at Ginny.

"Oh no," Ginny said. "You two killers go rally. I have to go back to Brooklyn, anyway. Excuse me, please."

Ginny walked off, on cue.

Three hours later, Hanna called her from the street outside the Helmsley Palace Hotel.

"I just walked out."

"Got it?" Ginny asked.

"Got it," Hanna said. "The self-involved schmuck never knew what hit him. I kept thinking, This is like a cartoon. He'll never go for it."

"Monica Lewinsky did more damage with less. You didn't actually have to take your clothes off, did you, Hanna?"

"Not really," Hanna said, snickering. "Give me an hour to get back. I think I saw a McDonald's around the corner."

"The mayor deserves a crushing public smack," Ginny said.

"Why?"

"He's trying to destroy a man I might love," Ginny said.

Five minutes later, the mayor telephoned from the hotel room down to his car, which was hidden in an alley between the hotel and the old *Daily News* building.

"I had some trouble," the mayor began. "I'm in room 1007."

"Yes, sir, I'll be right up, sir."

"Be discreet," the mayor said. "Bring me the blue suit in the trunk, and the shoes in the emergency bag."

"Shaving gear, too, sir?"

"The whole fucking kit!" the mayor suddenly screeched. "And don't forget the underwear."

"I'm on the way up, Mr. Mayor. Anything else, sir?"

"Bring my emergency hair, too," Caruso said, almost whimpering.

"Give me ten minutes, sir," the driver said. "We're all out of hair. The boys from Gracie will have to bring me another one."

Dillon Donovan, conspirator, had listened to the plan, and then Hanna's phone call. Even before the mayor called his car, she had an idea. She loved the plan because it was so deviously bawdy.

"I just thought of something," Dillon said, meeting Bridget at the door. "Give me five minutes, Nana. No questions."

"I'd love to see his *idjoit* face when he tries to explain," Bridget said. "Did you know I voted for him?"

"Yeah, yeah, whatever," Dillon said, slipping out the door on her secret task. She pulled Bridget's favorite green shawl from the hook and wrapped it around her neck and face. Then she walked to the corner pay phone. Dillon had the number written on her palm.

The phone rang twice before the switchboard girl answered, "Good afternoon, Helmsley Palace. How may I direct your call?"

"I would handle this call directly, wee miss," Dillon said in her best fake brogue. "You have the queen's wanker staying there. 'Tis a pity. The bomb will go off presently, dear. I'd make a run for the door myself, love."

"What's your name?" the operator said. She had already started to record the conversation and dial 911.

"Order of the Belfast Shawl," Dillon said before hanging up. "The code word is 'Cheers.'" Then the cop's daughter hung up, impressed with herself. The make-believe terrorist giggled as she turned from the phones and started to walk back down Avenue D. When you mainlined it, terror could be as much fun as smack.

She came up with the second idea as she passed another bank of phones. She saw a sticker pasted to the booth, suggesting that people with news to report call a toll-free number.

It was so easy. Dillon was in play again after one ring.

"*New York Post Standard*," Myron Byron said cheerfully. "City desk."

"Yeah," Dillon whispered. "Get a photographer over to the Helmsley Palace on Forty-second Street. The *Daily News* is already there. There's a bomb scare. The mayor will be coming out a back-door exit on Forty-first street after a sordid rendezvous. He will be easy to spot. Mr. Mayor will be wearing his nicest flower dress."

"Who is this?"

"A friend of his wife's," Dillon said, hanging up.

Myron put down the phone just as he heard the Emergency Service unit trucks, the marines of the NYPD, being ordered up the FDR Drive, past the United Nations, to the hotel.

"Photo!" Myron roared, holding the pink slip of information firmly in his hand. "I think we got the big one."

Evening, Navy Yard Warehouse, Brooklyn

Overnight, fifty detectives were culled from the best squads in the city. "The Rhubarb Task Force," as they were named, gathered in a shuttered room at the edge of the Brooklyn Navy Yard. Some of the old-timers were still there. Some of them had first met in this unmarked building twenty years ago. Others had been there ten years ago when the department was trying to catch the so-called Zodiac Killer.

Mickey Donovan stood before them chewing on an unlit cigar. All of the guys were tired, and some of them, the first-grade detectives, had their ties loosened on their shirts, like scarves. It was a practiced look. Donovan wore a pale green khaki suit, a blue short-sleeved shirt, and a yellow tie. He was one of the only people still wearing his jacket.

"This is our suspect," Donovan said. He handed a stack of photographs to a slack-jawed lieutenant who had just been borrowed again from Queens homicide. The old-timer, Gene Kelly, talked in codes and riddles because he suspected that every conversation on every telephone was being taped.

"You have to know what I'm talking about to know what I'm talking about," he routinely explained.

Donovan continued, "Lieutenant Kelly will pass them out. He is commanding this task force, but I will personally ride herd."

Kelly stood and slapped a clipboard on the table. "I see some faces from Son of Sam," Kelly said. "You're all old farts, like me, so let's ride one more time."

The cops laughed. They were edgy with the chase.

"There are some Zodiac veterans here, too," he continued. "We screwed that one up, also. Both cases, the greatest modern manhunts in this department's modern history, were solved by accident. Sam's traffic ticket. The other nitwit signed a piece of paper, years later, with his Zodiac signature. So we begin knowing that the little things solve the big cases."

"You have to let detectives detect," said a detective in the back of the room, a detective-union delegate borrowed from Manhattan North.

"True," Kelly said. "But if you talk again while I have the floor, without raising your hand, you'll be back in the bag tomorrow. Understood?"

Kelly paused, glaring at the room, then stepped back. He carried a pearl-handled pistol. "Inspector?"

Donovan stood up and took off his coat. He handed it to his brother, Ryan, who hadn't been invited to the meeting but had come anyway.

"Okay, detectives," he said. "I'm going to put it plainly, not in Kellyesque, as we call it; and anyone who has ever spoken to the lieutenant on the phone knows what we're talking about." Mickey then spoke in the whispering, conspiratorial voice of the legendary homicide lieutenant: "You know that blue thing? We never talk about it. Well, we really can't talk about it now because people are talking about it. Mr. Blue is back. A black blue was found where the sun don't shine. We're looking for a former tenant."

The room detonated with laughter.

"Exactly," Donovan said. "Translation: The umpire killer is back. He killed a black ump in New Jersey. We have identified the suspect as a former upstate prisoner."

He turned to Kelly again and smiled. "Did I leave anything out, Loo?"

"Yeah," Kelly said. "But I'll *not* talk to you about it later."

More laughter.

Donovan sat down and opened his folder, saying, "Dusty Vargas. White male, thirty-five. Five-feet eight, a hundred and eighty pounds. Scar on the right cheek. Badly scarred on the chin as a teenager when his older brother mistakenly sliced him while cutting windows in their igloo. Subsequently, the brother was found stabbed in the heart in the same icebox, his eye mutilated. Our boy does five years in a youth facility, emerges as a real animal. He moves from burglary to robbery to rape. Does seven the hard way in Attica. Very good athlete. Big drug dealer. Currently on parole for the rape and robbery of a teenaged tennis player in Utica. He was the dishwasher in her tennis camp. He brutalized the girl."

"Where is this tennis player now?"

"Deceased," Mickey replied. "She was shot while umping a softball game in the Bronx last year. Unsolved case. It seemed like a senseless, random act. Anyone here work it with me?"

"I did," a guy yelled from the back of the room. "Dennis Porridge. Four-seven Bronx PDU. We found some shells on the track. We figured a one-in-a-million shot from the train."

"Maybe," Donovan interrupted. "But, more likely, she was our first umpire to die. She's killed a week after Vargas comes home. I want a few of your Bronx guys to go back to some of those witnesses. Call The Cold-Case Squad."

"We had a nurse who said she saw a guy leave his subway car and then come back."

"Get up to her with the Vargas picture. We know this starts with that kill. Melanie Morgan testified against him."

"The witness lives on the Grand Concourse now, boss," Porridge said. "I see her regularly waiting for a bus outside the criminal-court building."

Donovan moved on to the next overwhelming question. He recognized a hand in the back of the room.

"So why does he hates umpires?" the detective asked.

"The shrinks will tell you they're versions of the prison guards who brutalized him and the cops who arrested him," Mickey said. "But I don't believe that. I don't think he gives two shits about umpires. He likes to rape and terrorize. He used to watch a lot of tennis upstate. Maybe he was hoping he'd see her show up in some tournament. He fixates on one woman, Ginny Glade."

"Why?" another detective asked.

"Why did Hinckley fixate on Foster?"

"She's a looker."

"Yeah. We know he follows her. Gets into her apartment. Ginny Glade is this guy's motivation. He kills the ump in New Hampshire because he wants to impress her. Oldest story in the world," Mickey Donovan said. "Boy sees girl. Boy kills to sway girl.

"That's what it looks like. Ms. Glade was at the camp. She says she saw him once or twice there. He kills Morgan. Then the tennis ump. Then the baseball ump. Then he kills the basketball ump to take the heat off Ms. Glade. But let's not assume anything with this guy. I think he even killed Sal Nesto, who was too slow to pay him for information on moving drugs through the airport. This guy can be invisible."

Someone yelled from the back, "Jesus, not another Wraith. So this whole sports-hater crap is bullshit?"

"And you are?"

"Ralph Steckowych, sir," the three-hundred-pound cop replied. "Brooklyn North homicide."

"I believe we met on the Yankee Stadium riot detail," Donovan said. "We always drag in the Brooklyn boys when there's a war to be fought."

"We're the department's humble blockers," Steckowych said, bowing quite awkwardly from the waist. "A gathering of simple offensive linemen, sir."

"Who would bite Tyson's ear off in a clinch," a Manhattan North delegate yelled.

The room laughed.

"Okay," Mickey continued, "his weapon of choice is a shiv, a snapped-off soup ladle. Crude, but effective. He thinks he's some sort of prison gladiator. Knows cars. Prefers nylon workout suits. He knows the city. A careful planner. A watcher. Since the basketball referee's murder, we also know he carries knockout gas and a gun with a gerry-rigged gas silencer. Tinker, sailor, soldier, stalker. Know that he is always close to this tennis player, Glade. And that he knows who is watching him."

"What does that mean?" a nattily dressed Queens detective asked.

"After he killed the last guy, he called my mother's home from a pay phone near the body. Just so I would know that he knows."

"Then he's a show-off—good," snarled the Queens cop.

"Hey, boss," Steckowych said. "I am an indelicate, plodding, fat ass but we heard some things."

"Yeah?"

"We heard the tennis player, this Glade female, is in Brooklyn, sir," the cop said. Everyone knew what was coming. "At your mother's house, Inspector."

Donovan did not smile. His brother, Ryan Donovan, coughed.

"She is at my mother's house," Donovan said. "Steckowych, you are going to guard her with your partner, Danny Hollie, as soon as we finish up. If you can't find me, beep Sergeant Francisco Camacho."

"Why didn't this Glade tell us about this Dusty character? Could they be a team?"

"I certainly hope not, gentlemen."

Donovan stared across the room at his brother. This was not going to be easy.

"There is one more thing, fellows," Mickey said. "I'm your boss. And I know many of you have worked with me as we have reclaimed this police department and city. Zero Tolerance has worked because you made it work. But I have a confession, ladies and gentlemen. I may have helped you save the city, but I nearly lost my little girl doing it. She's a heroin addict. And she is in the middle of this case. Ginny Glade has sort of reclaimed my kid. It's only been a couple of weeks, but maybe even saved her life, really. But now that she's on her way to being reclaimed, this Vargas fellow knows about her. He has threatened to hurt her and has broken into Ginny's apartment where they were staying to leave a poisoned bag of junk for my kid to find. They ran. He followed. He called my mother because he knows where they are. We did not save my girl to have her be hurt by this maniac."

Donovan brought a hand to his face, and wiped away a tear. "Gee, it's hot," he said. "My eyes are sweating. I know this is personal, but I thought you should know it."

"We did know it, sir," Steckowych said gently. "And we also know that your friend the mayor was threatening to make your anguish public, boss. We cannot, and will not, have that."

"All of our families have been touched by a version of the same tragedy," Lieutenant Kelly said. "A daughter, a cousin, an uncle, or an aunt. We just don't, ahem, talk about alcoholics and drug addicts, sir."

A couple of the older detectives, familiar with the guy's dark sense of humor, managed to laugh. Mickey reset himself. Ryan had come to the front of the room. He stood behind his brother, his hands balled into fists.

"That is all, detectives," Donovan said, grabbing his jacket. "Happy hunting."

TWENTY-TWO

Helmsley Hotel, East Forty-second Street, Manhattan

Francisco heard the reports as he headed down Second Avenue toward the Thirty-fourth Street entrance to the FDR Drive. He made a right on East Forty-first Street as the NYPD's Special Operations Division ordered everything short of helicopters onto the block. The helicopters were in the air over the United Nations Building, just two blocks east, in case of an international incident. Ever since some loonies had started to plant two sets of bombs in abortion clinics and gay bars—one to blow up the place and a second to injure the responding federal officers—the rules were new.

Everyone in the fire zone wore body armor. It was a war until you heard different. Inspector Seamus Larkins was the man in charge. He was the first set of boots at the back door. He had an empty city bus waiting.

"Everyone in this hotel goes right on the bus," he yelled at his battle-ready cops. "Take them two blocks away. Get identification. No one is released until we know who and what we got."

The back door was about to be opened when he pressed his jackboot against it. "Assume that everyone you meet is a suspect until you see different."

"Open this fucking door," someone screamed from behind the door. It was a vaguely familiar voice.

"Got it?" Larkins asked.

The cops nodded.

"Okay, then," Larkins said, pressing the door closed.

"Yes, inspector," the platoon sergeant replied. "Open the door."

They stood back and the black door opened. The man who had been pushing on it burst through and toppled at their feet. One cop grabbed him and pulled him to his feet. The bald fellow stood there, a bathroom towel wrapped around his waist. He was wearing a ladies' tennis skirt. The cop stood back as Larkins peered at the man.

"Mr. Mayor?" Inspector Larkins asked. "Is that you, sir?"

Before he could answer, the cameras were flashing. One heavily shouldered fellow shone a light on Vito Caruso, an extremely diminished man. The setup was beautiful. This kind of thing worked easily. The reporters never minded being set up. The pictures were always deadly and delicious. Anyone and everyone who convinced themselves that they were bullet-proof could be similarly set up. The mayor, a cartoon figure in dancing pumps, was easy to capture.

"Mr. Mayor," the fellow from Channel One yelled, "what were you doing in there?"

This was lunacy, but Larkins still had an emergency. He handed the mayor a baseball cap and pushed him toward the waiting bus. The mayor's driver grabbed him, but not before the cameras caught him. In another second the bus was filled.

After an hour, the frightened hotel guests were all allowed to leave. The hotel was only half full, but a hundred people needed to be evacuated. There was no bomb, of course. No disaster. No injuries. No news.

So all anyone cared about was the mayor. The newspapers were mad to interview the bellhops, maids, doormen, and room service.

The *Post Standard* and the *Daily News* ran the same series of photographs the next day. The bald mayor in ladies' tennis skirt was a lot to explain.

Mickey Donovan called Inspector Larkins at six A.M. the following morning. They were old friends who had grown up together in East Flatbush. They both agreed that the last picture of the mayor, the one showing him running for his limo in the skirt, said it all. The cops, still working without a contract, were laughing in every patrol car in the city when they saw the foppish mayor with his new hat.

The letters on the top of the cap handed to the mayor by the toughest cop in the NYPD said it all. After he'd seen the mayor wearing a similar cap at Bellevue, he now carried a box of them at all times. Over the last month, Inspector Larkins had slapped a similar cap on the head of every murderer, child killer, and rapist he'd arrested and walked in front of the television cameras in Manhattan South. The logo on the cap read:

FDNY.

The mayor's publicist tried to claim he was practicing for another drag appearance in the city hall variety show, but no one was buying that story. The *Post Standard* editorial writers were calling him the most embarrassing mayor since Jimmy Walker. Vito Caruso's national plans suffered a major setback.

At lunch that day, Mickey returned to his parish office and found an envelope on his desk.

"Your mother dropped it off," the priest said.

"My mother came here?" Mickey said. "She hasn't been here in five years."

Mickey waited until his assistant left the room, then opened the manila envelope. A single five-by-seven photograph fell out. He reached into the envelope further and felt something hairy. He recoiled, then looked at the photograph again and let the mangy black toupee fall on his desk. In the photo, His Honor was standing in his hotel room wearing spikes and chains. He had a mask on top of his head.

Three minutes later, an aide answered the mayor's hot-line phone at city hall. Youngblood was winded and barely audible.

"Yeah, this is Youngblood. What the hell do you want?"

"I want to see His Honor this afternoon. Confidentially. I found something."

"What?"

"His hair. But I have something else, too."

"What?"

"I'll discuss that with the mayor."

———————

That afternoon they met on the veranda at Gracie Mansion. The mayor was not doing well at all. As soon as he saw the inspector, he screamed.

"Where's your commissioner, Inspector Donovan?" the mayor asked.

"He is not one for gloating, sir," Mickey said.

"Bullshit," the mayor said. "You guys set me up, right down to that fireman's hat. You are gone. Your daughter is going in the papers tomorrow as a junkie. I know you have Ginny Glade in your house. You got her to set me up with her doubles partner in the hotel."

"The girls tell me the hotel was your idea, sir," Mickey said. "They're incorrigible. Ginny is no longer a suspect, incidentally, so you can't hurt her. And my daughter is just beginning to understand the true meaning of zero tolerance. Every cop in the city knows my family problems. And they known about your threats, too. So they're gonna catch me an umpire killer."

"So what?"

"So you are out of cards, sir."

"This is blackmail; I'll have you arrested in the driveway."

"No, and I assume you have this room wired for sound, Mr. Mayor," Mickey said. "If you don't you should. You decide what you are going to do. I don't want anything."

The cop laid the bulky envelope on the table. On cue, the obsequious assistant scurried into the room and tried to grab the envelope. Mickey slapped his hand, hard. The gofer reeled.

"You can leave now," Mickey said.

The mayor waved his assistant out of the room.

"The girls did this on their own," Mickey said. "They're naughty. But don't threaten me again."

The mayor opened the envelope and saw the picture; he had been expecting it. Hanna had snapped it with a disposable Kodak camera. He had been expecting to see the photograph since he had come out of the hotel bathroom and discovered Hanna gone, along with his clothes and hair.

"Check, checkmate," the mayor said.

"I was thinking stalemate," Mickey said.

The mayor sighed and watched the cop jiggling his hairpiece. "I can live with a stalemate, Inspector," the mayor said, putting the photograph in his coat pocket. "But I want the negative, too."

"Mr. Mayor, you, thanks to the new term limits, are a lame-duck mayor. I'll mail it to you on your last day in office."

Mickey stood up. "One more thing," he said, and pulled a cassette from his pocket. "The commissioner mailed me this tape from Key West. He told me to give it to you. It's the only copy. He said it's the only break you deserve for letting us save the city."

The mayor stood up and took the tape. "We are done, Inspector. Go catch the bad guy."

Mickey stood up to depart. He got to the door, but then stopped. Maybe a greater man would just have left. Maybe a bigger man would just have let the mayor stew in his defeat. But Mickey wouldn't go down to victory that quietly.

"Just one question, sir," Mickey said.

"Careful," the mayor said.

"I was just wondering, Mr. Mayor, about the outfit," Mickey said, scratching his head. "Was the dress yours, sir? Or did she provide it?"

"Piss off, cop."

"With all due respect, Mr. Mayor, I imagine you make firemen in this city proud," Donovan said, tipping his NYPD cap.

East Flatbush

The next afternoon the six-foot-two, three-hundred-pound cop, on loan from Brooklyn North to the Sore Loser Task Force, was sitting in Bridget's vestibule, his gun hanging from a shoulder harness. He was too big for the house. He was too big for the block. Maybe he was too big for the city on this humid October day. No one could explain the heat. It was like one of those wonderful spring days in February that the detective remembered Robert Penn Warren having written—something—a short story about when country kids feel chunks of ice between their bare toes.

Detective Steckowych could remember only two summer days as a kid. The season started the first time in April you could wear a T-shirt outside. It ended the last time you could go shirtless.

"What is this?" the detective said, sighing. "Blackberry summer?"

Bridget had an air conditioner in the living room. She had turned it on only twice in the 1990s.

"These things cause blackouts," Bridget explained. "I wouldn't do that to my city, Detective."

"I'm kind of dying here," Steckowych said. "This heat is impossible."

He had a wet towel over his balding head. For fun, he rode motorcycles on the weekends. Sitting in Bridget's apartment was not unlike sitting on the Garden State Parkway on the way to the New Jersey Shore at about eight P.M. on a Friday night. He was soup.

"Maybe we could turn it on low, Mrs. Donovan," Steckowych said in a voice that whined like the broken clutch on his Harley Indian.

"Soon enough, young man," Bridget said. "Maybe after the eleven o'clock news. Con Edison says it's okay after that."

The absurd Indian-summer weather had the detective melting in his shoes. It was eighty-seven degrees with ninety percent humidity. The news wasn't on for another five hours.

"You are such a dear," the detective said, smiling through his sweat.

At the end of the block, he suddenly heard the chimes. And then the squeal of kids. Francisco Camacho arrived just then at the door. He was buzzed in and Ginny saw the ice cream truck behind him. This was probably the last ice cream night of the year in New York City. Dillon pointed to the truck. Ginny was sitting on the couch watching the Mets baseball game on the Classic Sports Network. Hanna was back in Boston, her mission happily, and successfully, completed.

"Please, Francisco," Dillon said. "You know I got a major sugar jones."

"You grandmother has stuff in the freezer," Ginny said.

"Not the soft shit," Dillon said.

The detectives whispered and tried to cool themselves in the living room as the ladies sat and chatted. They laughed as the bell moved up the block. Dillon got up and walked to the door.

"Oh great," Dillon said, walking toward the screen door. "Mr. Rocky."

Steckowych stood up, leaving a wet spot on his chair. "Hold on, young lady," he said. "I don't want anything, but I have to go with you."

"Stay here with Ginny, Detective," Camacho said. "I'll walk her out."

They walked to the Yummy Ice Cream truck. The lime-green-and-white truck smelled especially sour tonight, not unlike a sanitation truck parked in the sun. Its air conditioner was whirring. A bald white man, completely barren of eyebrows, with the silly white cap on his head, served the kids. He was in his forties and about six-five with awkward, skinny legs and painfully thin arms. Camacho studied him and saw a version of every scumbag carney he had ever watched work a Ferris wheel or carnival booth. He had that "I'm only working between three-day binge drunks" look.

"Hey, Mister Yummy," the kid in front of them yelled. "Where Rocky at?"

The man with the newly shaved head said, "Oh, his summer is over. Rocky always takes off for Florida the first week of October."

"He do?"

"Of course, kid. You just never noticed."

"Oh, well, tell him I said hi," the kid, about seven years old, said. "What do we call you?"

The ice cream man turned his hat sideways, and bent to the side so that he looked as if he was wearing a pair of paper antlers. "Bull-winkle," the ice cream man said.

The kids screamed. Dillon stepped in next. Camacho was at her side with his back to the truck. A gray van was coming down the street slowly. He didn't like that and tensed as it approached. He was watching the parked cars on East Thirty-eighth Street, too, to make sure no one stepped out of them. The suspect could be anywhere. Camacho wasn't going to lose Mickey's kid while getting an ice cream cone.

"I want a vanilla cone," Dillon said, "with rainbow sprinkles. And my friend here wants a chocolate."

The ice cream man filled the wafer cone with vanilla ice cream and spooned red, blue, green, and yellow sprinkles on top. He handed it to Dillon in a napkin and then filled the other cone with milky chocolate ice cream. He spooned black and yellow sprinkles onto the cop's cone.

"One-fifty," Mr. Bullwinkle said.

Dillon gasped. "I forgot my money."

"I'll wait," the ice cream man said.

Camacho turned to the window and said, "That's okay, Bullwinkle. I got it."

He handed the guy two one-dollar bills.

"Hey," the cop said, "but I didn't want chocolate sprinkles."

"Those are our new hazelnut sprinkles," Bullwinkle said. "But give it back. I'll give you a new one."

The ice cream guy had his hand out. It was a worn, sour hand, a carney hand.

"Never mind," the cop said. "It's too hot to wait."

"Thank you, sir," Bullwinkle continued. "I have to eat my mistakes."

"I'll eat this one," the cop said. "Keep the change."

The truck rolled off as they climbed the steps.

"Here," Dillon said. "Take my cone. I like hazelnut."

They switched cones. Camacho took his first lick before they entered the door. He took a second lick as he took his jacket off and sat down next to Steckowych, who was sipping an iced tea. Dillon sat on the couch and offered Ginny a lick.

"No thanks, kid," Ginny said, patting her stomach. "Now that I'm no longer public enemy number one, I'd like to make a run at making number forty on the women's tennis ranking."

The detectives watched the truck roll off the block.

"That guy must have some racket," Steckowych said. "I should just rent a truck."

"The guy Rocky has been here for thirty years," Bridget said. "Mickey used to buy ice cream from him."

Camacho took another lick. "What's he do during the winter, when he goes to Florida?" Camacho asked. It was just conversation.

Bridget raised an eyebrow and gave him an amused look. She studied the cop as he ate the last sprinkle.

"Well, I don't know who gave you that information, Detective," Bridget said. "Rocky doesn't go to Florida in the winter."

"Oh shit," Camacho said. And stopped licking.

"Rocky lives across the street from what used to be the Farragut pool," Bridget continued, leaning into the cop's surprise. "I saw his wife, Carmella, at the Little Flower bingo game last week. Rocky switches to the grinder truck as soon as it gets cold. He was out here sharpening knives and scissors just yesterday."

Camacho coughed once with a terrible realization and reached for Dillon. He began to tremble. Then he gasped with complete understanding and terror. Steckowych stood staring at Camacho's cone and understood completely. The sergeant dropped the cone and grabbed Mickey's daughter.

"Dillon, no . . . ," he said, reaching.

Francisco Camacho was unconscious twenty seconds after he hit the carpeted floor. He died staring up at a framed color photo of Deputy Inspector Mickey Donovan. Dillon, who'd eaten the wrong cone, cried for the first time in five years.

Mickey was just getting on the exit to the Brooklyn Bridge from the southbound FDR Drive when the scanner began to beep and whistle.

"Ten-thirteen. MOS down. Six thirty-eight East Thirty-eighth Street. Between Avenue D and Foster. Send a bus."

"I'll have you at Mom's in seven minutes," his new driver, Ryan Donovan, said. He already had the cherry on top of the car. The siren was wailing.

"Straight to Atlantic and then down to Flatbush—all the way."

The dispatcher was talking nonstop. "MOS in cardiac arrest," she continued. "Caller says he may have been poisoned. Units are advised that the suspect vehicle is a Mister Yummy truck. Detective on the scene describes the suspect shooter as a bald white male wearing a white smock."

"Jesus, what's happening?"

Ryan dialed Bridget's phone. It was busy. He hit Redial. Busy again. She had never wanted to spend the extra five bucks for call waiting. Ryan called the next-door neighbor and handed the phone to Mickey.

"The Tedescos. It's ringing."

The phone was answered on the tenth ring. Anthony Tedesco,

the father, had been watering the rosebushes in the back, pretending not to look.

"The girls are fine," Tedesco reported. "Bridget is cursing. I just saw Dillon. She's with some attractive woman. But the cop—I went in and looked; he's dead."

"A detective or the sergeant?"

"It's your friend, the one I see you with here all the time, Camacho."

Mickey dropped the phone.

On the police radio, the dispatcher was cool and controlled. "No further at East Thirty-eighth and Foster Avenue," she said. "Slow it down. Division advises no further."

There was just chatter. Some cop had left his key button open and you could hear him racing through the Brooklyn streets.

"No, no, make a right. Jesus, watch that bus."

"Check your radios," the dispatcher said. "We got an open key."

The frantic driver fell silent. This was followed by more deliberate quiet.

That was never good news.

"Any further word on the condition of the MOS?" a cop asked. He was speaking for the ten thousand working that shift.

No response. That was answer enough. She came back on fifteen minutes later. "MOS was DOA at King's County. Notifications being made."

As they drove from Brooklyn back to Manhattan, the inspector sat in the backseat with Ginny Glade. She had been incredibly poised when he'd first arrived on the scene. They had quickly driven to a precinct on Coney Island to hide from the press. By the time the reporters figured out the cops were conducting their murder investigation on the ass end of South Brooklyn, the cops were done.

There wasn't much to investigate, really. He had left his prints everywhere. He knew that they knew who he was. Vargas was daring them to catch him. Mickey hadn't expected such a bold move. The guy killed the cop just to show off. The scary thing was that he could have parked at the end of the block and walked back with a gun.

"He could have killed everyone in the house," Ginny said. "He likes the terror of this."

"Yes, he does," Mickey said. "We can't underestimate him again."

Ryan Donovan was driving. Dillon was sullen and silent. When the teenager had gotten in the car, she'd turned off the radio.

"You know, Dad, when I was getting high, I never gave two shits about dying. AIDS. Overdose. I never cared."

"Yeah, we noticed," Mickey said.

"Well, I didn't decide to live just to be killed by some maniac. I don't want to die, Daddy."

"You're not going to," Mickey said. "We're not going to."

Ryan playfully grabbed Dillon's thigh. He pulled off the FDR Drive onto Canal Street. After a couple of blocks, they were surrounded by people with purple hair and cheek earrings. Ryan parked outside a store on East Thirteenth Street called Pierced Arse.

"Come on," Ryan said. "I'll buy you a dog collar."

They got out, leaving Ginny and Mickey sitting in the backseat. After a long moment of uncomfortable silence, Mickey spoke. "We are going to need you to capture him," Mickey said. "I need a plan. But you're the key. We found a note in the ice cream truck, under the seat. This one was handwritten. He pasted it with a bloody fingerprint just so we'd know it was his work."

"What did it say?" Ginny asked. She didn't have an ounce of cool or patience left.

"I brought a copy."

He felt inside his coat and unfolded the copy of the note. It was written in neat block lettering.

GINNY,

I DID SO MUCH FOR YOU. THEN YOU BETRAYED ME. FOR A COP. *IACTA ALEA EST*. YOU DIE NEXT. 1000631K

Ginny dropped the letter on the seat. She was shaking. Mickey held her by the shoulders, saying, "The Latin is pretty simple. *The die is cast*. It's supposed to be what Caesar said when he crossed the Rubicon. 'You made your choice. Now you pay the price.' The number is his Attica prison ID."

"I want a gun," Ginny said.

"I've got five guns, Ginny. We don't need guns, we need a plan."

"Meaning what?"

"Meaning we have to set a trap," Mickey continued. "What is the one thing we know about this guy? He likes you. So you have to be the bait. I have a plan."

"We go back to my apartment and have sex again?"

"Ginny, please. We can't ever do that again. I was wrong."

"Maybe we were wrong. I can live with that. As long as I have the memory."

"Now, the plan."

Ryan returned to the car with his niece a few minutes later.

"There's more than just the note," the head of the narcotics unit told Ginny. "We found Rocky dead on a bench in a park near Newkirk Avenue. He had a spike in his arm. He was killed by a heroin overdose."

"There's junk all over this place," Dillon said. She did not sound disappointed.

"Our lab did an analysis and just called me," Ryan said. "It's called China Blue. New stuff. Been on the street for about a month. Strictly East Village. We may get lucky. Mickey and I have our best people down here looking."

Mickey cut in. "Why is he buying smack, Ryan?" Mickey asked.

"I imagine he's doing that with Dillon in mind. But this may be just counterintelligence. Dusty Vargas may have left the body to be found with the spike, knowing we would trace the heroin back to the East Village. Assume he's watching us."

"Great," Mickey said.

"One more thing," Ryan added. "They found stilts in his ice cream truck. He made himself taller just to screw up Camacho's chances of making him. This guy is an accomplished chameleon."

"Is this the best we can do?" Ginny said.

"It's all the lead we've got," Ryan continued. "The man is a vapor, a ghostly apparition."

"Hey, Dad," Dillon said, laughing. "This town is only big enough for one Wraith."

———

The attraction was wrong, Mickey realized, and not just because he was a cop. It was wrong because it was dangerous. The cemeteries on either side of the Jackie Robinson Parkway running through Brooklyn and Queens were filled with cops who'd thought with their cocks. Mickey didn't trust himself when he saw Ginny Glade. It was hard not to. At the beginning of this investigation, back when Commissioner Mason and Mayor Caruso were desperate to throw a leg over the glorious tennis player, Mickey hadn't dared look at her.

That night, after Steckowych had moved his daughter, with ten detectives, into a secret suite the police commissioner kept atop a tower in the World Trade Center for just such an emergency, Mickey took Ginny to a Grand Hyatt hotel on East Forty-second Street for the night. The hotel gave the cop and his witness a floor to themselves. Mickey had the emergency services unit—the marines of the NYPD—posted at either end of the hallway.

"I am so sorry," Ginny said. "I'm not sure I even know what loyalty is. But he was your friend."

"He was my arms and legs," Mickey said.

They ate dinner in the room. Mickey personally ordered it in from Chin Chin's. He spoke directly to the chef and had him bring it over to the hotel. The meal never left his sight, from wok to customer.

"Eat," Mickey said. "It may be the only safe meal in the world."

This time they ate before they made love. They even feel asleep in each other's arms for a whole hour. Then the terror awakened them.

TWENTY-THREE

A Policeman's Funeral, Brooklyn

They held the policeman's funeral at the Our Lady of Most Precious Blood church in Bensonhurst. It was an odd church, the church of the Chief of Detectives and Sammy "the Bull" Gravano. Cop and gangster shared the same pew. Some of them even worked together as altar boys. Every parishioner knew about the cop's son who'd served in the funeral mass of a great Gambino soldier. And every priest and nun in the parish knew of the gangster's son who had carried the communion dish at a cop's funeral.

An odd ritual had become legend in the church years before. No one knew how it had begun, really. But tradition had it that the gangsters always sat on the bride's side of the altar—on the left, facing the front of the church, while the cops sat on the groom's side.

Detective Francisco Camacho had been shoehorned into a powder-blue casket.

A police funeral, when you happen on it, is a frightening event. In Manhattan, when they buried a cop, they shut down the streets for ten blocks in each direction. And the truck driver who beeped his horn was asking for a serious beating. In the Bronx, people tended to ignore them. In Queens, they usually closed the streets for an hour. In Brooklyn, it depended on the neighborhood. In Sunset Park, citizens were only marginally patient. But in Bensonhurst and most of South Brooklyn, the entire neighborhood dropped to one knee.

The thunder of the motorcycles could be heard. Camacho's Harley followed on a trailer with his blue helmet strapped to the empty seat. There were twenty bikes in all, slowly rumbling past. The pavement seemed to shake, and the skies thundered with passing helicopters. The police bagpipers, culled from the Emerald Society, came next, the drummers beating an ungodly, lonely beat. They played "Amazing Grace."

Then came the cars and the black limousines and the gray hearse. Six uniformed pallbearers waited. The cops in the funeral detail all wore skin tight, white cotton gloves and creased blue tunics with polished brass buttons. They hoisted Camacho's NYPD-blue casket onto their uniformed shoulders and clicked into the church.

The widow, and this one even wore black lace gloves, followed up the steps with two fatherless children.

The mayor waited at the center of the line with the Police Commissioner and Inspector Mickey Donovan. The mayor had the grace to step off the church property before asking for the death penalty.

"When we catch this guy, I want him to meet God as quickly as Detective Sergeant Francisco Camacho," Mayor Caruso said. "The only thing standing between this killer and the big needle is one last set of umpires. His jury."

"He just killed him to show that he could do it," Mickey whispered to the mayor as they entered. "He likes the terror."

Dillon and Ginny sat in a back row of the church feeling like exposed conspirators. Mourners had the grace not to blame them publicly. It was odd for an adult her age, but Ginny hadn't attended many funerals. The last service she'd attended had been for Arthur Ashe in Manhattan. She could still hear him saying all those years ago, "Your legacy isn't the tournaments you've won, it is the people you help, the society you change."

"None of this would have happened if it wasn't for me," Ginny whispered. "Francisco was killed by some guy who wants to prove something to me. Why me? Why him?"

Dillon had attended dozens of cop funerals. She had two sets of mourning clothes in a closet that included only one nightgown. The funeral was part of the cop life. It was part of what she hated.

"An effin' ice cream," Dillon said, loud enough for several mourners to turn around glaring. "The bastard killed him with an ice cream."

"Did they ever find the truck?" Ginny asked.

"Yeah," Dillon said. "He left it parked outside the park, near the subway on Foster Avenue. People said he just jumped out and shouted, 'Free ice cream. Take whatever you want.' There was nearly a riot. He took the plastic bin of sprinkles with him. They found it in the trash at the entrance to the subway."

"Quiet," Ginny said, "here comes your father."

Mickey Donovan walked in behind the mayor. He was shamed by the murder. To have lost a cop in his mother's house was preposterous, almost as horrid as coming home from a drug raid to find heroin in your kid's nightstand. He nodded to his daughter and Ginny Glade. Ralphie Steckowych stood at the entrance with the ushers. The three-hundred-pound cop would never swallow another scoop of ice cream.

Clockworks Restaurants, Park Slope, Brooklyn

The inspector smelled of perspiration and Brut. Mickey Donovan needed a shave and a shower. By design, he was meeting his informant half a world from the East Village. He sat in a tiny restaurant named Clockworks in Park Slope. The guy had called saying he had information. He'd picked the spot and the hour.

Twenty years before, the former cop had to be told where to go. He used to meet the internal affairs cops up the block at the end of his midnight tour. They could see anyone coming through Prospect Park. The informant would always have the body recorder off by the time they met. Mickey would take the tape and give the cop a new one.

He could still remember the old conversations. He knew them by rote. Mickey would begin, "At this time I am testing an Olympus micro recorder, model number L200, serial number 211417. This recorder is to be used to record conversation by Officer Peter Herod during a tour of duty on this date in the Ninety-ninth Precinct. Officer, do you realize that once this recorder is activated, it will record any conversations by you or directed toward you?"

"Yes," Peter had always replied.

"Officer," Mickey Donovan asked, "are you willing to record all conversations of your own free will?"

"Yes."

"Have you been instructed in the proper use of this recorder?"

"Yes, I have."

"This is your primary recorder, to be used during your tour of duty. I ask that you have nothing in your pocket that would interfere with that recording. Is that understood?"

"Yes."

"End of this portion of the tape."

He could still hear those conversations as he nursed his beer and watched a storm hammer Twelfth Street a rivulet of fouled rainwater rushing toward the sewer. A biting wind slapped sheets of rain against the windowpane.

Mickey wasn't sure what to expect.

In outlining the ground rules for the meeting, Peter Heroin, apostle of the East Village, had made a simple request. "No tape recorders," he had said. "I don't do that anymore."

"Neither do I," Mickey had said.

As Mickey studied the street, the silvery-haired man in a blue pickup truck drove past, then stopped. Peter sat in the cab, smoking, the motor still running. For a moment, Mickey thought he would drive off.

"Come on, Peter," Mickey murmured to himself. "Find the cop in you."

Peter finished his cigarette and climbed out of the car. He gathered a brown suede coat against the rain and ran into the bar. He walked over to the table, took off his coat, and smiled. Mickey did not get up.

"I couldn't resist making you wait here the way I used to wait," Peter Heroin said. "Turnaround in games of torture is fair play."

"You can hate me all you want," Mickey said. "But you can't hate my kid."

"Sure I can, Mickey D.," Peter said.

The inspector hated that crude nickname. No one had called him that to his face after he'd made the rank of lieutenant, thanks to Peter Heroin and the Ninety-ninth Precinct corruption cases ten years before.

"I will beg for my daughter's life if you need to see me do that, Peter," Mickey said.

Peter Heroin held up his hand and waved to the bartender, who was working the small room alone.

"Two Budweisers, please," Peter said.

Mickey suddenly recognized the old paradox in Peter Heroin. He could be engaging and confident in one moment, bewildered and vengeful the next. Mostly he wanted to be liked. Going to a cop when you needed help wasn't much different than going to a drug dealer when you needed to get high. Cop and dealer provided comfort.

Sometimes Mickey had seen Peter cry. Sometimes he had seen him laugh. It all came back to one choice Peter Heroin had made. He could have gone to jail, sure. He could have gone with ten years' hard on his head. He'd be out now. He hadn't become a rat like Sammy Gravano because it was easy. He had wanted to help all those years ago, Mickey always believed, because he saw it as one last chance to do right. He had wanted to do a noble thing.

It hadn't worked. He'd been chewed up, like every informant past and present, by the prosecutors. He was nothing in the end, just a free man turned by his own legacy. He wasn't just a corrupt cop. He was a rat fuck. And he knew it.

"You used to get up from this table and go to the newspapers, Mickey," Heroin said. "You called me a rogue in the newspaper stories. Do you know what the word 'rogue' means? I looked it up in the dictionary the night my wife left me. It's like calling someone a worthless criminal. Do you think that's the way I'll be remembered?"

Mickey sipped his beer, paused a full beat, then looked up. "That's not the way I remember you, Peter. In another life, you were a good cop."

"I don't remember that guy."

Heroin slapped a palm on the table, rattling the beer bottles. Mickey didn't flinch. He had been expecting an outburst.

"Stop the happy horse shit," Peter Heroin said.

Mickey said nothing. Peter sat back and pulled a cigarette from his pack of Newports. Mickey recognized the brand from the projects. The black kids smoked Newports. It was the one habit Heroin had carried across from the Brooklyn precinct to the East Village.

"This is our last meeting, ever," Peter Heroin began, blowing smoke.

"Granted."

"You aren't in a position to grant shit anymore," Peter said, bristling.

"Probably not."

He blew some more smoke. "I am going to talk to you for one reason, Mickey," Peter Heroin said. "You have a conscience. And I have a conscience. So now you suffer. I am going to solve this thing for you. And you will have to wake up every day for the rest of your life knowing that you owe your daughter's life, and your fucking complete career, to Peter Heroin. I want nothing. No money. No help. Your suffering is all the payback I need."

"You're a sick fuck," Mickey said truthfully. "But hold on a second. I just wanted to see how you were going to play this. I have a couple of cards left. So, here's how this goes. We have you in a drug conspiracy out of Kennedy with the priest, who was using coke and heroin as payment for sex. I talked to my brother and he says the feds will do it, so you will fall under the new drug kingpin laws and get a life bit. You paid the priest to put on his best collar and carry the stuff through customs. He knew all the agents because they caught Mass in his parish on their way to work. Very ingenious."

"Nice story, but you ain't got shit with a dead priest."

"We didn't have shit, but the dopey priest kept a fucking diary. He believed in confession, but in this case, you have to do the priest's penance."

"I can beat the credibility of a dead gay priest."

"Maybe you can. But we also got a videotape from the airport. See the priest walking. See the priest hand the bag to the ex-cop."

"You don't have the bag, so who's to say what's in it?"

"Take your chances with the feds in the eastern district."

"Okay, what do I have to do? Drug cases aren't you, Donovan."

"There's more. We just got this piece last night. One day we see Dustin Vargas take the bag from you outside the American international terminal. This is Sal Nesto's videotape. He keeps copies of all these tapes in his basement. He is working you. He is using Vargas to get you."

"Yeah, okay. But I had nothing to do with the Sal's murder."

"I know, Peter. This crazy fuck just likes to kill people. Sal is late with some informant money, so our boy Dusty just kills him for the fun of it. We've since learned that Dusty was also a DEA informant and a registered FBI informant. He is using their money to chase Ginny Glade around the world."

"That's the way I figure it, too. I'll help you with your kid."

"Go."

"Yeah, I'm a rogue," Pete said, "but even with a bullshit federal case hanging over my head, I'm *your* worthless animal now. I can live with that so long as I know you're unhappy."

He stopped to guzzle the remainder of his beer, then spoke again. "Besides, the needle may kill your kid. Ten years later you're over that. But this way . . ."

Mickey clenched his fist, but said nothing more.

". . . I just love the agony of it." Peter Heroin sighed and snuffed out his cigarette in the tin ashtray. He spoke then in a dead, colorless voice. "Your boy Vargas copped China blue on Monday night at the Micro Bar on Avenue C," Peter said. "See a guy there they call the Growler. He bought an eighth, and unless Vargas is going to get Dillon extremely fucking high, and dead, I'm betting your friend is a user. Anyway, the Growler has two guys follow your boy to West Fourth Street and on the F train back to Brooklyn. After the business with Sal Nesto, the Growler thinks Vargas is more than just a CI. Maybe he's a cop. As of two days ago, Dusty is living in Park Slope. He lives on one of those pretty brownstone blocks off Prospect Avenue that dead-end into Eighth Avenue. Here's the address." Peter Heroin slipped the white scrap of paper across the table.

Mickey grabbed it, and read 17 Rutherford. He started to get up. "This is ten blocks west of here. Thank you, Peter." He offered his hand. Peter just stared at it.

"Let the suffering begin," Peter said. He dipped a hand into the pocket in his dirty suede coat and came up with a small machine. Mickey recognized it as his old Panasonic micro recorder. And it was rolling.

"Son of a bitch," Mickey said.

"I'll send you a copy every Christmas," the disgraced cop said, getting up.

Peter Heroin walked away without saying another word.

TWENTY-FOUR

Dustin Vargas's Apartment, Rutherford Street, Park Slope,
Brooklyn

He lived in the garden apartment. The cops parked the black-and-blue vans on either end of the block. Mickey Donovan was in the one marked NYNEX. The cops sat in the back as darkness fell on Brooklyn. They were wearing night-vision goggles, watching the apartment. The upstairs neighbors, a young law student and his wife, an emergency-room nurse at Methodist Hospital, answered the phone in their apartment and agreed to meet the cops at the Greek diner on Seventh Avenue.

"Tell us about your downstairs neighbor," Mickey began. They had to be cautious but not secretive.

"What did he do?"

"We believe multiple murders." Mickey slid the front page of the *Post Standard* across the table. Dusty Vargas smiled up from the page at his upstairs neighbors.

"Jesus," the guy said. "We didn't leave the apartment today. Didn't turn on the television."

"What about him?"

"He moved in about a year ago, from around Buffalo."

"Close," Mickey said. "Try Attica. Do you see him much?"

"He works at night. I assume he sleeps during the day. We share the garden, but he never comes out. I see a lot of beer cans in the garbage. He didn't recycle."

"When did you see him last?"

"This afternoon," the guy said. "In our common vestibule. He was carrying a small knapsack. He said, 'Have a nice weekend.' Then he left."

Mickey leaned forward and asked the guy if they could use his apartment for surveillance. At that point, the law student was nervous. He was studying search and seizure that semester at Pace University, just on the other side of the Brooklyn Bridge.

A sergeant assigned to the criminal had just rushed over from the judge's house on Montague Street in Brooklyn Heights. The warrant was signed by the chief Brooklyn judge, Roy Andretti. When the kid protested, Ryan handed the young man his cell phone.

"Call the judge yourself, sir. Here is his card," Ryan said. "His home number is on the back."

The kid called the judge, who answered the call himself, in his bedroom.

"What year of law school are you in?" the judge asked after the kid had apologized for getting him out of bed.

"My last year, sir."

"Then you should know that it doesn't hurt to know a judge, son. What kind of law do you want to do?"

"Criminal, Your Honor."

"Well, we have lots of criminals in Brooklyn, young man," the judge replied. "Some of them are lawyers. Some are cops. Deputy Inspector Mickey Donovan is an estimable man. And now you know a judge. Do what you can to help these police officers. They know the law."

The kid gave them the keys to the apartment.

"Who lives on the top floor?" Donovan said.

"A fireman," the woman replied. "His name is Gates McKenzie. He is a sergeant-at-arms with the Uniformed Fireman's Association."

"I know him," Ryan said. "His brother is a sergeant with ESU."

"Get him here," Mickey said.

The law student was looking at the paper, then at Ginny. "She looks familiar," he said.

"She better not," his wife said.

Mike McAlary

"I've seen her in the paper. She practically lives on Page Six."

Within fifteen minutes the young law student and his wife were being driven by a detective to the Ramada Inn by LaGuardia for the night. Another young man and his girlfriend walked arm in arm to the suspect's three-story brownstone. They unlocked the door, climbed the stairs, entered the apartment above the suspect, and turned the stereo on, loudly. The guy had *Lollapalooza* in the CD player. Maybe this would end that easily. Maybe Vargas would come upstairs to ask the two people posing as neighbors to turn down Pearl Jam.

Unlikely, but possible.

In the back of the van, Inspector Donovan watched the detectives from the tactical-response unit monitoring the phones. There was no sign of the suspect.

Just before night fell on Brooklyn, five kids were playing stickball in the street. One of them hit a long ball, beyond the sewer, and the pink rubber ball smacked off the side of the van.

The van fell silent. The kid ran up, inspected the dent, and said, "Where did this van come from? I wonder what they got behind all these smoky windows."

The kid tried the door lock, but the other kids screamed for the ball. The kid left. He was a jock, not a thief.

"If it had been a football, we would have had to kill him," one of the cops said. "Like they did in the Bronx." The cops laughed at the cop humor.

Mickey picked up his handheld radio and whispered, "Ryan? Whaddaya got?"

Ryan was in the yard behind the suspect's apartment. He was lying on his belly under a tarp, studying the suspect's living room. There was a light on in the dining room. "There isn't anyone home; I can see his bedroom door. It's open. I stopped at the Prospect Park Ninth Street station on the way in. We have undercover guys everywhere. In the booth, conducting the train. Very limited uniform presence. We're in place at the other end of the park in the IRT station, too. If he comes home by train, we got him."

"He won't," said Mickey. "I want to check the apartment."

They met in front of the apartment five minutes later. The landlord gave them the keys. They stepped into the apartment. It was clean and neat, which is how guys who spent more than five years in prison kept a place. There was an answering machine hooked up to the phone. It was blinking red.

Vargas had one place setting of silverware and one plate. These dried in a yellow rack by the sink. He had one coffee cup and a single water glass. They were on the shelf above the stove. He owned one pot. It was on the stove, next to the kettle.

His bills were stacked neatly by the phone. Mickey thumbed through them. No long-distance calls. No personal correspondence. No cards. No address book.

He was just an anonymous, dangerous obsession.

Ryan stepped past Mickey and opened the refrigerator. Just some yogurt and milk. The expiration dates were two days away. There was a jar of pickles on the middle shelf. Ryan started to close the door, but then froze. He looked again at the pickle jar. "I see you, mister," he said. There were two eyeballs in the brine.

"Mickey," Ryan said. "This gets him the big needle."

Mickey stepped to the door and saw.

A couple of minutes later, Mickey opened the cabinet under the sink. The silver caught the light and he saw the collection. Six sharpened shivs remained.

"He left them there for us to see," Mickey said. "This is all choreographed."

He walked into the bedroom and snapped on the light. This was Ginny's room. Her pictures covered every inch of the wall. Some of them were five years old. The old advertisement stuff was there. The *Vogue* ads featuring Ginny during her funky Mediterranean period. The centerpiece of the lusty collage was a color poster of Ginny in her Fila outfit. Ryan opened the closet door and shined his light on the only garment on a hanger: the black-and-white Fila jacket.

Ryan pointed to an autographed color photo on the wall. It read, "Dear D. Keep trying. Ginny Glade. U.S. Open, 1985."

"What do you make of that?"

"Forgery," Mickey said. He pointed to a jar of Vaseline under the bed and said, "Whatever works for these guys."

Mickey opened the dresser drawer and saw the gun. The silencer was still attached. The heroin was in his sock drawer, with his works. There was blood in the needle.

Mike McAlary

"He is a user," Mickey said. "There is only one thing I don't like," he continued. "I don't see a spittoon."

Ryan walked back out into the kitchen and opened the freezer. There were a half dozen bags of Red Man in the ice bin.

"Too perfect," Ryan said.

Mickey pointed to the blinking red light. Ryan pressed the Play button.

"Hello, Inspector Donovan. This is Dusty. Don't mess up the place too bad or my landlord will keep my security deposit. Oh yeah, I'm with Ginny. Say hello, Ginny. '*Uggggh.*' She don't talk too good no more. I just slit her throat."

Mickey and Ryan both ran for the door.

TWENTY-FIVE

Basement, East Wind Towers, Manhattan

Ginny was doing her laundry.

A cop was posted at the front door to the East Wind Towers on East Eighty-first Street. He was a burly rookie cop who hadn't quite learned the art of swinging his baton. He kept smacking it against his thigh.

The cute girls walked by him and rolled their eyes. This section of Manhattan's East Side was filled with flight attendants and UN trash. A New York City cop didn't do much for the neighborhood. Especially an uncoordinated one.

"Stop that," Victor the doorman said. "You're scaring off the residents."

Another cop sat in the lobby, thumbing through the magazines. He was surprised by how many people in the building subscribed to *Playboy*. One resident subscribed to *Out*, *Hustler*, and *Architectural Digest*. He couldn't figure out how that combination worked.

"She's a bored AC-DC psychoanalyst with a leaky roof in the Hamptons," the doorman explained.

"I was going to guess that," the cop said.

———

Ginny answered the phone just before going out to get on the elevator.

"You okay?" Mickey asked.

"I'm fine."

"Vargas left a message for us to find on his machine. He put it there just to scare us. He couldn't have known we were there."

"I'm going to do the laundry, then," Ginny said.

"Go ahead, do the laundry."

Three minutes later she got off the elevator in the lobby. The cop saw her and dropped his magazine.

"I'll carry that, Ms. Glade," the cop said.

"You will not."

She checked her mailbox, took out a package, and placed it in the laundry bag. Then she walked to the stairwell and down the last flight, into the basement. The laundry room was empty. She placed her bag on the Formica table and turned to the only machine not in use. She opened the lid and saw a metal rod inside. By then she had already smelled the cheap cologne again. It was the same across all those years.

She did not hesitate. She reached down and pulled the rod out of the basket. It was thin, and perhaps eighteen inches long. The end was sharpened. She studied it for a moment, then noticed a word engraved into the middle of the shaft: Cutco.

Ginny placed it on the table and grabbed her clothes. She dropped them into the washing machine. Behind her, a door to the huge tumble dryer opened. The room was too noisy to hear. A hand was revealed, then a leg. Then Dusty Vargas stepped out of the dryer. Ginny, blind to his emergence, started her machine. As she turned, the killer grabbed the shiv off the table between them.

"Hello, Ginny," Dusty said. His bald head was wet and covered with lint.

Ginny was holding her bag. She calmly placed it on the table. "That couldn't have been fun," she said. She was ice.

The coolness of Ginny's response surprised him. This wasn't a tennis match. This was real horror. He was disappointed that she hadn't fainted.

"It's a trick I learned in the prison laundry," he said.

"How did you get past the cops?" she asked. Her easy conversation continued to surprise him.

"Just walked in the side door and around to the freight elevator," he said. "I was in your apartment last night, too, waiting."

"Didn't mean to stand you up," Ginny said. "I know how that offends you."

"I don't like you and the cop," he said, almost growling. "I did more for you than he did. Will he kill for you, Ginny?"

"I doubt it." She turned back to her machine and began to talk over her shoulder. Her coolness in this situation was intimidating. "So how is this gonna go?" she asked.

"I am going to kill you right here," Dusty said, raising the shiv.

She didn't flinch. "I don't see that happening," Ginny replied. "The cops are in your bedroom."

"Yeah," he cackled. "That's why I left them the heroin trail to follow in the park. I needed them to drop their guard."

"Is it going to be like the last time, Dusty, like in Utica?"

He lowered the shiv. He had been caught flat-footed, like so many of her opponents. "The cops know about us?" he asked.

"There is no us, you delusional freak," Ginny snapped. "You raped me. I was never the same. Ice grew on me."

"You liked it," Dusty said, smiling through ginger-colored teeth. "I used to see you when I was working in the kitchen. I could tell."

Ginny snickered and brought her hand to her face. "Oh, you pathetic man," Ginny said. "I wanted to win Wimbledon, not the summer-camp dishwasher."

"Did you tell the cops?"

"That you had two victims that summer?" Ginny said. "Melanie Morgan and me? No, I never told them."

"The only reason I grabbed the other girl was because I thought it would make you jealous," he said. And then added, "Melanie Morgan wasn't shit."

"So why kill her when you got paroled. Why?"

"Because she thought she was tougher than me. So she paid for the price for testifying against me. If every woman I ever raped had the balls to testify against me, I would have been in prison years ago."

"So you shot her from a train?"

"I practiced making that shot for a week. No one heard as I rattled past that park in the Bronx. Did you know it was me when it happened, Ginny? Did you feel me coming for you again?"

"I was mad after you raped me, Dusty," Ginny said. "I wanted vengeance across all these years. I was hoping you would come."

"You wanted me?"

"I wanted the chance to kill you."

"That's big talk for a woman."

"You know what I think about when I'm losing a match? I think of your soiled hands on me, the tobacco juice in your frothing mouth, and I think, 'Losing is nothing compared to that.' So I waited. I can still smell your cologne. Ice Blue Aqua Velva. Once, I passed it in the pharmacy and began to shudder. I couldn't move. Thank God no one wears it anymore."

"I still wear it, Ginny. I have it on now."

"I smelled you when I came into the room. I'm actually glad you still wear it."

"Huh?"

"You leave a trail," she said. "I knew you were a weak man. I knew you would get out and try again. I planned on it. I used to send you those photographs in prison. And then after I realized that you were the one who shot Melanie Morgan from the subway train, I knew you would come for me."

Ginny looked him dead in the eye.

"So what are you say-saying?" the killer stammered.

"I'm saying I played you like the dumb animal you are," Ginny said. "I was able to trap you because you couldn't control your pathetic lust. I always hated you but I didn't understand how much you had ruined me until after I lost the baby. I'm damaged. Still, it took me a while to realize I had you on the line. At the diner, I just figured you were following me. Then, when I heard about the murder weapons, I knew it was you. Shivs. You used a shiv on us in Utica, too, stole them from the kitchen."

"I like the blunt steel on the skin," he said.

"The tobacco juice was the giveaway. You did the same thing to me."

"I like knives," he said. "And spitting on whores."

"Yeah, you are an animal of routine, Dusty." Ginny sighed, turning to face her washing machine again. "Frankly, I expected more of a show from you. But having you here, now, like this, is perfect."

Ginny was still facing the machines. She pressed a lint panel on a dryer and a nine-millimeter pistol popped out. She turned and faced him, training the gun at his midsection. She looked as calm as she did when she was waiting to return a serve. But instead of a racquet, she had both hands on the gun.

"Donovan put it in there for me last night," Ginny said. She grabbed a chain on her neck with her left hand and pulled out a small ladybug charm, holding it up for him to see. There was a button on the bug's back.

"I pressed this as soon as I saw the shiv," Ginny said. "I'd say this victim's-rights class is about to end."

"I underestimated you, Ginny," Dusty Vargas said.

"You won't do that again."

She fired the gun and his chest exploded. The shiv rattled to the floor. Ginny fired again and again, until the gun was empty.

The moment the last shot was fired, Mickey and Ryan Donovan burst through the door.

"He was coming at me," Ginny lied. "I had no choice."

A uniformed cop took her spent gun away, then, taking her by the elbow, he began to walk her out of the room. Mickey Donovan reached over and hugged her.

"That's my girl," he said.

"But I'm not your girl, Detective," she said coolly.

"Just a figure of speech, Ginny," Donovan said. "I'm glad we spent an afternoon at the range test-firing that Glock."

"Yes," she said. The cop led her out.

As soon as the door closed, Mickey Donovan stepped over the body and walked to Ginny's laundry bag. He took out the brown paper package and tore it open, revealing a four-inch tape recorder. It was motion-activated, state-of-the-art stuff. He'd picked it up from internal affairs a couple of days before. Donovan had placed it in Ginny's mailbox that morning. It was the only part of Mickey Donovan's elaborate trap that he hadn't discussed with Ginny Glade.

He placed the conversation in his pocket and left.

EPILOGUE

The Voice of Deputy Inspector Mickey Donovan, NYPD

The tape made it pretty clear that while Ginny Glade wasn't a murderer, she was a killer. It even turned out that she had followed the guy for a while when he'd gotten out of prison. She'd heard he was out and then gotten a friend to run his name through the state motor vehicle computer. Ginny came up with the Brooklyn address from his license. When I finally asked her about this six months later, she admitted having walked by him in a crowded Brooklyn saloon one night. It was a cop bar, Snookey's, on Seventh Avenue in Brooklyn, so the maniac was frozen. But it was still a ballsy, cold-blooded move. She told me, "Oh, yeah. I wanted to put the hook in his mouth." I asked her about the rape after I heard the tape. She said she had been fifteen and ashamed. She hadn't known what to do. And then Dusty Vargas had attacked her best friend. He was quickly arrested, and she hadn't wanted to be shamed further. She hadn't seen any point in the bother.

She sent him stuff in prison, only I don't think Ginny even started to think about killing the guy until he got out. A lot of that had to do with her life. Ginny was falling. The husband wouldn't save her. The women on the tour were grotesque. Then he killed Melanie Morgan, and she knew.

She had a slate to clean.

Dusty Vargas was no match for Ginny Glade. None of us were.

We walked through the plan ten times the day before. We knew he would come. I put two knuckleheaded cops on the door, and told them to stay put. He came in the entrance we wanted. He waited in the basement because he knew her routine. Saturday was laundry day. The gun in the laundry trap was my brother Ryan's idea. He came up with it after Ginny asked, "What do I do if it goes wrong and you guys don't bust through the door in time?" We knew she'd grown up in New Hampshire knowing how to shoot. We figured, okay.

It may have been her greatest move.

She planned the whole thing, right down to the last bullet.

Ginny Glade moved out of New York City. The last I heard she was teaching tennis at a girls' camp in Austin, Texas. She does some color commentary for ESPN on the women's indoor tour during the winter. Ginny says they're both great gigs. She still talks to me and my daughter, Dillon, on the phone. Bridget writes her letters. The kid is doing better and the counselors say she may even make it. She is off methadone and back in school. I never told Dillon the truth about what happened in that room. My brother knows something isn't right, but he had the grace not to press. He keeps saying, "Boss, you know I can't find that autographed picture we took out of Dusty's room. Could that have been for real?"

Technically, I know, Ginny murdered the guy. But no jury was going to convict. He'd killed her years ago. No prosecutor would ever indict. Hell, they renamed a mountain after her in New Boston after the case died down. Ginny wasn't going to jail. And when the *Post Standard* finally learned that Vargas had raped Ginny twenty years before, they decided not to write the story for fear of backlash from women's groups.

Did I love her? I guess I did. I burned the tape after seeing her off to Texas. Does that make me a hypocrite? I still believe in zero tolerance. But I'd have to be a hell of a lot colder than Ginny ever pretended to be to apply those standards to her.

People died in this case, you'll probably say, And what about that? Well, what about it? Ginny didn't kill them. Blinky Hammond would have woken up with a splitting headache in an hour. That was Ginny's only crime. When I think about the baseball umpire who died in the park and the referee on the train in New Jersey, I get mad again. But Ginny didn't know about that. She couldn't have prevented it. In the end, this case is sort of like life. Once it gets rolling, and fate happens, there is not a damn thing you can do about it.

Sport and crime are on the upswing again. Eventually, the Yankees and the Mets started to win games on their own again. The mayor went away. I'm working on another case. And if you go to a ballpark tonight, somewhere, you'll probably hear the scream.

In America, once again it's safe to yell, "Kill the Umpire."